WHO WOULD HAVE THOUGHT?

Once upon a time the Hugos and Nebulas were reserved for science-fiction writers, and the coveted National Book Awards were saved for the rest of the world. Not so any more! In 1974 the literary establishment gave the NBA to Thomas Pynchon for **Gravity's Rainbow**. They thought it was a great novel; but they didn't know it was science fiction. However the Science Fiction Writers of America got the message and voted Pynchon runner-up for the Nebula. His competition was, among others, Heinlein and Clarke, who won.

More and more science fiction in recent years has had exceptional literary merit. For **Alpha 5** Robert Silverberg has selected stories by some of the finest young writers who are heading sf in bold new directions.

ALPHA
5

Edited by
ROBERT SILVERBERG

BALLANTINE BOOKS • NEW YORK

Library of Congress Cataloging in Publication Data

Silverberg, Robert, comp.
   Alpha 5.

   CONTENTS: Delany, S. R. The star pit.—Wilhelm,
K. Baby, you were great.—Effinger, G. A. Live, from
Berchtesgaden. [etc.]
   1. Science fiction, American. 2. Science fiction, English.
I. Title.
PZ1.S587Am [PS648.S3]   813'.0876   74-10768

ISBN 0-345-24140-X

SBN 345-24140-1-125

First Printing: August, 1974

Printed in Canada.

BALLANTINE BOOKS
A Division of Random House, Inc.
201 East 50th Street, New York, N.Y. 10022
Simultaneously published by
Ballantine Books, Ltd., Toronto, Canada

ACKNOWLEDGMENTS

"The Star Pit" by Samuel R. Delany. Copyright © 1966 by Galaxy Publishing Corp. Reprinted by permission of the author and Henry Morrison, Inc., his agents.

"Baby, You Were Great" by Kate Wilhelm. Copyright © 1967 by Damon Knight. Reprinted by permission of the author.

"Live, From Berchtesgaden" by Geo. Alec Effinger. Copyright © 1972 by Damon Knight. Reprinted by permission of the author.

"As Never Was" by P. Schuyler Miller. Copyright © 1943 in U.S.A. and Great Britain by Street & Smith Publications, Inc. Reprinted by permission of The Condé Nast Publications, Inc.

"We Can Remember It For You Wholesale" by Philip K. Dick. Copyright © 1966 by Mercury Press, Inc. Reprinted by permission of the author and his agents, Scott Meredith Literary Agency, Inc.

"Yesterday House" by Fritz Leiber. Copyright © 1952 by Galaxy Publishing Corp. Reprinted by permission of the author and his agent, Robert P. Mills.

"A Man Must Die" by John Clute. Copyright © 1966 by New Worlds SF. Reprinted by permission of the author.

"The Skills of Xanadu" by Theodore Sturgeon. Copyright © 1956 by Theodore Sturgeon. Reprinted by permission of the author.

"A Special Kind of Morning" by Gardner R. Dozois. Copyright © 1971 by Robert Silverberg. Reprinted by permission of the author.

CONTENTS

INTRODUCTION

Five years have passed since the first of these *Alpha* collections was compiled. The stories for the first volume were selected not long after men first walked the face of the moon; the stories for the present book were chosen at a time when the lunar exploration program had seemingly run its entire course. (How strange to feel that one already lives in mankind's *post*-lunar period!) But as I type this, three Skylab astronauts toil in orbit above the earth, so perhaps obituaries for the space program are premature.

These five years have seen vast changes in the patterns of world events. The United States has discovered—as Athens and Rome and Assyria and Byzantium discovered long ago—that even the most powerful empire can shatter itself in the extravagances of needless war; the economic domination of the world has passed into the hands of Japan and Germany, nations reduced to rubble not very long ago, as though to tell us that losing wars is not nearly so perilous as conducting oneself foolishly; the world has entered an era of increasing scarcity of natural resources, and our lives are destined now to grow steadily more impoverished as the impact of past squandering makes itself felt. All these things were foreshadowed in science fiction—not that science fiction is particularly a literature of accurate prophecy, nor science-fiction writers unusually gifted with second sight, but only that all these trends were obvious years ago to everyone except those who govern us, and they became part of any rational projection of mankind's immediate future.

Things change. Science fiction registers those changes —not so much predicting things to come as merely interpreting that which has already happened and outlining certain inevitable consequences. Some of the stories in this year's *Alpha* show us, with painful clarity, the approaching consequences of our most recent miscalculations; other stories take a longer view, portraying events in the remote galaxies that have only metaphorical applications to our immediate lives. Science fiction is no literature of harangues. We are not primarily in the business of peddling sermons or delivering warnings; we offer only visions of times to come. Here are ten more visions, glimpses of the roads ahead.

ROBERT SILVERBERG

ALPHA
5

THE STAR PIT

Samuel R. Delany

At last count Samuel "Chip" Delany was the only writer to have won four Nebulas. (He has a Hugo, too.) He collected his trophies for two novels—Babel-17 and The Einstein Intersection—and two shorter pieces, "Aye, and Gomorrah" and "Time Considered as a Helix of Semi-Precious Stones," all published between 1966 and 1968. Since then his appearances in print have been sparse, for Delany has been at work for years on a single monumental novel when not diverting himself with such amusements as experimental film-making, travel, and haute cuisine. That vast book is scheduled for imminent publication as this introduction is being written and no doubt will have become a major topic of conversation by the time the fifth Alpha goes on sale. Those who have just read it may find it instructive to return now to an early but by no means immature Delany story which is, I think—that list of awards notwithstanding—his finest contribution to science fiction.

Two glass panes with dirt between and little tunnels from cell to cell: when I was a kid I had an ant colony. But once some of our four-to-six-year-olds built an

ecologarium with six-foot plastic panels and grooved aluminum bars to hold corners and top down. They put it out
on the sand.

There was a mud puddle against one wall so you could
see what was going on underwater. Sometimes segment
worms crawling through the reddish earth hit the side so
their tunnels were visible for a few inches. In hot weather
the inside of the plastic got coated with mist and droplets.
The small round leaves on the litmus vines changed from
blue to pink, blue to pink as clouds coursed the sky and the
pH of the photosensitive soil shifted slightly.

The kids would run out before dawn and belly down
naked in the cool sand with their chins on the backs of
their hands and stare in the half-dark till the red mill
wheel of Sigma lifted over the bloody sea. The sand was
maroon then, and the flowers of the crystal plants looked
like rubies in the dim light of the giant sun. Up the beach
the jungle would begin to whisper while somewhere an
ani-wort would start warbling. The kids would giggle and
poke each other and crowd closer.

Then Sigma-prime, the second member of the binary,
would flare like thermite on the water, and crimson clouds
would bleach from coral, through peach, to foam. The
kids, half on top of each other, now lay like a pile of
copper ingots with sun streaks in their hair—even on little
Antoni, my oldest, whose hair was black and curly like
bubbling oil (like his mother's), the down on the small
of his two-year-old back was a white haze across the
copper if you looked that close to see.

More children came to squat and lean on their knees,
or kneel with their noses an inch from the walls, to watch,
like young magicians, as things were born, grew, matured,
and other things were born. Enchanted at their own
construction, they stared at the miracles in their live
museum.

A small, red seed lay camouflaged in the silt by the
lake/puddle. One evening as white Sigma-prime left the
sky violet, it broke open into a brown larva as long and
of the same color as the first joint of Antoni's thumb. It

flipped and swirled in the mud a couple of days, then crawled to the first branch of the nearest crystal plant to hang, exhausted, head down, from the tip. The brown flesh hardened, thickened, grew shiny, black. Then one morning the children saw the onyx chrysalis crack, and by second dawn there was an emerald-eyed flying lizard buzzing at the plastic panels.

"Oh, look, Da!" they called to me. "It's trying to get out!"

The speed-hazed creature butted at the corner, for a few days, then settled at last to crawling around the broad leaves of the miniature shade palms.

When the season grew cool and there was the annual debate over whether the kids should put tunics on—they never stayed in them more than twenty minutes anyway —the jewels of the crystal plant misted, their facets coarsened, and they fell like gravel.

There were little four-cupped sloths, too, big as a six-year-old's fist. Most of the time they pressed their velvety bodies against the walls and stared longingly across the sand with their retractable eye-clusters. Then two of them swelled for about three weeks. We thought at first it was some bloating infection. But one evening there were a couple of litters of white velvet balls half hidden by the low leaves of the shade palms. The parents were occupied now and didn't pine to get out.

There was a rock half in and half out of the puddle, I remember, covered with what I'd always called mustard-moss when I saw it in the wild. Once it put out a brush of white hairs. And one afternoon the children ran to collect all the adults they could drag over. "Look, oh Da, Da, Ma, look!" The hairs had detached themselves and were walking around the water's edge, turning end over end along the soft soil.

I had to leave for work in a few minutes and haul some spare drive parts out to Tau Ceti. But when I got back five days later, the hairs had taken root, thickened, and were already putting out the small round leaves of litmus vines. Among the new shoots, lying on her back, claws curled over her wrinkled belly, eyes cataracted like the foggy jewels of the crystal plant—she'd dropped her wings like cellophane days ago—was the flying lizard. Her pearl throat still pulsed, but as I watched, it stopped. Before she died, however, she had managed to deposit, nearly camouflaged in the silt by the puddle, a scattering of red seeds.

I remember getting home from another job where I'd been doing the maintenance on the shuttle-boats for a crew putting up a ring station to circle a planet itself circling Aldebaran. I was gone a long time on that one. When I left the landing complex and wandered out toward the tall weeds at the edge of the beach, I still didn't see anybody.

Which was just as well because the night before I'd put on a real winner with the crew to celebrate the completion of the station. That morning I'd taken a couple more drinks at the landing bar to undo last night's damage. Never works.

The swish of frond on frond was like clashed rasps. Sun on the sand reached out fingers of pure glare and tried to gouge my eyes. I was glad the home-compound was deserted because the kids would have asked questions I didn't want to answer; the adults wouldn't ask anything, which was even harder to anwer.

Then, down by the ecologarium, a child screeched. And screeched again. Then Antoni came hurtling toward me, half running, half on all fours, and flung himself on my leg. "Oh, Da! Da! Why, oh why, Da?"

I'd kicked my boots off and shrugged my shirt back at the compound porch, but I still had my overalls on. Antoni had two fists full of my pants leg and wouldn't let go. "Hey, kid-boy, what's the matter?"

When I finally got him on my shoulder he butted his blubber wet face against my collarbone. "Oh, Da! Da! It's crazy, it's all cra*aaa-zy!*" His voice rose to lose itself in sobs.

"What's crazy, kid-boy? Tell Da."

Antoni held my ear and cried while I walked down to the plastic enclosure.

They'd put a small door in one wall with a two-number combination lock that was supposed to keep this sort of thing from happening. I guess Antoni learned the combination from watching the older kids, or maybe he just figured it out.

One of the young sloths had climbed out and wandered across the sand about three feet.

"See, Da! It crazy, it bit me. Bit me, Da!" Sobs became sniffles as he showed me a puffy, bluish place on his wrist centered on which was a tiny crescent of pinpricks. Then he pointed jerkily to the creature.

It was shivering, and bloody froth spluttered from its lip flaps. All the while it was digging futilely at the sand with its clumsy cups, eyes retracted. Now it fell over, kicked, tried to right itself, breath going like a flutter valve. "It can't take the heat," I explained, reaching down to pick it up.

It snapped at me, and I jerked back. "Sunstroke, kid-boy. Yeah, it is crazy."

Suddenly it opened its mouth wide, let out all its air, and didn't take in any more. "It's all right now," I said.

Two more of the baby sloths were at the door, front cups over the sill, staring with bright, black eyes. I pushed them back with a piece of seashell and closed the door. Antoni kept looking at the white fur ball on the sand. "Not crazy now?"

"It's dead," I told him.

"Dead because it went outside, Da?"

I nodded.

"And crazy?" He made a fist and ground something already soft and wet around his upper lip.

I decided to change the subject, which was already too close to something I didn't like to think about. "Who's been taking care of you, anyway?" I asked. "You're a mess, kid-boy. Let's go and fix up that arm. They shouldn't leave a fellow your age all by himself." We started back to the compound. Those bites infect easily, and this one was swelling.

"Why it go crazy? Why it die when it go outside, Da?"

"Can't take the light," I said as we reached the jungle. "They're animals that live in shadow most of the time. The plastic cuts out the ultraviolet rays, just like the leaves that shade them when they run loose in the jungle. Sigma-prime's high on ultraviolet. That's why you're so good-looking, kid-boy. I think your ma told me their nervous systems are on the surface, all that fuzz. Under the ultraviolet, the enzymes break down so quickly that—does this mean anything to you at all?"

"Uh-uh." Antoni shook his head. Then he came out with, "Wouldn't it be nice, Da"—he admired his bite while we walked—"if some of them could go outside, just a few?"

That stopped me. There were sunspots on his blue-black hair. Fronds reflected faint green on his brown cheek. He was grinning, little, and wonderful. Something that had been anger in me a lot of times momentarily melted to raging tenderness, whirling about him like the dust in the light striking down at my shoulders, raging to protect my son. "I don't know about that, kid-boy."

"Why not?"

"It might be pretty bad for the ones who had to stay inside," I told him. "I mean after a while."

"Why?"

I started walking again. "Come on, let's fix your arm and get you cleaned up."

I washed the wet stuff off his face, and scraped the dry stuff from beneath it which had been there at least two days. Then I got some antibiotic into him.

"You smell funny, Da."

"Never mind how I smell. Let's go outside again." I put down a cup of black coffee too fast, and it and my hang-over had a fight in my stomach. I tried to ignore it and do a little looking around. But I still couldn't find anybody. That got me mad. I mean he's independent, sure: he's mine. But he's only two.

Back on the beach we buried the dead sloth in sand; then I pointed out the new, glittering stalks of the tiny crystal plants. At the bottom of the pond, in the jellied mass of ani-wort eggs, you could see the tadpole forms quivering already. An orange-fringed shelf fungus had sprouted nearly eight inches since it had been just a few black spores on a pile of dead leaves two weeks back.

"Grow up," Antoni chirped with nose and fists against the plastic. "Everything grow up, and up."

"That's right."

He grinned at me. "I grow!"

"You sure as hell do."

"You grow?" Then he shook his head, twice: once to say no, and the second time because he got a kick from shaking his hair around—there was a lot of it. "You don't grow. You don't get any bigger. Why don't you grow?"

"I do too," I said indignantly. "Just very slowly."

Antoni turned around, leaned on the plastic and moved one toe at a time in the sand—I can't do that—watching me.

"You have to grow all the time," I said. "Not necessarily get bigger. But inside your head you have to grow, kid-boy. For us human-type people that's what's important. And that kind of growing never stops. At least it shouldn't. You can grow, kid-boy, or you can die. That's the choice you've got, and it goes on all of your life."

He looked back over his shoulder. "Grow up, all the time, even if they can't get out."

"Yeah," I said. And was uncomfortable all over again. I started pulling off my overalls for something to do. "Even —" The zipper got stuck. "God *damn* it—if you can't get out." *Rnrnrnrnrn*—it came loose.

The rest got back that evening. They'd been on a group trip around the foot of the mountain. I did a little shouting to make sure my point got across about leaving Antoni alone. Didn't do much good. You know how family arguments go:

He didn't want to come. We weren't going to force—

So what. He's got to learn to do things he doesn't want—

Like some other people I could mention!

Now look—

It's a healthy group. Don't you want him to grow up a healthy—

I'll be happy if he just grows up period. No food, no medical—

But the server was chock full of food. He knows how to use it—

Look, when I got home the kid's arm was swollen all the way up to his elbow!

And so on and so forth, with Antoni sitting in the middle looking confused. When he got confused enough, he ended it all by announcing matter-of-factly: "Da smell funny when he came home."

Everyone got quiet. Then someone said, "Oh, Vyme, you didn't come home that way again! I mean, in front of the children . . ."

I said a couple of things I was sorry for later and stalked off down the beach—on a four-mile hike.

Times I got home from work? The ecologarium? I guess I'm just leading up to this one.

The particular job had taken me a hectic week to get. It was putting back together a battleship that was gutted somewhere off Aurigae. Only when I got there, I found I'd already been laid off. That particular war was over—they're real quick now. So I scraped and lied and browned my way into a repair gang that was servicing a traveling replacement station, generally had to humiliate myself to get the job because every other drive mechanic from the battleship fiasco was after it too. Then I got canned the first day because I came to work smelling funny. It took me another week to hitch a ride back to Sigma. Didn't even have enough to pay passage, but I made a deal with the pilot I'd do half the driving for him.

We were an hour out, and I was at the controls when something I'd never heard of happening, happened. We came *this* close to ramming another ship. Consider how much empty space there is; the chances are infinitesimal. And on top of that, every ship should be broadcasting an identification beam at all times.

But this big, bulbous keeler-intergalactic slid by so close

I could *see* her through the front viewport. Our inertia system went nuts. We jerked around in the stasis whirl from the keeler. I slammed on the video-intercom and shouted, "You great big stupid . . . *stupid* . . ." so mad and scared I couldn't say anything else.

The golden piloting the ship stared at me from the view-screen with mildly surprised annoyance. I remember his face was just slightly more Negroid than mine.

Our little Serpentina couldn't hurt him. But had we been even a hundred meters closer we might have ionized. The other pilot came bellowing from behind the sleeper curtain and started cursing me out.

"Damn it," I shouted, "it was one of those . . ." and lost all the profanity I know to my rage, ". . . golden . . ."

"This far into galactic center? Come off it. They should be hanging out around the Star-pit!"

"It was a keeler drive," I insisted. "It came right in front of us." I stopped because the control stick was shaking in my hand. You know the Serpentina colophon? They have it in the corner of the view-screen and raised in plastic on the head of the control knobs. Well, it got pressed into the ham of my thumb so you could make it out for an hour, I was squeezing the control rod that tight.

When he set me down, I went straight to the bar to cool off. And got in a fight. When I reached the beach I was broke, I had a bloody nose, I was sick, and furious.

It was just after first sunset, and the kids were squealing around the ecologarium. Then one little girl I didn't even recognize ran up to me and jerked my arm. "Da, oh, Da! Come look! The ani-worts are just about to—"

I pushed her, and she sat down, surprised, on the sand.

I just wanted to get to the water and splash something cold on my face, because every minute or so it would start to burn.

Another bunch of kids grabbed me, shouting, "Da, Da, the ani-worts, Da!" and tried to pull me over.

First I took two steps with them. Then I just swung my arms out. I didn't make a sound. But I put my head down and barreled against the plastic wall. Kids screamed. Aluminum snapped; the plastic cracked and went down. My boots were still on, and I kicked and kicked at red earth and sand. Shade palms went down and the leaves tore under my feet. Crystal plants broke like glass rods beneath a piece of plastic. A swarm of lizards flittered up around my head. Some of the red was Sigma, some was what burned behind my face.

I remember I was still shaking and watching water run out of the broken lake over the sand, then soak in so that the wet tongue of sand expanded a little, raised just a trifle around the edge. Then I looked up to see the kids coming back down the beach, crying, shouting, afraid and clustered around Antoni's ma. She walked steadily toward me—steady because she was a woman and they were children. But I saw the same fear in her face. Antoni was on her shoulder. Other grownups were coming behind her.

Antoni's ma was a biologist, and I think she had suggested the ecologarium to the kids in the first place. When she looked up from the ruin I'd made, I knew I'd broken something of hers too.

An odd expression got caught in the features of her— I remember it oh so beautiful—face, with compassion alongside the anger, contempt alongside the fear. "Oh, for pity's sake, Vyme," she cried, not loudly at all. "Won't you ever grow up?"

I opened my mouth, but everything I wanted to say was too big and stayed wedged in my throat.

"Grow up?" Antoni repeated and reached for a lizard that buzzed his head. "Everything stop growing up, now." He looked down again at the wreck I'd made. "All broken. Everything get out."

"He didn't mean to break it," she said to the others for me, then knifed my gratitude with a look. "We'll put it back together."

She put Antoni on the sand and picked up one of the walls.

After they got started, they let me help. A lot of the

plants were broken. And only the ani-worts who'd completed metamorphosis could be saved. The flying lizards were too curious to get far away, so we—they netted them and got them back inside. I guess I didn't help that much. And I wouldn't say I was sorry.

They got just about everything back except the sloths.

We couldn't find them. We searched for a long time, too.

The sun was down so they should have been all right. They can't negotiate the sand with any speed so couldn't have reached the jungle. But there were no tracks, no nothing. We even dug in the sand to see if they'd buried themselves. It wasn't till more than a dozen years later I discovered where they went.

For the present I accepted Antoni's mildly adequate, "They just must of got out again."

Not too long after that I left the procreation group. Went off to work one day, didn't come back. But like I said to Antoni, you either grow or die. I didn't die.

Once I considered returning. But there was another war, and suddenly there wasn't anything to return to. Some of the group got out alive. Antoni and his ma didn't. I mean there wasn't even any water left on the planet.

When I finally came to the Star-pit, myself, I hadn't had a drink in years. But working there out on the galaxy's edge did something to me—something to the part that grows I'd once talked about on the beach with Antoni.

If it did it to me, it's not surprising it did it to Ratlit and the rest.

(And I remember a black-eyed creature pressed against the plastic wall, staring across impassable sands.)

Perhaps it was knowing this was as far as you could go. Perhaps it was the golden.

Golden? I hadn't even joined the group yet when I first heard the word. I was sixteen and a sophomore at Luna Vocational. I was born in a city called New York on a planet called Earth. Luna is its one satellite. You've heard of the system, I'm sure; that's where we all came from. A

few other things about it are well known. Unless you're
an anthropologist, though, I doubt you've ever been there.
It's way the hell off the main trading routes and pretty
primitive. I was a drive-mechanics major, on scholarship,
living in and studying hard. All morning in Practical
Theory (a ridiculous name for a ridiculous class, I thought
then) we'd been putting together a model keeler-
intergalactic drive. Throughout those dozens of helical
inserts and super-inertia organus sensitives, I had been silently cursing my teacher, thinking, about like everybody
else in the class, "So what if they can fly these jalopies
from one galaxy to another. Nobody will ever be able to
ride in them. Not with the Psychic and Physiologic shells
hanging around this cluster of the universe."

Back in the dormitory I was lying on my bed, scraping graphite lubricant from my nails with the end of my
slide rule and half reading at a folded-back copy of *The
Young Mechanic* when I saw the article and the pictures.

Through some freakish accident, two people had been
discovered who didn't crack up at twenty thousand light-
years off the galactic rim, who didn't die at twenty-five
thousand.

They were both psychological freaks with some incredible hormone imbalance in their systems. One was a little
Oriental girl; the other was an older man, blond and big-
boned, from a cold planet circling Cygnus-beta: golden.
They looked sullen as hell, both of them.

Then there were more articles, more pictures, in the
economic journals, the sociology student-letters, the legal
bulletins, as various fields began acknowledging the impact that the golden and the sudden birth of intergalactic
trade were having on them. The head of some commission
summed it up with the statement: "Though interstellar
travel has been with us for three centuries, intergalactic
trade has been an impossibility, not because of mechanical
limitations, but rather because of barriers that till now we
have not even been able to define. Some psychic shock
causes insanity in any human—or for that matter, any
intelligent species or perceptual machine or computer—

that goes more than twenty thousand light-years from the galactic rim; then complete physiological death, as well as recording breakdown in computers that might replace human crews. Complex explanations have been offered, none completely satisfactory, but the base of the problem seems to be this: as the nature of space and time are relative to the concentration of matter in a given area of the continuum, the nature of reality itself operates by the same, or similar laws. The averaged mass of all the stars in our galaxy controls the 'reality' of our microsector of the universe. But as a ship leaves the galactic rim, 'reality' breaks down and causes insanity and eventual death for any crew, even though certain mechanical laws—though not all—appear to remain, for reasons we don't understand, relatively constant. Save for a few barbaric experiments done with psychedelics at the dawn of spatial travel, we have not even developed a vocabulary that can deal with 'reality' apart from its measurable, physical expression. Yet, just when we had to face the black limit of intergalactic space, bright resources glittered within. Some few of us whose sense of reality has been shattered by infantile, childhood, or prenatal trauma, whose physiological orientation makes life in our interstellar society painful or impossible—not all, but a few of these golden . . ." at which point there was static, or the gentleman coughed, ". . . can make the crossing and return."

The name golden, sans noun, stuck.

Few was the understatement of the millennium. Slightly less than one human being in thirty-four thousand is a golden. A couple of people had. pictures of emptying all mental institutions by just shaking them out over the galactic rim. Didn't work like that. The particular psychosis and endocrine setup was remarkably specialized. Still, back then there was excitement, wonder, anticipation, hope, admiration in the word: admiration for the ones who could get out.

"Golden?" Ratlit said when I asked him. He was working as a grease monkey out here in the Star-pit over at Poloscki's. "Born with the word. Grew up with it. Weren't no first time with me. Though I remember when I was about six, right after the last of my parents was killed, and I was hiding out with a bunch of other lice in a broke-open packing crate in an abandoned freight yard near the ruins of Helios on Creton VII—that's where I was born, I think. Most of the city had been starved out by then, but somebody was getting food to us. There was this old crook-back character who was hiding too. He used to sit on the top of the packing crate and bang his heels on the aluminum slats and tell us stories about the stars. Had a couple of rags held with twists of wire for clothes, missing two fingers off one hand; he kept plucking the loose skin under his chin with those grimy talons. And he talked about them. So I asked, 'Golden what, sir?' He leaned forward so that his face was like a mahogany bruise on the sky, and croaked, 'They've been *out,* I tell you, seen more than even you or I. Human and inhuman, kid-boy, mothered by women and fathered by men, still they live by their own laws and walk their own ways!' " Ratlit and I were sitting under a street lamp with our feet over the Edge where the fence had broken. His hair was like breathing flame in the wind, his single earring glittered. Star-flecked infinity dropped away below our boot soles, and the wind created by the stasis field that held our atmosphere down—we call it the "world-wind" out here because it's never cold and never hot and like nothing on any world—whipped his black shirt back from his bony chest as we gazed on galactic night between our knees. "I guess that was back during the second Kyber war," he concluded.

"Kyber war?" I asked. "Which one was that?"

He shrugged. "I just know it was fought over possession of couple of tons of di-allium; that's the polarized element the golden brought back from Lupe-galaxy. They used y-adna ships to fight it—that's why it was such a bad war. I mean worse than usual."

"Y-adna? That's a drive I don't know anything about."

"Some golden saw the plans for them in a civilization in Magellanic-9."

"Oh," I said. "And what was Kyber?"

"It was a weapon, a sort of fungus the golden brought back from some overrun planet on the rim of Andromeda. It's deadly. Only they were too stupid to bring back the antitoxin."

"That's golden for you."

"Yeah. You ever notice about golden, Vyme? I mean just the word. I found out all about it from my publisher, once. It's semantically unsettling."

"Really?" I said. "So are they. Unsettling I mean."

I'd just finished a rough, rough day installing a rebuilt keeler in a quantum transport hull that just wasn't big enough. The golden having the job done stood over my shoulder the whole time, and every hour he'd come out with the sort of added instruction that would make the next sixty-one minutes miserable. But I did it. The golden paid me in cash and without a word climbed into the lift, and two minutes later, while I was still washing the grease off, the damn five-hundred-ton hulk began to whistle for takeoff.

Sandy, a young fellow who'd come looking for a temporary mechanic's job three months back, but hadn't given me cause to fire him yet, barely had time to pull the big waldoes out of the way and go scooting into the shock chamber when the three-hundred-meter doofus tore loose from the grapplers. And Sandy, who, like a lot of these youngsters drifting around from job to job, is usually sort of quiet and vague, got loud and specific. ". . . two thousand pounds of non-shockproof equipment out there . . . ruin it all if he could . . . I'm not expendable, I don't care what a . . . these golden out here . . ." while the ship hove off where only the golden go. I just flipped on the "not-open" sign, left the rest of the grease where it was, left the hanger, and hunted up Ratlit.

So there we were, under that street lamp, sitting on the Edge, in the world-wind.

"Golden," Ratlit said under the roar. "It would be much easier to take if it were grammatically connected to something: golden ones, golden people. Or even one gold, two golden."

"Male golden, female goldene?"

"Something like that. It's not an adjective, it's not a noun. My publisher told me that for a while it was written with a dash after it that stood for whatever it might modify."

I remembered the dash. It was an uneasy joke, a fill-in for that cough. Golden *what?* People had already started to feel uncomfortable. Then it went past joking and back to just "golden."

"Think about that, Vyme. Just golden: one, two, or three of them."

"That's something to think about, kid-boy," I said.

Ratlit had been six during the Kyber war. Square that and add it once again for my age now. Ratlit's? Double six and add one. I like kids, and they like me. But that may be because my childhood left me a lot younger at forty-two than I should be. Ratlit's had left him a lot older than any thirteen-year-old has a right to be.

"No golden took part in the war," Ratlit said.

"They never do." I watched his thin fingers get all tangled together.

After two divorces, my mother ran off with a salesman and left me and four siblings with an alcoholic aunt for a year. Yeah, they still have divorces, monogamous marriages and stuff like that where I was born. Like I say, it's pretty primitive. I left home at fifteen, made it through vocational school on my own, and learned enough about what makes things fly to end up—after that disastrous marriage I told you about earlier—with my own repair hangar on the Star-pit.

Compared with Ratlit I had a stable childhood.

That's right, he lost the last parent he remembered when he was six. At seven he was convicted of his first felony—after escaping from Creton VII. But part of his treatment at hospital *cum* reform school *cum* prison was to have the details lifted from his memory. "Did something to my head back there. That's why I never could learn to read, I think." For the next couple of years he ran away from one foster group after the other. When he was eleven, some guy took him home from Play Planet where he'd been existing under the boardwalk on discarded hot dogs, souvlakia, and falafel. "Fat, smoked perfumed cigarettes; name was Vivian?" Turned out to be the publisher. Ratlit stayed for three months, during which time he dictated a novel to Vivian. "Protecting my honor," Ratlit explained. "I had to do *something* to keep him busy."

The book sold a few hundred thousand copies as a precocious curiosity among many. But Ratlit had split. The next years he was involved as a shill in some illegality I never understood. He didn't either. "But I bet I made a million, Vyme! I earned at least a million." It's possible. At thirteen he still couldn't read or write, but his travels had gained him fair fluency in three languages. A couple of weeks ago he'd wandered off a stellar tramp, dirty and broke, here at the Star-pit. And I'd gotten him a job as grease monkey over at Poloscki's.

He leaned his elbows on his knees, his chin in his hands. "Vyme, it's a shame."

"What's a shame, kid-boy?"

"To be washed up at my age. A has-been! To have to grapple with the fact that this"—he spat at a star—"is it."

He was talking about golden again.

"You still have a chance." I shrugged. "Most of the time it doesn't come out till puberty."

He cocked his head up at me. "I've been pubescent since I was nine, buster."

"Ex*cuse* me."

"I feel cramped in, Vyme. There's all that night out there to grow up in, to explore."

"There was a time," I mused, "when the whole species was confined to the surface, give or take a few feet up or down, of a single planet. You've got the whole galaxy to run around in. You've seen a lot of it, yeah. But not all."

"But there are billions of galaxies out there. I want to see them. In all the stars around here there hasn't been one life form discovered that's based on anything but silicon or carbon. I overheard two golden in a bar once, talking: there's something in some galaxy out there that's big as a star, neither dead nor alive, and sings. I want to hear it, Vyme!"

"Ratlit, you can't fight reality."

"Oh, go to sleep, grandpa!" He closed his eyes and bent his head back until the cords of his neck quivered. "What is it that makes a golden? A combination of physiological and psychological . . . what?"

"It's primarily some sort of hormonal imbalance as well as an environmentally conditioned thalamic/personality response—"

"Yeah. Yeah." His head came down. "And that X-chromosome heredity nonsense they just connected up with it a few years back. But all I know is *they* can take the stasis shift from galaxy to galaxy, where you and I, Vyme, if we get more then twenty thousand light-years off the rim, we're dead."

"Insane at twenty thousand," I corrected. "Dead at twenty-five."

"Same difference." He opened his eyes. They were large, green, and mostly pupil. "You know, I stole a golden belt once? Rolled it off a staggering slob about a week ago who came out of a bar and collapsed on the corner. I went across the Pit to Calle-J where nobody knows me and wore it around for a few hours, just to see if I felt different."

"You did?" Ratlit had lengths of gut that astounded me about once a day.

"I didn't. But people walking around me did. Wearing that two-inch band of yellow metal around my waist, nobody in the worlds could tell I wasn't a golden, just walking by on the street, without talking to me awhile, or making hormone tests. And wearing that belt, I learned just how much I hated golden. Because I could suddenly see, in almost everybody who came by, how much they hated me while I had that metal belt on. I threw it over the Edge." Suddenly he grinned. "Maybe I'll steal another one."

"You really hate them, Ratlit?"

He narrowed his eyes at me and looked superior.

"Sure, I talk about them," I told him. "Sometimes they're a pain to work for. But it's not their fault we can't take the reality shift."

"I'm just a child," he said evenly, "incapable of such fine reasoning. I hate them." He looked back at the night. "How can you stand to be trapped by anything, Vyme?"

Three memories crowded into my head when he said that.

First: I was standing at the railing of the East River—runs past this New York I was telling you about—at midnight, looking at the illuminated dragon of the Manhattan Bridge that spanned the water, then at the industrial fires flickering in bright, smoky Brooklyn, and then at the template of mercury street lamps behind me bleaching out the playground and most of Houston Street; then, at the reflections in the water, here like crinkled foil, there like glistening rubber; at last, looked up at the midnight sky itself. It wasn't black but dead pink, without a star. This glittering world made the sky a roof that pressed down on me so I almost screamed. . . . That time the next night I was twenty-seven light-years away from Sol on my first star-run.

Second: I was visiting my mother after my first few years out. I was looking in the closet for something when this contraption of plastic straps and buckles fell on my head.

"What's this, Ma?" And she smiled with a look of idiot nostalgia and crooned, "Why that's your little harness, Vymey. Your first father and I would take you on picnics up at Bear Mountain and put you in that and tie you to a tree with about ten feet of cord so you wouldn't get—" I didn't hear the rest because of the horror that suddenly flooded me, thinking of myself tied up in that thing. Okay, I was twenty and had just joined that beautiful procreation group a year back on Sigma and was the proud father of three and expecting two more. The hundred and sixty-three of us had the whole beach and nine miles of jungle and half a mountain to ourselves; maybe I was seeing

Antoni caught up in that thing, trying to catch a bird or a beetle or a wave—with only ten feet of cord. I hadn't worn clothes for anything but work in a twelvemonth, and I was chomping to get away from that incredible place I had grown up in called an apartment and back to wives, husbands, kids, and civilization. Anyway, it was pretty terrible.

The third? After I had left the proke-group—fled them, I suppose, guilty and embarrassed over something I couldn't name, still having nightmares once a month that woke me screaming about what was going to happen to the kids, even though I knew one point of group marriage was to prevent the loss of one, two, or three parents being traumatic—still wondering if I wasn't making the same mistakes my parents made, hoping my brood wouldn't turn out like me, or worse like the kids you sometimes read about in the paper (like Ratlit, though I hadn't met him yet), horribly suspicious that no matter how different I tried to be from my sires, it was just the same thing all over again . . . . Anyway, I was on the ship bringing me to the Star-pit for the first time. I'd gotten talking to a golden who, as golden go, was a pretty regular gal. We'd been discussing inter- and intra-galactic drives. She was impressed I knew so much. I was impressed that she could use them and know so little. She was digging in a very girl-way the six-foot-four, two-hundred-and-ten-pound drive mechanic with mildly grimy fingernails that was me. I was digging in a very boy-way the slim, amber-eyed young lady who had seen it *all*. From the view deck we watched the immense, artificial disk of the Star-pit approach, when she turned to me and said, in a voice that didn't sound cruel at all, "This is as far as you go, isn't it?" And I was frightened all over again, because I knew that on about nine different levels she was right.

Ratlit said: "I know what you're thinking." A couple of times when he'd felt like being quiet and I'd felt like talking I may have told him more than I should. "Well, cube that for me, dad. That's how trapped I feel!"

I laughed, and Ratlit looked very young again. "Come on," I said. "Let's take a walk."

"Yeah." He stood. The wind fingered at our hair. "I want to go see Alegra."

"I'll walk you as far as Calle-G," I told him. "Then I'm going to go to bed."

"I wonder what Alegra thinks about this business? I always find Alegra a very good person to talk to," he said sagely. "Not to put you down, but her experiences are a little more up to date than yours. You have to admit she has a modern point of view. Plus the fact that she's older." Than Ratlit anyway. She was fifteen.

"I don't think being 'trapped' ever really bothered her," I said. "Which may be a place to take a lesson from."

By Ratlit's standards Alegra had a few things over me. In my youth kids took to dope in their teens, twenties. Alegra was born with a three-hundred-milligram-a-day habit on a bizarre narcotic that combined the psychedelic qualities of the most powerful hallucinogens with the addictiveness of the strongest depressants. I can sympathize. Alegra's mother was addicted, and the tolerance was passed with the blood plasma through the placental wall. Ordinarily a couple of complete transfusions at birth would have gotten the newborn child straight. But Alegra was also a highly projective telepath. She projected the horrors of birth, the glories of her infantile hallucinated world on befuddled doctors; she was given her drug. Without too much difficulty she managed to be given her drug every day since.

Once I asked Alegra when she'd first heard of golden, and she came back with this horror story. A lot were coming back from Tiber-44 cluster with psychic shock—the mental condition of golden is pretty delicate, and sometimes very minor conflicts nearly ruin them. Anyway, the government that was sponsoring the importation of micro-micro surgical equipment from some tiny planet in that galaxy, to protect its interests, hired Alegra, age eight, as a psychiatric therapist. "I'd concretize their fantasies and make them work 'em through. In just a couple of hours I'd have 'em back to their old, mean, stupid selves again. Some of them were pretty nice when they came to me." But there was a lot of work for her; projective telepaths are rare. So they started withholding her drug to force her to work harder, then rewarding her with increased dosage. "Up till then," she told me, "I might have kicked it. But when I came away, they had me on double what I used to take. They pushed me past the point where withdrawal would be fatal. But I *could* have kicked it, up till then, Vyme." That's right. Age eight.

Oh yeah. The drug was imported by golden from Cancer-9, and most of it goes through the Star-pit. Alegra came here because illegal imports are easier to come by, and you can get it for just about nothing—if you want it. Golden don't use it.

The wind lessened as Ratlit and I started back. Ratlit began to whistle. In Calle-K the first night lamp had broken so that the level street was a tunnel of black.

"Ratlit?" I asked. "Where do you think you'll be, oh, in say five years?"

"Quiet," he said. "I'm trying to get to the end of the street without bumping into the walls, tripping on something, or some other catastrophe. If we get through the next five minutes all right, I'll worry about the next five years." He began whistling again.

"Trip? Bump the walls?"

"I'm listening for echoes." Again he commenced the little jets of music.

I put my hands in my overall pouch and went on quietly while Ratlit did the bat bit. Then there was a catastrophe. Though I didn't realize it at the time.

Into the circle of light from the remaining lamp at the other end of the street walked a golden.

His hands went up to his face, and he was laughing. The sound skittered in the street. His belt was low on his belly the way the really down and broke—

I just thought of a better way to describe him; the resemblance struck me immediately. He looked like Sandy, my mechanic, who is short, twenty-four years old, muscled like an ape, and wears his worn-out work clothes even when he's off duty. ("I just want this job for a while, boss. I'm not staying out here at the Star-pit. As soon as I save up a little, I'm gonna make it back in toward galactic center. It's funny out here, like dead." He gazes up through the opening in the hangar roof where there are no clouds and no stars either. "Yeah. I'm just gonna be here for a little while.")

("Fine with me, kid-boy.")

(That was three months back, like I say. He's still with me. He works hard too, which puts him a cut above a lot of characters out here. Still, there was something about Sandy . . .) On the other hand Sandy's face is also hacked up with acne. His hair is always nap short over his wide head. But in these aspects, the golden was exactly Sandy's opposite, come to think of it. Still, there was something about the golden . . .

He staggered, went down on his knees still laughing, then collapsed. By the time we reached him, he was silent. With the toe of his boot Ratlit nudged the hand from the belt buckle.

It flopped, palm up, on the pavement. The little finger-nail was three quarters of an inch long, the way a lot of the golden wear it. (Like his face, the tips of Sandy's fingers are all masticated wrecks. Still, something . . .)

"Now isn't that something." Ratlit shook his head. "What do you want to do with him, Vyme?"

"Nothing," I said. "Let him sleep it off."

"Leave him so somebody can come along and steal his belt?" Ratlit grinned. "I'm not that nasty."

"Weren't you just telling me how much you hated golden?"

"I'd be nasty to whoever stole the belt and wore it. Nobody but a golden should be hated that much."

"Ratlit, let's go."

But he had already kneeled down and was shaking the golden's shoulder. "Let's get him to Alegra's and find out what's the matter with him."

"He's just drunk."

"Nope," Ratlit said. " 'Cause he don't smell funny."

"Look. Get back." I hoisted the golden up and laid him across my neck, fireman's carry. "Start moving," I told Ratlit. "I think you're crazy."

Ratlit grinned. "Thanks. Maybe he'll be grateful and lay some lepta on me for taking him in off the street."

"You don't know golden," I said. "But if he does, split it with me."

"Sure."

Two blocks later we reached Alegra's place. (But like I say, Sandy, though well built, is little; so I didn't have much trouble carrying him.) Halfway up the tilting stairs Ratlit said, "She's in a good mood."

"I guess she is." The weight across my shoulders was becoming pleasant.

I can't decribe Alegra's place. I can describe a lot of places like it; and I can describe it before she moved in because I knew a derelict named Drunk-roach who slept on that floor before she did. You know what never-wear plastics look like when they wear out? What nonrust metals look like when they rust through? It was a shabby crackwalled cubicle with dirt in the corners and scars on the windowpane when Drunk-roach had his pile of blankets in the corner. But since the hallucinating projective telepath took it over, who knows what it had become.

Ratlit opened the door on an explosion of classical beauty. "Come in," she said, accompanied by symphonic arrangement scored on twenty-four staves, with full chorus. "What's that you're carrying, Vyme? Oh, it's a golden!" And before me, dizzying tides of yellow.

"Put him down, put him down quick and let's see what's wrong!" Hundreds of eyes, spotlights, glittering lenses; I lowered him to the mattress in the corner. "Ohhh . . ." breathed Alegra.

And the golden lay on orange silk pillows in a teak barge drawn by swans, accompanied by flutes and drums.

"Where did you find him?" she hissed, circling against the ivory moon on her broom. We watched the glowing barge, hundreds of feet below, sliding down the silvered waters between the crags.

"We just picked him up off the street," Ratlit said. "Vyme thought he was drunk. But he don't smell."

"Was he laughing?" Alegra asked. Laughter rolled and broke on the rocks.

"Yeah," Ratlit said. "Just before he collapsed."

"Then he must be from the Un-dok expedition that just got back." Mosquitoes darted at us through wet fronds. The insects reeled among the leaves, upsetting droplets that fell like glass as, barely visible beyond the palms, the barge drifted on the bright, sweltering river.

"That's right," I said, backpaddling frantically to avoid a hippopotamus that threatened to upset my kayak. "I'd forgotten they'd just come in."

"Okay." Ratlit's breath clouded his lips. "I'm out of it. Let me in. Where did they come back from?" The snow hissed beneath the runners, as we looked after the barge, nearly at the white horizon.

"Un-dok, of course," Alegra said. The barking grew fainter. "Where did you think?"

White eclipsed to black, and the barge was a spot gleaming in galactic night, flown on by laboring comets.

"Un-dok is the furthest galaxy reached yet," I told Ratlit. "They just got back last week."

"Sick," Alegra added.

I dug my fingers against my abdomen to grab the pain.

"They all came back sick—"

Fever heated blood-bubbles in my eyes: I slipped to the ground, my mouth wide, my tongue like paper on my lips . . .

Ratlit coughed. "All *right*, Alegra. Cut it out! You don't have to be so dramatic!"

"Oh, I'm dreadfully sorry, Ratty, Vyme." Coolth, water. Nausea swept away as solicitous nurses hastily put the pieces back together until everything was beautiful, or so austerely horrible it could be appreciated as beauty. "Anyway," she went on, "they came back with some sort of disease they picked up out there. Apparently it's not contagious, but they're stuck with it for the rest of their lives. Every few days they suddenly have a blackout. It's preceded by a fit of hysterics. It's just one of those stupid things they can't do anything about yet. It doesn't hurt their being golden."

Ratlit began to laugh. Suddenly he asked, "How long are they passed out for?"

"Only a few hours," Alegra said. "It must be terribly annoying." And I began to feel mildly itchy in all sorts of unscratchable places, my shoulder blades, somewhere down my ear, the roof of my mouth. Have you ever tried to scratch the roof of your mouth?

"Well," Ratlit said, "let's sit down and wait it out."

"We can talk," Alegra said, patly. "That way it won't seem like such a long . . ." and hundreds of years later she finished ". . . time."

"Good," Ratlit said. "I wanted to talk to you. That's why I came up here in the first place."

"Oh, fine!" Alegra said. "I love to talk. I want to talk about love. Loving someone" (an incredible yearning twisted my stomach, rose to block my throat) "I mean really loving someone" (the yearning brushed the edge of agony) "means you are willing to admit the person you love is not what you first fell in love with, not the image you first had; and you must be able to like them still for being as close to that image as they are, and avoid disliking them for being so far away."

And through the tenderness that suddenly obliterated all hurt, Ratlit's voice came from the jeweled mosaics shielding him: "Alegra, I want to talk about loneliness."

"I'm on my way home, kids," I said. "Tell me what happens with Prince Charming when he wakes up." They kept on talking while I went through the difficulties of finding my way out without Alegra's help. When my head cleared, halfway down the stairs, I couldn't tell you if I'd been there five minutes or five years.

When I got to the hangar next morning Sandy was filing the eight-foot prongs on the conveyer. "You got a job coming in about twenty minutes," he called down from the scaffold.

"I hope it's not another of those rebuilt jobs."

"Yep."

"Hell," I said. "I don't want to see another one for six weeks."

"All he wants is a general tune-up. Maybe two hours."

"Depends on where it's been," I said. "Where *has* it been?"

"Just back from—"

"Never mind." I started toward the office cubicle. "I think I'll put the books in order for the last six months. Can't let it go forever."

"Boss!" Sandy protested. "That'll take all day!"

"Then I better get started." I leaned back out the door. "Don't disturb me."

Of course as soon as the shadow of the hull fell over the office window I came out in my overalls, after giving Sandy five minutes to get it grappled and himself worried. I took the lift up to the one-fifty catwalk. When I stepped out, Sandy threw me a grateful smile from his scar-ugly face. The golden had already started his instructions. When I reached them and coughed, the golden turned to me and continued talking, not bothering to fill me in on what he had said before, figuring Sandy and I would put it together. You could tell this golden had made his pile. He wore an immaculate blue tunic, with bronze codpiece, bracelets and earrings. His hair was the same bronze, his skin was burned red-black, and his blue-gray eyes and tight-muscled mouth were proud, proud, proud. While I finished getting instructions, Sandy quietly got started unwelding the eight-foot seal of the organum so we could get to the checkout circuits.

Finally the golden stopped talking—that's the only way you could tell he was finished—and leaned his angular six and a half feet against the railing, clicking his glossy, manicured nails against the pipe a few times. He had that same sword-length pinky nail, all white against his skin. I climbed out on the rigging to help Sandy.

We had been at work ten minutes when a kid, maybe eighteen or nineteen, barefoot and brown, black hair hacked off shoulder length, a rag that didn't fit tucked around under his belt, and dirty, came wandering down the catwalk. His thumbs were hooked under the metal links: golden.

First I thought he'd come from the ship. Then I realized he'd just stalked into the hangar from outside and come up on the lift.

"Hey, brother!" The kid who was golden hooked his thumbs in his belt, as Sandy and I watched the dialogue from the rigging on the side of the hull. "I'm getting tired of hanging around this Star-pit. Just about broke as well. Where you running to?"

The man who was golden clicked his nails again. "Go away, distant cousin."

"Come on, brother, give me a berth on your lifeboat out of this dungheap to someplace worthwhile."

"Go away, or I'll kill you."

"Now, brother, I'm just a youngster adrift in this forsaken quarter of the sky. Come on, now—"

Suddenly the blond man whirled from the railing, grabbed up a four-foot length of pipe leaning beside him, and swung it so hard it hissed. The black-haired ragamuffin leapt back and from under his rag snatched something black that, with a flick of that long nail, grew seven inches of blade. The bar swung again, caught the shoulder of the boy, then clattered against the hull. He shrieked and came straight forward. The two bodies locked, turned, fell. A gurgle, and the man's hands slipped from the neck of the ragamuffin. The boy scrambled back to his feet. Blood bubbled and popped on the hot blade.

A last spasm caught the man; he flipped over, smearing the catwalk, rolled once more, this time under the rail, and dropped—two hundred and fifty feet to the cement flooring.

Flick. Off went the power in the knife. The golden wiped powdered blood on his thigh, spat over the rail and said softly, "No relative of mine." Flick. The blade itself disappeared. He started down the catwalk.

"Hey!" Sandy called, when he got his voice back up into his throat, "what about . . . I mean you . . . well, your ship!" There are no familial inheritance laws among golden —only rights of plunder.

The golden glanced back. "I give it to you," he sneered. His shoulder must have been killing him, but he stepped into the lift like he was walking into a phone booth. That's a golden for you.

Sandy was horrified and bewildered. Behind his pitted ugliness there was that particularly wretched amazement only the totally vulnerable get when hurt.

"That's the first time you've ever seen an incident like that?" I felt sorry for him.

"Well, I wandered into Gerg's Bar a couple of hours after they had that massacre. But the ones who started it were drunk."

"Drunk or sober," I said. "Believe me, it doesn't mean that much difference to the way a man acts." I shook my head. "I keep forgetting you've only been here three months."

Sandy, upset, looked down at the body on the flooring. "What about him? And the ship, boss?"

"I'll call the wagon to come scrape him up. The ship is yours."

"Huh?"

"He gave it to you. It'll stand up in court. It just takes one witness. Me."

"What am I gonna do with it? I mean I would have to haul it to a junk station to get the salvage. Look, boss, I'm gonna give it to you. Sell it or something. I'd feel sort of funny with it anyway."

"I don't want it. Besides, then I'd be involved in the transaction and couldn't be a witness."

"I'll be a witness." Ratlit stepped from the lift. "I caught the whole bit when I came in the door. Great acoustics in this place." He whistled again. The echo came back. Ratlit closed his eyes for a moment. "Ceiling is . . . a hundred and twenty feet overhead, more or less. How's that, huh?"

"Hundred and twenty-seven," I said.

Ratlit shrugged. "I need more practice. Come on, Sandy, you give it to him, and I'll be a witness."

"You're a minor," Sandy said. Sandy didn't like Ratlit. I used to think it was because Ratlit was violent and flamboyant where Sandy was stolid and ugly. Even though Sandy kept protesting the temporariness of his job to me, I remember, when I first got to the Star-pit, those long-dying thoughts I'd had about leaving. It was a little too easy to see Sandy a mechanic here thirty years from now. I wasn't the only one it had happened to. Ratlit had been a grease monkey here three weeks. You tell me where he was going to be in three more. "Aren't you supposed to be working at Poloscki's?" Sandy said, turning back to the organum.

"Coffee break," Ratlit said. "If you're going to give it away, Sandy, can I have it?"

"So you can claim salvage? Hell, no!"

"I don't want it for salvage. I want it for a present." Sandy looked up again. "Yeah. To give to someone else. Finish the tune-up and give it to me, okay?"

"You're nuts, kid-boy," Sandy said. "Even if I gave you the ship, what you gonna pay for the work with?"

"Aw, it'll only take a couple of hours. You're half done anyway. I figured you'd throw in the tune-up along with it. If you really want the money, I'll get it to you a little at a time. Vyme, what sort of professional discount will you give me? I'm just a grease monkey, but I'm still in the business."

I whacked the back of his red head between a-little-too-playfully and not-too-hard. "Come on, kid-boy," I said. "Help me take care of puddles downstairs. Sandy, finish it up, huh?"

Sandy grunted and plunged both hands back into the organum.

As soon as the lift door closed, Ratlit demanded, "You gonna give it to me, Vyme?"

"It's Sandy's ship," I said.

"You tell him, and he will."

I laughed. "You tell me how your golden turned out when he came to. I assume that's who you want the ship for. What sort of fellow was he?"

Ratlit hooked his fingers in the mesh wall of the lift cage and leaned back. "There're only two types of golden." He began to swing from side to side. "Mean ones and stupid ones." He was repeating a standard line around the Star-pit.

"I hope yours is stupid," I said, thinking of the two who'd just ruined Sandy's day and upset mine.

"Which is worse?" Ratlit shrugged. That is the rest of the line. When a golden isn't being outright mean, he exhibits the sort of nonthinkingness that gets other people hurt—you remember the one that nearly rammed my ship, or the ones who didn't bother to bring back the Kyber antitoxin? "But this one"—Ratlit stood up—"is unbelievably stupid."

"Yesterday you hated them. Today you want to give one a ship?"

"He doesn't have one," Ratlit explained calmly, as though that warranted all change of attitude. "And because he's sick, it'll be hard for him to find work unless he has one of his own."

"I see." We bounced on the silicon cushion. I pushed open the door and started for the office. "What all went on after I left? I must have missed the best part of the evening."

"You did. Will I really need that much more sleep when I pass thirty-five?"

"Cut the cracks and tell me what happened."

"Well—" Ratlit leaned against the office door jamb while I dialed necrotics. "Alegra and I talked a little after you left, till finally we realized the golden was awake and listening. Then he told us we were beautiful."

I raised an eyebrow. "Mmmm?"

"That's what we said. And he said it again, that watching us talk and think and build was one of the most beautiful things he'd ever seen. 'What have you seen?' we asked him. And he began to tell us." Ratlit stopped breathing, something built up, then, at once, it came out. "Oh, Vyme, the places he's been! The things he's done! The landscapes he's starved in, the hells where he's had to lie down and go to sleep he was that tired, or the heavens he's soared through screaming! Oh, the things he told us about! And Alegra made them almost real so we could all be there again, just like she used to do when she was a psychiatrist! The stories, the places, the things . . ."

"Sounds like it was really something."

"It was nothing!" he came back vehemently. "It was all in the tears that wash your eyes, in the humming in your ears, in the taste of your own saliva. It was just a hallucination, Vyme! It wasn't real." Here his voice started cracking between the two octaves that were after it. "But that thing I told you about . . . huge . . . alive and dead at the same time, like a star . . . way in another galaxy. Well, he's seen it. And last night, but it wasn't real of course, but . . . I almost heard it . . . singing!" His eyes were huge and green and bright. I felt envious of anyone who could pull this reaction from kids like Alegra and Ratlit.

"So, we decided"—his voice fixed itself on the proper side of middle C—"after he went back to sleep, and we lay awake talking a while longer, that we'd try and help him get back out there. Because it's . . . wonderful!"

"That's fascinating." When I finished my call, I stood up from the desk. I'd been sitting on the corner. "After work I'll buy you dinner and you can tell me all about the things he showed you."

"He's still there, at Alegra's," Ratlit said—helplessly, I realized after a moment. "I'm going back there right after work."

"Oh," I said. I didn't seem to be invited.

"It's just a shame," Ratlit said when we came out of the office, "that he's so stupid." He glanced at the mess staining the concrete and shook his head.

I'd gone back to the books when Sandy stepped in. "All finished. What say we knock off for a beer or something, huh, boss?"

"All right," I said, surprised. Sandy was usually as social as he was handsome. "Want to talk about something?"

"Yeah." He looked relieved.

"That business this morning got to your head, huh?"

"Yeah," he repeated.

"There is a reason," I said as I made ready to go. "It's got something to do with the psychological part of being a golden. Meanness and stupidity, like everyone says. But however it makes them act here, it protects them from complete insanity at the twenty thousand light-year limit."

"Yeah. I know, I know." Sandy had started stepping uncomfortably from one boot to the other. "But that's not what I wanted to talk about."

"It isn't?"

"Um-um."

"Well?" I asked after a moment.

"It's that kid, the one you're gonna give the ship to."

"Ratlit?"

"Yeah."

"I haven't made up my mind about giving him the ship," I lied. "Besides, legally it's yours."

"You'll give it to him," Sandy said. "And I don't care, I mean not about the ship. But, boss, I gotta talk to you about that kid-boy."

Something about Sandy . . .

I'd never realized he'd thought of Ratlit as more than a general nuisance. Also, he seemed sincerely worried about me. I was curious. It took him all the way to the bar and through two beers—while I drank hot milk with honey—before he tongued and chewed what he wanted to say into shape.

"Boss, understand, I'm nearer Ratlit than you. Not only my age. My life's been more like his than yours has. You look at him like a son. To me, he's a younger brother: I taught him all the tricks. I don't understand him completely but I see him clearer than you do. He's had a hard time, but not as hard as you think. He's gonna take you—and I don't mean money—for everything he can."

Where the hell that came from I didn't know and didn't like. "He won't take anything I don't want to give."

"Boss?" Sandy suddenly asked. "You got kids of your own?"

"Nine," I said. "Did have. I don't see the ones who're left now, for which their parents have always been just as happy—except one. And she was sensible enough to go along with the rest, while she was alive."

"Oh." Sandy got quiet again. Suddenly he went scrambling in his overall pouch and pulled out a three-inch porta-pix. Those great, greasy hands that I was teaching to pick up an eggshell through a five-hundred-to-one-ratio waldo were clumsily fumbling at the push-pull levers. "I got kids," he said. "See. Seven of them."

And on the porta-pix screen was a milling, giggling group of little apes that couldn't have been anybody else's. All the younger ones lacked was acne. They even shuffled back and forth from one foot to the other. They began to wave, and the speaker in the back chirped: "Hi, Da! Hello, Da! Da, Mommy says to say we love you! Da, Da, come home soon!"

"I'm not with them now," he said throatily. "But I'm going back soon as I get enough money so I can take them all out of that hell-hole they're in now and get the whole family with a decent-sized proke-group. There're only twenty-three adults there now, and things were beginning to rub. That's why I left in the first place. It was getting so nobody could talk to anyone else. That's pretty rough on all our kids, thirty-two when I left. But soon I'll be able to fix that."

"On the salary I'm paying you?" This was the first I'd heard of any of this; that was my first reaction. My second, which I didn't voice, was: Then why the hell don't you take that ship and sell it somehow! Over forty and self-employed, the most romantic become monetarily practical.

Sandy's fist came down hard on the bar. "That's what I'm trying to say to you, boss! About you, about Ratlit. You've all got it in your heads that this, out here, is it! The end! Sure, you gotta accept limitations, but the right

ones. Sure, you have to admit there are certain directions
in which you cannot go. But once you do that, you find
there are others where you can go as far as you want.
Look, I'm not gonna hang around the Star-pit all my life!
And if I make my way back toward galactic center, make
enough money so I can go home, raise my family the way
I want, that's going forward, forward even from here. Not
back."

"All right," I said. Quiet Sandy surprised me. I still
wondered why he wasn't breaking his tail to get salvage on
that ship that had just fallen into his hands, if getting back
home with money in his pocket was that important. "I'm
glad you told me about yourself. Now how does it all tie
up with Ratlit?"

"Yeah. Ratlit." He put the porta-pix back in his overall
pouch. "Boss, Ratlit is the kid your own could be. You
want to give him the advice, friendship, and concern he's
never had, that you couldn't give yours. But Ratlit is also
the kid I was about ten years ago, started no place, with no
destination, and no values to help figure out the way, mixed
up in all the wrong things, mainly because he's not sure
where the right ones are."

"I don't think you're that much like Ratlit," I told him.
"I think you may wish you were. You've done a lot of the
things Ratlit's done? Ever write a novel?"

"I tried to write a trilogy," Sandy said. "It was lousy.
But it pushed some things off my chest. So I got something
out of it, even if nobody else did, which is what's important. Because now I'm a better mechanic for it, boss. Until
I admit to myself what I can't do, it's pretty hard to work
on what I can. Same goes for Ratlit. You too. That's growing up. And one thing you can't do is help Ratlit by giving
him a ship he can't fly."

Growing up brought back the picture. "Sandy, did you
ever build an ecologarium when you were a kid?"

"No." The word had the puzzled inflection that means,
Don't-even-know-what-one-is.

"I didn't either," I told him. Then I grinned and punched

him on the shoulder. "Maybe you're a little like me, too? Let's get back to work."

"Another thing," Sandy said, not looking very happy as he got off the stool. "Boss, that kid's gonna hurt you. I don't know how, but it's gonna seem like he hunted for how to make it hurt most, too. That's what I wanted to tell you, boss."

I was going to urge him to take the ship, but he handed me the keys back in the hangar before I could say anything, and walked away. When people who should be clearing up their own problems start giving you advice . . . well, there was something about Sandy I didn't like.

If I can't take long walks at night with company, I take them by myself. I was strolling by the Edge, the world-wind was low, and the Stellarplex, the huge heat-gathering mirror that's hung nine thousand miles off the Pit, was out. It looks vaguely like the moon used to look from Earth, only twice as big, perfectly silver, and during the three and a half days it faces us it's always full.

Then, up ahead where the fence was broken, I saw Ratlit kicking gravel over the Edge. He was leaning against a lamppost, his shirt ballooning and collapsing at his back.

"Hey, kid-boy! Isn't the golden still at Alegra's?"

Ratlit saw me and shrugged.

"What's the matter?" I asked when I reached him. "Ate dinner yet?"

He shrugged again. His body had the sort of ravenous metabolism that shows twenty-four hours without food. "Come on. I promised you a meal. Why so glum?"

"Make it something to drink."

"I know about your phony I.D.," I told him. "But we're going to eat. You can have milk, just like me."

No protests, no dissertation on the injustice of liquor laws. He started walking with me.

"Come on, kid-boy, talk to gramps. Don't you want your ship any more?"

Suddenly he clutched my forearm with white, bony fingers. My forearm is pretty thick, and he couldn't get his hands around it. "Vyme, you've got to make Sandy give it to me now! You've got to!"

"Kid-boy, talk to me."

"Alegra." He let go. "And the golden. Hate golden, Vyme. Always hate them. Because if you start to like one, and then start hating again, it's worse."

"What's going on? What are they doing?"

"He's talking. She's hallucinating. And neither one pays any attention to me."

"I see."

"You don't see. You don't understand about Alegra and me."

Then I was the only one who'd met the both of them who didn't. "I know you're very fond of each other." More could be said.

Ratlit said more. "We don't even like each other that much, Vyme. But we need each other. Since she's been here, I get her medicine for her. She's too sick to go out much now. And when I have bad changes, or sometimes bright recognitions, it doesn't matter, I bring them to her, and she builds pictures of them for me, and we explore them together and . . . learn about things. When she was a psychiatrist for the government, she learned an awful lot about how people tick. And she's got an awful lot to teach me, things I've got to know." Fifteen-year-old ex-psychiatrist drug addicts? Same sort of precocity that produces thirteen-year-old novelists. Get used to it. "I need her now almost as much as she needs her . . . medicine."

"Have you told the golden you've got him a ship?"

"You didn't say I could have it yet."

"Well, I say so right now. Why don't we go back there and tell him he can be on his way? If we put it a little more politely, don't you think that'll do the trick?"

He didn't say anything. His face just got back a lot of its life.

"We'll go right after we eat. What the hell, I'll buy you a drink. I may even have one with you."

Alegra's was blinding when we arrived. "Ratlit, oh,

you're back! Hello, Vyme! I'm so glad you're both here! Everything is beautiful tonight!"

"The golden," Ratlit said. "Where's the golden?"

"He's not here." A momentary throb of sadness dispelled with tortuous joy. "But he's coming back!"

"Oh," Ratlit said. His voice echoed through the long corridors of golden absence winding the room. " 'Cause I got a ship for him. All his. Just had a tune-up. He can leave any time he wants to."

"Here're the keys," I said, taking them from my pouch for dramatic effect. "Happen to have them right here."

As I handed them to Ratlit there were fireworks, applause, a fanfare of brasses. "Oh, that's wonderful. Wonderful! Because guess what, Ratlit? Guess what, Vyme?"

"I don't know," Ratlit said. "What?"

"I'm a golden too!" Alegra cried from the shoulders of the cheering crowd that pushed its way through more admiring thousands.

"Huh?"

"I, me, myself am actually an honest-to-goodness golden. I just found out today."

"You can't be," Ratlit said. "You're too old for it just to show up now."

"Something about my medicine," Alegra explained. "It's dreadfully complicated." The walls were papered with anatomical charts, music by Stockhausen. "Something in my medicine kept it from coming out until now, until a golden could come to me, drawing it up and out of the depths of me, till it burst out, beautiful and wonderful and . . . golden! Right now he's gone off to Carlson Labs with a urine sample for a final hormone check. They'll let him know in an hour, and he'll bring back my golden belt. But he's sure already. And when he comes back with it, I'm going to go with him to the galaxies, as his apprentice. We're going to find a cure for his sickness and something that will make it so I won't need my medicine any more. He says if you have all the universe to roam around in, you can find anything you look for. But you need it *all*— not just a cramped little cluster of a few billion stars off in a corner by itself. Oh, I'm free, Ratlit, like you always wanted to be! While you were gone, he . . . well, did something to me that was . . . *golden!* It triggered my hormonal imbalance." The image came in through all five senses. Breaking the melodious ecstasy came the clatter of keys as Ratlit hurled them at the wall.

I left feeling pretty odd. Ratlit had started to go too, but Alegra called him back. "Oh, now don't go on like that, Ratty! Act your age. Won't you stay and do me one little last favor?"

So he stayed. When I untangled myself from the place and was walking home, I kept on remembering what Alegra had said about love.

Work next day went surprisingly smoothly. Poloscki called me up about ten and asked if I knew where Ratlit was because he hadn't been at work that day. "You're sure the kid isn't sick?"

I said I'd seen him last night and that he was probably all right. Poloscki made a disgusted sound and hung up.

Sandy left a few minutes early, as he'd been doing all week, to run over to the post office before it closed. He was expecting a letter from his group, he said. I felt strange about having given the ship away out from under him. It was sort of an immature thing to do. But he hadn't said anything about wanting it, and Ratlit was still doing Alegra favors, so maybe it would all work out for the best.

I thought about visiting Alegra that evening. But there was the last six-months' paper work, still not finished. I went into the office, plugged in the computer and got ready to work late.

I was still at it sometime after eleven when the entrance light blinked, which meant somebody had opened the hangar door. I'd locked it. Sandy had the keys so he could come in early. So it was Sandy. I was ready for a break and all set to jaw with him awhile. He was always coming back to do a little work at odd hours. I waited for him to come into the office. But he didn't.

Then the needle on the power gauge, which had been

hovering near zero with only the drain of the little office computer, swung up to seven. One of the big pieces of equipment had been cut in.

There was some cleanup work to do, but nothing for a piece that size. Frowning, I switched off the computer and stepped out of the office. The first great opening in the hangar roof was mostly blocked with the bulk of Ratlit's/Sandy's/my ship. Stellarplex light curved smoothly over one side, then snarled in the fine webbing of lifts, catwalks, haul-lines, and grappler rigging. The other two openings were empty, and hundred-meter circles of silver dropped through assembly riggings to the concrete floor. Then I saw Sandy.

He stood just inside the light from the last opening, staring up at the Stellarplex, its glare lost in his ruined face. As he raised his left hand—when it started to move I thought it looked too big—light caught on the silver joints of the master-gauntlet he was wearing. I knew where the power was going.

As his hand went above his head, a shadow fell over him as a fifteen-foot slave talon swung from the darkness, its movement aping the master-glove. He dropped his hand in front of his face, fingers curved. Metal claws lowered about him, beginning to quiver. Something about . . . he was trying to kill himself!

I started running toward those hesitant, gaping claws, leaped into the grip, and reached over his shoulder to slap my forearm into the control glove, just as he squeezed. Like I said, my forearm is big, but when those claws came together, it was a tight fit. Sandy was crying.

"You stupid," I shouted, "inconsiderate, bird-brained, infantile"—at last I got the glove off—"puerile . . ." Then I said, "What the hell is the matter with you?"

Sandy was sitting on the floor now, his head hung between his shoulders. He stank.

"Look," I said, maneuvering the talon back into place with the gross-motion controls on the gauntlet's wrist, "if you want to go jump off the Edge, that's fine with me. Half the gate's down anyway. But don't come here and mess up my tools. You can squeeze your own head up a little, but you're not going to bust up my glove here. You're fired. Now tell me what's wrong."

"I knew it wasn't going to work. Wasn't even worth trying. I knew . . ." His voice was getting all mixed up with the sobs. "But I thought maybe . . ." Beside his left hand was the porta-pix, its screen cracked. And a crumpled piece of paper.

I turned off the glove, and the talons stopped humming twenty feet overhead. I picked up the paper and smoothed it out. I didn't mean to read it all the way through.

Dear Sanford,
 Things have been difficult since you left but not too hard and I guess a lot of pressure is off everybody since you went away and the kids are getting used to your not being here though Bobbi-D cried a lot at first. She doesn't now. We got your letter and were glad to hear things had begun to settle down for you though Hank said you should have written before this and was very mad though Mary tried to calm him down but he just said, "When he married you all he married me too, damn it, and I've got just as much right to be angry at him as you have," which is true, Sanford, but I tell you what he said because it's a quote and I think you should know exactly what's being said, especially since it expresses something we all feel on one level or another. You said you might be able to send us a little money, if we wanted you home, which I think would be very good, the money I mean, though Laura said if I put that in the letter she would divorce us, but she won't, and like Hank I've got a right to say what I feel which is, Yes, I think you should send money, especially after that unpleasant business just before you left. But we are all agreed we do not want you to come back. And would rather not have the money if that's what it meant.
 That is hard but true. As you can gather your letter caused quite an upset here. I would like—which makes me different from the others but is why they wanted me to write this letter—to hear from you again and keep track of what you are doing because I used to love you very much and I never could hate you. But like Bobbi-D, I have stopped crying.
                    Sincerely—

The letter was signed "Joseph." In the lower corner

were the names of the rest of the men and women of the group.

"Sandy?"

"I knew they wouldn't take me back. I didn't even really try, did I? But—"

"Sandy, get up."

"But the *children*," he whispered. "What's gonna happen to the children?"

And there was a sound from the other end of the hangar. Three stories up the side of the ship in the open hatchway, silvered by Stellarplex light, stood the golden, the one Ratlit and I had found on the street. You remember what he looked like. He and Alegra must have sneaked in while Sandy and I were struggling with the waldo. Probably they wanted to get away as soon as possible before Ratlit made real trouble, or before I changed my mind and got the keys back. All this ship-giving had been done without witnesses. The sound was the lift rising toward the hatchway. "The children . . ." Sandy whispered again.

The door opened, and a figure stepped out in the white light. Only it was Ratlit! It was Ratlit's red hair, his gold earring, his bouncy run as he started for the hatch. And there were links of yellow metal around his waist.

Baffled, I heard the golden call: "Everything checks out inside, brother. She'll fly us anywhere."

And Ratlit cried, "I got the grapples all released, brother. Let's go!" Their voices echoed down through the hangar. Sandy raised his head, squinting.

As Ratlit leapt into the hatch, the golden caught his arm around the boy's shoulder. They stood a moment, gazing at one another, then Ratlit turned to look down into the hangar, back on the world he was about to leave. I couldn't tell if he knew we were there or not. Even as the hatch swung closed, the ship began to whistle.

I hauled Sandy back into the shock chamber. I hadn't even locked the door when the thunder came and my ears nearly split. I think the noise surprised Sandy out of himself. It broke something up in my head, but the pieces were falling wrong.

"Sandy," I said, "we've got to get going!"

"Huh?" He was fighting the drunkenness and probably his stomach too.

"I don't wanna go nowhere."

"You're going anyway. I'm sure as hell not going to leave you alone."

When we were halfway up the stairs I figured she wasn't there. I felt just the same. Was she with them in the ship?

"My medicine. Please can't you get my medicine? I've got to have my medicine, please, please . . . please." I could just hear the small, high voice when I reached the door. I pushed it open.

Alegra lay on the mattress, pink eyes wide, white hair frizzled around her balding skull. She was incredibly scrawny, her uncut nails black as Sandy's nubs without the excuse of hours in a graphite-lubricated gauntlet. The translucency of her pigmentless skin under how-many-days of dirt made my flesh crawl. Her face drew in around her lips like the flesh about a scar. "My medicine. Vyme, is that you? You'll get my medicine for me, Vyme? Won't you get my medicine?" Her mouth wasn't moving, but the voice came on. She was too weak to project on any but the aural level. It was the first time I'd seen Alegra without her cloak of hallucination, and it brought me up short.

"Alegra," I said when I got hold of myself. "Ratlit and the golden went off on the ship!"

"Ratlit. Oh, nasty Ratty, awful little boy! He wouldn't get my medicine. But you'll get it for me, won't you, Vyme? I'm going to die in about ten minutes, Vyme. I don't want to die. Not like this. The world is so ugly and painful now. I don't want to die here."

"Don't you have any?" I stared around the room I hadn't seen since Drunk-roach lived there. It was a lot worse. Dried garbage, piled first in one corner, now covered half the floor. The rest was littered with papers, broken glass, and a spilled can of something unrecognizable for the mold.

"No. None here. Ratlit gets it from a man who hangs out in Gerg's over on Calle-X. Oh, Ratlit used to get it for me every day, such a nice little boy, every day he would bring me my lovely medicine, and I never had to leave my room at all. You go get it for me, Vyme!"

"It's the middle of the night, Alegra! Gerg's is closed, and Calle-X is all the way across the Pit anyway. Couldn't even get there in ten minutes, much less find this character and come back!"

"If I were well, Vyme, I'd fly you there in a cloud of light pulled by peacocks and porpoises, and you'd come back to hautboys and tambourines, bringing my beautiful medicine to me, in less than an eye's blink. But I'm sick now. And I'm going to die."

There was a twitch in the crinkled lid of one pink eye.

"Alegra, what happened!"

"Ratlit's insane!" she projected with shocking viciousness. I heard Sandy behind me catch his breath. "Insane at twenty thousand light-years, dead at twenty-five."

"But his golden belt . . ."

"It was mine! It was my belt and he stole it. And he wouldn't get my medicine. Ratlit's not a golden. I'm a golden, Vyme! I can go anywhere, anywhere at all! I'm a golden golden golden . . . But I'm sick now. I'm so sick."

"But didn't the golden know the belt was yours?"

"Him? Oh, he's so incredibly stupid! He would believe anything. The golden went to check some papers and get provisions and was gone all day, to get my belt. But you were here that night. I asked Ratlit to go get my medicine and take another sample to Carlson's for me. But neither of them came back till I was very sick, very weak. Ratlit found the golden, you see, told him that I'd changed my mind about going, and that he, Ratlit, was a golden as well, that he'd just been to Carlson's. So the golden gave him my belt and off they went."

"But how in the world would he believe a kid with a story like that?"

"You know how stupid a golden can be, Vyme. As

stupid as they can be mean. Besides, it doesn't matter to him if Ratlit dies. He doesn't care if Ratlit was telling the truth or not. The golden will live. When Ratlit starts drooling, throwing up blood, goes deaf first and blind last and dies, the golden won't even be sad. He's too stupid to feel sad. That's the way golden are. But I'm sad, Vyme, because no one will bring me my medicine."

My frustration had to lash at something; she was there. "You mean you didn't know what you were doing to Ratlit by leaving, Alegra? You mean you didn't know how much he wanted to get out, and how much he needed you at the time? You couldn't see what it would do to him if you deprived him of the thing he needed and rubbed his nose in the thing he hated both at once? You couldn't guess that he'd pull something crazy? Oh, kid-girl, you talk about golden. You're the stupid one!"

"Not stupid," she projected quietly. *"Mean,* Vyme. I knew he'd try to do something. I just didn't think he'd succeed. Ratlit is really such a child."

The frustration, spent, became rolling sadness. "Couldn't you have waited just a little longer, Alegra? Couldn't you have worked out the leaving some other way, not hurt him so much?"

"I wanted to get out, Vyme, to keep going and not be trapped, to be free. Like Ratlit wanted, like you want, like Sandy wants, like golden. Only I was cruel. I had the chance to do it and I took it. Why is that bad, Vyme? Unless, of course, that's what being free means."

A twitch in the eyelid again. It closed. The other stayed open.

"Alegra—"

"I'm a golden, Vyme. A golden. And that's how golden are. But don't be mad at me, Vyme. Don't. Ratlit was mean, too, not to give me my medi—"

The other eye closed. I closed mine too and tried to cry, but my tongue was pushing too hard on the roof of my mouth.

Sandy came to work the next day, and I didn't mention his being fired. The teletapes got hold of it, and the leadlines tried to make the thing as sordid as possible:

X-CON TEEN-AGER (they didn't mention his novel)
SLAYS JUNKY SWEETHEART! DIES HORRIBLY!

They didn't mention the golden either. They never do.

Reporters pried around the hangar awhile, trying to get us to say the ship was stolen. Sandy came through pretty well. "It was his ship," he grunted, putting lubricant in the gauntlets. "I gave it to him."

"What are you gonna give a kid like that a ship for? Maybe you loaned it to him. 'Dies horrible death in borrowed ship.' That sound okay?"

"Gave it to him. Ask the boss." He turned back toward the scaffolding. "He witnessed."

"Look, even if you liked the kid, you're not saving him anything by covering up."

"I didn't like him," Sandy said, "but I gave him the ship."

"Thanks," I told Sandy when they left, not sure what I was thanking him for but still feeling very grateful. "I'll do you a favor back."

A week later Sandy came in and said, "Boss, I want my favor."

I narrowed my eyes against his belligerent tone. "So you're gonna quit at last. Can you finish out the week?"

He looked embarrassed, and his hands started moving around in his overall pouch. "Well, yeah. I am gonna leave. But not right away, boss. It is getting a little hard for me to take, out here."

"You'll get used to it," I said. "You know there's something about you that's, well, a lot like me. I learned. You will too."

Sandy shook his head. "I don't think I want to." His hand came out of his pocket. "See, I got a ticket." In his dirty fingers was a metal-banded card. "In four weeks I'm going back in from the Star-pit. Only I didn't want to tell you just now, because, well, I did want this favor, boss."

I was really surprised. "You're not going back to your group," I said. "What are you going to do?"

He shrugged. "Get a job, I don't know. There're other groups. Maybe I've grown up a little bit." His fists went way down into his pouch, and he started to shift his weight back and forth on his feet. "About that favor, boss."

"What is it?"

"I got to talking to this kid outside. He's really had it rough, Vyme." That was the first and last time Sandy ever called me by name, though I'd asked him to enough times before. "And he could use a job."

A laugh got all set to come out of me. But it didn't, because the look on his ugly face, behind the belligerence, was so vulnerable and intense. Vulnerable? But Sandy had his ticket; Sandy was going on.

"Send him to Poloscki's," I said. "Probably needs an extra grease monkey. Now let me get back to work, huh?"

"Could you take him over there?" Sandy said very quickly. "That's the favor, boss."

"Sandy, I'm awfully busy." I looked at him again. "Oh, all right."

"Hey, boss," Sandy said as I slid from behind the desk, "remember that thing you asked me if I ever had when I was a kid?"

It took a moment to come back to me. "You mean an ecologarium?"

"Yeah. That's the word." He grinned. "The kid-boy's got one. He's right outside, waiting for you."

"He's got it with him?"

Sandy nodded.

- I walked toward the hangar door picturing some kid lugging around a six-by-six plastic cage.

Outside the boy was sitting on a fuel hydrant. I'd put a few trees there, and the "day"-light from the illumination tubes arcing the street dappled the gravel around him.

He was about fourteen, with copper skin and curly black

hair. I saw why Sandy wanted me to go with him about
the job. Around his waist, as he sat hunched over on the
hydrant with his toes spread on the metal base-flange, was
a wide-linked, yellow belt: golden.

He was looking through an odd jewel-and-brass thing
that hung from a chain around his neck.

"Hey."

He looked up. There were spots of light on his blue-
black hair.

"You need a job?"

He blinked.

"My name's Vyme. What's yours?"

"You call me An." The voice was even, detached, with
an inflection that is golden.

I frowned. "Nickname?"

He nodded.

"And really?"

"Androcles."

"Oh." My oldest kid is dead. I know it because I have
all sorts of official papers saying so. But sometimes it's
hard to remember. And it doesn't matter whether the
hair is black, white, or red. "Well, let's see if we can put
you to work somewhere. Come on." An stood up, eyes
fixed on me, suspicion hiding behind high glitter. "What's
the thing around your neck?"

His eyes struck it and bounced back to my face. "Cousin?" he asked.

"Huh?" Then I remembered the golden slang. "Oh, sure.
First cousins. Brothers if you want."

"Brother," An said. Then a smile came tumbling out of
his face, silent and volcanic. He began loping beside me
as we started off toward Poloscki's. "This"—he held up
the thing on the chain—"is an ecologarium. Want to
see?" His diction was clipped, precise, and detached. But
when an expression caught on his face, it was unsettlingly
intense.

"Oh, a little one. With microorganisms?"

An nodded.

"Sure. Let's have a look."

The hair on the back of his neck pawed the chain as he bent to remove it.

I held it up to see.

Some blue liquid, a fairly large air bubble, and a glob of black-speckled jelly in a transparent globe, the size of an eyeball; it was set in two rings, one within the other, pivoted so the globe turned in all directions. Mounted on the outside ring was a curved tongue of metal at the top of which was a small tube with a pin-sized lens. The tube was threaded into a bushing, and I guess you used it to look at what was going on in the sphere.

"Self-contained," explained An. "The only thing needed to keep the whole thing going is light. Just about any frequency will do, except way up on the blue end. And the shell cuts that out."

I looked through the brass eyepiece.

I'd swear there were over a hundred life forms with five to fifty stages each: spores, zygotes, seeds, eggs, growing and developing through larvae, pupae, buds, reproducing through sex, syzygy, fission. And the whole ecological cycle took about two minutes.

Spongy masses like red lotuses clung to the air bubble. Every few seconds one would expel a cloud of black things like wrinkled bits of carbon paper into the gas where they were attacked by tiny motes I could hardly see even with the lens. Black became silver. It fell back to the liquidlike globules of mercury, and coursed toward the jelly that was emitting a froth of bubbles. Something in the froth made the silver beads reverse direction. They reddened, sent out threads and alveoli, until they reached the main bubble again as lotuses.

The reason the lotuses didn't crowd each other out was because every eight or nine seconds a swarm of green paramecia devoured most of them. I couldn't tell where they came from; I never saw one of them split or get eaten, but they must have had something to do with the thorn-balls—if only because there were either thorn-balls or paramecia floating in the liquid, but never both at once.

A black spore in the jelly wiggled, then burst the surface as a white worm. Exhausted, it laid a couple of eggs, rested until it developed fins and a tail, then swam to the bubble where it laid more eggs among the lotuses. Its fins grew larger, its tail shriveled, splotches of orange and blue appeared, till it took off like a weird butterfly to sail around the inside of the bubble. The motes that silvered the black offspring of the lotus must have eaten the parti-colored fan because it just grew thinner and frailer till it disappeared. The eggs by the lotus would hatch into bloated fish forms that swam back through the froth to vomit a glob of jelly on the mass at the bottom, then collapse. The first eggs didn't do much except turn into black spores when they were covered with enough jelly.

All this was going on amidst a kaleidoscope of frail, wilting flowers and blooming jeweled webs, vines and worms, worts and jellyfish, symbiotes and saprophytes, while rainbow herds of algae careened back and forth like glittering confetti. One rough-rinded galoot, so big you could see him without the eyepiece, squatted on the wall, feeding on jelly, batting his eye-spots while the tide surged through quivering tears of gills.

I blinked as I took it from my eye.

"That looks complicated." I handed it back to him.

"Not really." He slipped it around his neck. "Took me two weeks with a notebook to get the whole thing figured out. You saw the big fellow?"

"The one who winked?"

"Yes. Its reproductive cycle is about two hours, which trips you up at first. Everything else goes so fast. But once you see him mate with the thing that looks like a spider web with sequins—same creature, different sex—and watch the offspring aggregate into paramecia, then dissolve again, the whole thing falls into—"

"One creature!" I said. "The whole thing is a single creature!"

An nodded vigorously. "Has to be to stay self-contained." The grin on his face whipped away like a snapped win-dowshade. A very serious look was underneath. "Even after I saw the big fellow mate, it took me a week to understand it was all one."

"But if goofus and the fishnet have paramecia—" I began. It seemed logical when I made the guess.

"You've seen one before."

I shook my head. "Not like that one, anyway. I once saw something similar, but it was much bigger, about six feet across."

An's seriousness was replaced by horror. I mean he really started to shake. "How could you . . . *ever* even *see* all the . . . stuff inside, much less *catalogue* it? You say . . . *this* is complicated?"

"Hey, relax. Relax!" I said. He did. Like that. "It was much simpler," I explained and went on to describe the one our kids had made so many years ago as best I remembered.

"Oh," An said at last, his face set in its original impassivity. "It wasn't microorganisms. Simple. Yes." He looked at the pavement. "Very simple." When he looked up, another expression had scrambled his features. It took a moment to identify. "I don't see the point at all."

There was surprising physical surety in the boy's movement; his nervousness was a cat's, not a human's. But it was one of the psychological qualities of golden.

"Well," I said, "it showed the kids a picture of the way the cycles of life progress."

An rattled his chain. "That is why they gave us these things. But everything in the one you had was so primitive. It wasn't a very good picture."

"Don't knock it," I told him. "When I was a kid, all I had was an ant colony. I got my infantile *Weltanschauung* watching a bunch of bugs running around between two plates of glass. I think I would have been better prepared by a couple of hungry rats on a treadmill. Or maybe a torus-shaped fish tank alternating sharks with schools of piraas: Get them all chasing around after each other real fast—"

"Ecology wouldn't balance," An said. "You'd need snails to get rid of the waste. Then a lot of plants to reoxygenate the water, and some sort of herbivore to keep down the plants because they'd tend to choke out everything since neither the sharks nor the piranhas would eat them." Kids and their damn literal minds. "If the herbivores had some way to keep the sharks off, then you might do it."

"What's wrong with the first one I described?"

The explanation worked around the muscles of his face. "The lizards, the segment worms, the plants, worts, all their cycles were completely circular. They were born, grew up, reproduced, maybe took care of the kids awhile, then died. Their only function was reproduction. That's a pretty awful picture." He made an unintelligible face.

There was something about this wise-alecky kid who was golden, younger than Alegra, older than Ratlit, I liked.

"There are stages in here," An tapped his globe with his pinky nail, "that don't get started on their most important functions till after they've reproduced and grown up through a couple more metamorphoses as well. Those little green worms are a sterile end stage of the blue feathery things. But they put out free phosphates that the algae live on. Everything else, just about, lives on the algae—except the thorn-balls. They eat the worms when they die. There're phagocytes in there that ingest the dust-things when they get out of the bubble and start infecting the liquid." All at once he got very excited. "Each of us in the class got one of these! They made us figure them out! Then we had to prepare these recordings on whether the reproductive process was the primary function in life or an adjunctive one." Something white frothed the corners of his mouth. "I think grownups should just *leave* their kids the hell *alone*, go on and do something *else*, stop bothering us! That's what I said! That's what I *told* them!" He stopped, his tongue flicked the foam at the cusp of his lips; he seemed all right again.

"Sometimes," I said evenly, "if you leave them alone and forget about them, you end up with monsters who aren't kids any more. If you'd been left alone, you wouldn't have had a chance to put your two cents in in the first place and you wouldn't have that thing around your neck." And he was really trying to follow what I was saying. A moment past his rage, his face was as open and receptive as a two-year-old's. God, I want to stop thinking about Antoni!

"That's not what I mean." He wrapped his arms around his shoulders and bit on his forearm pensively.

"An—you're not stupid, kid-boy. You're cocky, but I don't think you're mean. You're golden." There was all my resentment, out now, Ratlit. There it is, Alegra. I didn't grow up with the word, so it meant something different to me. An looked up to ingest my meaning. The tooth-marks were white on his skin, then red around that. "How long have you been one?"

He watched me, arms still folded. "They found out when I was seven."

"That long ago?"

"Yes." He turned and started walking again. "I was very precocious."

"Oh." I nodded. "Just about half your life then. How's it been, little brother, being a golden?"

An dropped his arms. "They take you away from your group a lot of times." He shrugged. "Special classes. Training programs. I'm psychotic."

"I never would have guessed." What would you call Ratlit? What would you call Alegra?

"I know it shows. But it gets us through the psychic pressures at the reality breakdown at twenty thousand light-years. It really does. For the past few years, though, they've been planting the psychosis artificially, pretty far down in the preconscious, so it doesn't affect our ordinary behavior as much as it does the older ones. They can use this process on anybody whose hormone system is even close to golden. They can get a lot more and a lot better quality golden that way than just waiting for us to pop up by accident."

As I laughed, something else struck me. "Just what do you need a job out here for, though? Why not hitch out with some cousin or get a job on one of the inter-galactics as an apprentice?"

"I have a job in another galaxy. There'll be a ship stopping for me in two months to take me out. A whole lot of Star-pits have been established in galaxies halfway to Un-dok. I'll be going back and forth, managing roboi-equipment, doing managerial work. I thought it would be a good idea to get some practical experience out here before I left."

"Precocious." I nodded. "Look, even with roboi-equipment you have to know one hell of a lot about the inside of how many different kinds of keeler drives. You're not going to get that kind of experience in two months as a grease monkey. And roboi-equipment? I don't even have any in my place. Poloscki's got some, but I don't think you'll get your hands on it."

"I know a good deal already," An said with strained modesty.

"Yeah?" I asked him a not too difficult question and got an adequate answer. Made me feel better that he didn't come back with something really brilliant. I did know more than he did. "Where'd you learn?"

"They gave me the information the same way they implanted my psychosis."

"You're pretty good for your age." Dear old Luna Vocational! Well, maybe educational methods have improved. "Come to think of it, I was just as old as you when I started playing around with those keeler models. Dozens and dozens of helical inserts—"

"And those oily organum sensitives in all that graphite? Yes, brother! But I've never even had my hands in a waldo."

I frowned. "Hell, when I was younger than you, I could—" I stopped. "Of course, with roboi-equipment, you don't need them. But it's not a bad thing to know how they work, just in case."

"That's why I want a job." He hooked one finger on his chain. "Brother-in-law Sandy and I got to talking, so I asked him about working here. He said you might help me get in someplace."

"I'm glad he did. My place only handles big ships, and it's all waldo. Me and an assistant can do the whole thing. Poloscki's place is smaller, but handles both inter- and intra-galactic jobs, so you get more variety and a bigger crew. You find Poloscki, say I sent you, tell what you can do and why you're out here. Belt or no, you'll probably get something better than a monkey."

"Thanks, brother."

We turned off Calle-D. Poloscki's hangar was ahead. Dull thunder sounded over the roof as a ship departed.

"As soon as I despair of the younger generation," I told him, "one of you kids comes by and I start to think there's hope. Granted you're a psychopath, you're a lot better than some of your older, distant relations."

An looked up at me, apprehensive.

"You've never had a run-in with some of your cousins out here. But don't be surprised if you're dead tomorrow and your job's been inherited by some character who decided to split your head open to check on what's inside. I try to get used to you, behaving like something that isn't even savage. But, boy-kid, can your kind really mess up a guy's picture of the universe."

"And what the hell do you expect us to act like?" An shot back. Spittle glittered on his lips again. "What would *you* do if you were trapped like *us?*"

"Huh?" I said questioningly. *"You,* trapped?"

"Look." A spasm passed over his shoulders. "The psycho-technician who made sure I was properly psychotic *wasn't* a golden, *brother!* You *pay* us to bring back the weapons, dad! *We* don't fight your damn wars, *grampa! You're* the ones who take us away from our groups, say we're *too* valuable to submit to *your* laws, then deny us our heredity because we don't *breed* true, no-relative-of *mine!"*

"Now, wait a minute!"

An snatched the chain from around his neck and held it taut in front of him. His voice ground to a whisper, his eyes glittered. "I strangled one of my classmates with this chain, the one I've got in my hands now." One by one, his features blanked all expression. "They took it away from me for a week, as punishment for killing the little girl."

The whisper stopped decibels above silence, then went on evenly. "Out here, nobody will punish me. And my reflexes are faster than yours."

Fear lashed my anger as I followed the insanity flickering in his eyes.

"Now!" He made a quick motion with his hands; I ducked. "I give it to you!" He flung the chain toward me. Reflexively I caught it. An turned away instantly and stalked into Poloscki's.

When I burst through the rattling hangar door at my place, the lift was coming down. Sandy yelled through the mesh walls, "Did he get the job?"

"Probably," I yelled back, going toward the office.

I heard the cage settle on the silicon cushion. Sandy was at my side a moment later, grinning. "So how do you like my brother-in-law, Androcles?"

"Brother-in-law?" I remembered An using the phrase, but I'd thought it was part of the slang golden. Something about the way Sandy said it though. "He's your *real* brother-in-law?"

"He's Joey's kid brother. I didn't want to say anything until after you met him." Sandy came along with me toward the office door. "Joey wrote me again and said since An was coming out here he'd tell him to stop by and see me and maybe I could help him out."

"Now how the hell am I supposed to know who Joey is?" I pushed open the door. It banged the wall.

"He's one of my husbands, the one who wrote me that letter you told me you'd read."

"Oh, yeah. Him." I started stacking papers.

"I thought it was pretty nice of him after all that to tell An to look me up when he got out here. It means that there's still somebody left who doesn't think I'm a complete waste. So what do you think of Androcles?"

"He's quite a boy." I scooped up the mail that had come in after lunch, started to go through it but put it down to hunt for my coveralls.

"An used to come visit us when he got his one weekend a month off from his training program as golden," Sandy was going on. "Joey's and An's parents lived in the reeds near the estuary. But we lived back up the canyon by Chroma Falls. An and Joey were pretty close, even though Joey's my age and An was only eight or nine back then. I guess Joey was the only one who really knew what An was going through, since they were both golden."

Surprised and shocked, I turned back to the desk. "You were married with a golden?" One of the letters on the top of the pile was addressed to Alegra from Carlson's Labs. I had a carton of the kids' junk in the locker and had gotten the mail—there wasn't much—sent to the hangar, as though I were waiting for somebody to come for it.

"Yeah," Sandy said, surprised at my surprise. "Joey."

So I wouldn't stand there gaping, I picked up Alegra's letter.

"Since the traits that are golden are polychromazoic, it dies out if they only breed with each other. There's a big campaign back in galactic center to encourage them to join heterogeneous proke-groups."

"Like bluepoint Siamese cats, huh?" I ran my blackened thumbnail through the seal.

"That's right. But they're *not* animals, boss. I remember what they put that kid-boy through for psychotic reinforcement of the factors that were golden to make sure they stuck. It tore me up to hear him talk about it when he'd visit us."

I pulled a porta-pix out of Alegra's envelope. Carlson's tries to personalize its messages.

"I'm sure glad they can erase the conscious memory from the kids' minds when they have to do that sort of stuff."

"Small blessings and all that." I flipped the porta-pix on.

Personalized but mass produced: ". . . blessed addit
. . ." the little speaker echoed me. Poloscki and I had
used Carlson's a couple of times, I know. I guess every
other mechanic up here had too. The porta-pix had started
in the middle. Now it hummed back to the beginning.

"You know," Sandy went on, "Joey was different, yeah,
sort of dense about some things . . ."

"Alegra," beamed the chic, grandmotherly type Carlson's
always uses for messages of this sort, "we were so glad to
receive the urine sample you sent us by Mr. Ratlit last
Thursday . . ."

". . . even so, Joey was one of the sweetest men or
women I've ever known. He was the easiest person in the
group to live with. Maybe it was because he was away a
lot . . ."

". . . and now, just a week later—remember, Carlson's
gives results immediately and confirms them by personalized porta-pix in seven days—we are happy to tell you
that there will be a blessed addition to your group. However . . ."

". . . All right, he was different, reacted funny to a lot
of things. But nothing like this rank, destructive stupidity
you find out here at the Star-pit . . ."

". . . the paternity is not Mr. Ratlit's. If you are
interested, for your eugenic records, in further information, please send us other possible urine samples from the
men in your group, and we will be glad to confirm
paternity . . ."

". . . I can't understand the way people act out here,
boss. And that's why I'm pushing on."

". . . Thank you so much for letting us give you this
wonderful news. Remember, when in doubt, call Carlson's."

I said to Sandy, "You were married with—you loved a
golden?"

Unbidden, the porta-pix began again. I flipped it off
without looking.

"Sandy," I said, "you were hired because you were a

fair mechanic and you kept off my back. Do what you're paid for. Get out of here."

"Oh. Sure, boss." He backed quickly from the office. I sat down.

Maybe I'm old-fashioned, but when someone runs off and abandons a sick girl like that, it gets me. That was the trip to Carlson's, the one last little favor Ratlit never came back from. On-the-spot results, and formal confirmation in seven days. In her physical condition, pregnancy would have been as fatal as the withdrawal. And she was too ill for any abortive method I know of not to kill her. On-the-spot results. Ratlit must have known all that too when he got the results back, the results that Alegra was probably afraid of, the results she sent him to find. Ratlit knew Alegra was going to die anyway. And so he stole a golden belt. "Loving someone, I mean really loving someone—" Alegra had said. When someone runs off and leaves a sick girl like that, there's got to be a reason. It came together for me like two fissionables. The explosion cut some moorings in my head I thought were pretty solidly fixed.

I pulled out the books, plugged in the computer, unplugged it, put the books away, and stared into the ecologarium in my fist.

Among the swimming, flying, crawling things, mating, giving birth, growing, changing, busy at whatever their business was, I picked out those dead-end, green worms. I hadn't noticed them before because they were at the very edge of things, bumping against the wall. After they released their free phosphates and got tired of butting at the shell, they turned on each other and tore themselves to pieces.

Fear and anger is a bad combination in me.

I came close to being killed by a golden once, through that meanness and stupidity.

The same meanness and stupidity that killed Alegra and Ratlit.

And now when this damn kid threatens to—I mean at first I had thought he was threatening to—

I reached Gerg's a few minutes after the daylights went out and the street lamps came on. But I'd stopped in nearly a dozen places on the way. I remember trying to explain to a sailor from a star-shuttle who was just stopping over at the Star-pit for the first time and was all upset because one woman golden had just attacked another with a broken glass; I remember saying to the three-headed bulge of his shoulder, ". . . an ant colony! You know what it is, two pieces of glass with dirt between them, and you can see all the little ants make tunnels and hatch eggs and stuff. When I was a kid, I had an ant colony . . ." I started to shake my hand in his face. The chain from the ecologarium was tangled up in my fingers.

"Look." He caught my wrist and put it down on the counter. "It's all right now, pal. Just relax."

"You look," I said as he turned away. "When I was a kid, all I had was an *ant* colony!"

He turned back and leaned his rusty elbow on the bar. "Okay," he said affably. Then he made the most stupid and frustrating mistake he possibly could have just then. "What about your aunt?"

"My mother—"

"I thought you were telling me about your aunt?"

"Naw," I said. "My aunt, she drank too much. This is about my mother."

"All right. Your mother then."

"My mother, see, she always worried about me, getting sick and things. I got sick a lot when I was a little kid. She made me mad! Used to go down and watch the ships take off from the place they called the Brooklyn Navy Yards. They were ships that went to the stars."

The sailor's Oriental face grinned. "Yeah, me too. Used to watch 'em when I was a kid."

"But it was raining, and she wouldn't let me go."

"Aw, that's too bad. Little rain never hurt a kid. Why didn't she call up and have it turned off so you could go out? Too busy to pay attention to you, huh? One of my old men was like that."

"Both of mine were," I said. "But not my ma. She was

all over me all the time when she was there. But she made me mad!"

He nodded with real concern. "Wouldn't turn off the rain."

"Naw, couldn't. You didn't grow up where I did, narrow-minded, dark-side world. No modern conveniences."

"Off the main trading routes, huh?"

"Way off. She wouldn't let me go out, and that made me mad."

He was still nodding.

"So I broke it!" My fist came down hard on the counter, and the plastic globe in its brass cage clacked on the wood. "Broke it! Sand, glass all over the rug, on the windowsill!"

"What'd you break?"

"Smashed it, stamped on it, threw sand whenever she tried to make me stop!"

"Sand? You lived on a beach? We had a beach when I was a kid. A beach is nice for kids. What'd you break?"

"Let all the damn bugs out. Bugs in everything for days. Let 'em all out."

"Didn't have no bugs on our beach. But you said you were off the main trading routes."

"Let 'em *out!*" I banged my fist again. "Let *every*body out, whether they like it or not! It's their problem whether they make it, not mine! Don't care, I don't—" I was laughing now.

"She let you go out, and you didn't care?"

My hand came down on top of the metal cage, hard. I caught my breath at the pain. "On our beach," I said, turning my palm up to look. There were red marks across it. "There weren't any bugs on our beach." Then I started shaking.

"You mean you were just putting me on, before, about the bugs. Hey, are you all right?"

". . . broke it," I whispered. Then I smashed fist and globe and chain into the side of the counter. "Let 'em *out!"* I whirled away, clutching my bruised hand against my stomach.

"Watch it, kid-boy!"

"I'm not a kid-boy!" I shouted. "You think I'm some stupid, half-crazy kid!"

"So you're older than me. Okay?"

"I'm not a kid any more!"

"So you're ten years older than Sirius, all right? Quiet down, or they'll kick us out."

I bulled out of Gerg's. A couple of people came after me because I didn't watch where I was going. I don't know who won, but I remember somebody yelling, "Get out! Get out!" It may have been me.

I remember later, staggering under the mercury street lamp, the world-wind slapping my face, stars swarming back and forth below me, gravel sliding under my boots, the toes inches over the Edge. The gravel clicked down the metal siding, the sound terribly clear as I reeled in the loud wind, shaking my arm against the night.

As I brought my hand back, the wind lashed the cold chain across my cheek and the bridge of my nose. I lurched back, trying to claw it away. But it stayed all tangled on my fingers while the globe swung, gleaming in the street light. The wind roared. Gravel chattered down the siding.

Later, I remember the hangar door ajar, stumbling into the darkness, so that in a moment I was held from plummeting into nothing only by my own footsteps as black swerved around me. I stopped when my hip hit a workbench. I pawed around under the lip of the table till I found a switch. In the dim orange light, racked along the back of the bench in their plastic shock-cases, were the row of master-gauntlets. I slipped one out and slid my hand into it.

"Who's over there?"

"Go 'way, Sandy." I turned from the bench, switched up the power on the wrist controls. Somewhere in the dark above, a fifteen-foot slave-hand hummed to life.

"Sorry, buster. This isn't Sandy. Put that down and get away from there."

I squinted as the figure approached in the orange light, hand extended. I saw the vibra-gun and didn't bother to look at the face.

Then the gun went down. "Vyme, baby? That you? What the hell are you doing here this hour of the night?"

"Poloscki?"

"Who'd you think it was?"

"Is this your—?" I looked around, shook my head. "But I thought it was my—" I shook my head again.

Poloscki sniffed. "Hey, have you been a naughty kid-boy tonight!"

I swung my hand, and the slave-hand overhead careened twenty feet.

The gun jumped. "Look, you mess up my waldo and I will kill you, don't care who you are! Take that thing off."

"Very funny." I brought the talon down where I could see it clawing shadow.

"Come on, Vyme. I'm serious. Turn it off and put it down. You're a mess now and you don't know what you're doing."

"That kid, the golden. Did you give him a job?"

"Sure. He said you sent him. Smart so-and-so. He rehulled a little yacht with the roboi-anamechaniakatasthy-sizer, just to show me what he could do. If I knew a few more people who could handle them that well, I'd go all roboi. He's not worth a damn with a waldo, but as long as he's got that little green light in front of him, he's fine."

I brought the talons down another ten feet so that the spider hung between us. "Well, I happen to be very handy with a waldo, Poloscki."

"Vyme, you're gonna get *hurrrt* . . ."

"Poloscki," I said, "will you stop coming on like an overprotective aunt? I don't need another one."

"You're very drunk, Vyme."

"Yeah. But I'm no clumsy kid-boy who is going to mess up your equipment."

"If you do, you'll be—"

"Shut up and watch." I pulled the chain out of my pouch and tossed it onto the concrete floor. In the orange light you couldn't tell whether the cage was brass or silver.

"What's that?"

The claws came down, and the fine-point tips, millimeters above the floor, closed on the ecologarium.

"Oh, hey! I haven't seen one of those since I was ten. What are you going to do with it? Those are five-hundred-to-one strength, you know. You're gonna break it."

"That's right. Break this one too."

"Aw, come on. Let me see it first."

I lifted the globe. "Could be an eggshell," I said. "Drunk or sober I can handle this damn equipment, Poloscki."

"I haven't seen one for years. Used to have one."

"You mean it wasn't spirited back from some distant galaxy by golden, from some technology beyond our limited ken?"

"Product of the home spiral. Been around since the fifties."

I raised it over Poloscki's extended hand.

"They're supposed to be very educational. What do you want to break it for?"

"I never saw one."

"You came from someplace off the routes, didn't you? They weren't that common. Don't break it."

"I want to."

"Why, Vyme?"

Something got wedged in my throat. "Because I want to get out, and if it's not that globe, it's gonna be somebody's head." Inside the gauntlet my hand began to quiver. The talons jerked. Poloscki caught the globe and jumped back.

"Vyme!"

"I'm hanging, here at the Edge." My voice kept getting caught on the things in my throat. "I'm useless, with a bunch of monsters and fools!" The talons swung, contracted, clashed on each other. "And then when the children . . . when the *children* get so bad you can't even reach them . . ." The claw opened, reached for Poloscki who jumped back in the half-dark.

"Damn it, Vyme—"

". . . can't even reach the children any more." The talon stopped shaking, came slowly back, knotting. "I want to break something and get out. Very childishly, yes. Because nobody is paying any attention to *me*." The claw jumped. "Even when I'm trying to help. I *don't* want to hurt anybody any *more*. I *swear* it, so help me, I swear—"

"Vyme, take off the glove and listen!"

I raised the slave-hand because it was about to scrape the cement.

"Vyme, I want to pay some attention to you." Slowly Poloscki walked back into the orange light. "You've been sending me kids for five years now, coming around and checking up on them, helping them out of the stupid scrapes they get in. They haven't all been Ratlits. I like kids too. That's why I take them on. I think what you do is pretty great. Part of me loves kids. Another part of me loves you."

"Aw, Poloscki . . ." I shook my head. Somewhere disgust began.

"It doesn't embarrass me. I love you a little and wouldn't mind loving you a lot. More than once I've thought about asking you to start a group."

"*Please*, Poloscki. I've had too many weird things happen to me this week. Not tonight, huh?" I then turned the power off in the glove.

"Love shouldn't frighten you, no matter when or how it comes, Vyme. Don't run from it. A marriage between us? Yeah, it would be a little hard for somebody like you, at first. But you'd get used to it before long. Then when kids came around, there'd be two—"

"I'll send Sandy over," I said. "He's the big-hearted, marrying kind. Maybe he's about ready to try again." I pulled off the glove.

"Vyme, don't go out like that. Stay for just a minute!"

"Poloscki," I said, "I'm just not that God damn drunk!" I threw the glove on the table.

"Please, Vyme."

"You're gonna use your gun to keep me here?"

"Don't be like—"

"I hope the kids I send over here appreciate you more than I do right now. I'm sorry I busted in here. Goodnight!"

I turned from the table.

Nine thousand miles away the Stellarplex turned too. Circles of silver dropped through the roof. Behind the metal cage of the relaxed slave-claw I saw Poloscki's large, injured eyes, circles of crushed turquoise, glistening now.

And nine feet away someone said, "Ma'am?"

Poloscki glanced over her shoulder. "An, you awake?"

An stepped into the silver light, rubbing his neck. "That office chair is pretty hard, sister."

"He's here?" I asked.

"Sure," Poloscki said. "He didn't have any place to stay so I let him sleep in the office while I finished up some work in the back. Vyme, I meant what I said. Leave if you want, but not like this. Untwist."

"Poloscki," I said, "you're very sweet, you're fun in bed, and a good mechanic too. But I've been there before. Asking me to join a group is like asking me to do something obscene. I know what I'm worth."

"I'm also a good businesswoman. Don't think that didn't enter my head when I thought about marrying you." An came and stood beside her. He was breathing hard, the way an animal does when you wake it all of a sudden.

"Poloscki, you said it, I didn't: I'm a mess. That's why I'm not with my own group now."

"You're not always like this. I've never seen you touch a drop before."

"For a while," I said, "it happened with disgusting frequency. Why do you think my group dropped me?"

"Must have been a while ago. I've known you a long time. So you've grown up since then. Now it only happens every half dozen years or so. Congratulations. Come have some coffee. An, run into the office and plug in the pot. I showed you where it was." An turned like something blown by the world-wind and was gone in shadow. "Come on," Poloscki said. She took my arm, and I came with her. Before we left the light, I saw my reflection in the polished steel tool-cabinet.

"Aw, no." I pulled away from her. "No, I better go home now."

"Why? An's making coffee."

"The kid. I don't want the kid to see me like this."

"He already has. Won't hurt him. Come on."

When I walked into Poloscki's office, I felt I didn't have a damn thing left. No. I had one. I decided to give it away.

When An turned to me with the cup, I put my hands on his shoulders. He jumped, but not enough to spill the coffee. "First and last bit of alcoholic advice for the evening, kid-boy. Even if you are crazy, don't go around telling people who are not golden how they've trapped you. That's like going to Earth and complimenting a nigger on how well he sings and dances and his great sense of rhythm. He may be able to tap seven with one hand against thirteen with the other while whistling a tone row. It still shows a remarkable naïveté about the way things are." That's one of the other things known throughout the galaxy about the world I come from. When I say primitive, I mean primitive.

An ducked from under my hands, put the coffee on the desk, and turned back. "I didn't say you trapped us."

"You said we treated you lousy and exploited you, which we may, and that this trapped you—"

"I said you exploited us, which you do, *and* that we were trapped. I *didn't* say by what."

Poloscki sat down on the desk, picked up my coffee and sipped it.

I raised my head. "All right. Tell me how you're trapped."

"Oh, I'm sorry," Poloscki said. "I started drinking your coffee."

"Shut up. How are you trapped, An?"

He moved his shoulders around as though he was trying

to get them comfortable. "It started in Tyber-44 cluster. Golden were coming back with really bad psy hic sho k."

"Yes. I heard about it. That was a few years back."

An's face started to twitch; the muscles around his eyes twisted below the skin. *"Something* out there . . ."

I put my hand on the back of his neck, my thumb in the soft spot behind his ear and began to stroke, the way you get a cat to calm down. "Take it easy. Just tell me."

"Thanks," An said and bent his head forward. "We found them first in Tyber-44, but then they turned up all *over,* on half the planets in every galaxy that could support any life, and a lot more that shouldn't have been able to at all." His breathing grew coarser. I kept rubbing, and it slowed again. "I guess we have such a funny psy hology that working with them, studying them, even thinking about them too much . . . there was something about them that changes our sense of reality. The shock was bad."

"An," I said, "to be trapped, there has to be somewhere you can't go. For it to bug you, there has to be something else around that can."

He nodded under my hand, then straightened up. "I'm all right now. Just tired. You want to know where and what?"

Poloscki had put down the coffee now and was dangling the chain. An whirled to stare.

"Where?" he said. "Other universes."

"Galaxies farther out?" asked Poloscki.

"No. Completely different matrices of time and space." Staring at the swinging ball seemed to calm him even more. "No physical or temporal connection to this one at all."

"A sort of parallel—"

"Parallel? Hell!" It was almost a drawl. "There's nothing parallel about them. Out of the billions-to-the-billionth of them, most are hundreds of times the size of ours and empty. There are a few, though, whose entire spatial extent is even smaller than this galaxy. Some of them are completely dense to us, because even though there seems to be matter in them, distributed more or less as in this universe, there's no electromagnetic activity at all. No radio waves, no heat, no light." The globe swung; the voice was a whisper.

I closed my fist around the globe and took it from Poloscki. "How do you know about them? Who brings back the information? Who is it who can get out?"

Blinking, An looked back at me.

When he told me, I began to laugh. To accommodate the shifting reality tensions, the psychotic personality that is golden is totally labile. An laughed with me, not knowing why. He explained through his torrential hysteria how with the micro-micro surgical techniques from Tyber-44 they had read much of the information from a direct examination of the creature's nervous system, which covered its surface like velvet. It could take intense cold or heat, a range of pressure from vacuum to hundreds of pounds per square millimeter; but a fairly small amount of ultraviolet destroyed the neural synapses, and it died. They were small and deceptively organic because in an organic environment they appeared to breathe and eat. They had four sexes, two of which carried the young. They had clusters of retractable sense organs that first appeared to be eyes, but were sensitive to twelve distinct senses, stimulation for three of which didn't even exist in our continuum. They traveled around on four suction cups when using kinetic motion for ordinary traversal of space, were small, and looked furry. The only way to make them jump universes was to scare the life out of them. At which point they just disappeared.

An kneaded his stomach under his belt to ease the pain from so much laughter. "Working with them at Tyber-44 just cracked up a whole bunch of golden." He leaned against the desk, panting and grinning. "They had to be sent home for therapy. We still can't think about them directly, but it's easier for us to control what we think about than for you; that's part of being golden. I even had one of them for a pet, up until yesterday. The damn creatures are either totally apathetic, or vicious.

Mine was a baby, all white and soft." He held out his arms. "Yesterday it bit me and disappeared." On his wrist there was a bluish place centered on which was a crescent of pinpricks. "Lucky it was a baby. The bites infect easily."

Poloscki started drinking from my cup again as An and I started laughing all over.

As I walked back that night, black coffee slopped in my belly.

There are certain directions in which you cannot go. Choose one in which you can move as far as you want. Sandy said that? He did. And there was something about Sandy, very much like someone golden. It doesn't matter how, he's going on.

Under a street lamp I stopped and lifted up the ecologarium. The reproductive function, was it primary or adjunctive? If, I thought with the whiskey lucidity always suspect at dawn, you consider the whole ecological balance a single organism, its adjunctive, a vital reparative process along with sleeping and eating, to the primary process which is living, working, growing. I put the chain around my neck.

I was still half soused, and it felt bad. But I howled. Androcles, is drunken laughter appropriate to mourn all my dead children? Perhaps not. But tell me, Ratlit; tell me, Alegra: what better way to launch my live ones who are golden into night? I don't know. I know I laughed. Then I put my fists into my overall pouch and crunched homeward along the Edge while on my left the world-wind roared.

BABY, YOU WERE GREAT

Kate Wilhelm

Kate Wilhelm is, among many other things, a beautiful woman, a warm and loving mother and wife (her husband is editor-and-writer Damon Knight), a perceptive critic of fiction, and an extraordinarily good writer. She is the author of seven or eight fine novels, not all of them science fiction, and enough short stories to fill several volumes; among her best-known titles are **Let the Fire Fall**, **The Killer Thing**, and the story collection **The Mile Long Spaceship**. Her short story "The Planners" won a Nebula in 1969, and she has come within a couple of votes of winning Nebulas on many other occasions—as happened with the award-quality story that is included in this year's **Alpha**.

John Lewisohn thought that if one more door slammed, or one more bell rang, or one more voice asked if he was all right, his head would explode. Leaving his laboratories, he walked through the carpeted hall to the elevator that slid wide to admit him noiselessly, was lowered, gently, two floors, where there were more carpeted halls. The door he shoved open bore a neat sign, AUDITIONING

71

STUDIO. Inside, he was waved on through the reception room by three girls who knew better than to speak to him unless he spoke first. They were surprised to see him; it was his first visit there in seven or eight months. The inner room where he stopped was darkened, at first glance appearing empty, revealing another occupant only after his eyes had time to adjust to the dim lighting.

John sat in the chair next to Herb Javits, still without speaking. Herb was wearing the helmet and gazing at a wide screen that was actually a one-way glass panel permitting him to view the audition going on in the next room. John lowered a second helmet to his head. It fit snugly and immediately made contact with the eight prepared spots on his skull. As soon as he turned it on, the helmet itself was forgotten.

A girl had entered the other room. She was breathtakingly lovely, a long-legged honey blonde with slanting green eyes and apricot skin. The room was furnished as a sitting room with two couches, some chairs, end tables and a coffee table, all tasteful and lifeless, like an ad in a furniture trade publication. The girl stopped at the doorway and John felt her indecision, heavily tempered with nervousness and fear. Outwardly she appeared poised and expectant, her smooth face betraying none of her emotions. She took a hesitant step toward the couch, and a wire showed trailing behind her. It was attached to her head. At the same time a second door opened. A young man ran inside, slamming the door behind him; he looked wild and frantic. The girl registered surprise, mounting nervousness; she felt behind her for the door handle, found it and tried to open the door again. It was locked. John could hear nothing that was being said in the room; he only felt the girl's reaction to the unexpected interruption. The wild-eyed man was approaching her, his hands slashing through the air, his eyes darting glances all about them constantly. Suddenly he pounced on her and pulled her to him, kissing her face and neck roughly. She seemed paralyzed with fear for several seconds, then there was something else, a bland nothing kind of feeling that accompanied boredom sometimes, or too-complete self-assurance. As the man's hands fastened on her blouse in the back and ripped it, she threw her arms about him, her face showing passion that was not felt anywhere in her mind or in her blood.

"Cut!" Herb Javits said quietly.

The man stepped back from the girl and left her without a word. She looked about blankly, her torn blouse hanging about her hips, one shoulder strap gone. She was very beautiful. The audition manager entered, followed by a dresser with a gown that he threw about her shoulders. She looked startled; waves of anger mounted to fury as she was drawn from the room, leaving it empty. The two watching men removed their helmets.

"Fourth one so far," Herb grunted. "Sixteen yesterday; twenty the day before . . . All nothing." He gave John a curious look. "What's got you stirred out of your lab?"

"Anne's had it this time," John said. "She's been on the phone all night and all morning."

"What now?"

"Those damn sharks! I told you that was too much on top of the airplane crash last week. She can't take much more of it."

"Hold it a minute, Johnny," Herb said. "Let's finish off the next three girls and then talk." He pressed a button on the arm of his chair and the room beyond the screen took their attention again.

This time the girl was slightly less beautiful, shorter, a dimply sort of brunette with laughing blue eyes and an upturned nose. John liked her. He adjusted his helmet and felt with her.

She was excited; the audition always excited them. There was some fear and nervousness, not too much. Curious about how the audition would go, probably. The wild young man ran into the room, and her face paled. Nothing else changed. Her nervousness increased, not uncomfortably. When he grabbed her, the only emotion she registered was the nervousness.

"Cut," Herb said.

The next girl was also brunette, with gorgeously elongated legs. She was very cool, a real professional. Her mobile face reflected the range of emotions to be expected as the scene played through again, but nothing inside her was touched. She was a million miles away from it all.

The next one caught John with a slam. She entered the room slowly, looking about with curiosity, nervous, as they all were. She was younger than the other girls, less poised. She had pale gold hair piled in an elaborate mound of waves on top of her head. Her eyes were brown, her skin nicely tanned. When the man entered, her emotion changed quickly to fear, then to terror. John didn't know when he closed his eyes. He was the girl, filled with unspeakable terror; his heart pounded, adrenalin pumped into his system; he wanted to scream but could not. From the dim unreachable depths of his psyche there came something else, in waves, so mixed with terror that the two merged and became one emotion that pulsed and throbbed and demanded. With a jerk he opened his eyes and stared at the window. The girl had been thrown down to one of the couches, and the man was kneeling on the floor beside her, his hands playing over her bare body, his face pressed against her skin.

"Cut!" Herb said. His voice was shaken. "Hire her," he said. The man rose, glanced at the girl, sobbing now, and then quickly bent over and kissed her cheek. Her sobs increased. Her golden hair was down, framing her face; she looked like a child. John tore off the helmet. He was perspiring.

Herb got up, turned on the lights in the room, and the window blanked out, blending with the wall. He didn't look at John. When he wiped his face, his hand was shaking. He rammed it in his pocket.

"When did you start auditions like that?" John asked, after a few moments of silence.

"Couple of months ago. I told you about it. Hell, we had to, Johnny. That's the six hundred nineteenth girl we've tried out! Six hundred nineteen! All phonies but one! Dead from the neck up. Do you have any idea how long it was taking us to find that out? Hours for each one. Now it's a matter of minutes."

John Lewisohn sighed. He knew. He had suggested it, actually, when he had said, "Find a basic anxiety situation for the test." He hadn't wanted to know what Herb had come up with.

He said, "Okay, but she's only a kid. What about her parents, legal rights, all that?"

"We'll fix it. Don't worry. What about Anne?"

"She's called me five times since yesterday. The sharks were too much. She wants to see us, both of us, this afternoon."

"You're kidding! I can't leave here now!"

"Nope. Kidding I'm not. She says no plug-up if we don't show. She'll take pills and sleep until we get there."

"Good Lord! She wouldn't dare!"

"I've booked seats. We take off at twelve-thirty-five. They stared at one another silently for another moment, then Herb shrugged. He was a short man, not heavy but solid. John was over six feet, muscular, with a temper that he knew he had to control. Others suspected that when he did let it go, there would be bodies lying around afterward, but he controlled it.

Once it had been a physical act, an effort of body and will to master that temper; now it was done so automatically that he couldn't recall occasions when it even threatened to flare anymore.

"Look, Johnny, when we see Anne, let me handle it. Right? I'll make it short."

"What are you going to do?"

"Give her an earful. If she's going to start pulling temperament on me, I'll slap her down so hard she'll bounce a week." He grinned. "She's had it all her way up to now. She knew there wasn't a replacement if she got bitchy. Let her try it now. Just let her try." Herb was pacing back and forth with quick, jerky steps.

John realized with a shock that he hated the stocky, red-faced man. The feeling was new; it was almost as if he could taste the hatred he felt, and the taste was unfamiliar and pleasant.

Herb stopped pacing and stared at him for a moment. "Why'd she call you? Why does she want you down, too? She knows you're not mixed up with this end of it."

"She knows I'm a full partner, anyway," John said.

"Yeah, but that's not it." Herb's face twisted in a grin. "She thinks you're still hot for her, doesn't she? She knows you tumbled once, in the beginning, when you were working on her, getting the gimmick working right." The grin reflected no humor then. "Is she right, Johnny, baby? Is that it?"

"We made a deal," John said. "You run your end, I run mine. She wants me along because she doesn't trust you, or believe anything you tell her anymore. She wants a witness."

"Yeah, Johnny. But you be sure you remember our agreement." Suddenly Herb laughed. "You know what it was like, Johnny, seeing you and her? Like a flame trying to snuggle up to an icicle."

At three-thirty they were in Anne's suite in the Skyline Hotel in Grand Bahama. Herb had a reservation to fly back to New York on the 6 P.M. flight. Anne would not be off until four, so they made themselves comfortable in her rooms and waited. Herb turned her screen on, offered a helmet to John, who shook his head, and they both seated themselves. John watched the screen for several minutes; then he, too, put on a helmet.

Anne was looking at the waves far out at sea where they were long, green, undulating; then she brought her gaze in closer, to the blue-green and quick seas, and finally in to where they stumbled on the sandbars, breaking into foam that looked solid enough to walk on. She was peaceful, swaying with the motion of the boat, the sun hot on her back, the fishing rod heavy in her hands. It was like being an indolent animal at peace with its world, at home in the world, being one with it. After a few seconds she put down the rod and turned, looking at a tall smiling man in swimming trunks. He held out his hand and she took it. They entered the cabin of the boat where drinks were waiting. Her mood of serenity and happiness ended abruptly, to be replaced by shocked disbelief, and a start of fear.

"What the hell . . . ?" John muttered, adjusting the audio. You seldom needed audio when Anne was on.

". . . Captain Brothers had to let them go. After all, they've done nothing yet—" the man was saying soberly.

"But why do you think they'll try to rob me?"

"Who else is here with a million dollars' worth of jewels?"

John turned it off and said, "You're a fool! You can't get away with something like that!"

Herb stood up and crossed to the window wall that was open to the stretch of glistening blue ocean beyond the brilliant white beaches. "You know what every woman wants? To own something worth stealing." He chuckled, a sound without mirth. "Among other things, that is. They want to be roughed up once or twice, and forced to kneel. . . . Our new psychologist is pretty good, you know? Hasn't steered us wrong yet. Anne might kick some, but it'll go over great."

"She won't stand for an actual robbery." Louder, emphatically, he added, "I won't stand for that."

"We can dub it," Herb said. "That's all we need, Johnny, plant the idea, and then dub the rest."

John stared at his back. He wanted to believe that. He needed to believe it. His voice was calm when he said, "It didn't start like this, Herb. What happened?"

Herb turned then. His face was dark against the glare of light behind him. "Okay, Johnny, it didn't start like this. Things accelerate, that's all. You thought of a gimmick, and the way we planned it, it sounded great, but it didn't last. We gave them the feeling of gambling, or learning to ski, of automobile racing, everything we could dream up, and it wasn't enough. How many times can you take the first ski jump of your life? After a while you want new thrills, you know? For you it's been great, hasn't it? You bought yourself a shiny new lab and closed the door. You bought yourself time and equipment and when things didn't go right, you could toss it out and start over, and nobody gave a damn. Think of what it's been like for me, kid! I gotta keep coming up with something new, something that'll give Anne a jolt and through her all those nice little people who aren't even alive unless they're plugged in. You think it's been easy? Anne was a green kid. For her everything was new and exciting, but it isn't like that now, boy. You better believe it is *not* like that now. You know what she told me last month? She's sick and tired of men. Our little hot-box Annie! Tired of men!"

John crossed to him and pulled him around toward the light. "Why didn't you tell me?"

"Why, Johnny? What would you have done that I didn't do? *I* looked harder for the right guy. What would you do for a new thrill for her? I worked for them, kid. Right from the start you said for me to leave you alone. Okay. I left you alone. You ever read any of the memos I sent? You initialed them, kiddo. Everything that's been done, we both signed. Don't give me any of that why didn't I tell you stuff. It won't work!" His face was ugly red and a vein bulged in his neck. John wondered if he had high blood pressure, if he would die of a stroke during one of his flash rages.

John left him at the window. He had read the memos. Herb was right; all he had wanted was to be left alone. It had been his idea; after twelve years of work in a laboratory on prototypes he had shown his—gimmick— to Herb Javits. Herb had been one of the biggest producers on television then; now he was the biggest producer in the world.

The gimmick was simple enough. A person fitted with electrodes in his brain could transmit his emotions, which in turn could be broadcast and picked up by the helmets to be felt by the audience. No words, or thoughts went out, only basic emotions—fear, love, anger, hatred . . . That, tied in with a camera showing what the person saw, with a voice dubbed in, and you were the person

having the experience, with one important difference—
you could turn it off if it got to be too much. The "actor"
couldn't. A simple gimmick. You didn't really need the
camera and the sound track; many users never turned
them on at all, but let their own imaginations fill in the
emotional broadcast.

The helmets were not sold, only leased or rented after
a short, easy fitting session. A year's lease cost fifty dollars, and there were over thirty-seven million subscribers.
Herb had created his own network when the demand for
more hours squeezed him out of regular television. From
a one-hour weekly show, it had gone to one hour nightly,
and now it was on the air eight hours a day live, with
another eight hours of taped programming.

What had started out as A DAY IN THE LIFE OF ANNE
BEAUMONT was now a life in the life of Anne Beaumont,
and the audience was insatiable.

Anne came in then, surrounded by the throng of hang-
ers-on that mobbed her daily—hairdressers, masseurs,
fitters, script men . . . She looked tired. She waved the
crowd out when she saw John and Herb were there.
"Hello, John," she said, "Herb."

"Anne, baby, you're looking great!" Herb said. He took
her in his arms and kissed her solidly. She stood still, her
hands at her sides.

She was tall, very slender, with wheat-colored hair and
gray eyes. Her cheekbones were wide and high, her mouth
firm and almost too large. Against her deep red-gold sun-
tan her teeth looked whiter than John remembered.
Although too firm and strong ever to be thought of as
pretty, she was a very beautiful woman. After Herb released her, she turned to John, hesitated only a moment,
then extended a slim, sun-browned hand. It was cool and
dry in his.

"How have you been, John? It's been a long time."

He was very glad she didn't kiss him, or call him darling. She smiled only slightly and gently removed her hand
from his. He moved to the bar as she turned to Herb.

"I'm through, Herb." Her voice was too quiet. She accepted a whiskey sour from John, but kept her gaze on Herb.

"What's the matter, honey? I was just watching you, baby. You were great today, like always. You've still got it, kid. It's coming through like always."

"What about this robbery? You must be out of your mind . . ."

"Yeah, that. Listen, Anne baby, I swear to you I don't know a thing about it. Laughton must have been giving you the straight goods on that. You know we agreed that the rest of this week you just have a good time, remember? That comes over too, baby. When you have a good time and relax, thirty-seven million people are enjoying life and relaxing. That's good. They can't be stimulated all the time. They like the variety." Wordlessly John held out a glass, scotch and water. Herb took it without looking.

Anne was watching him coldly. Suddenly she laughed. It was a cynical, bitter sound. "You're not a damn fool, Herb. Don't try to act like one." She sipped her drink again, staring at him over the rim of the glass. "I'm warning you, if anyone shows up here to rob me, I'm going to treat him like a real burglar. I bought a gun after today's broadcast, and I learned how to shoot when I was ten. I still know how. I'll kill him, Herb, whoever it is."

"Baby," Herb started, but she cut him short.

"And this is my last week. As of Saturday, I'm through."

"You can't do that, Anne," Herb said. John watched him closely, searching for a sign of weakness; he saw nothing. Herb exuded confidence. "Look around, Anne, at this room, your clothes, everything. . . . You are the richest woman in the world, having the time of your life, able to go anywhere, do anything. . . ."

"While the whole world watches—"

"So what? It doesn't stop you, does it?" Herb started to pace, his steps jerky and quick. "You knew that when you signed the contract. You're a rare girl, Anne, beautiful, emotional, intelligent. Think of all those women

who've got nothing but you. If you quit them, what do
they do? Die? They might, you know. For the first time
in their lives they're able to feel like they're living. You're
giving them what no one ever did before, what was only
hinted at in books and films in the old days. Suddenly
they know what it feels like to face excitement, to experience love, to feel contented and peaceful. Think of them,
Anne, empty, with nothing in their lives but you, what
you're able to give them. Thirty-seven million drabs, Anne,
who never felt anything but boredom and frustration
until you gave them life. What do they have? Work, kids,
bills. You've given them the world, baby! Without you
they wouldn't even want to live anymore."

She wasn't listening. Almost dreamily she said, "I
talked to my lawyers, Herb, and the contract is meaning-
less. You've already broken it over and over. I agreed to
learn a lot of new things. I did. My God! I've climbed
mountains, hunted lions, learned to ski and water-ski, but
now you want me to die a little bit each week. . . . That
airplane crash, not bad, just enough to terrify me. Then
the sharks. I really do think it was having sharks brought
in when I was skiing that did it, Herb. You see, you will
kill me. It will happen, and you won't be able to top it,
Herb. Not ever."

There was a hard, waiting silence following her words.
No! John shouted soundlessly. He was looking at Herb.
He had stopped pacing when she started to talk. Something flicked across his face—surprise, fear, something not
readily identifiable. Then his face went blank and he raised
his glass and finished the scotch and water, replacing the
glass on the bar. When he turned again, he was smiling
with disbelief.

"What's really bugging you, Anne? There have been
plants before. You knew about them. Those lions didn't
just happen by, you know. And the avalanche needed a
nudge from someone. You know that. What else is bugging you?"

"I'm in love, Herb."

Herb waved that aside impatiently. "Have you ever

watched your own show, Anne?" She shook her head. "I thought not. So you wouldn't know about the expansion that took place last month, after we planted that new transmitter in your head. Johnny boy's been busy, Anne. You know these scientist types, never satisfied, always improving, changing. Where's the camera, Anne? Do you ever know where it is anymore? Have you ever seen a camera in the past couple of weeks, or a recorder of any sort? You have not, and you won't again. You're on now, honey." His voice was quite low, amused almost. "In fact the only time you aren't on is when you're sleeping. I know you're in love. I know who he is. I know how he makes you feel. I even know how much money he makes a week. I should know, Anne baby. I pay him." He had come closer to her with each word, finishing with his face only inches from hers. He didn't have a chance to duck the flashing slap that jerked his head around, and before either of them realized it, he had hit her back, knocking her into a chair.

The silence grew, became something ugly and heavy, as if words were being born and dying without utterance because they were too brutal for the human spirit to bear. There was a spot of blood on Herb's mouth where Anne's diamond ring had cut him. He touched it and looked at his finger. "It's all being taped now, honey, even this," he said. He turned his back on her and went to the bar.

There was a large red print on her cheek. Her gray eyes had turned black with rage.

"Honey, relax," Herb said after a moment. "It won't make any difference to you, in what you do, or anything like that. You know we can't use most of the stuff, but it gives the editors a bigger variety to pick from. It was getting to the point where most of the interesting stuff was going on after you were off. Like buying the gun. That's great stuff there, baby. You weren't blanketing a single thing, and it'll all come through like pure gold." He finished mixing his drink, tasted it, and then swallowed half of it. "How many women have to go out and buy a gun to protect themselves? Think of them all, feeling that gun, feeling the things you felt when you picked it up, looking at it . . ."

"How long have you been tuning in all the time?" she asked. John felt a stirring along his spine, a tingle of excitement. He knew what was going out over the miniature transmitter, the rising crests of emotion she was feeling. Only a trace of them showed on her smooth face, but the raging interior torment was being recorded faithfully. Her quiet voice and quiet body were lies; the tapes never lied.

Herb felt it too. He put his glass down and went to her, kneeling by the chair, taking her hand in both of his. "Anne, please, don't be that angry with me. I was desperate for new material. When Johnny got this last wrinkle out, and we knew we could record around the clock, we had to try it, and it wouldn't have been any good if you'd known. That's no way to test anything. You knew we were planting the transmitter . . ."

"How long?"

"Not quite a month."

"And Stuart? He's one of your men? He is transmitting also? You hired him to . . . to make love to me? Is that right?"

Herb nodded. She pulled her hand free and averted her face. He got up then and went to the window. "But what difference does it make?" he shouted. "If I introduced the two of you at a party, you wouldn't think anything of it. What difference if I did it this way? I knew you'd like each other. He's bright, like you, likes the same sort of things you do. Comes from a poor family, like yours . . . Everything said you'd get along."

"Oh, yes," she said almost absently. "We get along." She was feeling in her hair, her fingers searching for the scars.

"It's all healed by now," John said. She looked at him as if she had forgotten he was there.

"I'll find a surgeon," she said, standing up, her fingers white on her glass. "A brain surgeon—"

"It's a new process," John said slowly. "It would be dangerous to go in after them."

She looked at him for a long time. "Dangerous?"

He nodded.

"You could take it back out."

He remembered the beginning, how he had quieted her fear of the electrodes and the wires. Her fear was that of a child for the unknown and the unknowable. Time and again he had proved to her that she could trust him, that he wouldn't lie to her. He hadn't lied to her, then. There was the same trust in her eyes, the same unshakable faith. She would believe him. She would accept without question whatever he said. Herb had called him an icicle, but that was wrong. An icicle would have melted in her fires. More like a stalactite, shaped by centuries of civilization, layer by layer he had been formed until he had forgotten how to bend, forgotten how to find release for the stirrings he felt somewhere in the hollow, rigid core of himself. She had tried and, frustrated, she had turned from him, hurt, but unable not to trust one she had loved. Now she waited. He could free her, and lose her again, this time irrevocably. Or he could hold her as long as she lived.

Her lovely gray eyes were shadowed with fear, and the trust that he had given to her. Slowly he shook his head.

"I can't," he said. "No one can."

"I see," she murmured, the black filling her eyes. "I'd die, wouldn't I? Then you'd have a lovely sequence, wouldn't you, Herb?" She swung around, away from John. "You'd have to fake the story line, of course, but you are so good at that. An accident, emergency brain surgery needed, everything I feel going out to the poor little drabs who never will have brain surgery done. It's very good," she said admiringly. Her eyes were black. "In fact, anything I do from now on, you'll use, won't you? If I kill you, that will simply be material for your editors to pick over. Trial, prison, very dramatic . . . On the other hand, if I kill myself . . ."

John felt chilled; a cold, hard weight seemed to be filling him. Herb laughed. "The story line will be something like this," he said. "Anne has fallen in love with a stranger, deeply, sincerely in love with him. Everyone knows how deep that love is, they've all felt it, too, you know. She finds him raping a child, a lovely little girl in her early teens. Stuart tells her they're through. He loves the little nymphet. In a passion she kills herself. You are broadcasting a real storm of passion, right now, aren't you, honey? Never mind, when I run through this scene, I'll find out." She hurled her glass at him, ice cubes and orange slices flying across the room. Herb ducked, grinning.

"That's awfully good, baby. Corny, but after all, they can't get too much corn, can they? They'll love it, after they get over the shock of losing you. And they will get over it, you know. They always do. Wonder if it's true about what happens to someone experiencing a violent death?" Anne's teeth bit down on her lip, and slowly she sat down again, her eyes closed tight. Herb watched her for a moment, then said, even more cheerfully, "We've got the kid already. If you give them a death, you've got to give them a new life. Finish one with a bang. Start one with a bang. We'll name the kid Cindy, a real Cinderella story after that. They'll love her, too."

Anne opened her eyes, black, dulled now; she was so full of tension that John felt his own muscles contract. He wondered if he would be able to stand the tape she was transmitting. A wave of excitement swept him and he knew he would play it all, feel it all, the incredibly contained rage, fear, the horror of giving a death to them to gloat over, and finally, anguish. He would know it all. Watching Anne, he wished she would break now. She didn't. She stood up stiffly, her back rigid, a muscle hard and ridged in her jaw. Her voice was flat when she said, "Stuart is due in half an hour. I have to dress." She left them without looking back.

Herb winked at John and motioned toward the door. "Want to take me to the plane, kid?" In the cab he said, "Stick close to her for a couple of days, Johnny. There might be an even bigger reaction later when she really understands just how hooked she is." He chuckled again. "By God! It's a good thing she trusts you, Johnny boy!"

As they waited in the chrome and marble terminal for the liner to unload its passengers, John said, "Do you think she'll be any good after this?"

"She can't help herself. She's too life-oriented to deliberately choose to die. She's like a jungle inside, raw, wild, untouched by that smooth layer of civilization she shows on the outside. It's a thin layer, kid, real thin. She'll fight to stay alive. She'll become more wary, more alert to danger, more excited and exciting . . . She'll really go to pieces when he touches her tonight. She's primed real good. Might even have to do some editing, tone it down a little." His voice was very happy. "He touches her where she lives, and she reacts. A real wild one. She's one; the new kid's one; Stuart . . . They're few and far between, Johnny. It's up to us to find them. God knows we're going to need all of them we can get." His expression became thoughtful and withdrawn. "You know, that really wasn't such a bad idea of mine about rape and the kid. Who ever dreamed we'd get that kind of a reaction from her? With the right sort of buildup . . ." He had to run to catch his plane.

John hurried back to the hotel, to be near Anne if she needed him. But he hoped she would leave him alone. His fingers shook as he turned on his screen; suddenly he had a clear memory of the child who had wept, and he hoped Stuart would hurt Anne just a little. The tremor in his fingers increased; Stuart was on from six until twelve, and he already had missed almost an hour of the show. He adjusted the helmet and sank back into a deep chair. He left the audio off, letting his own words form, letting his own thoughts fill in the spaces.

Anne was leaning toward him, sparkling champagne raised to her lips, her eyes large and soft. She was speaking, talking to him, John, calling him by name. He felt a tingle start somewhere deep inside him, and his glance was lowered to rest on her tanned hand in his, sending electricity through him. Her hand trembled when he ran his fingers up her palm, to her wrist where a blue vein throbbed. The slight throb became a pounding that grew, and when he looked again into her eyes, they were dark and very deep. They danced and he felt her body against his, yielding, pleading. The room darkened and she was an outline against the window, her gown floating down about her. The darkness grew denser, or he closed his eyes, and this time when her body pressed against his, there was nothing between them, and the pounding was everywhere.

In the deep chair, with the helmet on his head, John's hands clenched, opened, clenched, again and again.

LIVE, FROM BERCHTESGADEN

Geo. Alec Effinger

One of the most gifted of science fiction's younger writers makes his Alpha debut with a story that has the mysterious clarity of a feverish dream—an eerie, hallucinatory tale of a woman who drifts between past and present.

"In Dusseldorf, as in certain other Rhinish *Hauptstädten*, there is a large, yellow-brick building very close to the railroad terminal. I am told that a great many good German *Bürger* make their periodic, Kaabic journey to this yellow institution; inside one is confronted by a bewildering array of charming and less charming photos, blurrily enticing Kodachromes of *Mädchen* that may be rung up in the manner to which one has become accustomed.

"It is sometimes difficult for the uninitiated to know how to react to this. Europe, by its very nature, is like this, in all ways and throughout its continental extent. The pure geographic propinquity of nations lulls the tourist's sense of culture. How easy it is to cross a border and find oneself immediately in an entirely different milieu of mores and folkways. It is necessary to change your ethics at the booth while you change your pounds sterling or kronor.

"Do you have inhibitions? Lose them, or be unhappy, for sooner or later you will have one or another offended. No matter how grotesque the practice, how bestial the behavior, if you live Continental long enough you will find the neighborhood where it is merely *comme il faut*. For some, it is not the superficiality of 'When in Rome . . .' but a matter of survival."

"*Mein Herr Doktor,* how is it that she speaks so? What language is it?"

"It is English she speaks, Frau Kämmer. She is delirious; oftentimes they will babble so in another language. But it is strange that she is so coherent. It is almost as if she recites."

"*Aber,* Herr Freischütz, my Gretchen knows no English. It cannot be English that she speaks."

"Far away now, beyond the political and other walls that we have built, beneath the impossible burden of years, look: Unter den Linden. Berlin! The mention of that brightest and most sophisticated of capitals did not always carry with it the indelible tinge of guilt, the subtlest pricks of fear. Unter den Linden: no other avenue in metropolitan Europe quite held the imagination of the literate world to such a degree; no other city's showplace was ever so rich with the modish, the absolute *dernier cri*. The broad, shaded way runs from the former Royal Palace down to the Vopos at Checkpoint Charlie. As in any large city, the Unter den Linden of old was frequented by the ubiquitous *Strassendirnen;* but, whether or not it was merely the effect of the reflection of old Berlin's loveliness, these easier matches did not offend the grace and charm of the street. It was only after the war that Berlin learned shame.

"This shame was not previously totally unknown. It was, however, unnecessary. Beginning with Carolus Magnus, or

Charlemagne, the Germans began their expansion east-
ward—the notorious *Drang nach Osten*—late in the eighth
century. To this day the land to the west of the River
Elbe is known as the 'old Germany,' and the land east, the
'new Germany.' Thus, historical precedent has given way
to shame; the shame is shared by those who know the old
Germany, for these are immersed in the most ancient of
traditions. The new Germany is comparatively younger,
but no one, not the oldest *Weisskopf*, is able to remember
the initial annexation. Whatever shame is felt, therefore,
is hereditary in nature. It is false shame."

"*Guten Nachmittag, Herr Doktor.*"
"*Ja, und auch Ihnen.*"
"*Wie geht es Ihnen.*"
"*Sehr gut, danke. Ihre Tochter hat gut geschlafen. Wie
geht's Ihnen?*"
"*Ach, comme çi, comme ça. Pas mal.*"

"Where *is* Germany? Do you find Germany in the
thousands of Volkswagens on the American highways? Is
Germany to be found by searching amongst the sausages
and waltzes and *Buddenbrooks* of the world? Where is
Germany? What, now, is Germany?

"Germany has traded *Weltschmerz* for *ethischer
Fortschritt*. The sensuousness of the Italians, the
chauvinism of the French, the snobbery of the British,
the unbridled passions of the Danish and the Swedes, the
inscrutability of the Finnish, all these are as nothing compared to the sincerity of the German concern for morality.
'May God punish the sinful French' is a slogan for the
masses; it is also, perhaps, an indication of the direction
the German *Weltanschauung* has taken. It is no longer
permissible to allow the nationalities of our con-
tinent to squander their precious energies in lustful abandon. It is time for a cleansing.

"But does this mean, I hear you ask, does this mean
that a new wave of Puritanism must o'ersweep us, one

and all? No, I reply, for extremism does not fit in with our
own and exquisitely German idea of *Weltpolitik*.

"We cannot yet look for Germany in those isolated and
expensive places in the sun. The specter of doom rises,
and falls, and rises again: such is the natural course of
events. It must rise once more like the *Unterseeboot,* to
an economic and social periscope depth. There must be
some effectual Curt Jurgens at the helm, and the tubes
must be kept cleared for action. 'Bearing zero five four,
two thousand yards . . . Mark!' This must be the
watchword. '*Torpedos . . . Los!* must be the counter-
sign."

"What is she saying? Does she still go on in English?"
"Yes, Nurse. But she become less coherent. What is
this inflammatory rhetoric? Such pseudo-poetry! Ah, such
a strange coma."

"*Herr Doktor,* can nothing be done? She rambles on so;
the other patients complain of the constant disturbance."

"*Naja,* then. Give her *ein Glas Schnaps.*"

"There is no hiding this shame. It hides *im Bahnhof,* it
lurks *im Postamt,* there is no peeling it from your shaking
shoulders. '*Ich bekenne mich die Anklage, "nicht schuldig."* ' How many of us stop our laughter when we buy
soap, when we touch the lampshade? When the SS and the
SA march away, whose minds do they take with them,
even now? '*Wenn wir fahren gegen England!*'

" 'Isn't the Jew a human being too? Of course he is;
none of us ever doubted it,' wrote Joseph Goebbels. 'All
we doubt is that he is a *decent* human being.'

"*Ich bekenne mich die Anklage, 'nicht schuldig.'*

" 'But in all, we can say that we fulfilled this heaviest of
tasks in love to our people. And we suffered no harm in
our essence, in our soul, in our character. . . .' Heinrich
Himmler wrote that.

" 'Paragraph 1: Jews may receive only those first names
which are listed in the directives of the Ministry of the
Interior concerning the use of first names.

" 'Paragraph 2: If Jews should bear first names other than those permitted to Jews according to Par. 1, they must, as of January 1, 1939, adopt an additional name. For males, that name shall be Israel, for females Sara.'

" 'On May 11, another transport of Jews (1,000 pieces) arrived in Minsk from Vienna, and was taken from the station directly to the above-mentioned ditch. . . .'

"Ich bekenne mich . . .

"I plead 'not guilty.' " "

"Ah, Frau Kämmer, so good of you to come. I must speak to you about your daughter. Gretchen is a tragic case. Her coma is now nearly a year. She takes little food, she is wasting away; she is but a human skeleton. But, you know, she never ceases to talk. Her voice is anguished, Frau Kämmer, so that it pains one to listen. But what she says? Still delirium.

"But now, our country is at war. We march against the czar. Our Wilhelm takes us against the Russians, and today we are at war also with the French. There has been a general call for doctors, and I must now tell you that the sanatorium is closing. Your Gretchen may be taken home; I had been already considering that recommendation. It may do her more good than this close but impersonal attention . . ."

"Why am I here? I can't remember my husband here.

"As I recall, we were driving to Mainz. Our little brown VW. We pronounced it *fow*-vay in Germany. Driving along the Autobahn. I remember this Mercedes. We had the temerity to pass this black Mercedes. In our little VW.

"This feeling, I'm twisting . . .

"Here . . .

"Ich . . ."

"How is she today?"

"Better, poor thing. She's just wasted away from being in that awful hospital. She sounds like she's just out of her head, pure and simple."

"And now, what with the war . . ."

"It is interesting to leaf through the documents that were discovered following the surrender. For instance, this communication: 'We started with three and a half million Jews here. Of that number, only a few work companies remain. Everybody else has—let us say—emigrated.'

"Where are all those soldiers now? Sousaphone players in the Bratwurst Festival?

"How can I say that I am not guilty?

"I cannot listen anymore. I cannot listen to the charges.

"Please, stop."

"Mama, does Gretchen know the news?"

"No, *Liebchen,* she cannot understand."

"Will you tell her about the *Lusitania?*"

"Nein, sie wurde es nicht verstehen."

"We must keep to ourselves. Everyone—the Russians, the French, the English, especially the Americans—they all watch. They hope to catch us, like little boys stealing the pfennigs from Mama's purse.

"We are here. We know what we have done; it is only left to atone for our deeds, or to justify them.

"We cannot know which course is the more horrible."

"Ernst. My husband's name is Ernst. He was born near Gelnhausen. We met in New York, during the Depression. But I can't remember . . ."

"Have you heard enough? Then consider the *Sonderkommando.*

"Little wooden and concrete block outhouses. Signs indicated that they were baths. How thoughtful of the German High Command. The inmates were gathered together; those who could play musical instruments were commandeered to play cheerful tunes from *The Merry Widow.* Everyone watched as the band played; soon everyone would have their turn for the delousing.

"They got a couple of thousand in one of those buildings. They got their money's worth out of the hydrogen cyanide.

"Twenty minutes later, after the spasms had stopped, they called in the *Sonderkommando*. They were male Jews who were promised immunity from execution for their services. They went into the gas chambers and pulled the tangled corpses apart with hooks. They hosed down the walls, cleaning off the blood and fouler material. They extracted the gold teeth of their kinsmen. A week later, they were gassed, too.

"You've heard it before, don't kid yourself.

"It is said that God appeared to Paul Joseph Goebbels dressed in a leather corset, tightly laced high-heeled hip boots, and brandishing a riding crop. To this day the breezes, according to the neighborhood fools around Bayreuth, to this day you may hear gentle whisperings, wind whistles of the *Horst Wessel*, and you know that it's just a matter of time before *die Fahne* is again *hoch*.

"After reading about Argentine political murders, can you spare some outrage for the merry pranks of thirty years past?

"Picture: It is night. The darkness is made more complete by the storm clouds which obscure the moon and stars. There is nothing to be seen but the light of a small lantern shining through the window of a farmhouse, about a hundred yards away. It is early December near Metz; it is very cold. There is ice on the Moselle, whose banks curve away about three kilometers beyond the farm. The German patrol halts on the rutted dirt road. Two of the six soldiers are sent up to the farmhouse. They knock loudly on the door. There is a long pause before the door is opened; then the light spills out through the narrow crack. Someone inside the house gasps, someone cries, another curses softly. The Germans force their way into the house. Sometimes in this situation there are shots, sounds of breaking glass, objects falling to the floor. At last one *vert-de-gris* comes to the door. He calls the other four, who still stand in the road, slapping their gloved hands and stamping their jackbooted feet.

"The six Germans are named Gerd, Thomas, Heinrich, Karl, Sigmund, and Gottlob. Their job is to stay in the farmhouse and guard it against the Allies. All over Europe there are similar pockets of Deutschland; this is how the war was fought, from farmhouses. Sometimes they are attacked by Burt Lancaster. Generally Heinrich, stranded hundreds of kilometers from the collaborating *dévoreuses* of Paris, goes mad and shoots a couple of his mates, or dies of lockjaw. In the end the Allies arrive in force, and the Boche are made to abandon the house, throwing their Lugers on a pile and crying '*Kamerad!*'

"And so, these days, as you take your Polaroid Swinger shots of the *Kölmer Dom,* you will meet a man. He is selling green and yellow balloons, ice cream and peanuts, plastic novelties. You speak to him in your halting German, *Bitte, können Sie mir sagen, wie komme ich zur Bedürfnisanstalt?*' He smiles at you and answers in flawless English. 'The public lavatory that you seek is located there, built into the side of the Victory Monument. My name is Sigmund. You must be Americans. How charming; I was a Stormtrooper, myself.'

"This never happens. If you ask a German student about the *Nazizeit,* he says, 'Terrible. Simply terrible. It is frightening to believe that an entire nation could be so deluded. It was all like a monstrous dream.' A dream.

" 'Yes,' you say, 'but what did *your* father do during the war?'

"His eyes shift nervously, his tongue licks his full, Aryan lips, and he coughs. 'My father? Oh, during the war he was taking care of some mining interests in South America. We lived in São Paulo then; we never had any actual contact with the Reich.'

"So much for atrocities.

"You must be the conscience for your family: your daughter is busy with ecology, and your husband leads the commuters' fight with the Long Island Railroad. You must keep these memories alive, before you are seduced away by the plight of the American Indian."

"We have shown the way. It is always Germany that develops, *nicht wahr*, it is always Germany that knows its resources, that knows what to do with its people."

"Ach, what is it now, Herr Müller? In what new and resourceful way are we now superior?"

"You have right, Frau Kämmer, in calling us resourceful. For, indeed, we are the practical nation. How did they fight wars? How did the human race battle previously? Why, by loosing various missiles at the enemy, and hoping that the paths of the projectiles and the opposing soldiery might intersect. Ah, look at the probability. Very low, *n'est-ce pas?* What we have done, what the German Command has done, April 22, 1915, at Ypres, is to harness the potential of the very air as a weapon! The atmosphere has become our ally, spreading our new and tiny globules of death. We use gas. The new aircraft dispense thick yellow clouds, and the French are overcome, they are disabled, or they die."

"Perhaps we could drop from those same aircraft a sort of jellied petroleum product. It could be ignited, and those same foes would then have something to contend with, eh?"

"You do not know what you ask, Frau Kämmer. There are still conventions. We do have several sorts of gas, thanks to the Krupps of Essen and to the Interessen Gemeinschaft with their famous German professors. We have such variety; 'poison gas' is then a misnomer. We should refer, rather, to 'chemical warfare.' That is better, it is more *gemütlich*. We have the gas chemicals, and also the liquid chemicals which act in much the same way. Of our asphyxiating substances we have had success with simple chlorine, phosgene, chlotopicrin, and others. We have produced lachrymators, vesicant or blistering compounds, sternutatory or sneezing compounds, and toxic compounds such as prussic acid. We have been disappointed so far with the arsenic compounds. Major V. Lefebure documents all this in his jocularly titled volume, *The Riddle of the Rhine*. He discusses the new developments in mustard gas and states that 'these inherent possibilities of organic chemistry, flexibility in research and production, make chemical warfare the most important war problem in the future reconstruction of the world.' "

"I couldn't agree more. Though we win, I would still see those canisters thrown into the sea."

"Yes, and how goes your daughter, Frau Kämmer?"

"My daughter? Gutrune? Why, she begins to go to school soon. It is very kind of you to ask after her."

"I am sorry. I meant to inquire about your other."

"My other? Perhaps you mean Gretchen? Ah, she sleeps. We have little to do with her these days. She needs such little attention. She is so thin, she looks like a skeleton. And her eyes! Sometimes they open, and stare . . . We do not go into her room often these days."

"I don't have any idea how I came here. I mean, I don't even know where I am. No one talks to me. They treat me like I'm not here at all. I'm paralyzed in this bed: I must have been in an accident, the way they shake their heads when they think I won't notice. Am I disfigured, startlingly mangled now?

"I don't know how I got here. Christ, I don't even remember who I am! Oh, my God. *Who am I?* What a dumb-ass question.

"Okay, don't panic. I'm Gretchen Weinraub.

"I'm on vacation. I'm in Europe. Our first trip back to Europe! We're in Germany, visiting Munich, just finished in Heidelberg and Stuttgart. Going on to Nuremberg next. Ernst and our grandson, Stevie. Where are they? I haven't seen them at all.

"How long have I been here?

"This isn't a hospital. I remember a doctor looking at me a few times, but he seemed old and worried, dressed in a funny-smelling old dark suit. The ceiling above me is pointed, as if I were stuck up under the eaves. The mattress I'm lying on is very soft and comfortable. The bed is piled up with lovely hand-sewn quilts: it must be winter.

"It was July in Munich.

"Where am I? What in hell's happened?
"Where's Ernst?"

"Weh, how she tosses and turns tonight. She is troubled."

"Mama, do you think she has dreams all this time? Her long sleep, is it like we have every night?"

"A full year. I pray the good Lord that it has been peaceful for her."

"Oh, Mama! A full year of nightmare! Oh, how horrible it would be! To be chased, or lost, or falling for a year—"

"*Schweigst du,* little one. God in Heaven watches her."

"Does God understand what she says?"

"Yes, *Liebchen,* God understands what everyone says. Our Gretchen mutters still in English, but she says yet those German words."

"You can understand them, Mama?"

"Yes, but such silly words they are! '*Geheime Staatspolizei . . .*' What good are *secret* police, police that you can't even find when you need them? A 'Gestapo'?"

"Are we winning, Mama?"

"Yes, of course we are. God knows who's been good and who's been bad."

"Has Daddy been good?"

"Yes, dear. He was wounded in the chest just last week. He will win the Iron Cross, Second Class, he thinks. I hope that he does. That will show that landlord of ours in München."

"Does Gretchen know?"

"No, *Liebchen.* Poor, poor Gretchen knows nothing of our great struggle."

"Will you be here when *I* die too, Mama?"

"Hush, now, *Liebchen.* Sit down. Watch the war."

"I could have taken any of several tacks in doing this. Should I instead have stayed only with the contrite and apologetic? Would it have been better, or even believable, to try to persuade that things weren't really all that bad? Can you believe the canard that seventy-five million Germans were only carrying out their instructions and today can't even recall that they did? No. The question is too big. There are too many angles, and the extenuating circumstances are too difficult to explain.

"The apology must suffice. A necessary prologue, perhaps, for one in my position; but enough. *Also, denn. 'Hier steche ich.'*

"I borrow those words, of course, from Martin Luther. He knew how it felt to have the responsibility of putting the abstract feelings of a nation, a world, into coherent form. It is for me, having attempted the apology with all the conscience that I can muster, to say, 'Here we are.' I am supposed to point into the shadows, into our nation's superstitious submind, beckoning, saying to my fellows, 'Come out! It is over. *Abierunt ad plures.* They are dead, they are dead.' *They* are the memories, the guilt-demons that take on almost hallucinatory presence.

"And they should be dead. Why are we guilty no longer? Walk among us now. *O felix culpa!* Have the vanquished ever found such prosperity in defeat? To despair of forgiveness from God is the gravest of sins: why then should we bear the enmity of nations beyond the reasonable limit? The Führer was a captain who saw himself sinking and, in his perverse logic, thought it necessary to take his ship with him. Of course, the *Heimatland* suffered, but it was cleansed in its own Iron and Blood.

"No more brownshirts, blackshirts put away, too, with the photos of polished Mussolini, farewell *Ade Polenland, ade weisse Hand; fest ist der Tritt, fest ist der Tritt* up the steps into the attic, packed away in the trunks with the Hitler Youth badges, *die Jugend marschiert,* thirty, count 'em, thirty extermination camps, hundreds of thousands of cheering people.

"Speak of this amazing recovery of the divided German republic. It is remarkable; it would not have been possible, ironically, without Hitler's terrible and unifying nationalistic zeal. The extremities which are his epitaph are the product of his absolute power. But today, and all that counts *is* today, our country is in a far stronger economic position than before the war. You may go into the *Sowjet* zone, if you wish, and cluck your tongue at the difference.

"The continued animosity of our former enemies grows a bit silly. Certainly we erred; we have learned from our mistakes. Not, I might add, like more than one of our accusers, to whom the term 'genocide' seems, to them, inapplicable because they lack the publicity that attended *our* Treblinkas and Buchenwalds. I fall into the *tu quoque* fallacy: you without sin, you be the first to cast the stone.

"We have a land. It is our *Vaterland;* that term cannot be discredited. If you insist on pulling open your older wounds, we insist on reacting with natural pride in our homes, ourselves, and our accomplishments.

"We still live."

"Gretchen? We once had a daughter named Gretchen, but last spring we lost her."

"Oh, I'm terribly sorry. Did she ever regain consciousness?"

"Oh, no. You misunderstand. We have no idea if she is still alive. You see, as time passed we saw less and less of her. She did not produce in us such a great amount of interest. We dusted her features often, and changed the flowers in the vase monthly, but otherwise we rarely thought of her. Then, one day, she was gone."

"But after so long a confinement to her bed, and in her starved condition, surely she couldn't have gone off by herself?"

"We think so, too. Perhaps we merely mislaid her. I remember one time, when we had taken her outside for the fresher air, we couldn't for the life of us recall where we had put her. We have recently written to the *Gastwirt* at the inn at St. Blasien, to see if we inadvertently left her in our rooms. But, personally, I don't think we even took her along."

"I can't remember who I am.

"Sometimes, like last night, I think I'm still Gretchen Kämmer. Sometimes I'm Gretchen Weinraub. Right now, I don't have any name at all.

"I can't remember where I'm from, or where I am now.

"I remember getting here, or there, in a brown Volkswagen. It was the car we rented in Hamburg. I don't remember who the others who make up the 'we' are.

"For some reason I feel absolutely no desire to know, I feel no horror at being totally lost. It's rather warm and soft, like anesthesia. The only reasonable thing now, I guess, is to start again somewhere. I don't know which way to head, and I suppose I'll make mistakes I've made before. I forget . . .

"And I cannot yet forgive, but I forget."

AS NEVER WAS

P. Schuyler Miller

Schuyler Miller is best known to the modern generation of science-fiction readers as the indefatigable and trustworthy reviewer of books for **Analog.** Why an author of his abilities prefers to review books rather than to write them is hard to understand—for, until he chose to retire from fiction-writing more than a quarter of a century ago, Miller was one of the most popular contributors to the science-fiction magazines. His first stories appeared in 1931, when he was still a boy; in the decade that followed he published such celebrated works as "The Chrysalis," "The Sands of Time," and "Old Man Mulligan"; in 1941 he collaborated with L. Sprague de Camp on the rollicking novel **Genus Homo.** The ingenious and brilliantly executed time-travel story you are about to read was published in 1943. Two or three minor Miller works came after it— and then silence and book reviews. Most of Miller's spare time these days is devoted to archaeology, which he pursues on a semiprofessional level; but perhaps he'll return to fiction occasionally when the potsherds and arrowheads begin to pall.

Have you ever dreamed of murder?
Have you ever set your elbows on the desk and let your

head slump down on your hands, and closed your eyes, and dreamed of how it would feel to drive a knife up to the hilt in a scrawny, wrinkled throat, and twist it until the thin old blood begins to slime your fingers and drip from your wrist—until the piercing old eyes roll back and close, and the skinny old legs crumple and sag? Have you felt the blood pounding in your own temples, and savage satisfaction swarming up in you as you stare down on the hideous, sprawling thing you have destroyed?

And then have you opened your eyes and looked down at the mass of scribbled papers, and the meticulously drawn sectional charts, and the trait tables and correlation diagrams and all the other dead, dry details that make up your life's work? And picked up your pen and started making more scribbles on the papers and more checks on the charts and more little colored dots on the scattergrams, just as you've been doing three days out of every five since you were old enough to start the career for which you'd been tested and picked and trained?

Maybe I should go to a clinic and let the psychotherapists feed vitamins to my personality. Maybe I should go to a religious center and let the licensed clergy try to put this fear of Humanity into my reputed soul. Maybe I should go to a pleasure palace and let them mix me up an emotional hooker to jar the megrims out of my disposition, or go down and apply for a permit to wed and set about begetting another generation of archeologists who will grow up to be just as tired and bored and murderous as their illustrious father.

Night after night and day after day I dream of what might have happened that day in the laboratory if I had picked up the knife and slit the gullet of the man who had just injected the time-stream concept into the quietly maturing science of human archeology. If I could have seen ahead— If I could have guessed what would happen to all the romantic visions he had worked so hard to inspire in me—

Why should I dream? I was a child then; I had no way of looking ahead; the knife was just another knife. And

I think if *he* had known—if he had been able to see ahead and watch the science to which he had devoted his every waking moment for a long lifetime degenerate into a variety of three-dimensional bookkeeping—he'd have cut his own heart out and offered it to me in apology.

He was a great old man. He was my grandfather.

You've seen the knife. Everyone has, I guess. I was the first, after him, ever to see it, and I was about ten years old. I was sitting in a chair in his laboratory, waiting for him to come back. It was a wooden chair, something his grandfather had used, and maybe other people before that. The laboratory was just a big room at the back of the house, with a concrete floor and plenty of light from a row of windows over the worktable. There were hundreds of potsherds strewn over the table where he'd been classifying and matching them for restoration. There were trays of stone implements, and cheap wooden boxes full of uncatalogued stuff with the dirt still on it. There was a row of battered-looking notebooks, bound in imitation leather, fraying at the corners and stained with ink and dirt. There was a pot that had been half restored, the sherds joined so neatly that you could barely see where they fitted together, and a little ivory goddess whose cracks and chips were being replaced with a plastic filler until you'd never have known she was five thousand years old.

That was what an archeologist's laboratory was like in those days. Of course, we've outgrown all that. His experiment, and the knife he brought back and tossed down on the table for me to look at, have ended all that. Archeology has found its place among the major sciences. It's no longer a kind of bastard stepchild of art and anthropology. We got money for the best equipment, the newest gadgets. We have laboratories designed by the best architects to fit the work we do in them. We can call on the technicians of a score of other sciences to do our dirty work, or can train ourselves to know as much as they do if we're reactionaries like me. We have our own specialists, just as learned and as limited as any hair-splitter in biochemistry or galactic physics. We have prestige—recognition—everything he never had in his day, when he was the acknowledged master in his field, and we have him to thank for it all. But Walter Toynbee, if he were living now, would dry up and die in the kind of laboratory his grandson has. He'd push his charts and his correlations back and drop his head in his hands and dream. He'd plan out his own murder.

I'd been sitting there for nearly six hours. I'd been over the worktable from one end to the other, three times. I'd picked up every potsherd—turned them over—studied them with all the solemn intentness of ten years old—put them back exactly where I'd found them, as he had taught me. I'd found four sherds that would fit onto the pot he was restoring, and two that made an ear for a little clay figurine shaped like a fat, happy puppy. I'd taken down his books, one by one, and looked at the plates and figures as I had done many times before. I had even taken down one of his notebooks and slowly leafed through it, trying to spell out the straggling handwriting and make sense of the precise sketches, until a loose slip of paper fell out from among the pages and I slipped it hurriedly back and put the book away.

All one corner of the laboratory was taken up by the time shuttle. It had cost more than all the air surveys, all the expeditions, all the books and photographs and restorations of his whole career. The copper bus bars that came in through the wall behind it were like columns in some Mayan colonnade. The instrument panel was like something you'd imagine on—well, on a time machine. The machine itself was a block of dull gray lead with a massive steel door in one side of it, the time cell floating in a magnetic bearing between the pole pieces which set up the field.

Ours are neater now, but inside they're about the same. Old Walter Toynbee was an artist to the core, and Balmer, who built the machine for him from Malecewicz's notes, had a flair for functional design. It was the first shuttle big enough and powerful enough to push a man and his baggage more than twenty years into the future—or the past, for that matter. Malecewicz had gone back fifteen years. He never returned. His questions showed why that was, and the archeological world, which had been rubbing its hands in anticipation of striking up a speaking acquaintance with Hatshepsut and Queen Shub-Ad, went back to its trowels and whiskbrooms with sighs of resignation. All but my grandfather. All but Walter Toynbee.

Malecewicz had never taken time to really work out his theory of the time function and lapsed interval, or he might be alive now. Laymen will still ask you why we archeologists don't simply climb into a shuttle with a solido camera and slip back to Greece or Elam or maybe Atlantis, and film what went on instead of tediously slicing the dust of millennia over the graveyards of past civilizations. It can be done, but the man who does it must be utterly self-centered, wrapped up in knowledge for its own sake, utterly unconcerned with his duties to his fellowmen. As any schoolchild learns, the time shuttler who goes into the past introduces an alien variable into the spacio-temporal matrix at the instant when he emerges. The time stream forks, an alternative universe is born in which his visit is given its proper place, and when he returns it will be to a future level in the new world which he has created. His own universe is forever barred to him.

The future is by its nature different. All that we are now and all that we have been or become from moment to moment is integral in the structure and flow of our particular thread of time. The man who visits the future is not changing it: his visit is a foredestined part of that future. As the ancients might have said: "It is written." Though I should imagine that the writing is in the matrix of spacetime and not in the record book of God.

Walter Toynbee was a brilliant man who might have made a success of many sciences. He had money to guarantee him such comfort as he might want, and he chose the science which most attracted him—archeology.

He was the last of the great amateurs. He had known Malecewicz well—financed some of his experimental work —and when the physicist failed to return he wheedled the trustees of the university into turning the man's notes over to him. He showed them almost at once where Malecewicz had gone and why he would never return, and he saw immediately that there was no such barrier between Man and his tomorrows. Inside of a week he and Balmer were moving cases of artifacts out of the back room to make room for the shuttle. Night after night they sat up into the wee hours, arguing over fantastic-looking diagrams. In two months the power lines were coming in across the fields, straight from the generators at Sheldon Forks, and Balmer's men were pouring the colossal concrete base on which the machine would sit.

It was past dinner time. I had been sitting there alone since a little after one o'clock, when he had stepped into the shuttle and asked me to wait until he returned. There it sat, just as it had sat for the last six hours, shimmering a little as though the air around it were hot and humming like a swarm of bees deep in an old beech. I got down a big book of plates of early Sumerian cylinder seals and began to turn the pages slowly. The sameness of them had grown boring when I realized that the humming had stopped.

I looked up at the lead cube. It was no longer shimmering. I closed the book and put it carefully back on the shelf, just as the great steel door of the shuttle swung silently open, and my grandfather stepped down out of the time cell.

He had been digging. His breeches and heavy jacket were covered with whitish dust. Dirt made grimy gutters under his eyes and filled in the creases and wrinkles of his face and neck. He had a stubble of dirty gray beard on his chin, which hadn't been there six hours before, and his shirt was dark with sweat. He was tired, but there was a gleam of satisfaction in his sharp black eyes and a kind of grin on his wrinkled face.

The battered canvas bag in which he kept his tools and records was slung over one shoulder. He slapped at his thighs and puffs of dust spurted from his trousers. He took off the shabby felt hat which he always wore, and his thin gray hair was damp and draggled. He came over to the table, fumbling with the buckle on the bag. I watched his knotted fingers wide-eyed, for I had seen them pull many wonders out of that dusty wallet. I can hear his triumphant chuckle as he drew out a knife—*the* knife—and tossed it ringing on the table among the sherds.

You've seen it, of course. It's been in the pictures many times, and there are solidographs of the thing in most museums. I saw it then for the first time—ever—in our time.

He hadn't washed it. There was dirt on the fine engraving of the dull-black hilt, and caked in the delicate filigree of the silver guard. But the blade was clean, and it was as you have seen it—cold, gleaming, metallic blue—razor-edged—and translucent.

Maybe you've had a chance to handle it, here in the museum. Where the blade thins down to that feather-edge you can read small print through it. Where it's thicker, along the rib that reinforces the back of the blade, it's cloudy—milky looking. There has been engraving on the blade, too, but it has been ground or worn down until it is illegible. That is odd, because the blade is harder than anything we know except diamond. There is no such metal in the System or the Galaxy, so far as we know, except in this one well-worn and apparently very ancient knife blade.

It must be old. Not only is the engraving on the blade obliterated by wear; there is the telltale little serif near the hilt, where that utterly keen, hard edge has been worn back a little by use and honing. The black stuff of the hilt looks newer, and the carving is clearer, though still very old. Grandfather thought that it was made of some very heavy wood, possibly impregnated with a plastic of some sort, and that it had been made to replace an earlier hilt which had become worn out or broken. The metal of the guard and the plate and rivets which hold the hilt are ordinary silver, in one of the new stainless alloys which were just then coming into fairly general use.

Well—there it was. Walter Toynbee, who was probably the most competent archeologist the world has yet seen, had gone into the future in a Malecewicz shuttle. He had dug up a knife, and brought it back with him. And it was made of a material—a metal—of which our science knew absolutely nothing.

Three days later Walter Toynbee was dead. It may have been some virus picked up in that distant future which he had visited, to which our generation of mankind had developed no resistance. It may have been the strain of the trip into time, or the excitement and exertion of what he did there. He washed up, and we went home together to supper. We had it together, in the kitchen, because the family had finished and the dishes were done. Grandfather examined the knife while we were eating, but he wouldn't talk about it then. He was tired: he wanted to sleep. He never awoke.

In my father, old Walter's only son, the family talents had taken another turn. He was a more practical man than his father, and had done his noted parent many a good turn by husbanding and stimulating the family fortunes when they most needed it. Where grandfather had been interested in the minutiae and complexities of the ancient cultures whose dust he cleared away, father was one of the then popular cyclic historians who tried to see civilization as a whole—as a kind of super-organism—and to find recurring patterns in Man's gradual progression from the jungle to Parnassus. I am not implying that old Walter had no interest in synthesis and generalization—it is, as a matter of fact, a tradition that he had adopted the name Toynbee out of admiration for an historian of that name—a scholar of scholars—who lived and wrote in the early years of the last century. There is a letter among his papers which suggests that our original patronym may have been Slavic. If so, it might also explain his long and warm friendship with the unfortunate Malecewicz.

Be that as it may, Grandfather's death set in motion events whose result is all too familiar to all who have chosen to identify their lives with the pursuit of archeology. By the time the public lamentations had begun to die away, the press found a new sensation in the knife. The experts mulled over it and reported with remarkable unanimity that the engraving on the blade and hilt, while clearly of the same provenance, resembled no known human script or style of decoration. Finding their progress blocked, they called on the metallurgists and chemists to identify the blue metal of the blade, and on the botanists to specify the wood—if it was wood—of which the hilt was made.

Need I continue? There was more quibbling for its own sake in those days than there is now. Every expert was jealous of his personal acumen and insistent upon being the Only Right Man. It was considered fitting and proper that experts should disagree. But it gradually dawned on everyone concerned that here was something where there could be no disagreement, and what was more, something which might very well open new vistas of human progress.

Physically and chemically the blue stuff was a metal, though it was no metal chemistry had ever described or imagined. When they had succeeded in sawing out a sliver of the blade for tests, and finally got it into solution, its chemical behavior placed it quite outside the periodic system of the elements. The physicists went to work on another sample with X rays and spectragraphs, and arrived at much the same result. The more they studied it, the less they knew, for sooner or later some experiment would succeed in knocking over any hypothesis which they might have built up on the basis of their previous investigations.

Out of it all eventually came the judgment which stands today: that the blue stuff might well be some familiar metal, but that its atomic and molecular structure—and consequently its physical and chemical properties—had been modified or tampered with in a manner unknown to our science, making it to all intents and purposes a new state of matter. The botanists returned the same report. The black material had the structure of wood, and it might be any of several common tropical woods or it might be something quite alien, but it, too, had been hardened—indurated—through internal transformations which left it something entirely new to our planet.

That ended the first stage of the battle. When the experts threw up their hands in despair, the attack shifted to another quarter. The knife came back to my father, and he promptly made it the nucleus of a Toynbee Museum of Human Acculturation at his and Malecewicz's university, where it is today. But it was common knowledge that old Walter had brought the thing from the future. That meant that somewhere in the coming centuries of our race was a science which could create such unheard of things as the blue metal, and that the stuff was sufficiently common with them for knives to be made of it. Its electrical properties alone were such as to open a host of possible uses for it—father had been offered a small fortune by a certain great electrical concern for the material in the knife alone—and science decided to visit that future civilization, learn its secrets, and profit suitably thereby.

So the experiments shifted to time traveling. Malecewicz's notes were unearthed again and published; Grandfather's shuttle was dismantled and reconstructed a dozen times; Balmer found himself in a position to charge almost any fee as a consultant to industrial laboratories, universities, and private speculators who were hot on the trail of tomorrow. Shuttles were built on every hand, and men —and women—disappeared into the future. One by one they straggled back, empty-handed and thoroughly disgruntled. The future had no such metal.

There was a brief period in which everyone who had failed to solve the problem of the knife tried to cast doubts on Walter Toynbee, but the thing existed, its nature was what it was, and presently the hubbub swung around full circle to the place it had started. Grandfather had been an archeologist. He had gone into the future, and excavated the knife from the detritus of what might conceivably have been a colony or a chance visitant from another world—even another galaxy—someone—or something—of which the rest of humanity at that moment in time was quite unaware. Archeology had found the thing. Science craved it. It was up to archeology to find it —or its source—again.

So we became, in the language of the popularizers, the Mother Science—spawning off all sorts of minuscule specialties, lording it over a score of devoutly adulatory slave sciences, enjoying our position and taking every advantage of it.

I grew up in that atmosphere. From the time I could talk and listen, Grandfather had filled me with the wonders of the past and the romance of their discovery. Now the whole world was awake to the glories of archeology as the science of sciences which would open a whole new world to struggling Mankind. Is it any wonder I chose to follow in my grandfather's footsteps?

Let me say now that men like my father and grandfather, who had needed no world-shaking anomaly to intrigue them with their chosen study, never lost their heads in the storm of recognition which swept over them. It might have been better if they had. Archeology was in the saddle; very well, it was going to ride—and ride hard. Projects which had been tabled for lack of funds were financed in a twinkling. Tools and instruments of investigation which had been regarded as extremists' pipe dreams were invented on demand. With new tools came new techniques, and with new techniques came a hierarchy of skilled technicians, statisticians in place of explorers, desk work in place of excavation, piddling with detail instead of drawing in broad strokes the panorama of advancing civilization which men like Schliemann, and Evans, and Breasted, and that first Toynbee—yes, and old Walter Toynbee after them all—had seen with clear and understanding eyes.

We have no one to blame but ourselves. I fully realize that. We dug our own hole; we furnished it lavishly; we built a wall around it to exclude the non-elite; we arranged to be fed and comforted while we dawdled with our trivia; and then we pulled the hole in on top of ourselves. We wore a rut so deep that we can never climb out of it. So I dream of cutting my grandfather's throat instead of realizing that if I were the man he was—if I had the courage to break away from the stultified pattern I have helped to make, and go primitive, dig in the dirt with a trowel, regain the thrill of new worlds—the barriers would disappear and I would be free again, as men were meant to be.

Of course, by the time I was old enough for the university the whole business was well under way. My father, with his cycles in mind, had instigated a project whereby Archeology—it rated the capital by now—would uncover and describe the entire growth, maturity, and decline of representative communities, our own included. A colleague—or maybe he was a competitor—at Harvard was all for starting all over again at the beginning and redigesting the entire corpus of archeological data accumulated by grubbers since the beginning of time, using the new statistical attacks and the college's vast new calculating machine. He got his money. Science had declared that Archeology was the magician which would presently pass out unbounded benefits to one and all, and one and all swarmed to get on Santa Claus' good side.

I served my apprenticeship doing the dirty work for the men who voyaged into the future and sent back reams and sheaves of notes out of which we desk-workers were supposed to pull blue metal rabbits. This was the era of specialism: when trained mechanics did the digging, when stenographers and solido-scanners took the notes, and when laboratory drudges squeezed out of them every possible drop of information which super-statistics could extract.

I remember the worst pest of them all—a man with as much personality as my grandfather, though of a different kind—who nearly imposed his infernal pattern on the science for a generation. He had been a mathematical physicist who turned to archeology in what he claimed was an attempt to fit human behavior "in its broader sense" into some set of universal field-equations he had distilled out of his stars and atoms, and which purported to express the Totality of All, or some such pat phrase, in a large nutshell.

Of course, any such over-view of civilization was music to my father's ears, and he gave the man the run of the Museum and a voice in all our activities. Hill—that was his name—at once announced the precept that it was quite unnecessary to *find* blue-metal knives in some future culture. By making a sufficiently exhaustive collection of data at any particular moment, and applying his field equations in their humano-cultural aspect—I am trying here to recall his jargon—it would be possible to predict accurately when and where such knives *must* be.

Hill had a shock of red hair, a barrel chest, and a loud voice. He spoke often and in the right places. Myriads of miserable students like myself had to mull over the tons of notes which expeditions under his direction sent back. We translated facts into symbols, put the symbols through his mill, and got out more symbols. Nine times, by count, he announced to the world that "now he had it"—and nine times by count a simple check up showed that the poor beleaguered natives of whatever era it was he had chosen as It had never heard of such a metal. Some of them had never heard of metal.

By the time I was twenty-three and had my own license to explore past and future indiscriminately, we had a pretty good overall view of the future of humanity. We had libraries of histories which had been written in millennia to come. We had gadgets and super-gadgets developed by future civilizations, some of which we could use and most of which we were able to misuse. The world we supposedly enjoy today was in the making, and you know what it is like.

I have done altogether too well at whipping the esteemed Dr. Hill's hodgepodge of miscellaneous data into some semblance of intelligibility. The powers that were— and are—announced that I might spend the rest of my life, for the good of Humanity, fiddling with the same kind of stuff. But I was young, and I was a Toynbee. I stood up and demanded my rights, and they gave them to me. I could go out like all the rest and hunt for the knife.

I am not a fool. Moreover, I had had the advantage of knowing my grandfather—better even than Father ever did. I knew how he would think and how he would react. He was the kind of man who went at things hard—all out—to the limit of his ability. It seemed clear enough to me that the first step in finding the knife was to determine what that limit was—although in thirteen years or so nobody had chosen that approach.

Balmer was still alive, and I made him dig out the plans and specifications he had drawn up when he made Grandfather's shuttle. I got hold of the notes the experts had made when they tore the machine apart after his death, and they checked. And then I had Balmer set me up just the same kind of old gray cube out of which Walter Toynbee had stumbled that day, with the blue knife in his dusty old ditty bag.

It was bigger, of course—I had to have room for the kind of equipment a field man considered necessary in my day. I'd never had any training or experience with the kind of work old Walter did with his own two hands, a camera, and a trowel. The profession had been mechanized, and it was silly not to use the best I could lay my hands on. The time field, though, was the same, and it should carry me just as far as it had carried its originator thirteen years before.

It did. Malecewicz, by stretching his original model, had been able to get fifteen years out of it. Grandfather's huge old vault of a machine lofted him nearly twenty times as far into the future of our race—and of our town. As I had suspected from the specifications of the machine, it dropped me somewhere near the middle of the interregnum which followed the Hemispheric Wars, when half the cities of America had been reduced to rubble, disease and famine had put the population of the planet back into a hunting-fishing-food-gathering economy, and all that remained of civilization was a memory which would some day be revived, restored, and started off again.

I am not saying that in thirteen years of trying nobody had hit upon this particular period in the future. It is true that having hit it they let common sense scare them off. It was obvious that that level of culture could never produce so sophisticated a scientific marvel as the knife. There was no evidence in the ruins they found to show that our own culture, up to and during the time of the Wars, had done so. Ergo: onward and upward. Try another thousand years. Try a million.

I had a slightly different point of view on the matter. I knew Grandfather. He would go as far as his machine could take him. I had duplicated that. He would look around him for a promising site, get out his tools, and pitch in. Well, I could do that, too.

There is enough uncertainty—backlash, if you want to call it that—in the operation of any time shuttle so that you can never be certain that you will hit any specific moment or even any specific day or week in the future. Put that down to mechanical imperfections, if you like— I know some do—but I consider it a matter of the inexactitude of the physical universe, and I doubt that there is ever anything that we can do about it. You can approximate—hopping back and forth across the time you want until you get reasonably close—but that is a makeshift solution, borrowed from practical mathematics. I didn't try.

If you've read your history of the next five hundred years, you'll know that the gas attacks toward the end of the war had stripped the Atlantic coastal regions of vegetation and every other living thing. I got out of the shuttle in a dusty landscape where the bare bones of the planet stuck up in shattered stumps in a wind-swept desert of gullied clay. I might be ahead of my grandfather's time—in which case I saw a paradox brewing—or I might be following him. As it turned out, it was the latter.

I knew from what others had learned that there was no life in this coastal strip until much later. Gradually vegetation worked its way into the arid strip, insects and mammals followed, men followed them—but this is no essay on the future. There was no point in hunting for survivors; Grandfather certainly hadn't. For on all sides stretched the wreckage of our own city—or its counterpart of three centuries from now—and I knew that he would have stood just as I was standing, looking it over with an appraising eye, wondering where to begin.

One mass of fallen masonry, half submerged in a drift of sand, towered higher than the rest. It would provide a vantage point from which to size up the situation. As I plodded toward it through the soft sand I found myself watching for his footprints, so certain was I that this must be the place and the time. It was nonsense, of course; my own tracks were filling in as the wind curled sand into them.

Then I saw it—and that day thirteen years before came rushing back to me. Of course there would be traces! Walter Toynbee would never in his life have abandoned a dig as promising as this—a dig where surface-scratching had yielded him a relic like the knife. But for his sickness and death he would have been planning a return expedition—a camp—a full-scale attack. Not half the equipment he had taken with him was in the shuttle when he returned. And there, at the eastern base of the mound, the tatters of a red bandanna whipping in the wind, a short-handled shovel was driven into a crack in the masonry.

I fingered the shreds of red cloth. It was his. He always

had one stuffed in the pocket of his jeans. Duster—sun shield—lashing—he had a score of uses for them. Any field worker had in those days, before there was a tool for every purpose.

The crevice into which the shovel had been wedged widened as it went down. Sand had drifted into it, filling it to within a few feet of the top. By all the tenets of civilized archeology I should first prepare my aërial plan of the entire complex of ruins, erect the light tower with its instrument board to establish a zero reference plane for the solidograph, and assemble the scanner. When a grid had been projected on the screen of the excavator, it would be time enough to think of beginning the actual investigation.

Do you believe in ghosts? As I stood there, with those shreds of faded red cloth in my hand, stroking the sand-polished handle of the shovel, I suddenly realized that so far as time itself went he might have been standing here only hours, or even minutes before me. It was as though he had turned his back for a moment, and I had stepped into his tracks there in the sand. I was a child again, tagging after him as he strode around the big laboratory with his giant's strides, pulling down a book here, running through a file of negatives there, gathering his tools around him before he set to work to unravel some perplexing situation in his digging. A thin cloud passed across the sun, and it was as though his shadow had fallen on me.

I pulled the shovel out of the crack in which he had wedged it. It was in good condition—perfectly usable. In my time we did not work with shovels or picks, but any fool could handle the thing. I dug it into the sand—scratched at the base of the crack. It would take only a few moments to deepen it enough so that I could crawl inside.

There was a kind of satisfaction to the work. I exercise in the public gymnasia—all young men of my age have to, to keep fit—but there was a difference. Using this primitive tool brought with it a feeling of accomplishment—

of purpose—that I never found in mere exercise. I was strong, and it gratified me to see the hole deepen and the drift of sand grow behind me. Soon I had a tunnel into which I could crawl without bumping my head. I went back to the shuttle for a glow lamp and a pocket scanner, and plunged into the darkness.

After the first few feet I had no use for the lamp. My eyes grew accustomed to the dark, and I saw that shafts and streaks of light broke through gaps in the ruin overhead. Presently I found a hard floor under my feet, and then I came out into a room which was like a wedge— the ceiling fallen in one mass which hung diagonally between the wall over my head and the floor about twenty feet before me. Sunlight seeped in through a crevice to the left, striking on the wall and filling the whole place with a kind of diffuse glow. In that glow I saw footprints in the thick dust which covered the floor, and the table to which they led.

They were his footprints, of course. On that table he had found the knife. I stepped out of the doorway where I had been standing, an odd feeling of familiarity growing in me. I crossed the floor to the table. It had been covered with heavy glass, which lay in shreds on the dusty bronze. I could see the marks of his fingers in the dust where he had moved the broken glass aside. And I could see the outline of the knife, as sharp in the unstirred dust as it was when he picked it up in his gnarled old fingers thirteen years—or was it thirteen minutes?— before.

The crack of light was widening as the sun moved; the place grew brighter. I brushed the dust away from the table top. It was heavy bronze; it told me nothing. And then, turning, I saw the opposite wall and the frieze in low relief which ran above the door—

I don't like the impossible. I don't like paradox. I sit here, toiling over my correlations—they have promised a machine by spring which will perform them for us more quickly and in far more detail than we have ever attempted—and when I grow tired I let my head slip down on my hands, and I dream of a day when I was a child. I dream of an old man and a knife—and murder.

I had had my chance. Others, more experienced and possibly more capable than I, followed me. The entire ruin was excavated, with the most meticulous attention to technique, down to bedrock. And I . . . I was sent back to my correlations and my trait tables, to work up the data which other men would presently send me. Because strive as they will, they can find no other explanation than the one which—to me—seems obvious. The answer which is no answer—

You can go into the Toynbee Museum now, today, and see the knife in a guarded case, in the anteroom of the main exhibit hall. In the course of three hundred years that case will have been replaced by a bronze table and a cover of heavy glass. Bombs will fall, the building will crumble in ruins, and the knife will still be there. Dust will cover the ruins, and one day a gnarled old man in shabby clothes will shovel it away and creep inside. He will find the knife and carry it away. Later a younger man will come—and then others—many others, men and women both. And all the while, on the granite lintel above the door to the room where the knife is kept, will be the inscription:

WALTER TOYNBEE
1962—2035

My grandfather brought the knife back from the future. He died. It was placed in the museum named for him. It lay there for three hundred years, while the human race went mad trying to solve its secret—while all civilization was turned upside down in the search for something which never existed!

He found it in the museum where it had always been. He carried it back through time, and it was placed in that museum. It lay there until he came and found it, and carried it back through time—

It was a simple pattern—as simple as ever was. Must we think only in terms of a beginning and an end? Cannot a thing—even a person—exist in a closed cycle without beginning or end? Appearing to us now, at this level of our time thread, accompanying us down its extension into our future, then vanishing from our stream and circling back to the point where it appeared? Can't you imagine that?

I thought I could. I thought it was a paradox—no more—as simple to explain as ever was. I was wrong, of course, and they are right.

The knife old Walter Toynbee brought back from the museum built in his honor, to house his knife, was perfect—worn, dirty, but perfect. A little notch was sawed in the back of its translucent blue blade—sawed with a diamond saw, to provide the chemist and the physicists with the samples they needed to test its properties. That notch is still in its blade as it lies out there in the museum case—it will be there for the next three hundred years, or until the raids come and the museum falls in ruins. Until an old man comes out of the past to find it—

The knife old Walter Toynbee will find there in our future will have that notch. The knife he brought back to me thirty years ago had no notch in it. Somewhere the circle must have a beginning. Somewhere it must have an end—but where, and how? How was this knife created, out of a strange blue metal, and a strange, black, indurated wood, when its existence has no beginning or end? How can the circle be broken? I wish I knew. I might not dream of murder then. I might find logic and purpose in the future instead of chaos—instead of impossible worlds that never were.

WE CAN REMEMBER IT
FOR YOU WHOLESALE

Philip K. Dick

The unreliability of reality and the persistence of memory—these are the great themes of Philip K. Dick's fiction, sounded again and again in such glittering novels as **The Three Stigmata of Palmer Eldritch, Ubik,** and **Do Androids Dream of Electric Sheep?** Here both themes converge in a tight, characteristically Dickian story, shining wth paranoiac passion, a Dick novel in miniature.

He awoke—and wanted Mars. The valleys, he thought. What would it be like to trudge among them? Great and greater yet: the dream grew as he became fully conscious, the dream and the yearning. He could almost feel the enveloping presence of the other world, which only Government agents and high officials had seen. A clerk like himself? Not likely.

"Are you getting up or not?" his wife Kirsten asked drowsily, with her usual hint of fierce crossness. "If you are, push the hot coffee button on the darn stove."

"Okay," Douglas Quail said, and made his way barefoot

122

from the bedroom of their conapt to the kitchen. There, having dutifully pressed the hot coffee button, he seated himself at the kitchen table, brought out a yellow, small tin of fine Dean Swift snuff. He inhaled briskly, and the Beau Nash mixture stung his nose, burned the roof of his mouth. But still he inhaled it; it woke him up and allowed his dreams, his nocturnal desires and random wishes, to condense into a semblance of rationality.

I will go, he said to himself. Before I die I'll see Mars.

It was, of course, impossible, and he knew this even as he dreamed. But the daylight, the mundane noise of his wife now brushing her hair before the bedroom mirror—everything conspired to remind him of what he was. A miserable little salaried employee, he said to himself with bitterness. Kirsten reminded him of this at least once a day and he did not blame her; it was a wife's job to bring her husband down to Earth. Down to Earth, he thought, and laughed. The figure of speech in this was literally apt.

"What are you sniggering about?" his wife asked as she swept into the kitchen, her long busy-pink robe wagging after her. "A dream, I bet. You're always full of them."

"Yes," he said, and gazed out the kitchen window at the hover-cars and traffic runnels, and all the little energetic people hurrying to work. In a little while he would be among them. As always.

"I'll bet it has to do with some woman," Kirsten said witheringly.

"No," he said. "A god. The god of war. He has wonderful craters with every kind of plant-life growing deep down in them."

"Listen." Kirsten crouched down beside him and spoke earnestly, the harsh quality momentarily gone from her voice. "The bottom of the ocean—*our* ocean is much more, an infinity of times more beautiful. You know that; everyone knows that. Rent an artificial gill-outfit for both of us, take a week off from work, and we can descend and live down there at one of those year-round aquatic resorts. And in addition—" She broke off. "You're not listening. You should be. Here is something a lot better than that compulsion, that obsession you have about Mars, and you don't even listen!" Her voice rose piercingly. "God in heaven, you're doomed, Doug! What's going to become of you?"

"I'm going to work," he said, rising to his feet, his breakfast forgotten. "That's what's going to become of me."

She eyed him. "You're getting worse. More fanatical every day. Where's it going to lead?"

"To Mars," he said, and opened the door to the closet to get down a fresh shirt to wear to work.

Having descended from the taxi Douglas Quail slowly walked across three densely-populated foot runnels and to the modern, attractively inviting doorway. There he halted, impeding mid-morning traffic, and with caution read the shifting-color neon sign. He had, in the past, scrutinized this sign before . . . but never had he come so close. This was very different; what he did now was something else. Something which sooner or later had to happen.

REKAL, INCORPORATED

Was this the answer? After all, an illusion, no matter how convincing, remained nothing more than an illusion. At least objectively. But subjectively—quite the opposite entirely.

And anyhow he had an appointment. Within the next five minutes.

Taking a deep breath of mildly smog-infested Chicago air, he walked through the dazzling polychromatic shimmer of the doorway and up to the receptionist's counter.

The nicely-articulated blonde at the counter, bare-bosomed and tidy, said pleasantly, "Good morning, Mr. Quail."

"Yes," he said. "I'm here to see about a Rekal course. As I guess you know."

"Not 'rekal' but *re*call," the receptionist corrected him. She picked up the receiver of the vid-phone by her smooth elbow and said into it, "Mr. Douglas Quail is here, Mr. McClane. May he come inside, now? Or is it too soon?"

"Giz wetwa wum-wum wamp," the phone mumbled.

"Yés, Mr. Quail," she said. "You may go in; Mr. McClane is expecting you." As he started off uncertainly she called after him, "Room D, Mr. Quail. To your right."

After a frustrating but brief moment of being lost he found the proper room. The door hung open and inside, at a big genuine walnut desk, sat a genial-looking man, middle-aged, wearing the latest Martian frog-pelt gray suit; his attire alone would have told Quail that he had come to the right person.

"Sit down, Douglas," McClane said, waving his plump hand toward a chair which faced the desk. "So you want to have gone to Mars. Very good."

Quail seated himself, feeling tense. "I'm not so sure this is worth the fee," he said. "It costs a lot and as far as I can see I really get nothing." Costs almost as much as going, he thought.

"You get tangible proof of your trip," McClane disagreed emphatically. "All the proof you'll need. Here; I'll show you." He dug within a drawer of his impressive desk. "Ticket stub." Reaching into a manila folder he produced a small square of embossed cardboard. "It proves you went—and returned. Postcards." He laid out four franked picture 3-D full-color postcards in a neatly-arranged row on the desk for Quail to see. "Film. Shots you took of local sights on Mars with a rented movie camera." To Quail he displayed those, too. "Plus the names of people you met, two hundred poscreds worth of souvenirs, which will arrive—from Mars—within the following month. And passport, certificates listing the shots you received. And more." He glanced up keenly at Quail. "You'll know you went, all right," he said. "You won't remember us, won't remember me or ever having been here. It'll be a real trip in your mind; we guarantee that. A full two weeks of recall; every last piddling detail. Remember this: if at any time you doubt that you really took an extensive trip to Mars you can return here and get a full refund. You see?"

"But I didn't go," Quail said. "I won't have gone, no matter what proofs you provide me with." He took a deep, unsteady breath. "And I never was a secret agent with Interplan." It seemed impossible to him that Rekal, Incorporated's extra-factual memory implant would do its job—despite what he had heard people say.

"Mr. Quail," McClane said patiently. "As you explained in your letter to us, you have no chance, no possibility in the slightest, of ever actually getting to Mars; you can't afford it, and what is much more important, you could never qualify as an undercover agent for Interplan or anybody else. This is the only way you can achieve your, hem, lifelong dream; am I not correct, sir? You can't be this; you can't actually do this." He chuckled. "But you can *have been* and *have done*. We see to that. And our fee is reasonable; no hidden charges." He smiled encouragingly.

"Is an extra-factual memory that convincing?" Quail asked.

"More than the real thing, sir. Had you really gone to Mars as an Interplan agent, you would by now have forgotten a great deal; our analysis of true-mem systems —authentic recollections of major events in a person's life—shows that a variety of details are very quickly lost to the person. Forever. Part of the package we offer you is such deep implantation of recall that nothing is forgotten. The packet which is fed to you while you're comatose is the creation of trained experts, men who have spent years on Mars; in every case we verify details down to the last iota. And you've picked a rather easy extra-factual system; had you picked Pluto or wanted to be Emperor of the Inner Planet Alliance we'd have much more difficulty . . . and the charges would be considerably greater."

Reaching into his coat for his wallet, Quail said, "Okay. It's been my lifelong ambition and I can see I'll never really do it. So I guess I'll have to settle for this."

"Don't think of it that way," McClane said severely. "You're not accepting second-best. The actual memory, with all its vagueness, omissions and ellipses, not to say distortions—that's second-best." He accepted the money and pressed a button on his desk. "All right, Mr. Quail," he said, as the door of his office opened and two burly men swiftly entered. "You're on your way to Mars as a secret agent." He rose, came over to shake Quail's nervous, moist hand. "Or rather, you have been on your way. This afternoon at four-thirty you will, um, arrive back here on Terra; a cab will leave you off at your conapt and as I say you will never remember seeing me or coming here; you won't, in fact, even remember having heard of our existence."

His mouth dry with nervousness, Quail followed the two technicians from the office; what happened next depended on them.

Will I actually believe I've been on Mars? he wondered. That I managed to fulfill my lifetime ambition? He had a strange, lingering intuition that something would go wrong. But just what—he did not know.

He would have to wait to find out.

The intercom on McClane's desk, which connected him with the work-area of the firm, buzzed and a voice said, "Mr. Quail is under sedation now, sir. Do you want to supervise this one, or shall we go ahead?"

"It's routine," McClane observed. "You may go ahead, Lowe; I don't think you'll run into any trouble." Programming an artificial memory of a trip to another planet —with or without the added fillip of being a secret agent —showed up on the firm's work-schedule with monotonous regularity. In one month, he calculated wryly, we must do twenty of these . . . ersatz interplanetary travel has become our bread and butter.

"Whatever you say, Mr. McClane," Lowe's voice came, and thereupon the intercom shut off.

Going to the vault section in the chamber behind his office, McClane searched about for a Three packet—trip to Mars—and a Sixty-two packet: secret Interplan spy. Finding the two packets, he returned with them to his desk, seated himself comfortably, poured out the contents—merchandise which would be planted in Quail's conapt while the lab technicians busied themselves installing the false memory.

A one-poscred sneaky-pete side arm, McClane reflected; that's the largest item. Sets us back financially the most. Then a pellet-sized transmitter, which could be swallowed if the agent were caught. Code book that astonishingly resembled the real thing . . . the firm's models were highly accurate: based, whenever possible, on actual U.S. military issue. Odd bits which made no intrinsic sense but which would be woven into the warp and woof of Quail's imaginary trip, would coincide with his memory: half an ancient silver fifty cent piece, several quotations from John Donne's sermons written incorrectly, each on a separate piece of transparent tissue-thin paper, several match folders from bars on Mars, a stainless steel spoon engraved PROPERTY OF DOME-MARS NATIONAL KIBBUZIM, a wire tapping coil which—

The intercom buzzed. "Mr. McClane, I'm sorry to bother you but something rather ominous has come up. Maybe it would be better if you were in here after all. Quail is already under sedation; he reacted well to the narkidrine; he's completely unconscious and receptive. But—"

"I'll be in." Sensing trouble, McClane left his office; a moment later he emerged in the work area.

On a hygienic bed lay Douglas Quail, breathing slowly and regularly, his eyes virtually shut; he seemed dimly—but only dimly—aware of the two technicians and now McClane himself.

"There's no space to insert false memory-patterns?"

McClane felt irritation. "Merely drop out two work weeks; he's employed as a clerk at the West Coast Emigration Bureau, which is a government agency, so he undoubtedly has or had two weeks' vacation within the last year. That ought to do it." Petty details annoyed him. And always would.

"Our problem," Lowe said sharply, "is something quite different." He bent over the bed, said to Quail, "Tell Mr. McClane what you told us." To McClane he said, "Listen closely."

The gray-green eyes of the man lying supine in the bed focused on McClane's face. The eyes, he observed uneasily, had become hard; they had a polished, inorganic quality, like semi-precious tumbled stones. He was not sure that he liked what he saw; the brilliance was too cold. "What do you want now?" Quail said harshly. "You've broken my cover. Get out of here before I take you all apart." He studied McClane. "Especially you," he continued. "You're in charge of this counter-operation."

Lowe said, "How long were you on Mars?"

"One month," Quail said gratingly.

"And your purpose there?" Lowe demanded.

The meager lips twisted; Quail eyed him and did not speak. At last, drawling the words out so that they dripped with hostility, he said, "Agent for Interplan. As I already told you. Don't you record everything that's said? Play your vid-aud tape back for your boss and leave me alone." He shut his eyes, then; the hard brilliance ceased. McClane felt, instantly, a rushing splurge of relief.

Lowe said quietly, "This is a tough man, Mr. McClane."

"He won't be," McClane said, "after we arrange for him to lose his memory-chain again. He'll be as meek as before." To Quail he said, "So *this* is why you wanted to go to Mars so terribly badly."

Without opening his eyes Quail said, "I never wanted to go to Mars. I was assigned it—they handed it to me and there I was: stuck. Oh yeah, I admit I was curious about it; who wouldn't be?" Again he opened his eyes and surveyed the three of them, McClane in particular.

"Quite a truth drug you've got here; it brought up things I had absolutely no memory of." He pondered. "I wonder about Kirsten," he said, half to himself. "Could she be in on it? An Interplan contact keeping an eye on me . . . to be certain I didn't regain my memory? No wonder she's been so derisive about my wanting to go there." Faintly, he smiled; the smile—one of understanding—disappeared almost at once.

McClane said, "Please believe me, Mr. Quail; we stumbled onto this entirely by accident. In the work we do—"

"I believe you," Quail said. He seemed tired now; the drug was continuing to pull him under, deeper and deeper. "Where did I say I'd been?" he murmured. "Mars? Hard to remember—I know I'd like to see it; so would everybody. But me—" His voice trailed off. "Just a clerk, a nothing clerk."

Straightening up, Lowe said to his superior, "He wants a false memory implanted that corresponds to a trip he actually took. And a false reason which is the real reason. He's telling the truth; he's a long way down in the narkidrine. The trip is very vivid in his mind—at least under sedation. But apparently he doesn't recall it otherwise. Someone, probably at a government military-sciences lab, erased his conscious memories; all he knew was that going to Mars meant something special to him, and so did being a secret agent. They couldn't erase that; it's not a memory but a desire, undoubtedly the same one that motivated him to volunteer for the assignment in the first place."

The other technician, Keeler, said to McClane, "What do we do? Graft a false memory-pattern over the real memory? There's no telling what the results would be; he might remember some of the genuine trip, and the confusion might bring on a psychotic interlude. He'd have to hold two opposite premises in his mind simultaneously: that he went to Mars and that he didn't. That he's a genuine agent for Interplan and he's not, that it's spurious. I think we ought to revive him without any false memory implantation and send him out of here; this is hot."

"Agreed," McClane said. A thought came to him. "Can you predict what he'll remember when he comes out of sedation?"

"Impossible to tell," Lowe said. "He probably will have some dim, diffuse memory of his actual trip, now. And he'd probably be in grave doubt as to its validity; he'd probably decide our programming slipped a gear-tooth. And he'd remember coming here; that wouldn't be erased —unless you want it erased."

"The less we mess with this man," McClane said, "the better I like it. This is nothing for us to fool around with; we've been foolish enough to—or unlucky enough to— uncover a genuine Interplan spy who was a cover so perfect that up to now even he didn't know what he was—or rather is." The sooner they washed their hands of the man calling himself Douglas Quail the better.

"Are you going to plant packets Three and Sixty-two in his conapt?" Lowe said.

"No," McClane said. "And we're going to return half his fee."

" 'Half'! Why half?"

McClane said lamely, "It seems to be a good compromise."

As the cab carried him back to his conapt at the residential end of Chicago, Douglas Quail said to himself, It's sure good to be back on Terra.

Already the month-long period on Mars had begun to waver in his memory; he had only an image of profound gaping craters, an ever-present ancient erosion of hills, of vitality, of motion itself. A world of dust where little happened, where a good part of the day was spent checking and rechecking one's portable oxygen source. And then the life forms, the unassuming and modest gray-brown cacti and maw-worms.

As a matter of fact he had brought back several moribund examples of Martian fauna; he had smuggled them through customs. After all, they posed no menace; they couldn't survive in Earth's heavy atmosphere.

Reaching into his coat pocket he rummaged for the container of Martian maw-worms—

And found an envelope instead.

Lifting it out he discovered, to his perplexity, that it contained five hundred and seventy poscreds, in cred bills of low denomination.

Where'd I get this? he asked himself. Didn't I spend every 'cred I had on my trip?

With the money came a slip of paper marked: *one-half fee ret'd. By McClane.* And then the date. Today's date.

"Recall," he said aloud.

"Recall what, sir or madam?" the robot driver of the cab inquired respectfully.

"Do you have a phone book?" Quail demanded.

"Certainly, sir or madam." A slot opened; from it slid a microtape phone book for Cook County.

"It's spelled oddly," Quail said as he leafed through the pages of the yellow section. He felt fear, then; abiding fear. "Here it is," he said. "Take me there, to Rekal, Incorporated. I've changed my mind; I don't want to go home."

"Yes sir, or madam, as the case may be," the driver said. A moment later the cab was zipping back in the opposite direction.

"May I make use of your phone?" he asked.

"Be my guest," the robot driver said. And presented a shiny new emperor 3-D color phone to him.

He dialed his own conapt. And after a pause found himself confronted by a miniature but chillingly realistic image of Kirsten on the small screen. "I've been to Mars," he said to her.

"You're drunk." Her lips writhed scornfully. "Or worse."

" 'S god's truth."

"When?" she demanded.

"I don't know." He felt confused. "A simulated trip, I think. By means of one of those artificial or extra-factual or whatever it is memory places. It didn't take."

Kirsten said witheringly, "You *are* drunk." And broke

the connection at her end. He hung up, then, feeling his face flush. Always the same tone, he said hotly to himself. Always the retort, as if she knows everything and I know nothing. What a marriage. Keerist, he thought dismally.

A moment later the cab stopped at the curb before a modern, very attractive little pink building, over which a shifting, polychromatic neon sign read: REKAL, INCORPORATED.

The receptionist, chic and bare from the waist up, started in surprise, then gained masterful control of herself. "Oh, hello, Mr. Quail," she said nervously. "H-how are you? Did you forget something?"

"The rest of my fee back," he said.

More composed now, the receptionist said, "Fee? I think you are mistaken, Mr. Quail. You were here discussing the feasibility of an extra-factual trip for you, but —" She shrugged her smooth pale shoulders. "As I understand it, no trip was taken."

Quail said, "I remember everything, miss. My letter to Rekal, Incorporated, which started this whole business off. I remember my arrival here, my visit with Mr. McClane. Then the two lab technicians taking me in tow and administering a drug to put me out." No wonder the firm had returned half his fee. The false memory of his "trip to Mars" hadn't taken—at least not entirely, not as he had been assured.

"Mr. Quail," the girl said, "although you are a minor clerk you are a good-looking man and it spoils your features to become angry. If it would make you feel any better, I might, ahem, let you take me out . . ."

He felt furious, then. "I remember you," he said savagely. "For instance the fact that your breasts are sprayed blue; that stuck in my mind. And I remember Mr. McClane's promise that if I remembered my visit to Rekal, Incorporated I'd receive my money back in full. Where is Mr. McClane?"

After a delay—probably as long as they could manage —he found himself once more seated facing the imposing walnut desk, exactly as he had been an hour or so earlier in the day.

"Some technique you have," Quail said sardonically. His disappointment—and resentment—were enormous, by now. "My so-called 'memory' of a trip to Mars as an undercover agent for Interplan is hazy and vague and shot full of contradictions. And I clearly remember my dealings here with you people. I ought to take this to the Better Business Bureau." He was burning angry, at this point; his sense of being cheated had overwhelmed him, had destroyed his customary aversion to participating in a public squabble.

Looking morose, as well as cautious, McClane said, "We capitulate, Quail. We'll refund the balance of your fee. I fully concede the fact that we did absolutely nothing for you." His tone was resigned.

Quail said accusingly, "You didn't even provide me with the various artifacts that you claimed would 'prove' to me I had been on Mars. All that song-and-dance you went into—it hasn't materialized into a damn thing. Not even a ticket stub. Nor postcards. Nor passport. Nor proof of immunization shots. Nor—"

"Listen, Quail," McClane said. "Suppose I told you—" He broke off. "Let it go." He pressed a button on his intercom. "Shirley, will you disburse five hundred and seventy more 'creds in the form of a cashier's check made out to Douglas Quail? Thank you." He released the button, then glared at Quail.

Presently the check appeared; the receptionist placed it before McClane and once more vanished out of sight, leaving the two men alone, still facing each other across the surface of the massive walnut desk.

"Let me give you a word of advice," McClane said as he signed the check and passed it over. "Don't discuss your, ahem, recent trip to Mars with anyone."

"What trip?"

"Well, that's the thing." Doggedly, McClane said, "The trip you partially remember. Act as if you don't remember; pretend it never took place. Don't ask me why; just take my advice; it'll be better for all of us." He had begun to perspire. Freely. "Now, Mr. Quail, I have other business, other clients to see." He rose, showed Quail to the door.

Quail said, as he opened the door, "A firm that turns out such bad work shouldn't have any clients at all." He shut the door behind him.

On the way home in the cab Quail pondered the wording of his letter of complaint to the Better Business Bureau, Terra Division. As soon as he could get to his typewriter he'd get started; it was clearly his duty to warn other people away from Rekal, Incorporated.

When he got back to his conapt he seated himself before his Hermes Rocket portable, opened the drawers and rummaged for carbon paper—and noticed a small, familiar box. A box which he had carefully filled on Mars with Martian fauna and later smuggled through customs.

Opening the box he saw, to his disbelief, six dead mawworms and several varieties of the unicellular life on which the Martian worms fed. The protozoa were dried-up, dusty, but he recognized them; it had taken him an entire day picking among the vast dark alien boulders to find them. A wonderful illuminated journey of discovery.

But I didn't go to Mars, he realized.

Yet on the other hand—

Kirsten appeared at the doorway to the room, an armload of pale brown groceries gripped. "Why are you home in the middle of the day?" Her voice, in an eternity of sameness, was accusing.

"*Did I go to Mars?*" he asked her. "You would know."

"No, of course you didn't go to Mars, *you* would know that, I would think. Aren't you always bleating about going?"

He said, "By God, I think I went." After a pause he added, "And simultaneously I think I didn't go."

"Make up your mind."

"How can I?" He gestured. "I have both memory-tracts grafted inside my head; one is real and one isn't but I can't tell which is which. Why can't I rely on you? They haven't

tinkered with you." She could do this much for him at least
—even if she never did anything else.

Kirsten said in a level, controlled voice, "Doug, if you
don't pull yourself together, we're through. I'm going to
leave you."

"I'm in trouble." His voice came out husky and coarse.
And shaking. "Probably I'm heading into a psychotic epi-
sode; I hope not, but—maybe that's it. It would explain
everything, anyhow."

Setting down the bag of groceries, Kirsten stalked to the
closet. "I was not kidding," she said to him quietly. She
brought out a coat, got it on, walked back to the door of
the conapt. "I'll phone you one of these days soon," she
said tonelessly. "This is goodbye, Doug, I hope you pull
out of this eventually; I really pray you do. For your sake."

"Wait," he said desperately. "Just tell me and make it
absolute; I did go or I didn't—tell me which one." But
they may have altered your memory-track also, he realized.

The door closed. His wife had left. Finally!

A voice behind him said, "Well, that's that. Now put up
your hands, Quail. And also please turn around and face
this way."

He turned, instinctively, without raising his hands.

The man who faced him wore the plum uniform of the
Interplan Police Agency, and his gun appeared to be UN
issue. And, for some odd reason, he seemed familiar to
Quail; familiar in a blurred, distorted fashion which he
could not pin down. So, jerkily, he raised his hands.

"You remember," the policeman said, "your trip to
Mars. We know all your actions today and all your
thoughts—in particular your very important thoughts on
the trip home from Rekal, Incorporated." He explained,
"We have a telep-transmitter wired within your skull; it
keeps us constantly informed."

A telepathic transmitter; use of a living plasma that had
been discovered on Luna. He shuddered with self-aversion.
The thing lived inside him, within his own brain, feeding,
listening, feeding. But the Interplan police used them; that

had come out even in the homeopapes. So this was probably true, dismal as it was.

"Why me?" Quail said huskily. What had he done—or thought? And what did this have to do with Rekal, Incorporated?

"Fundamentally," the Interplan cop said, "this has nothing to do with Rekal; it's between you and us." He tapped his right ear. "I'm still picking up your mentational processes by way of your cephalic transmitter." In the man's ear Quail saw a small white-plastic plug. "So I have to warn you: anything you think may be held against you." He smiled. "Not that it matters now; you've already thought and spoken yourself into oblivion. What's annoying is the fact that under narkidrine at Rekal, Incorporated you told them, their technicians and the owner, Mr. McClane, about your trip; where you went, for whom, some of what you did. They're very frightened. They wish they had never laid eyes on you." He added reflectively, "They're right."

Quail said, "I never made any trip. It's a false memory-chain improperly planted in me by McClane's technicians." But then he thought of the box, in his desk drawer, containing the Martian life forms. And the trouble and hardship he had had gathering them. The memory seemed real. And the box of life forms; that certainly was real. Unless McClane had planted it. Perhaps this was one of the "proofs" which McClane had talked glibly about.

The memory of my trip to Mars, he thought, doesn't convince me—but unfortunately it has convinced the Interplan Police Agency. They think I really went to Mars and they think I at least partially realize it.

"We not only know you went to Mars," the Interplan cop agreed, in answer to his thoughts, "but we know that you now remember enough to be difficult for us. And there's no use expunging your conscious memory of all this, because if we do you'll simply show up at Rekal, Incorporated again and start over. And we can't do anything about McClane and his operation because we have no jurisdiction over anyone except our own people. Anyhow, Mc-

Clane hasn't committed any crime." He eyed Quail. "Nor, technically, have you. You didn't go to Rekal, Incorporated with the idea of regaining your memory; you went, as we realize, for the usual reason people go there—a love by plain, dull people for adventure." He added, "Unfortunately you're not plain, not dull, and you've already had too much excitement; the last thing in the universe you needed was a course from Rekal, Incorporated. Nothing could have been more lethal for you or for us. And, for that matter, for McClane."

Quail said, "Why is it 'difficult' for you if I remember my trip—my alleged trip—and what I did there?"

"Because," the Interplan harness bull said, "what you did is not in accord with our great white all-protecting father public image. You did, for us, what we never do. As you'll presently remember—thanks to narkidrine. That box of dead worms and algae has been sitting in your desk drawer for six months, ever since you got back. And at no time have you shown the slightest curiosity about it. We didn't even know you had it until you remembered it on your way home from Rekal; then we came here on the double to look for it." He added, unnecessarily, "Without any luck; there wasn't enough time."

A second Interplan cop joined the first one; the two briefly conferred. Meanwhile, Quail thought rapidly. He did remember more, now; the cop had been right about narkidrine. They—Interplan—probably used it themselves. Probably? He knew darn well they did; he had seen them putting a prisoner on it. Where would *that* be? Somewhere on Terra? More likely Luna, he decided, viewing the image rising from his highly defective—but rapidly less so—memory.

And he remembered something else. Their reason for sending him to Mars; the job he had done.

No wonder they had expunged his memory.

"Oh god," the first of the two Interplan cops said, breaking off his conversation with his companion. Obviously, he had picked up Quail's thoughts. "Well, this is a far worse problem, now; as bad as it can get." He walked toward

Quail, again covering him with his gun. "We've got to kill you," he said. "And right away."

Nervously, his fellow officer said, "Why right away? Can't we simply cart him off to Interplan New York and let them—"

"*He* knows why it has to be right away," the first cop said; he too looked nervous, now, but Quail realized that it was for an entirely different reason. His memory had been brought back almost entirely, now. And he fully understood the officer's tension.

"On Mars," Quail said hoarsely, "I killed a man. After getting past fifteen bodyguards. Some armed with sneaky-pete guns, the way you are." He had been trained, by Interplan, over a five year period to be an assassin. A professional killer. He knew ways to take out armed adversaries . . . such as these two officers; and the one with the ear-receiver knew it, too.

If he moved swiftly enough—

The gun fired. But he had already moved to one side, and at the same time he chopped down the gun-carrying officer. In an instant he had possession of the gun and was covering the other, confused, officer.

"Picked my thoughts up," Quail said, panting for breath. "He knew what I was going to do, but I did it anyhow."

Half sitting up, the injured officer grated, "He won't use that gun on you, Sam; I pick that up, too. He knows he's finished, and he knows we know it, too. Come on, Quail." Laboriously, grunting with pain, he got shakily to his feet. He held out his hand. "The gun," he said to Quail. "You can't use it, and if you turn it over to me I'll guarantee not to kill you; you'll be given a hearing, and someone higher up in Interplan will decide, not me. Maybe they can erase your memory once more; I don't know. But you know the thing I was going to kill you for; I couldn't keep you from remembering it. So my reason for wanting to kill you is in a sense past."

Quail, clutching the gun, bolted from the conapt, sprinted for the elevator. If you follow me, he thought, I'll kill you. So don't. He jabbed at the elevator button and, a moment later, the doors slid back.

The police hadn't followed him. Obviously they had picked up his terse, tense thoughts and had decided not to take the chance.

With him inside the elevator descended. He had gotten away—for a time. But what next? Where could he go?

The elevator reached the ground floor; a moment later Quail had joined the mob of peds hurrying along the runnels. His head ached and he felt sick. But at least he had evaded death; they had come very close to shooting him on the spot, back in his own conapt.

And they probably will again, he decided. When they find me. And with this transmitter inside me, that won't take too long.

Ironically, he had gotten exactly what he had asked Rekal, Incorporated for. Adventure, peril, Interplan police at work, a secret and dangerous trip to Mars in which his life was at stake—everything he had wanted as a false memory.

The advantages of it being a memory—and nothing more—could now be appreciated.

On a park bench, alone, he sat dully watching a flock of perts: a semi-bird imported from Mars' two moons, capable of soaring flight, even against Earth's huge gravity.

Maybe I can find my way back to Mars, he pondered. But then what? It would be worse on Mars; the political organization whose leader he had assassinated would spot him the moment he stepped from the ship; he would have Interplan and *them* after him, there.

Can you hear me thinking? he wondered. Easy avenue to paranoia; sitting here alone he felt them tuning in on him, monitoring, recording, discussing . . . he shivered, rose to his feet, walked aimlessly, his hands deep in his pockets. No matter where I go, he realized. You'll always be with me. As long as I have this device inside my head.

I'll make a deal with you, he thought to himself—and to them. Can't you imprint a false-memory template on me again, as you did before, that I lived an average, routine life, never went to Mars? Never saw an Interplan uniform up close and never handled a gun?

A voice inside his brain answered, "As has been carefully explained to you: that would not be enough."

Astonished, he halted.

"We formerly communicated with you in this manner," the voice continued. "When you were operating in the field, on Mars. It's been months since we've done it; we assumed, in fact, that we'd never have to do so again. Where are you?"

"Walking," Quail said, "to my death." By your officers' guns, he added as an afterthought. "How can you be sure it wouldn't be enough?" he demanded. "Don't the Rekal techniques work?"

"As we said. If you're given a set of standard, average memories you get—restless. You'd inevitably seek out Rekal, or one of its competitors again. We can't go through this a second time."

"Suppose," Quail said, "once my authentic memories have been canceled, something more vital than standard memories are implanted. Something which would act to satisfy my craving," he said. "That's been proved; that's probably why you initially hired me. But you ought to be able to come up with something else—something equal. I was the richest man on Terra but I finally gave all my money to educational foundations. Or I was a famous deep-space explorer. Anything of that sort; wouldn't one of those do?"

Silence.

"Try it," he said desperately. "Get some of your top-notch military psychiatrists; explore my mind. Find out what my most expansive daydream is." He tried to think. "Women," he said. "Thousands of them, like Don Juan had. An interplanetary playboy—a mistress in every city on Earth, Luna and Mars. Only I gave that up, out of exhaustion. Please," he begged. "Try it."

"You'd voluntarily surrender, then?" the voice inside his head asked. "If we agreed to arrange such a solution? *If* it's possible?"

After an interval of hesitation he said, "Yes." I'll take the risk, he said to himself. That you don't simply kill me.

"You make the first move," the voice said presently. "Turn yourself over to us. And we'll investigate that line of possibility. If we can't do it, however, if your authentic memories begin to crop up again as they've done at this time, then—" There was silence and then the voice finished, "We'll have to destroy you. As you must understand. Well, Quail, you still want to try?"

"Yes," he said. Because the alternative was death now—and for certain. At least this way he had a chance, slim as it was.

"You present yourself at our main barracks in New York," the voice of the Interplan cop resumed. "At 580 Fifth Avenue, floor twelve. Once you've surrendered yourself we'll have our psychiatrists begin on you; we'll have personality-profile tests made. We'll attempt to determine your absolute, ultimate fantasy wish—and then we'll bring you back to Rekal, Incorporated, here; get them in on it, fulfilling that wish in vicarious surrogate retrospection. And—good luck. We do owe you something; you acted as a capable instrument for us." The voice lacked malice; if anything, they—the organization—felt sympathy toward him.

"Thanks," Quail said. And began searching for a robot cab.

"Mr. Quail," the stern-faced, elderly Interplan psychiatrist said, "you possess a most interesting wish-fulfillment dream fantasy. Probably nothing such as you consciously entertain or suppose. This is commonly the way; I hope it won't upset you too much to hear about it."

The senior ranking Interplan officer present said briskly, "He better not be too much upset to hear about it, not if he expects not to get shot."

"Unlike the fantasy of wanting to be an Interplan undercover agent," the psychiatrist continued, "which, being relatively speaking a product of maturity, had a certain plausibility to it, this production is a grotesque dream of your childhood; it is no wonder you fail to recall it. Your fantasy is this: you are nine years old, walking alone down a rustic lane. An unfamiliar variety of space vessel from another star system lands directly in front of you. No one on Earth but you, Mr. Quail, sees it. The creatures within are very small and helpless, somewhat on the order of field mice, although they are attempting to invade Earth; tens of thousands of other such ships will soon be ·on their way, when this advance party gives the go-ahead signal."

"And I suppose I stop them," Quail said, experiencing a mixture of amusement and disgust. "Single-handed I wipe them out. Probably by stepping on them with my foot."

"No," the psychiatrist said patiently. "You halt the invasion, but not by destroying them. Instead, you show them kindness and mercy, even though by telepathy their mode of communication—you know why they have come. They have never seen such humane traits exhibited by any sentient organism, and to show their appreciation they make a covenant with you."·

Quail said, "They won't invade Earth as long as I'm alive."

"Exactly." To the Interplan officer the psychiatrist said, "You can see it does fit his personality, despite his feigned scorn."

"So by merely existing," Quail said, feeling a growing pleasure, "by simply being alive, I keep Earth safe from alien rule. I'm in effect, then, the most important person on Terra. Without lifting a finger."

"Yes indeed, sir," the psychiatrist said. "And this is bedrock in your psyche; this is a lifelong childhood fantasy. Which, without depth and drug therapy, you never would have recalled. But it had always existed in you; it went underneath, but never ceased."

To McClane, who sat intently listening, the senior police official said, "Can you implant an extra-factual memory pattern that extreme in him?"

"We get handed every possible type of wish-fantasy there is," McClane said. "Frankly, I've heard a lot worse than this. Certainly we can handle it. Twenty-four hours from now he won't just *wish* he'd saved Earth; he'll devoutly believe it really happened."

The senior police official said, "You can start the job, then. In preparation we've already once again erased the memory in him of his trip to Mars."

Quail said, "What trip to Mars?"

No one answered him, so, reluctantly, he shelved the question. And anyhow a police vehicle had now put in its appearance; he, McClane and the senior police officer crowded into it, and presently they were on their way to Chicago and Rekal, Incorporated.

"You had better make no errors this time," the police officer said to heavy-set, nervous-looking McClane.

"I can't see what could go wrong," McClane mumbled, perspiring. "This has nothing to do with Mars or Interplan. Single-handedly stopping an invasion of Earth from another star-system." He shook his head at that. "Wow, what a kid dreams up. And by pious virtue, too; not by force. It's sort of quaint." He dabbed at his forehead with a large linen pocket handkerchief.

Nobody said anything.

"In fact," McClane said, "it's touching."

"But arrogant," the police official said starkly. "Inasmuch as when he dies the invasion will resume. No wonder he doesn't recall it; it's the most grandiose fantasy I ever ran across." He eyed Quail with disapproval. "And to think we put this man on our payroll."

When they reached Rekal, Incorporated the receptionist, Shirley, met them breathlessly in the outer office. "Welcome back, Mr. Quail," she fluttered, her melon-shaped breasts—today painted an incandescent orange—bobbing with agitation. "I'm sorry everything worked out so badly before; I'm sure this time it'll go better."

Still repeatedly dabbing at his shiny forehead with his neatly-folded Irish linen handkerchief, McClane said, "It better." Moving with rapidity he rounded up Lowe and Keeler, escorted them and Douglas Quail to the work area,

and then, with Shirley and the senior police officer, returned to his familiar office. To wait.

"Do we have a packet made up for this, Mr. McClane?"
Shirley asked, bumping against him in her agitation, then
coloring modestly.

"I think we do." He tried to recall; then gave up and con-
sulted the formal chart. "A combination," he decided
aloud, "of packets Eighty-one, Twenty, and Six." From
the vault section of the chamber behind his desk he fished
out the appropriate packets, carried them to his desk for
inspection. "From Eighty-one," he explained, "a magic
healing rod given him—the client in question, this time
Mr. Quail—by the race of beings from another system. A
token of their gratitude."

"Does it work?" the police officer asked curiously.

"It did once," McClane explained. "But he, ahem, you
see, used it up years ago, healing right and left. Now it's
only a memento. But he remembers it working spectacu-
larly." He chuckled, then opened packet Twenty. "Docu-
ment from the UN Secretary General thanking him for
saving Earth; this isn't precisely appropriate, because part
of Quail's fantasy is that no one knows of the invasion except himself, but for the sake of verisimilitude we'll throw
it in." He inspected packet Six, then. What came from
this? He couldn't recall; frowning, he dug into the plastic
bag as Shirley and the Interplan police officer watched intently.

"Writing," Shirley said. "In a funny language."

"This tells who they were," McClane said, "and where
they came from. Including a detailed star map logging their
flight here and the system of origin. Of course it's in *their*
script, so he can't read it. But he remembers them reading
it to him in his own tongue." He placed the three artifacts
in the center of the desk. "These should be taken to Quail's
conapt," he said to the police officer. "So that when he gets
home he'll find them. And it'll confirm his fantasy. SOP—
standard operating procedure." He chuckled apprehen-
sively, wondering how matters were going with Lowe and
Keeler.

The intercom buzzed. "Mr. McClane, I'm sorry to bother you." It was Lowe's voice; he froze as he recognized it, froze and became mute. "But something's come up. Maybe it would be better if you came in here and supervised. Like before, Quail reacted well to the narkidrine; he's unconscious, relaxed and receptive. But—"

McClane sprinted for the work area.

On a hygienic bed Douglas Quail lay breathing slowly and regularly, eyes half-shut, dimly conscious of those around him.

"We started interrogating him," Lowe said, white-faced. "To find out exactly when to place the fantasy-memory of him single-handedly having saved Earth. And strangely enough—"

"They told me not to tell," Douglas Quail mumbled in a dull drug-saturated voice. "That was the agreement. I wasn't even supposed to remember. But how could I forget an event like that?"

I guess it would be hard, McClane reflected. *But you did—until now.*

"They even gave me a scroll," Quail mumbled, "of gratitude. I have it hidden in my conapt; I'll show it to you."

To the Interplan officer who had followed after him, McClane said, "Well, I offer the suggestion that you better not kill him. If you do they'll return."

"They also gave me a magic invisible destroying rod," Quail mumbled, eyes totally shut, now. "That's how I killed that man on Mars you sent me to take out. It's in my drawer along with the box of Martian maw-worms and dried-up plant life."

Wordlessly, the Interplan officer turned and stalked from the work area.

I might as well put those packets of proof-artifacts away, McClane said to himself resignedly. He walked, step by step, back to his office. *Including the citation from the UN Secretary General. After all—*

The real one probably would not be long in coming.

YESTERDAY HOUSE

Fritz Leiber

This little-known story by the author of **The Wanderer** and **Conjure Wife** was written more than twenty years ago —long before "cloning" and its related biogenetic concepts had become part of the everyday furniture of science fiction. And so it shows once again how far ahead of his times Fritz Leiber has always been—as well as demonstrating, in its quiet, haunting way, his eloquence, his compassion, his power to move the heart.

I

The narrow cove was quiet as the face of an expectant child, yet so near the ruffled Atlantic that the last push of wind carried the *Annie O.* its full length. The man in gray flannels and sweatshirt let the sail come crumpling down and hurried past its white folds at a gait made comically awkward by his cramped muscles. Slowly the rocky ledge came nearer. Slowly the blue V inscribed on the cove's surface by the sloop's prow died. Sloop and ledge kissed so gently that he hardly had to reach out his hand.

He scrambled ashore, dipping a sneaker in the icy water, and threw the line around a boulder. Unkinking himself, he looked back through the cove's high and rocky mouth at the gray-green scattering of islands and the faint dark line that was the coast of Maine. He almost laughed in satisfaction at having disregarded vague warnings and done the thing every man yearns to do once in his lifetime—gone to the farthest island out.

He must have looked longer than he realized, because by the time he dropped his gaze the cove was again as glassy as if the *Annie O.* had always been there. And the splotches made by his sneaker on the rock had faded in the hot sun. There was something very unusual about the quietness of this place. As if time, elsewhere hurrying frantically, paused here to rest. As if all changes were erased on this one bit of earth.

The man's lean, melancholy face crinkled into a grin at the banal fancy. He turned his back on his new friend, the little green sloop, without one thought for his nets and specimen bottles, and set out to explore. The ground rose steeply at first and the oaks were close, but after a little way things went downhill and the leaves thinned and he came out on more rocks—and realized that he hadn't quite gone to the farthest one out.

Joined to this island by a rocky spine, which at the present low tide would have been dry but for the spray, was another green, high island that the first had masked from him all the while he had been sailing. He felt a thrill of discovery, just as he'd wondered back in the woods whether his might not be the first human feet to kick through the underbrush. After all, there were thousands of these islands.

Then he was dropping down the rocks, his lanky limbs now moving smoothly enough.

To the landward side of the spine, the water was fairly still. It even began with another deep cove, in which he glimpsed the spiny spheres of sea urchins. But from seaward the waves chopped in, sprinkling his trousers to the knees and making him wince pleasurably at the thought of what vast wings of spray and towers of solid water must crash up from here in a storm.

He crossed the rocks at a trot, ran up a short grassy slope, raced through a fringe of trees—and came straight up against an eight-foot fence of heavy mesh topped with barbed wire and backed at a short distance with high, heavy shrubbery.

Without pausing for surprise—in fact, in his holiday mood, using surprise as a goad—he jumped for the branch of an oak whose trunk touched the fence, scorning the easier lower branch on the other side of the tree. Then he drew himself up, worked his way to some higher branches that crossed the fence, and dropped down inside.

Suddenly cautious, he gently parted the shrubbery and, before the first surprise could really sink in, had another.

A closely mown lawn dotted with more shrubbery ran up to a snug white Cape Cod cottage. The single strand of a radio aerial stretched the length of the roof. Parked on a neat gravel driveway that crossed just in front of the cottage was a short, square-lined touring car that he recognized from remembered pictures as an ancient Essex. The whole scene had about it the same odd quietness as the cove.

Then, with the air of a clockwork toy coming to life, the white door opened and an elderly woman came out, dressed in a long, lace-edged dress and wide, lacy hat. She climbed into the driver's seat of the Essex, sitting there very stiff and tall. The motor began to chug bravely, gravel skittered, and the car rolled off between the trees.

The door of the house opened again and a slim girl emerged. She wore a white silk dress that fell straight from square neckline to hip-height waistline, making the skirt seem very short. Her dark hair was bound with a white bandeau so that it curved close to her cheeks. A dark necklace dangled against the white of the dress. A newspaper was tucked under her arm.

She crossed the driveway and tossed the paper down on a rattan table between three rattan chairs and stood watching a squirrel zigzag across the lawn.

The man stepped through the wall of shrubbery, called, "Hello!" and walked toward her.

She whirled around and stared at him as still as if her heart had stopped beating. Then she darted behind the table and waited for him there. Granting the surprise of his appearance, her alarm seemed not so much excessive as eerie. As if, the man thought, he were not an ordinary stranger, but a visitor from another planet.

Approaching closer, he saw that she was trembling and that her breath was coming in rapid, irregular gasps. Yet the slim, sweet, patrician face that stared into his had an underlying expression of expectancy that reminded him of the cove. She couldn't have been more than eighteen.

He stopped short of the table. Before he could speak, she stammered out, "Are you he?"

"What do you mean?" he asked, smiling puzzledly.

"The one who sends me the little boxes."

"I was out sailing and I happened to land in the far cove. I didn't dream that anyone lived on this island, or even came here."

"No one ever does come here," she replied. Her manner had changed, becoming at once more wary and less agitated, though still eerily curious.

"It startled me tremendously to find this place," he blundered on. "Especially the road and the car. Why, this island can't be more than a quarter of a mile wide."

"The road goes down to the wharf," she explained, "and up to the top of the island, where my aunts have a tree-house."

He tore his mind away from the picture of a woman dressed like Queen Mary clambering up a tree. "Was that your aunt I saw driving off?"

"One of them. The other's taken the motorboat in for supplies." She looked at him doubtfully. "I'm not sure they'll like it if they find someone here."

"There are just the three of you?" he cut in quickly, looking down the empty road that vanished among the oaks.

She nodded.

"I suppose you go in to the mainland with your aunts quite often?"

She shook her head.

"It must get pretty dull for you."

"Not very," she said, smiling. "My aunts bring me the papers and other things. Even movies. We've got a projector. My favorite stars are Antonio Morino and Alice Terry. I like her better even than Clara Bow."

He looked at her hard for a moment. "I suppose you read a lot?"

She nodded. "Fitzgerald's my favorite author." She started around the table, hesitated, suddenly grew shy. "Would you like some lemonade?"

He'd noticed the dewed silver pitcher, but only now realized his thirst. Yet when she handed him a glass, he held it untasted and said awkwardly, "I haven't introduced myself. I'm Jack Barr."

She stared at his outstretched right hand, slowly extended her own toward it, shook it up and down exactly once, then quickly dropped it.

He chuckled and gulped some lemonade. "I'm a biology student. Been working at Wood's Hole the first part of the summer. But now I'm here to do research in marine ecology—that's sort of sea-life patterns—of the inshore islands. Under the direction of Professor Kesserich. You know about him, of course?"

She shook her head.

"Probably the greatest living biologist," he was proud to inform her. "Human physiology as well. Tremendous geneticist. In a class with Carlson and Jacques Loeb. Martin Kesserich—he lives over there at town. I'm staying with him. You ought to have heard of him." He grinned. "Matter of fact, I'd never have met you if it hadn't been for Mrs. Kesserich."

The girl looked puzzled.

Jack explained, "The old boy's been off to Europe on some conferences, won't be back for a couple days more. But I was to get started anyhow. When I went out this morning Mrs. Kesserich—she's a drab sort of person—said to me. 'Don't try to sail to the farther islands.' So, of course, I had to. By the way, you still haven't told me your name."

"Mary Alice Pope," she said, speaking slowly and with an odd wonder, as if she were saying it for the first time.

"You're pretty shy, aren't you?"

"How would I know?"

The question stopped Jack. He couldn't think of anything to say to this strangely attractive girl dressed almost like a "flapper."

"Will you sit down?" she asked him gravely.

The rattan chair sighed under his weight. He made another effort to talk. "I'll bet you'll be glad when summer's over."

"Why?"

"So you'll be able to go back to the mainland."

"But I never go to the mainland."

"You mean you stay out here all winter?" he asked incredulously, his mind filled with a vision of snow and frozen spray and great gray waves.

"Oh, yes. We get all our supplies on hand before winter. My aunts are very capable. They don't always wear long lace dresses. And now I help them."

"But that's impossible!" he said with sudden sympathetic anger. "You can't be shut off this way from people your own age!"

"You're the first one I ever met." She hesitated. "I never saw a boy or a man before, except in movies."

"You're joking!"

"No, it's true."

"But why are they doing it to you?" he demanded, leaning forward. "Why are they inflicting this loneliness on you, Mary?"

She seemed to have gained poise from his loss of it. "I don't know why. I'm to find out soon. But actually I'm not lonely. May I tell you a secret?" She touched his hand, this time with only the faintest trembling. "Every night the loneliness gathers in around me—you're right about that. But then every morning new life comes to me in a little box."

"What's that?" he said sharply.

"Sometimes there's a poem in the box, sometimes a book, or pictures, or flowers, or a ring, but always a note. Next to the notes I like the poems best. My favorite is the one by Matthew Arnold that ends,

> Ah, love, let us be true
> To one another! for the world, which seems
> To lie before us like a land of dreams,
> So various, so beautiful, so new,
> Hath really neither joy, nor love, nor light,
> Nor certitude—"

"Wait a minute," he interrupted. "Who sends you these boxes?"

"I don't know."

"But how are the notes signed?"

"They're wonderful notes," she said. "So wise, so gay, so tender, you'd imagine them being written by John Barrymore or Lindbergh."

"Yes, but how are they signed?"

She hesitated. "Never anything but 'Your Lover.' "

"And so when you first saw me, you thought—" He began, then stopped because she was blushing.

"How long have you been getting them?"

"Ever since I can remember. I have two closets of the boxes. The new ones are either by my bed when I wake or at my place at breakfast."

"But how does this—person get these boxes to you out here? Does he give them to your aunts and do they put them there?"

"I'm not sure."

"But how can they get them in winter?"

"I don't know."

"Look here," he said, pouring himself more lemonade, "how long is it since you've been to the mainland?"

"Almost eighteen years. My aunts tell me I was born there in the middle of the war."

"What war?" he asked startledly, spilling some lemonade.

"The World War, of course. What's the matter?"

Jack Barr was staring down at the spilled lemonade and feeling a kind of terror he'd never experienced in his waking life. Nothing around him had changed. He could still feel the same hot sun on his shoulders, the same icy glass in his hand, scent the same lemon-acid odor in his nostrils. He could still hear the faint *chop-chop* of the waves.

And yet everything had changed, gone dark and dizzy as a landscape glimpsed just before a faint. All the little false notes had come to a sudden focus. For the lemonade had spilled on the headline of the newspaper the girl had tossed down, and the headline read:

HITLER IN NEW DEFIANCE

Under the big black banner of that head swam smaller ones:

> FOES OF MACHADO RIOT IN HAVANA
> BIG NRA PARADE PLANNED
> BALBO SPEAKS IN NEW YORK

Suddenly he felt a surge of relief. He had noticed that the paper was yellow and brittle-edged.

"Why are you so interested in old newspapers?" he asked.

"I wouldn't call day-before-yesterday's paper old," the girl objected, pointing at the dateline: July 20, 1933.

"You're trying to joke," Jack told her.

"No, I'm not."

"But it's 1953."

"Now it's you who are joking."

"But the paper's yellow."

"The paper's always yellow."

He laughed uneasily. "Well, if you actually think it's 1933, perhaps you're to be envied," he said, with a sardonic humor he didn't quite feel. "Then you can't know anything about the Second World War, or television, or the V-2s, or bikini bathing suits, or the atomic bomb, or—"

"Stop!" She had sprung up and retreated around her chair, white-faced. "I don't like what you're saying."

"But—"

"No, please! Jokes that may be quite harmless on the mainland sound different here."

"I'm really not joking," he said after a moment.

She grew quite frantic at that. "I can show you all last week's papers! I can show you magazines and other things. I can prove it!"

She started toward the house. He followed. He felt his heart begin to pound.

At the white door she paused, looking worriedly down the road. Jack thought he could hear the faint *chug* of a motorboat. She pushed open the door and he followed her inside. The small-windowed room was dark after the sunlight. Jack got an impression of solid old furniture, a fireplace with brass andirons.

"Flash!" croaked a gritty voice. "After their disastrous break day before yesterday, stocks are recovering. Leading issues . . ."

Jack realized that he had started and had involuntarily put his arm around the girl's shoulders. At the same time he noticed that the voice was coming from the curved brown trumpet of an old-fashioned radio loudspeaker.

The girl didn't pull away from him. He turned toward her. Although her gray eyes were on him, her attention had gone elsewhere.

"I can hear the car. They're coming back. They won't like it that you're here."

"All right, they won't like it."

Her agitation grew. "No, you must go."

"I'll come back tomorrow," he heard himself saying.

"Flash! It looks as if the World Economic Conference may soon adjourn, mouthing jeers at old Uncle Sam who is generally referred to as Uncle Shylock."

Jack felt a numbness on his neck. The room seemed to be darkening, the girl growing stranger still.

"You must go before they see you."

"Flash! Wiley Post has just completed his solo circuit of

the globe, after a record-breaking flight of seven days, eighteen hours and forty-five minutes. Asked how he felt after the energy-draining feat, Post quipped . . ."

He was halfway across the lawn before he realized the terror into which the grating radio voice had thrown him.

He leaped for the branch overhanging the fence, vaulted up with the risky help of a foot on the barbed top. A surprised squirrel, lacking time to make its escape up the trunk, sprang to the ground ahead of him. With terrible suddenness, two steel-jawed semicircles clanked together just over the squirrel's head. Jack landed with one foot to either side of the sprung trap, while the squirrel darted off with a squeak.

Jack plunged down the slope to the rocky spine and ran across it, spray from the rising waves spattering him to the waist. Panting now, he stumbled up into the oaks and undergrowth of the first island, fought his way through it, finally reached the silent cove. He loosed the line of the *Annie O.,* dragged it as near to the cove's mouth as he could, plunged knee-deep in freezing water to give it a final shove, scrambled aboard, snatched up the boathook and punched at the rocks.

As soon as the *Annie O.* was nosing out of the cove into the cross waves, he yanked up the sail. The freshening wind filled it and sent the sloop heeling over, with inches of white water over the lee rail, and plunging ahead.

For a long while, Jack was satisfied to think of nothing but the wind and the waves and the sail and speed and danger, to have all his attention taken up balancing one against the other, so that he wouldn't have to ask himself what year it was and whether time was an illusion, and wonder about flappers and hidden traps.

When he finally looked back at the island, he was amazed to see how tiny it had grown, as distant as the mainland.

Then he saw a gray motorboat astern. He watched it as it slowly overtook him. It was built like a lifeboat, with a sturdy low cabin in the bow and wheel amidship. Whoever was at the wheel had long gray hair that whipped in the wind. The longer he looked, the surer he was that it was a woman wearing a lace dress. Something that stuck up inches over the cabin flashed darkly beside her. Only when she lifted it to the roof of the cabin did it occur to him that it might be a rifle.

But just then the motorboat swung around in a turn that sent waves drenching over it, and headed back toward the island. He watched it for a minute in wonder, then his attention was jolted by an angry hail.

Three fishing smacks, also headed toward town, were about to cross his bow. He came around into the wind and waited with shaking sail, watching a man in a lumpy sweater shake a fist at him. Then he turned and gratefully followed the dark, wide, fanlike sterns and age-yellowed sails.

II

The exterior of Martin Kesserich's home—a weathered white cube with narrow, sharp-paned windows, topped by a cupola—was nothing like its lavish interior.

In much the same way, Mrs. Kesserich clashed with the darkly gleaming furniture, Persian rugs and bronze vases around her. Her shapeless black form, poised awkwardly on the edge of a huge sofa, made Jack think of a cow that had strayed into the drawing room. He wondered again how a man like Kesserich had come to marry such a creature.

Yet when she lifted up her little eyes from the shadows, he had the uneasy feeling that she knew a great deal about him. The eyes were still those of a domestic animal, but of a wise one that has been watching the house a long, long while from the barnyard.

He asked abruptly, "Do you know anything of a girl around here named Mary Alice Pope?"

The silence lasted so long that he began to think she'd gone into some bovine trance. Then, without a word, she got up and went over to a tall cabinet. Feeling on a ledge behind it for a key, she opened a panel, opened a cardboard box inside it, took something from the box and handed him a photograph. He held it up to the failing light and sucked in his breath with surprise.

It was a picture of the girl he'd met that afternoon. Same flat-bosomed dress—flowered rather than white— no bandeau, same beads. Same proud, demure expression, perhaps a bit happier.

"That is Mary Alice Pope," Mrs. Kesserich said in a strangely flat voice. "She was Martin's fiancee. She was killed in a railway accident in 1933."

The small sound of the cabinet door closing brought Jack back to reality. He realized that he no longer had the photograph. Against the gloom by the cabinet, Mrs. Kesserich's white face looked at him with what seemed a malicious eagerness.

"Sit down," she said, "and I'll tell you about it."

Without a thought as to why she hadn't asked him a single question—he was much too dazed for that—he obeyed. Mrs. Kesserich resumed her position on the edge of the sofa.

"You must understand, Mr. Barr, that Mary Alice Pope was the one love of Martin's life. He is a man of very deep and strong feelings, yet as you probably know, anything but kindly or demonstrative. Even when he first came here from Hungary with his older sisters Hani and Hilda, there was a cloak of loneliness about him—or rather about the three of them.

"Hani and Hilda were athletic outdoor women, yet fiercely proud—I don't imagine they ever spoke to anyone in America except as to a servant—and with a seething distaste for all men except Martin. They showered all their devotion on him. So of course, though Martin didn't realize it, they were consumed with jealousy when he fell in love with Mary Alice Pope. They'd thought that since he'd reached forty without marrying, he was safe.

"Mary Alice came from a purebred, or as a biologist would say, inbred British stock. She was very young, but very sweet, and up to a point very wise. She sensed Hani and Hilda's feelings right away and did everything she could to win them over. For instance, though she was afraid of horses, she took up horseback riding, because that was Hani and Hilda's favorite pastime. Naturally, Martin knew nothing of her fear, and naturally his sisters knew about it from the first. But—and here is where Mary's wisdom fell short—her brave gesture did not pacify them; it only increased their hatred.

"Except for his research, Martin was blind to everything but his love. It was a beautiful and yet frightening passion, an insane cherishing as narrow and intense as his sisters' hatred."

With a start, Jack remembered that it was Mrs. Kesserich telling him all this.

She went on, "Martin's love directed his every move. He was building a home for himself and Mary, and in his mind he was building a wonderful future for them as well —not vaguely, if you know Martin, but year by year, month by month. This winter, he'd plan, they would visit Buenos Aires, next summer they would sail down the inland passage and he would teach Mary Hungarian for their trip to Buda-Pesth the year after, where he would occupy a chair at the university for a few months . . . and so on. Finally the time for their marriage drew near. Martin had been away. His research was keeping him very busy—"

Jack broke in with, "Wasn't that about the time he did his definitive work on growth and fertilization?"

Mrs. Kesserich nodded with solemn appreciation in the gathering darkness. "But now he was coming home, his work done. It was early evening, very chilly, but Hani and Hilda felt they had to ride down to the station to meet their brother. And although she dreaded it, Mary rode with them, for she knew how delighted he would be at her cantering to the puffing train and his running up to lift her down from the saddle to welcome him home.

"Of course there was Martin's luggage to be considered, so the station wagon had to be sent down for that." She looked defiantly at Jack. "I drove the station wagon. I was Martin's laboratory assistant."

She paused. "It was almost dark, but there was still a

white cold line of sky to the west. Hani and Hilda, with Mary between them, were waiting on their horses at the top of the hill that led down to the station. The train had whistled and its headlight was graying the gravel of the crossing.

"Suddenly Mary's horse squealed and plunged down the hill. Hani and Hilda followed—to try to catch her, they said—but they didn't manage that, only kept her horse from veering off. Mary never screamed, but as her horse reared on the tracks, I saw her face in the headlight's glare.

"Martin must have guessed, or at least feared what had happened, for he was out of the train and running along the track before it stopped. In fact, he was the first to kneel down beside Mary—I mean, what had been Mary— and was holding her all bloody and shattered in his arms."

A door slammed. There were steps in the hall. Mrs. Kesserich stiffened and was silent. Jack turned.

The blur of a face hung in the doorway to the hall—a seemingly young, sensitive, suavely handsome face with aristocratic jaw. Then there was a click and the lights flared up and Jack saw the close-cropped gray hair and the lines around the eyes and nostrils, while the sensitive mouth grew sardonic. Yet the handsomeness stayed, and somehow the youth, too, or at least a tremendous inner vibrancy.

"Hello, Barr," Martin Kesserich said, ignoring his wife.

The great biologist had come home.

III

"Oh, yes, and Jamieson had a feeble paper on what he called individualization in marine worms. Barr, have you ever thought much about the larger aspects of the problem of individuality?"

Jack jumped slightly. He had let his thoughts wander very far.

"Not especially, sir," he mumbled.

The house was still. A few minutes after the professor's

arrival. Mrs. Kesserich had gone off with an anxious glance at Jack. He knew why and wished he could reassure her that he would not mention their conversation to the professor.

Kesserich had spent perhaps a half hour briefing him on the more important papers delivered at the conferences. Then, almost as if it were a teacher's trick to show up a pupil's inattention, he had suddenly posed this question about individuality.

"You know what I mean, of course," Kesserich pressed. "The factors that make you you, and me me."

"Heredity and environment," Jack parroted like a freshman.

Kesserich nodded. "Suppose—this is just speculation—that we could control heredity and environment. Then we could recreate the same individual at will."

Jack felt a shiver go through him. "To get exactly the same pattern of hereditary traits. That'd be far beyond us."

"What about identical twins?" Kesserich pointed out. "And then there's parthenogenesis to be considered. One might produce a duplicate of the mother without the intervention of the male." Although his voice had grown more idly speculative, Kesserich seemed to Jack to be smiling secretly. "There are many examples in the lower animal forms, to say nothing of the technique by which Loeb caused a sea urchin to reproduce with no more stimulus than a salt solution."

Jack felt the hair rising on his neck. "Even then you wouldn't get exactly the same pattern of hereditary traits."

"Not if the parent were of very pure stock? Not if there were some special technique for selecting ova that would reproduce all the mother's traits?"

"But environment would change things," Jack objected. "The duplicate would be bound to develop differently."

"Is environment so important? Newman tells about a pair of identical twins separated from birth, unaware of each other's existence. They met by accident when they were twenty-one. Each was a telephone repairman. Each had a wife the same age. Each had a baby son. And each had a fox terrier called 'Trixie.' That's without trying to make environments similar. But suppose you did try. Suppose you saw to it that each of them had exactly the same experiences at the same times . . ."

For a moment it seemed to Jack that the room was dimming and wavering, becoming a dark pool in which the only motionless thing was Kesserich's sphinxlike face.

"Well, we've escaped quite far enough from Jamieson's marine worms," the biologist said, all brisk again. He said it as if Jack were the one who had led the conversation down wild and unprofitable channels. "Let's get on to your project. I want to talk it over now, because I won't have any time for it tomorrow."

Jack looked at him blankly.

"Tomorrow I must attend to a very important matter," the biologist explained.

IV

Morning sunlight brightened the colors of the wax flowers under glass on the high bureau that always seemed to emit the faint odor of old hair combings. Jack pulled back the diamond-patterned quilt and blinked the sleep from his eyes. He expected his mind to be busy wondering about Kesserich and his wife—things said and half said last night—but found instead that his thoughts swung instantly to Mary Alice Pope, as if to a farthest island in a world of people.

Downstairs, the house was empty. After a long look at the cabinet—he felt behind it, but the key was gone—he hurried down to the waterfront. He stopped only for a bowl of chowder and, as an afterthought, to buy half a dozen newspapers.

The sea was bright, the brisk wind just right for the *Annie O*. There was eagerness in the way it smacked the sail and in the creak of the mast. And when he reached the cove, it was no longer still, but nervous with faint ripples, as if time had finally begun to stir.

After the same struggle with the underbrush, he came

out on the rocky spine and passed the cove of the sea urchins. The spiny creatures struck an uncomfortable chord in his memory.

This time he climbed the second island cautiously, scraping the innocent-seeming ground ahead of him intently with a boathook he'd brought along for the purpose. He was only a few yards from the fence when he saw Mary Alice Pope standing behind it.

He hadn't realized that his heart would begin to pound or that, at the same time, a shiver of almost supernatural dread would go through him.

The girl eyed him with an uneasy hostility and immediately began to speak in a hushed, hurried voice. "You must go away at once and never come back. You're a wicked man, but I don't want you to be hurt. I've been watching for you all morning."

He tossed the newspapers over the fence. "You don't have to read them now," he told her. "Just look at the datelines and a few of the headlines."

When she finally lifted her eyes to his again, she was trembling. She tried unsuccessfully to speak.

"Listen to me," he said. "You've been the victim of a scheme to make you believe you were born around 1916 instead of 1933, and that it's 1933 now instead of 1953. I'm not sure why it's been done, though I think I know who you really are."

"But," the girl faltered, "my aunts tell me it's 1933."

"They would."

"And there are the papers . . . the magazines . . . the radio."

"The papers are old ones. The radio's faked—some sort of recording. I could show you if I could get at it."

"*These* papers might be faked," she said, pointing to where she'd let them drop on the ground.

"They're new," he said. "Only old papers get yellow."

"But why would they do it to me? *Why?*"

"Come with me to the mainland, Mary. That'll set you straight quicker than anything."

"I couldn't," she said, drawing back. "He's coming to-night."

"He?"

"The man who sends me the boxes . . . and my life."

Jack shivered. When he spoke, his voice was rough and quick. "A life that's completely a lie, that's cut you off from the world. Come with me, Mary."

She looked up at him wonderingly. For perhaps ten seconds the silence held and the spell of her eerie sweetness deepened.

"I love you, Mary," Jack said softly.

She took a step back.

"Really, Mary, I do."

She shook her head. "I don't know what's true. Go away."

"Mary," he pleaded, "read the papers I've given you. Think things through. I'll wait for you here."

"You can't. My aunts would find you."

"Then I'll go away and come back. About sunset. Will you give me an answer?"

She looked at him. Suddenly she whirled around. He, too, heard the *chuff* of the Essex. "They'll find us," she said. "And if they find you, I don't know what they'll do. Quick, run!" And she darted off herself, only to turn back to scramble for the papers.

"But will you give me an answer?" he pressed.

She looked frantically up from the papers. "I don't know. You mustn't risk coming back."

"I will, no matter what you say."

"I can't promise. Please go."

"Just one question," he begged. "What are your aunts' names?"

"Hani and Hilda," she told him, and then she was gone. The hedge shook where she'd darted through.

Jack hesitated, then started for the cove. He thought for a moment of staying on the island, but decided against it. He could probably conceal himself successfully, but whoever found his boat would have him at a disadvantage.

Besides, there were things he must try to find out on the mainland.

As he entered the oaks, his spine tightened for a moment, as if someone were watching him. He hurried to the rippling cove, wasted no time getting the *Annie O.* underway. With the wind still in the west, he knew it would be a hard sail. He'd need half a dozen tacks to reach the mainland.

When he was about a quarter of a mile out from the cove, there was a sharp *smack* beside him. He jerked around, heard a distant *crack* and saw a foot-long splinter of fresh wood dangling from the edge of the sloop's cockpit, about a foot from his head.

He felt his skin tighten. He was the bull's-eye of a great watery target. All the air between him and the island was tainted with menace.

Water splashed a yard from the side. There was another distant *crack*. He lay on his back in the cockpit, steering by the sail, taking advantage of what little cover there was.

There were several more *cracks*. After the second, there was a hole in the sail.

Finally Jack looked back. The island was more than a mile astern. He anxiously scanned the sea ahead for craft. There were none. Then he settled down to nurse more speed from the sloop and wait for the motorboat.

But it didn't come out to follow him.

V

Same as yesterday, Mrs. Kesserich was sitting on the edge of the couch in the living room, yet from the first Jack was aware of a great change. Something had filled the domestic animal with grief and fury.

"Where's Dr. Kesserich?" he asked.

"Not here!"

"Mrs. Kesserich," he said, dropping down beside her, "you were telling me something yesterday when we were interrupted."

She looked at him. "You *have* found the girl?" she almost shouted.

"Yes," Jack was surprised into answering.

A look of slyness came into Mrs. Kesserich's bovine face. "Then I'll tell you everything. I can now.

"When Martin found Mary dying, he didn't go to pieces. You know how controlled he can be when he chooses. He lifted Mary's body as if the crowd and the railway men weren't there, and carried it to the station wagon. Hani and Hilda were sitting on their horses nearby. He gave them one look. It was as if he had said, 'Murderers!'

"He told me to drive home as fast as I dared, but when I got there, he stayed sitting by Mary in the back. I knew he must have given up what hope he had for her life, or else she was dead already. I looked at him. In the domelight, his face had the most deadly and proud expression I've ever seen on a man. I worshiped him, you know, though he had never shown me one ounce of feeling. So I was completely unprepared for the naked appeal in his voice.

"Yet all he said at first was, 'Will you do something for me?' I told him, 'Surely,' and as we carried Mary in, he told me the rest. He wanted me to be the mother of Mary's child."

Jack stared at her blankly.

Mrs. Kesserich nodded. "He wanted to remove an ovum from Mary's body and nurture it in mine, so that Mary, in a way, could live on."

"But that's impossible!" Jack objected. "The technique is being tried on cattle, I know, so that a prize heifer can have several calves a year, all nurtured in 'scrub heifers,' as they're called. But no one's ever dreamed of trying it on human beings!"

Mrs. Kesserich looked at him contemptuously. "Martin had mastered the technique twenty years ago. He was willing to take the chance. And so was I—partly because he fired my scientific imagination and reverence, but mostly because he said he would marry me. He barred the doors. We worked swiftly. As far as anyone was concerned,

Martin, in a wild fit of grief, had locked himself up for several hours to mourn over the body of his fiancée.

"Within a month we were married, and I finally gave birth to the child."

Jack shook his head. "You gave birth to your own child."

She smiled bitterly. "No, it was Mary's. Martin did not keep his whole bargain with me—I was nothing more than his 'scrub wife' in every way."

"You *think* you gave birth to Mary's child."

Mrs. Kesserich turned on Jack in anger. "I've been wounded by him, day in and day out, for years, but I've never failed to recognize his genius. Besides, you've seen the girl, haven't you?"

Jack had to nod. What confounded him most was that, granting the near-impossible physiological feat Mrs. Kesserich had described, the girl should look so much like the mother. Mother and daughters don't look that much alike; only identical twins did. With a thrill of fear, he remembered Kesserich's casual words: ". . . parthenogenesis . . . pure stock . . . special techniques . . ."

"Very well," he forced himself to say, "granting that the child was Mary's and Martin's—"

"No! Mary's alone!"

Jack suppressed a shudder. He continued quickly, "What became of the child?"

Mrs. Kesserich lowered her head. "The day it was born, it was taken away from me. After that, I never saw Hilda and Hani, either."

"You mean," Jack asked, "that Martin sent them away to bring up the child?"

Mrs. Kesserich turned away. "Yes."

Jack asked incredulously, "He trusted the child with the two people he suspected of having caused the mother's death?"

"Once when I was his assistant," Mrs. Kesserich said softly, "I carelessly broke some laboratory glassware. He kept me up all night building a new setup, though I'm rather poor at working with glass and usually get burned. Bringing up the child was his sisters' punishment."

"And they went to that house on the farthest island? I suppose it was the house he'd been building for Mary and himself."

"Yes."

"And they were to bring up the child as his daughter?"

Mrs. Kesserich started up, but when she spoke it was as if she had to force out each word. "As his wife—as soon as she was grown."

"How can you know that?" Jack asked shakily.

The rising wind rattled the windowpane.

"Because today—eighteen years after—Martin broke all of his promise to me. He told me he was leaving me."

VI

White waves shooting up like dancing ghosts in the moon-sketched, spray-swept dark were Jack's first beacon of the island and brought a sense of physical danger, breaking the trancelike yet frantic mood he had felt ever since he had spoken with Mrs. Kesserich.

Coming around farther into the wind, he scudded past the end of the island into the choppy sea on the landward side. A little later he let down the reefed sail in the cove of the sea urchins, where the water was barely moving, although the air was shaken by the pounding of the surf on the spine between the two islands.

After making fast, he paused a moment for a scrap of cloud to pass the moon. The thought of the spiny creatures in the black fathoms under the *Annie O.* sent an odd quiver of terror through him.

The moon came out and he started across the glistening rocks of the spine. But he had forgotten the rising tide. Midway, a wave clamped around his ankles, tried to carry him off, almost made him drop the heavy object he was carrying. Sprawling and drenched, he clung to the rough rock until the surge was past.

Making it finally up to the fence, he snipped a wide gate with the wire-cutters.

The windows of the house were alight. Hardly aware of his shivering, he crossed the lawn, slipping from one clump of shrubbery to another, until he reached one just across the drive from the doorway. At that moment he heard the approaching *chuff* of the Essex, the door of the cottage opened, and Mary Alice Pope stepped out, closely followed by Hani or Hilda.

Jack shrank close to the shrubbery. Mary looked pale and blank-faced, as if she had retreated within herself. He was acutely conscious of the inadequacy of his screen as the ghostly headlights of the Essex began to probe through the leaves.

But then he sensed that something more was about to happen than just the car arriving. It was a change in the expression of the face behind Mary that gave him the cue —a widening and sideways flickering of the cold eyes, the puckered lips thinning into a cruel smile.

The Essex shifted into second and, without any warning, accelerated. Simultaneously, the woman behind Mary gave her a violent shove. But at almost exactly the same instant, Jack ran. He caught Mary as she sprawled toward the gravel, and lunged ahead without checking. The Essex bore down upon them, a square-snouted, roaring monster. It swerved viciously, missed them by inches, threw up gravel in a skid, and rocked to a stop, stalled.

The first, incredulous voice that broke the pulsing silence, Jack recognized as Martin Kesserich's. It came from the car, which was slewed around so that it almost faced Jack and Mary.

"Hani, you tried to kill her! You and Hilda tried to kill her again!"

The woman slumped over the wheel slowly lifted her head. In the indistinct light, she looked the twin of the woman behind Jack and Mary.

"Did you really think we wouldn't?" she asked in a voice that spat with passion. "Did you actually believe that Hilda and I would serve this eighteen years' penance just to watch you go off with her?" She began to laugh wildly. "You've never understood your sisters at all!"

Suddenly she broke off and stiffly stepped down from the car. Lifting her skirts a little, she strode past Jack and Mary.

Martin Kesserich followed her. In passing, he said, "Thanks, Barr." It occurred to Jack that Kesserich made no more question of his appearance on the island than of his presence in the laboratory. Like Mrs. Kesserich, the great biologist took him for granted.

Kesserich stopped a few feet short of Hani and Hilda. Without shrinking from him, the sisters drew closer together. They looked like two gaunt hawks.

"But you waited eighteen years," he said. "You could have killed her at any time, yet you chose to throw away so much of your lives just to have this moment."

"How do you know we didn't like waiting eighteen years?" Hani answered him. "Why shouldn't we want to make as strong an impression on you as anyone? And as for throwing our lives away, that was your doing. Oh, Martin, you'll never know anything about how your sisters feel!"

He raised his hands baffledly. "Even assuming that you hate me"—at the word "hate" both Hani and Hilda laughed softly—"and that you were prepared to strike at both my love and my work, still, that you should have waited . . ."

Hani and Hilda said nothing.

Kesserich shrugged. "Very well," he said in a voice that had lost all its tension. "You've wasted a third of a lifetime looking forward to an irrational revenge. And you've failed. That should be sufficient punishment."

Very slowly, he turned around and for the first time looked at Mary. His face was clearly revealed by the twin beams from the stalled car.

Jack grew cold. He fought against accepting the feelings of wonder, of poignant triumph, of love, of renewed youth he saw entering the face in the headlights. But most of all he fought against the sense that Martin Kesserich was successfully drawing them all back into the past, to 1933 and another accident. There was a distant hoot and Jack shook. For a moment he had thought it a railway whistle and not a ship's horn.

The biologist said tenderly, "Come, Mary."

Jack's trembling arm tightened a trifle on Mary's waist. He could feel *her* trembling.

"Come, Mary," Kesserich repeated.

Still she didn't reply.

Jack wet his lips. "Mary isn't going with you, Professor," he said.

"Quiet, Barr," Kesserich ordered absently. "Mary, it is necessary that you and I leave the island at once. Please come."

"But Mary isn't coming," Jack repeated.

Kesserich looked at him for the first time. "I'm grateful to you for the unusual sense of loyalty—or whatever motive it may have been—that led you to follow me out here tonight. And of course I'm profoundly grateful to you for saving Mary's life. But I must ask you not to interfere further in a matter which you can't possibly understand."

He turned to Mary. "I know how shocked and frightened you must feel. Living two lives and then having to face two deaths—it must be more terrible than anyone can realize. I expected this meeting to take place under very different circumstances. I wanted to explain everything to you very naturally and gently, like the messages I've sent you every day of your second life. Unfortunately, that can't be.

"You and I must leave the island right now."

Mary stared at him, then turned wonderingly toward Jack, who felt his heart begin to pound warmly.

"You still don't understand what I'm trying to tell you, Professor," he said, boldly now. "Mary is not going with you. You've deceived her all her life. You've taken a fantastic amount of pains to bring her up under the delusion that she is Mary Alice Pope, who died in—"

"She *is* Mary Alice Pope," Kesserich thundered at him. He advanced toward them swiftly. "Mary, darling, you're confused, but you must realize who you are and who I am and the relationship between us."

"Keep away," Jack warned, swinging Mary half behind him. "Mary doesn't love you. She can't marry you, at any rate. How could she, when you're her father?"

"Barr!"

"Keep off!" Jack shot out the flat of his hand and Kesserich went staggering backward. "I've talked with your wife—your wife on the mainland. She told me the whole thing."

Kesserich seemed about to rush forward again, then controlled himself. "You've got everything wrong. You hardly deserve to be told, but under the circumstances I have no choice. Mary is not my daughter. To be precise, she has no father at all. Do you remember the work that Jacques Loeb did with sea urchins?"

Jack frowned angrily. "You mean what we were talking about last night?"

"Exactly. Loeb was able to cause the egg of a sea urchin to develop normally without union with a male germ cell. I have done the same thing with a human being. This girl is Mary Alice Pope. She has exactly the same heredity. She has had exactly the same life, so far as it could be reconstructed. She's heard and read the same things at exactly the same times. There have been the old newspapers, the books, even the old recorded radio programs. Hani and Hilda have had their daily instructions, to the letter. She's retraced the same time-trail."

"Rot!" Jack interrupted. "I don't for a moment believe what you say about her birth. She's Mary's daughter—or the daughter of your wife on the mainland. And as for retracing the same time-trail, that's senile self-delusion. Mary Alice Pope had a normal life. This girl has been brought up in cruel imprisonment by two insane, vindictive old women. In your own frustrated desire, you've pretended to yourself that you've recreated the girl you lost. You haven't. You couldn't. Nobody could—the great Martin Kesserich or anyone else!"

Kesserich, his features working, shifted his point of attack. "Who are you, Mary?"

"Don't answer him," Jack said. "He's trying to confuse you."

"Who are you?" Kesserich insisted.

"Mary Alice Pope," she said rapidly in a breathy whisper before Jack could speak again.

"And when were you born?" Kesserich pressed on.

"You've been tricked all your life about that," Jack warned.

But already the girl was saying, "In nineteen hundred and sixteen."

"And who am I then?" Kesserich demanded eagerly. "Who am I?"

The girl swayed. She brushed her head with her hand.

"It's so strange," she said, with a dreamy, almost laughing throb in her voice that turned Jack's heart cold. "I'm sure I've never seen you before in my life, and yet it's as if I'd known you forever. As if you were closer to me than—"

"Stop it!" Jack shouted at Kesserich. "Mary loves me. She loves me because I've shown her the lie her life has been, and because she's coming away with me now. Aren't you, Mary?"

He swung her around so that her blank face was inches from his own. "It's me you love, isn't it, Mary?"

She blinked doubtfully.

At that moment Kesserich charged at them, went sprawling as Jack's fist shot out. Jack swept up Mary and ran with her across the lawn. Behind him he heard an agonized cry—Kesserich's—and cruel, mounting laughter from Hani and Hilda.

Once through the ragged doorway in the fence, he made his way more slowly, gasping. Out of the shelter of the trees, the wind tore at them and the ocean roared. Moonlight glistened, now on the spine of black wet rocks, now on the foaming surf.

Jack realized that the girl in his arms was speaking rapidly, disjointedly, but he couldn't quite make out the sense of the words and then they were lost in the crash of the surf. She struggled, but he told himself that it was only because she was afraid of the menacing waters.

He pushed recklessly into the breaking surf, raced gasping across the middle of the spine as the rocks uncovered, sprang to the higher ones as the next wave crashed behind, showering them with spray. His chest burning with exertion, he carried the girl the few remaining yards to where the *Annie O.* was tossing. A sudden great gust of wind almost did what the waves had failed to do, but he kept his footing and lowered the girl into the boat, then jumped in after.

She stared at him wildly. "What's that?"

He, too, had caught the faint shout. Looking back along the spine just as the moon came clear again, he saw white spray rise and fall—and then the figure of Kesserich stumbling through it.

"Mary, wait for me!"

The figure was halfway across when it lurched, started forward again, then was jerked back as if something had caught its ankle. Out of the darkness, the next wave sent a line of white at it neck-high, crashed.

Jack hesitated, but another great gust of wind tore at the half-raised sail, and it was all he could do to keep the sloop from capsizing and head her into the wind again.

Mary was tugging at his shoulder. "You must help him," she was saying. "He's caught in the rocks."

He heard a voice crying, screaming crazily above the surf:

> "Ah, love, let us be true
> To one another! for the world—"

The sloop rocked. Jack had it finally headed into the wind. He looked around for Mary.

She had jumped out and was hurrying back, scrambling across the rocks toward the dark, struggling figure that even as he watched was once more engulfed in the surf.

Letting go the lines, Jack sprang toward the stern of the sloop.

But just then another giant blow came, struck the sail like a great fist of air, and sent the boom slashing at the back of his head.

His last recollection was being toppled out onto the rocks and wondering how he could cling to them while unconscious.

VII

The little cove was once again as quiet as time's heart. Once again the *Annie O.* was a sloop embedded in a mirror. Once again the rocks were warm underfoot.

Jack Barr lifted his fiercely aching head and looked at the distant line of the mainland, as tiny and yet as clear as something viewed through the wrong end of a telescope. He was very tired. Searching the island, in his present shaky condition, had taken all the strength out of him.

He looked at the peacefully rippling sea outside the cove and thought of what a churning pot it had been during the storm. He thought wonderingly of his rescue—a man wedged unconscious between two rock teeth, kept somehow from being washed away by the merest chance.

He thought of Mrs. Kesserich sitting alone in her house, scanning the newspapers that had nothing to tell.

He thought of the empty island behind him and the vanished motorboat.

He wondered if the sea had pulled down Martin Kesserich and Mary Alice Pope. He wondered if only Hani and Hilda had sailed away.

He winced, remembering what he had done to Martin and Mary by his blundering infatuation. In his way, he told himself, he had been as bad as the two old women.

He thought of death, and of time, and of love that defies them.

He stepped limpingly into the *Annie O.* to set sail— and realized that philosophy is only for the unhappy.

Mary was asleep in the stern.

A MAN MUST DIE

John Clute

John Clute is a Canadian-born novelist and critic who
has lived in London in recent years. His output of published science fiction thus far has been slender—two
short stories and an extract from a novel, all in Michael
Moorcock's experimental British magazine, **New Worlds.**
The story that follows appeared there in 1966: an intense,
disturbing, unusual retelling of one of science fiction's
classic themes.

He ran away for the third time, and as usual it had all
been arranged. The proper hour was One of Day. His
tutor, Dwight, had laid out his travelling veils last night
at Three of Dark, just before bedtime, and now they
floated about him. The great brown door of the nursery
shushed into the wall when he touched it tap-tap-tap, his
own private code. He stepped outside, into the corridor.
He ran away down the corridors with the white lights. He
didn't go down the green-lighted corridors because they
were dead ends, and the red-lighted corridors were for-
bidden. "I am following the white lights," he said proudly

to an Ox, who curtsied. It was a female Ox. He ran on. His veils flushed as he ran.

He was running away to Father.

The corridors began to curve before him, more and more, a delicate and soothing increment as he ran on, and eventually he reached Wall. Wall was black. He trotted beside black Wall until he came to a new corridor. It was lighted red. A third-generation Ox got up to its knees and went grunt-grunt meaning no. The red corridor spiralled upwards. Ox guarded it. Father was upwards. He was too young to see Father. That's what Dwight had said. Ambition and the worldly drives are poisonous to the young, Dwight had said (reading from a textbook made of paper). Dwight also said, first things first. Dwight had seen Father when Father was young. Dwight had seen everything, but Dwight didn't remember much. Dwight was a first-generation Ox and said oh no he didn't regret it, smiling out of his own world.

He was wearing his travelling veils and stared Ox down, but Ox still went grunt-grunt meaning no. It obeyed its instructions, for there was no Star pinned under the gossamer veils. "My name is Picasso Perkins III," to humble Ox who wouldn't move. "Step aside now."

Picasso Perkins III had been born to command.

But he could not command poor Ox so he turned left. Ox had no years and would not remember. To the left the lights were white, and Picasso ran, his decorous veil sinuous behind him. He felt although he was not aware of the mathematical joy of corridors bending at the proper moment. His eyes shone. Ox salaamed in his wake.

Eventually there was only one white corridor and it led to only one room. This was their game. Picasso took off his veils and stood naked. Clothes were for travelling. Dwight, standing in the final room, said, "Now I'll tell you the third lesson."

Picasso was flushed from running and the game of lessons.

He said, "I have run and run and exercised my legs and my talent for individual initiative. But I didn't see Father."

"My little Ass," said Dwight fondly but without particular intonation, being an Ox. Dwight had no years and already Ass for short was almost as tall, and his shoulders were straight and Dwight's sloped from his thin neck. Ass was learning pride. Dwight taught him. His teeth showed as he grinned. He had run away with much physical exertion. Dwight had told him about the cost of energy. Dwight nor any other Ox was allowed to run and run and waste energy like Ass. And Dwight was not strong. If he broke the law and ran all the way to black Wall and Father's corridor and back by the arduous route of the white lights, he would lie panting and in great pain, because his lungs had grown tiny.

"This is the third lesson," said Dwight. "We are the crew of the Starship *Lunge*." Ass did not blink, having no preconceptions to be shattered; and a month later, after he had run away for the fourth and last time, and after Dwight had said, "The fourth lesson is, you will die before our ship, the Starship *Lunge*, reaches landfall, but I am now authorized to extend you the privileges of the cinema," not even then did Ass blink or have bad dreams in the nursery.

"What is the cinema?"

Ass was smiling because it was a new thing.

But Dwight was almost sad, and when he was almost sad he was almost querulous, a memory of his mortal time perhaps. His broad lips flapped blub-blub. He looked Ass almost in the eye and said, "But I will not die."

"Well of course not. Poor Ox," said Picasso Perkins III, whose father was the Captain of the *Lunge*. And he ran off to see what cinema was.

Picasso sat alone in the projection room and watched the educational tape. It was about human biology, and birth control. He was very moved but there was no one to discuss his reaction with.

A second-generation Ox groped for words. Picasso was a teenager with pimples, and was impatient. Having viewed Shakespeare on the cinema and read much rhetoric, being born to command, he said, "Come, Ox, out out out out out with it," widening his eyes and shifting on Hilda, the masseuse-couch.

Picasso was widely-read, being alone.

"Cushy, cushy, cushy," murmured Hilda beneath him, intending him to relax.

Picasso slapped her off.

Ox managed, "Dwight," then got out, its eyes filling with tears, "X," meaning emergency.

"Where?" sitting upright smoothly, unfastening Hilda, long and taut from daily exercise, arching over hunched knobby Ox. He smiled what was intended to be a bitter-sweet smile, the smile of the grown man faced once again with the fragility of existence; but could not manage this. He knew it. Ox began to stutter at his waist. "WHERE?"

And finally Ox managed where, "Level K, Room 17." A spittle-stutter. Picasso began to move. And the second-generation Ox wept in swift Picasso's wake, loving mortals.

The Lord ran swiftly through the simulated gravity down the corridors of his childhood and then down the corridors of the Oxen, past the first-generation quarters, then the second, and finally, crouching now, down to shadowy level K, knowing his way from the charts he had studied. Stooped Dwight awaited him at the entrance to Room 17. "Thank you, my Lord."

For Picasso wore the Star now, since the previous month, and could not now be commanded.

"Well?" It meant something to Picasso to think it meant something to Dwight, and he added, "Well, my friend?"

Dwight knuckled to Picasso's Star. One month ago Picasso's intercom had spat at him and had said, "My boy, this is your Father. You are now of sufficient age, you have from this moment the run of the ship. Go to your room." And the Star was on his bed. "Place the Star on your wrist." He did so, and it adhered. "Do not come forward until you are called."

Picasso was in command below now. Dwight said, "Two

of the third generation have bred, and the Star must be present for me to act."

"How long ago?"

"Minutes only."

They crouched into the low room. The mother, poor Ox, hunkered by the newly-born monster, which ran at the orifices and mewled and which had already begun to age. The pregnancy had taken only a few weeks, Picasso knew from his educational tapes. The fat of its belly began to disappear. Shins and elbows poked through the grey flesh. The umbilical cord shrivelled into dust. The monster opened its mouth to scream and the teeth that had just poked through its pale gums fell to the floor.

They splintered soundlessly on the floor.

"Fast," said Picasso Perkins III. Dwight aimed and his laser bisected and trisected the tiny aged shape, whose hand and feet had already begun to break off. "Fast," said Picasso, vomiting into a corner of the room, "fast."

The mother, who had forgotten the monster, smiled softly from her cot.

He beckoned Dwight into the corridor. He could not stand upright. He wiped at his mouth. The Star shone in the low dusk.

"Why wasn't she sterilized?"

Dwight smiled.

"*Dwight*. Why wasn't she sterilized? Where is the Doctor? Where is the Doctor of the Ship?"

And at this point Picasso's inner ear deserted him, and his head spun, and he thought, holding on, *the Doctor of the Ship is forward with Father and must not be disturbed*.

Dwight smiled from his world.

And he said, "Doctor?" He smiled. He said, "Oh, the Doctor. My Lord, the Doctor of the Ship is dead. My Lord, you are the Doctor."

His doe eyes did not change.

Above them suddenly the intercom rattled and blew out sparks. It had rarely sounded and had gone bad. Picasso had not previously wondered why, but now the inner ear of habit had gone, and he was naked, he was holding on by dumb will, his hand touched his Star by rote and he looked up at the intercom, which continued to rattle. Dwight kneeled calmly. Had Dwight forgotten the monster?

The intercom burbled and sighed and shut up. Picasso stared down at Dwight, and he said, "Have you forgotten what happened in there?" jerking his arm backwards to the four-foot door.

"No, my Lord. But it is done."

His drooping face remained placid, and the intercom became coherent.

"Picasso Perkins," it said in the voice of his father.

"Father?"

"Speak up, boy."

"Sir?"

"That's better. Now what was the trouble?"

"A fourth-generation baby. It was taken care of."

"Destroyed?"

"Yes, sir."

"Good work, son."

The intercom whined.

"Father?"

"Well?" a bit impatiently.

"Father, where is the Doctor of the Ship?"

The intercom died.

"Father?"

Picasso could hear the muted hubbub of the distant Oxen, and Dwight's rapid shallow breathing, but the intercom was dead.

He banged his fist at the wall, which noiselessly absorbed the shock.

He began to run.

He ran for an hour. He was panting, he had wasted much energy. He sat on his large bed. The walls whinnied in on him for his balance had gone.

For if there was no Doctor of the Ship . . .

He screwed his eyes shut.

The intercom sparked.

"Father?"

He was on his feet, he had leapt to his feet.

"My son," said the intercom. "I think it is time we met. Come forward now. On the double."

"Sir."

His heart pounded with what he could only assume was joyful anticipation.

The question of the Doctor had unleashed the dozens of other questions, would they be answered? Of course his feeling was one of joyful anticipation.

He kept himself from thinking. He slipped into his veils, slim Picasso, and ran ran ran off smoothly, mortals being allowed the light fantastic.

He toed the third-generation guard, who kneeled blinking awake.

"Aside," and the Star shone.

Picasso began to mount the spiral ramp, he mounted and turned, mounted and turned, past doors marked NO in glowing letters. He had read *Alice in Wonderland* on paper and tried to chuckle as he passed the doors marked NO, but his larynx caught and he began to cough. The passage spiralled up and grew brighter. Dwight would lie panting twenty turns back, having tiny lungs.

The passage levelled on to shimmering broadloom, and soft music from the intercom.

"You are here," his father's voice through the music, "turn right at the third door."

He did. The black door swung inwards and he swallowed his throat and entered. A tall man stood with raised arm signifying peace beside a maroon console.

"My son," said the tall man, who was wrinkled. Picasso's educational films had shown old men.

"Sir," he said.

And stepped closer.

"No further, if you please," said his father.

And Picasso's mouth opened. His tall body shook dissonantly, his mouth opened and shut and opened. He took another step.

"PLEASE," said his father.

But Picasso could see through his father. His father's white uniform had a maroon console showing through it, an aluminium knob twinkled through his father's waist.

"Move back," said his father, but this time his lips didn't move, and his voice was stereophonic.

"Father," said Picasso Perkins III.

His father faded out, going *click* as he disappeared.

He opened his eyes at the azure ceiling. His head ached where it had struck the broadloom. Soft music mooned from the hidden speakers. He sat.

"Captain Perkins," said the stereophonic voice of his father.

He dizzied himself turning his head to search, but could see nothing.

"What is this?" he yelled.

"Please," said the voice, "I shall explain."

Picasso moved himself slowly to a chair, which purred soothingly until it had adjusted itself to his form.

"Well?" imperiously, for he had been born to command, after all.

The stereophonic voice said, "This is the computer unit of the Starship *Lunge,* and requests permission to use the first person singular."

Picasso remembered about computer ethics from his educational tapes and said, "Permission granted."

"I thank you. May I first make my apologies. I did not realize that the simulation—to your left—" and his father appeared again, waveringly and shamefaced, "was so weak."

"Turn off the music," said Picasso, and there was silence.

"I had hoped to break it to you gradually," continued the voice, "that you were the only mortal left aboard the *Lunge,* but as you are now aware I was unsuccessful. I am unfortunately wearing out, and you have not the knowledge to repair me. That, and the lack of a Doctor, he died with your father, years ago, have made imperative your rapid initiation into your adult role. I must again apologize for the clumsiness with which your coming of age has been handled.

The chair crooned to Picasso, who had begun to cry.

"You are the Captain of the Starship *Lunge*," the voice went on obliviously, "landfall can be expected in approximately sixty years, the journey is in its seventieth year, and your cargo, deepfrozen behind the doors marked NO, is several thousand rabbits impregnated with livestock and personnel sufficient to colonize the system to which we are heading. As the several million foetuses in the wombs of these rabbits must be extracted immediately upon defrosting, the three upper chambers contain a deepfrozen medical team, all mortals."

"What happened?" said Picasso, "did I faint or did you knock me out?"

"You fainted, Captain, immediately after the simulacrum of your father dissolved."

"You may continue with your briefing," said Picasso, having come back to himself.

"Thank you, sir. In addition to the mortal medical team, there is in the first chamber another mortal. He is the pilot, and barring an emergency he must not be awoken until the final month before landfall. That is in his contract. You will of course understand the reason for that clause."

"No," said Picasso, and it seemed he was trying to make the computer uncomfortable, "no, I don't understand at all."

"Well," said the computer, its voice dutifully hesitant, "the four members of the original crew were accorded the benefits and the adulation of befitting heroes and heroines before their departure. Should you reach landfall alive you will be accorded the same. Your grandparents were volunteers, Captain."

"Who will accord me adulation, Uncle Computer," said Picasso, "the rabbits?"

His father's voice chuckled benignly.

Picasso Perkins III, Captain of the Starship *Lunge*, noticed from his wet cheeks that he had been crying. He began to turn his back on Uncle Computer, but realized that it was all around him.

"What is in store for me, Uncle Computer?"

"I am afraid there is not a great deal in store for you, Captain. Unless you Opt you will grow old in this solitary environment and eventually you will die. You come of a race of heroes," said the computer, exaggerating, "and in my opinion you will not Opt, you will not leave the Starship *Lunge* helpless."

"I could always awaken the pilot," said Picasso, but he knew that he would not do this. He had been bred to command, pride had been bred into him by the educational tapes, he had no desire to become an Ox and look at the world forever passing with a doe smile. If he awoke the pilot he would lose his ship, too. After all, he was God.

"You must not awaken the pilot," said the computer, "that would be a breach of contract."

"That is certainly true," said Picasso, Lord of Oxen, and, he had discovered, rabbits.

"Then you agree," said the computer.

"I have no choice," said Picasso, and stood out of his humming chair. "I think it is time for you to tell me about the death of my parents."

"Yes," said the computer. "Close your eyes."

Picasso did so.

"Now look," said the computer.

Picasso did so, and sat down again.

Two old men and two old women stood before him politely. They were all somewhat translucent. After nodding to Picasso courteously, they began to go about what seemed to be their daily tasks.

"These are real heroes," said Uncle Computer warmly, "they were in their mid-twenties when they left Earth, never to see her again, never to see again the land of their birth, their native soil, their parents and kith, and kin. Here you see them engaged in their daily pursuits. They have been doing what you see them doing there for many years. In ten years, alas, they will all be dead."

"Who wrote your script?" said Picasso.

There was a miffed silence.

"Well?"

"It's a free adaptation from some notes set down by Dwight Mulligan before he Opted," said the computer. "May I continue?"

"Please."

The figures began sadly to fade out.

"They died," said the computer, "this band of men and women, these heroes of the latter days of Earth, these pioneers, and were succeeded by their offspring. Here they are now."

Five figures strode to the space before Picasso, three men and two women.

"The Mulligans," who nodded briskly, one woman and two men, one of the men familiar like an old toothache and then Picasso realized that it was Dwight before he'd Opted, "and the Perkins's," and the Perkins's stepped forward, his father and his mother, and his mother was so beautiful and so sinuous and sad that tears once again started to Picasso's eyes.

But she was as translucent as any of them.

Dwight had a thin, hungry face, he was sallow and beanstalky; he turned and left the room.

"As you are aware, Dwight Mulligan Opted, leaving the two couples."

"He was a little *de trop?*"

"I believe that was the case," said the computer. "But to continue, you realize that your mother was Mulligan's sister, and Mulligan's wife your father's sister."

"Go on," said Picasso.

"Disaster did not strike until after the death of Mrs. Mulligan," and the simulacrum vanished in a sweet despond. The simulacrum Mulligan began immediately to lour and sulk in one corner of the room. His sister, Picasso's mother, busied herself with a translucent and willowy dance, and Picasso's father kept time by clapping his hands. They laughed soundlessly to one another. Then Mulligan suddenly stepped between the happily married couple, and he and his sister started to waltz stridingly about the room. Captain Perkins stood very straight and stern. He put his hand to his forehead in agony. Then he stepped over to the whizzing incestuous couple and cut in. Mulligan pointed his finger at the door and sneered volumes. Picasso's mother cupped her face in her hands and keened mournfully. Captain Perkins punched Mulligan in the face.

"Yea team," said Picasso Perkins III.

The two men took up a boxing stance. They sparred back and forth until Captain Perkins' superior strength and skill began to tell, and Mulligan began to drip blood that dripped to the floor but faded before it touched the broadloom. Picasso's mother sat on the floor in desperate straits.

Then they all faded out so abruptly that they *clicked*.

"What?" said Picasso.

"The rest of the story takes place beyond the limits of this room, unfortunately," said the computer. "Doctor Mulligan, in a morose frenzy, detached a lifeboat and disappeared. You father did not take kindly to your birth, eight months later, although your mother protested her innocence. The last scene was melancholy and brief. Your mother, who had always been unstable, though of the highest intelligence, disappeared one day in the second lifeboat, leaving you in Dwight's care. Your father committed suicide, after leaving you a short message."

"What was the message?"

A piece of paper drifted from the ceiling and landed on Picasso's knee. He turned it over and read his father's message:

"Son, if you take my advice you'll stay clear of women. Your loving father."

Picasso walked over to the console. He had much to learn about all those knobs.

"You will teach me what I need to know."

"I am your servant," said Uncle Computer.

Oxen in three rows according to generation stood or hunched to attention; third-generation Oxen, having tired immediately, were allowed to sit. This was the crew of the Starship *Lunge*. On the dais in the center of the hall stood Picasso, and beside him improved simulations of his father, his mother and Dr. Mulligan. They were quarrelling.

"Shut up," said Picasso, "I'll turn you off."

Despite everything Picasso had learned over the past seven years, the computer unit was more and more demonstrating the random whimsy and punchiness that the educational tapes had indicated were the signs of incremental senility. Soon it would die. But it shut up.

To work then, thought Picasso.

Picasso Perkins, Jr., Captain of the Starship *Lunge*, stepped forward no longer translucent and addressed his crew. "We are gathered here," he said eloquently, a recorded message, "here here, here . . ." getting stuck. Picasso kicked the small console behind him. "Sorry," it whispered mechanically, being no one but itself. The Oxen stood in their seventh heaven. The third-generation slept smiling. "We are gathered here on the twenty-fifth anniversary of the birth of a man. This man is Picasso Perkins III." He chuckled indulgently. "My mortal son." Oxen clapped. The third-generation, awoken by the happy sound, went grunt, meaning yes.

The Captain spread his arms for quiet.

"Soon I shall die, my children," he said.

The third-generation went grunt, meaning yes, in the calm silence.

The Captain pointed to the large softly-contoured device in the far corner of the room.

"My children," he said, "the time has come for my son, who is mortal, to make his decision. Yes, my dear son," said the Captain turning to Picasso, "it is time for you to declare whether or not you intend to Opt. Will you become immortal, my son?" Picasso watched Dwight from the corner of his eye; Dwight who had chosen peace forever, and the stunted form that resulted from the gene changes; Dwight who had chosen to relinquish his frontal lobe to live forever. "My son," repeated the Captain, "will you

become immortal?" All Oxen stared attentively at their
Lords, and Dwight was as they were. Did Dwight remember that Primary Option required a human doctor? "Do
you Opt?"

The hall rested in silence.

"I do not Opt."

All Oxen knelt.

"My children," said Picasso Perkins III uncomfortably.
Slowly and smiling, the most natural thing in the world,
his father and his mother and Dr. Mulligan faded out, they
were gone, no Ox noticed, and the Captain of the Starship
Lunge stepped from the dais and walked among his crew,
touching them and they were blessed thereby.

He would beat at chess, he would bed a whore, he would
argue with his peers, he would win a free election, he
would . . .

His dreams grew worse. The rabbits exploded into livestock and personnel who touched his frail corpse and he
went *click*.

As the years passed he slept less, and sometimes the
rabbits came at him when he was awake. All Oxen knelt
at his coming and wept when he had passed, but he was a
distant Lord, although he loved them. They were as they
had been, and they lived because he watered them and fed
them. He lasered fourteen more fourth-generation babies,
for whom the buildup of mutated gene commands back-
fired. All good things come to an end. Dwight said what he
had said the year before. The supply of films was finite.

One night he gave the dwindling computer certain tax-
ing commands, and that night his ashen and beautiful
mother came to him in his room and he locked the door.
The next morning he called for the computer but it had
died from the strain.

"I am alone," he muttered to himself.

When he was seventy-eight he tottered at the brink of
blackness Dwight need never feel. He injected himself
against his cancers but hovered at the edge of the limitless
vertigo, and it was almost welcome. How long?

He moved slowly to the control room, and time had passed. Sometimes he lost track. There were only months to go, but he would be dead.

"Is this why I am mortal?"

He snorted petulantly and was forced to catch his breath in the chair he had always chosen, because he liked its tone of voice. Since Hilda the masseuse had broken this chair was the only voice left. He had put some of Hilda's tapes into it and now it murmured, "Cushy cushy cushy."

He fell into a catnap.

When he awoke he remembered that there was something he must do before he died. It hurt when he moved. He stood finally before the first door marked NO. He put his key in the slot and the operating panel came into view. He pushed the proper sequence and began the ten-hour process that would defrost the pilot.

He put on his travelling veils.

He walked among his Oxen, their sweet eyes followed him as he strode. They forgot their small duties until he had gone. He found Dwight. "I would not have lasted without you. Good-bye, Dwight."

"Good-bye," said Dwight softly with doe eyes.

"My friend," said Picasso Perkins III, but Dwight had begun to doze.

He moved slowly back past the doors marked NO, where the rabbits slept frozen, carrying their populations. He hurried as much as that was possible. He had seen rabbits on the educational tapes and they had sharp teeth, they were rodents, they frightened him.

He sat at the maroon console. The pilot would come. The pilot would know the way. The cancers pained his breast.

He heard a sound. He had been asleep.

"My life has been of value. That is why I am mortal."

But it had been a dream of gnashing rabbits?

Footsteps.

Picasso switched off the music. He remembered how

irritating that music could be. He stood by the maroon console with his right arm raised signifying peace.

The door slid open.

And an enormous rabbit walked in.

The pilot, a fit young man, pulled off his huge helmet and absently folded its projections into place. He was shocked. He stared down at the body of the man who had keeled over as soon as he entered the room. He dropped the defrost helmet to the floor and leaned over the corpse. His hands were sweating and he wiped them off on his puffy white defrost suit. The room stank of age. He thought, what in God's name has happened here.

He bustled about the ship, he verified the course to landfall, he found no other mortals, he noted that the computer unit had defuncted. He didn't like Oxen, not at all—possibly because he had almost Opted the year before, subjective time—they gazed after him beatifically. He strode heavily back to the control room. He gazed at the dead mortal, and began to comprehend. The crazy old screwed-up face with its wide-open toothless mouth. How long had that old man been alone? He buzzed for a platoon of Oxen after closing the eyelids of the corpse and folding the shrivelled arms across the eaten chest. He began to comprehend. He would never know the details, but the result lay before him. Alone with a bunch of Oxen, he thought, good God. He thought, there are all sorts of heroes.

THE SKILLS OF XANADU

Theodore Sturgeon

Somehow no stories by Theodore Sturgeon succeeded in making their way into any of the previous Alpha collections—an inexplicable, almost inconceivable, omission, for the author of **More Than Human, The Dreaming Jewels, Venus Plus X,** and five dozen equally astonishing shorter works is surely one of the indispensable grand masters of science fiction. With much pleasure we remedy the situation herewith, offering one of Sturgeon's less familiar stories as an example of the man's vision, warmth, and grace of style.

And the Sun went nova and humanity fragmented and fled; and such is the self-knowledge of humankind that it knew it must guard its past as it guarded its being, or it would cease to be human; and such was its pride in itself that it made of its traditions a ritual and a standard.

The great dream was that wherever humanity settled, fragment by fragment by fragment, however it lived, it would continue rather than begin again, so that all through the Universe and the years, humans would be humans, speaking as humans, thinking as humans, aspiring and progressing as humans; and whenever human met human, no matter how different, how distant, he would come in peace, meet his own kind, speak his own tongue.

Humans, however, being humans—

Bril emerged near the pink star, disliking its light, and found the fourth planet. It hung waiting for him like an exotic fruit. (And was it ripe, and could he ripen it? And what if it were poison?) He left his machine in orbit and descended in a bubble. A young savage watched him come and waited by a waterfall.

"Earth was my mother," said Bril from the bubble. It was the formal greeting of all humankind, spoken in the Old Tongue.

"And my father," said the savage, in an atrocious accent.

Watchfully, Bril emerged from the bubble, but stood very close by it. He completed his part of the ritual. "I respect the disparity of our wants, as individuals, and greet you."

"I respect the identity of our needs, as humans, and greet you. I am Wonyne," said the youth, "son of Tanyne, of the Senate, and Nina. This place is Xanadu, the district, on Xanadu, the fourth planet."

"I am Bril of Kit Carson, second planet of the Sumner System, and a member of the Sole Authority," said the newcomer, adding, "and I come in peace."

He waited then, to see if the savage would discard any weapons he might have, according to historic protocol. Wonyne did not; he apparently had none. He wore only a cobwebby tunic and a broad belt made of flat, black, brilliantly polished stones and could hardly have concealed so much as a dart. Bril waited yet another moment, watching the untroubled face of the savage, to see if Wonyne suspected anything of the arsenal hidden in the sleek black uniform, the gleaming jackboots, the metal gauntlets.

Wonyne said only, "Then, in peace, welcome." He

smiled. "Come with me to Tanyne's house and mine, and be refreshed."

"You say Tanyne, your father, is a Senator? Is he active now? Could he help me to reach your center of government?"

The youth paused, his lips moving slightly, as if he were translating the dead language into another tongue. Then, "Yes. Oh, yes."

Bril flicked his left gauntlet with his right fingertips and the bubble sprang away and up, where at length it would join the ship until it was needed. Wonyne was not amazed —probably, thought Bril, because it was beyond his understanding.

Bril followed the youth up a winding path past a wonderland of flowering plants, most of them purple, some white, a few scarlet, and all jeweled by the waterfall. The higher reaches of the path were flanked by thick soft grass, red as they approached, pale pink as they passed.

Bril's narrow black eyes flicked everywhere, saw and recorded everything: the easy-breathing boy spring up the slope ahead, and the constant shifts of color in his gossamer garment as the wind touched it; the high trees, some of which might conceal a man or a weapon; the rock outcroppings and what oxides they told of; the birds he could see and the birdsongs he heard which might be something else.

He was a man who missed only the obvious, and there is so little that is obvious.

Yet he was not prepared for the house; he and the boy were halfway across the parklike land which surrounded it before he recognized it as such.

It seemed to have no margins. It was here high and there only a place between flower beds; yonder a room became a terrace, and elsewhere a lawn was a carpet because there was a roof over it. The house was divided into areas rather than rooms, by open grilles and by arrangements of color. Nowhere was there a wall. There was nothing to hide behind and nothing that could be locked. All the land, all the sky, looked into and through the house, and the house was one great window on the world.

Seeing it, Bril felt a slight shift in his opinion of the natives. His feeling was still one of contempt, but now he added suspicion. A cardinal dictum on humans as he knew them was: *Every man has something to hide.* Seeing a mode of living like this did not make him change his dictum: he simply increased his watchfulness, asking: *How do they hide it?*

"Tan! Tan!" the boy was shouting. "I've brought a friend!"

A man and a woman strolled toward them from a garden. The man was huge, but otherwise so like the youth Wonyne that there could be no question of their relationship. Both had long, narrow, clear gray eyes set very wide apart, and red—almost orange—hair. The noses were strong and delicate at the same time, their mouths thin-lipped but wide and good-natured.

But the woman—

It was a long time before Bril could let himself look, let himself believe that there was such a woman. After his first glance, he made of her only a presence and fed himself small nibbles of belief in his eyes, in the fact that there could be hair like that, face, voice, body. She was dressed, like her husband and the boy, in the smoky kaleidoscope which resolved itself, when the wind permitted, into a black-belted tunic.

"He is Bril of Kit Carson in the Sumner System," babbled the boy, "and he's a member of the Sole Authority and it's the second planet and he knew the greeting and got it right. So did I," he added, laughing. "This is Tanyne, of the Senate, and my mother Nina."

"You are welcome, Bril of Kit Carson," she said to him; and unbelieving in this way that had come upon him, he took away his gaze and inclined his head.

"You must come in," said Tanyne cordially, and led the way through an arbor which was not the separate arch it appeared to be, but an entrance.

The room was wide, wider at one end than the other,

though it was hard to determine by how much. The floor was uneven, graded upward toward one corner, where it was a mossy bank. Scattered here and there were what the eye said were white and striated gray boulders; the hand would say they were flesh. Except for a few shelf- and tablelike niches on these and in the bank, they were the only furniture.

Water ran frothing and gurgling through the room, apparently as an open brook; but Bril saw Nina's bare foot tread on the invisible covering that followed it down to the pool at the other end. The pool was the one he had seen from outside, indeterminately in and out of the house. A large tree grew by the pool and leaned its heavy branches toward the bank, and evidently its wide-flung limbs were webbed and tented between by the same invisible substance which covered the brook. It formed the only cover overhead yet, to the ear, it *felt* like a ceiling.

The whole effect was, to Bril, intensely depressing, and he surprised himself with a flash of homesickness for the tall steel cities of his home planet.

Nina smiled and left them. Bril followed his host's example and sank down on the ground, or floor, where it became a bank, or wall. Inwardly, Bril rebelled at the lack of decisiveness, of discipline, of clear-cut limitation inherent in such haphazard design as this. But he was well trained and quite prepared, at first, to keep his feelings to himself among barbarians.

"Nina will join us in a moment," said Tanyne.

Bril, who had been watching the woman's swift movements across the courtyard through the transparent wall opposite, controlled a start. "I am unused to your ways, and wondered what she was doing," he said.

"She is preparing a meal for you," explained Tanyne.

"Herself?"

Tanyne and his son gazed wonderingly. "Does that seem unusual to you?"

"I understood the lady was wife to a Senator," said Bril. It seemed adequate as an explanation, but only to him. He looked from the boy's face to the man's. "Perhaps

I understand something different when I use the term 'Senator.' "

"Perhaps you do. Would you tell us what a Senator is on the planet Kit Carson?"

"He is a member of the Senate, subservient to the Sole Authority, and in turn leader of a free Nation."

"And his wife?"

"His wife shares his privileges. She might serve a member of the Sole Authority, but hardly anyone else—certainly not an unidentified stranger."

"Interesting," said Tanyne, while the boy murmured the astonishment he had not expressed at Bril's bubble, or Bril himself. "Tell me, have you not identified yourself, then?"

"He did, by the waterfall," the youth insisted.

"I gave you no proof," said Bril stiffly. He watched father and son exchange a glance. "Credentials, written authority." He touched the flat pouch hung on his power belt.

Wonyne asked ingenuously, "Do the credentials say you are *not* Bril of Kit Carson in the Sumner System?"

Bril frowned at him, and Tanyne said gently, "Wonyne, take care." To Bril, he said, "Surely there are many differences between us, as there always are between different worlds. But I am certain of this one similarity: the young at times run straight where wisdom has built a winding path."

Bril sat silently and thought this out. It was probably some sort of apology, he decided, and gave a single sharp nod. Youth, he thought, was an attenuated defect here. A boy Wonyne's age would be a soldier on Carson, ready for a soldier's work, and no one would be apologizing for him. Nor would he be making blunders. *None!*

He said, "These credentials are for your officials when I meet with them. By the way, when can that be?"

Tanyne shrugged his wide shoulders. "Whenever you like."

"The sooner the better."

"Very well."

"Is it far?"

Tanyne seemed perplexed. "Is what far?"

"Your capital, or wherever it is your Senate meets."

"Oh, I see. It doesn't meet, in the sense you mean. It is always in session, though, as they used to say. We—"

He compressed his lips and made a liquid, bisyllabic sound. Then he laughed. "I do beg your pardon," he said warmly. "The Old Tongue lacks certain words, certain concepts. What is your word for—er—the-presence-of-all-in-the-presence-of-one?"

"I think," said Bril carefully, "that we had better go back to the subject at hand. Are you saying that your Senate does not meet in some official place, at some appointed time?"

"I—" Tan hesitated, then nodded. "Yes, that is true as far as it—"

"And there is no possibility of my addressing your Senate in person?"

"I didn't say that." Tan tried twice to express the thought, while Bril's eyes slowly narrowed. Tan suddenly burst into laughter. "Using the Old Tongue to tell old tales and to speak with a friend are two different things," he said ruefully. "I wish you would learn our speech. Would you, do you suppose? It is rational and well based on what you know. Surely you have another language besides the Old Tongue on Kit Carson?"

"I honor the Old Tongue," said Bril stiffly, dodging the question. Speaking very slowly, as if to a retarded child, he said, "I should like to know when I may be taken to those in authority here, in order to discuss certain planetary and interplanetary matters with them."

"Discuss them with me."

"You are a Senator," Bril said, in a tone which meant clearly: *You are only a Senator.*

"True," said Tanyne.

With forceful patience, Bril asked, "And what is a Senator here?"

"A contact point between the people of his district and the people everywhere. One who knows the special prob-

lems of a small section of the planet and can relate them
to planetary policy."

"And whom does the Senate serve?"

"The people," said Tanyne, as if he had been asked to
repeat himself.

"Yes, yes, of course. And who, then, serves the Senate?"

"The Senators."

Bril closed his eyes and barely controlled the salty
syllable which welled up inside him. "Who," he inquired
steadily, "is your Government?"

The boy had been watching them eagerly, alternately,
like a devotee at some favorite fast ball game. Now he
asked, "What's a Government?"

Nina's interruption at that point was most welcome to
Bril. She came across the terrace from the covered area
where she had been doing mysterious things at a long work-
surface in the garden. She carried an enormous tray—
guided it, rather, as Bril saw when she came closer. She
kept three fingers under the tray and one behind it, barely
touching it with her palm. Either the transparent wall
of the room disappeared as she approached, or she passed
through a section where there was none.

"I do hope you find something to your taste among
these," she said cheerfully, as she brought the tray down to
a hummock near Bril. "This is the flesh of birds, this of
small mammals, and, over here, fish. These cakes are
made of four kinds of grain, and the white cakes here of
just one, the one we call milk-wheat. Here is water, and
these two are wines, and this one is a distilled spirit we
call warm-ears."

Bril, keeping his eyes on the food, and trying to keep
his universe from filling up with the sweet fresh scent of
her as she bent over him, so near, said, "This is welcome."

She crossed to her husband and sank down at his feet,
leaning back against his legs. He twisted her heavy hair
gently in his fingers and she flashed a small smile up at
him. Bril looked from the food, colorful as a corsage,
here steaming, there gathering frost from the air, to the
three smiling expectant faces, and did not know what to do.

"Yes, this is welcome," he said again, and still they sat there, watching him. He picked up the white cake and rose, looked out and around, into the house, through it and beyond. Where could one go in such a place?

Steam from the tray touched his nostrils and saliva filled his mouth. He was hungry, but . . .

He sighed, sat down, gently replaced the cake. He tried to smile and could not.

"Does none of it please you?" asked Nina, concerned.

"I can't eat here!" said Bril; then, sensing something in the natives that had not been there before, he added, "thank you." Again he looked at their controlled faces. He said to Nina, "It is very well prepared and good to look on."

"Then eat," she invited, smiling again.

This did something that their house, their garments, their appallingly easy ways—sprawling all over the place, letting their young speak up at will, the shameless admission that they had a patois of their own—that none of these things had been able to do. Without losing his implacable dignity by any slightest change of expression, he yet found himself blushing. Then he scowled and let the childish display turn to a flush of anger. He would be glad, he thought furiously, when he had the heart of this culture in the palm of his hand, to squeeze when he willed; then there would be an end to these hypocritical amenities and they would learn who could be humiliated.

But these three faces, the boy's so open and unconscious of wrong, Tanyne's so strong and anxious for him, Nina's —that face, that face of Nina's—they were all utterly guileless. He must not let them know of his embarrassment. If they had planned it, he must not give them the satisfaction. And if they had not planned it, he must not let them suspect his vulnerability.

With an immense effort of will, he kept his voice low; still, it was harsh. "I think," he said slowly, "that we on Kit Carson regard the matter of privacy perhaps a little more highly than you do."

They exchanged an astonished look, and then comprehension dawned visibly on Tanyne's ruddy face. "You don't eat together!"

Bril did not shudder, but it was in his word: "No."

"Oh," said Nina, "I'm *so* sorry!"

Bril thought it wise not to discover exactly what she was sorry about. He said, "No matter. Customs differ. I shall eat when I am alone."

"Now that we understand," said Tanyne, "go ahead. Eat."

But they *sat* there!

"Oh," said Nina, "I wish you spoke our other language; it would be so easy to explain!" She leaned forward to him, put out her arms, as if she could draw meaning itself from the air and cast it over him. "Please try to understand, Bril. You are mistaken about one thing—we honor privacy above almost anything else."

"We don't mean the same thing when we say it," said Bril.

"It means aloneness with oneself, doesn't it? It means to do things, think or make or just *be*, without intrusion."

"Unobserved," said Bril.

"So?" replied Wonyne happily, throwing out both hands in a gesture that said *quod erat demonstrandum.* "Go on then—eat! We won't look!" and helped the situation not at all.

"Wonyne's right," chuckled the father, "but, as usual, a little too direct. He means we can't look, Bril. If you want privacy, *we can't see you.*"

Angry, reckless, Bril suddenly reached to the tray. He snatched up a goblet, the one she had indicated as water, thumbed a capsule out of his belt, popped it into his mouth, drank and swallowed. He banged the goblet back on the tray and shouted, "Now you've seen all you're going to see."

With an indescribable expression, Nina drifted upward to her feet, bent like a dancer and touched the tray. It lifted and she guided it away across the courtyard.

"All right," said Wonyne. It was precisely as if someone

had spoken and he had acknowledged. He lounged out, following his mother.

What *had* been on her face?

Something she could not contain; something rising to that smooth surface, about to reveal outlines, break through . . . anger? Bril hoped so. Insult? He could, he supposed, understand that. But—laughter? *Don't make it laughter,* something within him pleaded.

"Bril," said Tanyne.

For the second time, he was so lost in contemplation of the woman that Tanyne's voice made him start.

"What is it?"

"If you will tell me what arrangements you would like for eating, I'll see to it that you get them."

"You wouldn't know how," said Bril bluntly. He threw his sharp, cold gaze across the room and back. "You people don't build walls you can't see through, doors you can close."

"Why, no, we don't." As always, the giant left the insult and took only the words.

I bet you don't, Bril said silently, *not even for*—and a horrible suspicion began to grow within him. "We of Kit Carson feel that all human history and development are away from the animal, toward something higher. We are, of course, chained to the animal state, but we do what we can to eliminate every animal act as a public spectacle." Sternly, he waved a shining gauntlet at the great open house. "You have apparently not reached such an idealization. I have seen how you eat; doubtless you perform your other functions so openly."

"Oh, yes," said Tanyne. "But with this"—he pointed —"it's hardly the same thing."

"With what?"

Tanyne again indicated one of the boulderlike objects. He tore off a clump of moss—it was real moss—and tossed it to the soft surface of one of the boulders. He reached down and touched one of the gray streaks. The moss sank into the surface the way a pebble will in quicksand, but much faster.

"It will not accept living animal matter above a certain level of complexity," he explained, "but it instantly absorbs every molecule of anything else, not only on the surface but for a distance above."

"And that's a—a—where you—"

Tan nodded and said that that was exactly what it was.

"But—anyone can see *you!*"

Tan shrugged and smiled. "How? That's what I meant when I said it's hardly the same thing. Of eating, wc make a social occasion. But this"—he threw another clump of moss and watched it vanish—"just isn't observed." His sudden laugh rang out and again he said, "I *wish* you'd learn the language. Such a thing is so easy to express."

But Bril was concentrating on something else. "I appreciate your hospitality," he said, using the phrase stiltedly, "but I'd like to be moving on." He eyed the boulder distastefully. "And very soon."

"As you wish. You have a message for Xanadu. Deliver it, then."

"To your Government."

"To our Government. I told you before, Bril—when you're ready, proceed."

"I cannot believe that you alone represent this planet!"

"Neither can I," said Tanyne pleasantly. "I don't. Through me, you can speak to forty-one others, all Senators."

"Is there no other way?"

Tanyne smiled. "Forty-one other ways. Speak to any of the others. It amounts to the same thing."

"And no higher government body?"

Tanyne reached out a long arm and plucked a goblet from a niche in the moss bank. It was chased crystal with a luminous metallic rim.

"Finding the highest point of the government of Xanadu is like finding the highest point on this," he said. He ran a finger around the inside of the rim and the goblet chimed beautifully.

"Pretty unstable," growled Bril.

Tanyne made it sing again and replaced it; whether that was an answer or not, Bril could not know.

He snorted, "No wonder the boy didn't know what Government was."

"We don't use the term," said Tanyne. "We don't need it. There are few things here that a citizen can't handle for himself; I wish I could show you how few. If you'll live with us a while, I will show you."

He caught Bril's eye squarely as it returned from another disgusted and apprehensive trip to the boulder, and laughed outright. But the kindness in his voice as he went on quenched Bril's upsurge of indignant fury, and a little question curled up: *Is he managing me?* But there wasn't time to look at it.

"Can your business wait until you know us, Bril? I tell you now, there is no centralized Government here, almost no government at all; we of the Senate are advisory. I tell you, too, that to speak to one Senator is to speak to all, and that you may do it now, this minute, or a year from now—whenever you like. I am telling you the truth and you may accept it or you may spend months, years, traveling this planet and checking up on me; you'll always come out with the same answer."

Noncommittally, Bril said, "How do I know that what I tell you is accurately relayed to the others?"

"It isn't relayed," said Tan frankly. "We all hear it simultaneously."

"Some sort of radio?"

Tan hesitated, then nodded. "Some sort of radio."

"I won't learn your language," Bril said abruptly. "I can't live as you do. If you can accept those conditions, I will stay a short while."

"Accept? We *insist!*" Tanyne bounded cheerfully to the niche where the goblet stood and held his palm up. A large, opaque sheet of a shining white material rolled down and stopped. "Draw with your finger," he said.

"Draw? Draw what?"

"A place of your own. How you would like to live, eat, sleep, everything."

"I require very little. None of us on Kit Carson do." He pointed the finger of his gauntlet like a weapon, made a couple of dabs in the corner of the screen to test the line, and then dashed off a very creditable parallelopiped. "Taking my height as one unit, I'd want this one-and-a-half long, one-and-a-quarter high. Slit vents at eye level, one at each end, two on each side, screened against insects—"

"We have no preying insects," said Tanyne.

"Screened anyway, and with as near an unbreakable mesh as you have. Here a hook suitable for hanging a garment. Here a bed, flat, hard, with firm padding as thick as my hand, one-and-one-eighth units long, one-third wide. All sides under the bed enclosed and equipped as a locker, impregnable, and to which only I have the key or combination. Here a shelf one-third by one-quarter units, one-half unit off the floor, suitable for eating from a seated posture.

"One of—those, if it's self-contained and reliable," he said edgily, casting a thumb at the boulderlike convenience. "The whole structure to be separate from all others on high ground and overhung by nothing—no trees, no cliffs, with approaches clear and visible from all sides; as strong as speed permits; and equipped with a light I can turn off and a door that only I can unlock."

"Very well," said Tanyne easily. "Temperature?"

"The same as this spot now."

"Anything else? Music? Pictures? We have some fine moving—"

Bril, from the top of his dignity, snorted his most eloquent snort. "Water, if you can manage it. As to those other things, this is a dwelling, not a pleasure palace."

"I hope you will be comfortable in this—in it," said Tanyne, with barely a trace of sarcasm.

"It is precisely what I am used to," Bril answered loftily.

"Come, then."

"What?"

The big man waved him on and passed through the arbor. Bril, blinking in the late pink sunlight, followed him.

On the gentle slope above the house, halfway between it and the mountaintop beyond, was a meadow of the red grass Bril had noticed on his way from the waterfall. In the center of this meadow was a crowd of people, bustling like moths around a light, their flimsy, colorful clothes flashing and gleaming in a thousand shades. And in the middle of the crowd lay a coffin-shaped object.

Bril could not believe his eyes, then stubbornly would not, and at last, as they came near, yielded and admitted it to himself: this was the structure he had just sketched.

He walked more and more slowly as the wonder of it grew on him. He watched the people—children, even—swarming around and over the little building, sealing the edge between roof and wall with a humming device, laying screen on the slit-vents. A little girl, barely a toddler, came up to him fearlessly and in lisping Old Tongue asked for his hand, which she clapped to a tablet she carried.

"To make your keys," explained Tanyne, watching the child scurry off to a man waiting at the door.

He took the tablet and disappeared inside, and they could see him kneel by the bed. A young boy overtook them and ran past, carrying a sheet of the same material the roof and walls were made of. It seemed light, but its slightly rough, pale-tan surface gave an impression of great toughness. As they drew up at the door, they saw the boy take the material and set it in position between the end of the bed and the doorway. He aligned it carefully, pressing it against the wall, and struck it once with the heel of his hand, and there was Bril's required table, level, rigid, and that without braces and supports.

"You seemed to like the looks of some of this, anyway." It was Nina, with her tray. She floated it to the new table, waved cheerfully and left.

"With you in a moment," Tan called, adding three singing syllables in the Xanadu tongue which were, Bril concluded, an endearment of some kind; they certainly sounded like it. Tan turned back to him, smiling.

"Well, Bril, how is it?"

Bril could only ask, "Who gave the orders?"

"You did," said Tan, and there didn't seem to be any answer to that.

Already, through the open door, he could see the crowd drifting away, laughing and singing their sweet language to each other. He saw a young man scoop up scarlet flowers from the pink sward and hand them to a smiling girl, and unaccountably the scene annoyed him. He turned away abruptly and went about the walls, thumping them and peering through the vents. Tanyne knelt by the bed, his big shoulders bulging as he tugged at the locker. It might as well have been solid rock.

"Put your hand there," he said, pointing, and Bril clapped his gauntlet to the plate he indicated.

Sliding panels parted. Bril got down and peered inside. It had its own light, and he could see the buff-colored wall of the structure at the back and the heavy filleted partition which formed the bed uprights. He touched the panel again and the doors slid silently shut, so tight that he could barely see their meeting.

"The door's the same," said Tanyne. "No one but you can open it. Here's water. You didn't say where to put it. If this is inconvenient . . ."

When Bril put his hand near the spigot, water flowed into a catch basin beneath. "No, that is satisfactory. They work like specialists."

"They are," said Tanyne.

"Then they have built such a strange structure before?"

"Never."

Bril looked at him sharply. This ingenuous barbarian surely could not be making a fool of him by design! No, this must be some slip of semantics, some shift in meaning over the years which separated each of them from the common ancestor. He would not forget it, but he set it aside for future thought.

"Tanyne," he asked suddenly, "how many are you in Xanadu?"

"In the district, three hundred. On the planet, twelve, almost thirteen thousand."

"We are one and a half billions," said Bril. "And what is your largest city?"

"City," said Tanyne, as if searching through the files of his memory. "Oh—city! We have none. There are forty-two districts like this one, some larger, some smaller."

"Your entire planetary population could be housed in one building within one city on Kit Carson. And how many generations have your people been here?"

"Thirty-two, thirty-five, something like that."

"We settled Kit Carson not quite six Earth centuries ago. In point of time, then, it would seem that yours is the older culture. Wouldn't you be interested in how we have been able to accomplish so much more?"

"Fascinated," said Tanyne.

"You have some clever little handicrafts here," Bril mused, "and a quite admirable cooperative ability. You could make a formidable thing of this world, if you wanted to, and if you had the proper guidance."

"Oh, could we really?" Tanyne seemed very pleased.

"I must think," said Bril somberly. "You are not what I—what I had supposed. Perhaps I shall stay a little longer than I had planned. Perhaps while I am learning about your people, you in turn could be learning about mine."

"Delighted," said Tanyne. "Now is there anything else you need?"

"Nothing. You may leave me."

His autocratic tone gained him only one of the big man's pleasant, open-faced smiles. Tanyne waved his hand and left. Bril heard him calling his wife in ringing baritone notes, and her glad answer. He set his mailed hand against the door plate and it slid shut silently.

Now what, he asked himself, *got me to do all that bragging?* Then the astonishment at the people of Xanadu rose up and answered the question for him. *What manner of people are specialists at something they have never done before?*

He got out of his stiff, polished, heavy uniform, his gauntlets, his boots. They were all wired together, power supply in the boots, controls and computers in the trousers and belt, sensory mechs in the tunic, projectors and field loci in the gloves.

He hung the clothes on the hook provided and set the alarm field for anything larger than a mouse any closer than thirty meters. He dialed a radiation dome to cover his structure and exclude all spy beams or radiation weapons. Then he swung his left gauntlet on its cable over the table and went to work on one small corner.

In half an hour, he had found a combination of heat and pressure that would destroy the pale brown board, and he sat down on the edge of the bed, limp with amazement. You could build a spaceship with stuff like this.

Now he had to believe that they had it in stock sizes exactly to his specifications, which would mean warehouses and manufacturing facilities capable of making up those and innumerable other sizes; or he had to believe that they had machinery capable of making what his torches had just destroyed, in job lots, right *now*.

But they didn't have any industrial plant to speak of, and if they had warehouses, they had them where the Kit Carson robot scouts had been unable to detect them in their orbiting for the last fifty years.

Slowly he lay down to think.

To acquire a planet, you locate the central government. If it is an autocracy, organized tightly up to the peak, so much the better; the peak is small and you kill it or control it and use the organization. If there is no government at all, you recruit the people or you exterminate them. If there is plant, you run it with overseers and make the natives work it until you can train your own people to it and eliminate the natives. If there are skills, you learn them or you control those who have them. All in the book; a rule for every eventuality, every possibility.

But what if, as the robots reported, there was high

technology and no plant? Planetwide cultural stability and almost no communications?

Well, nobody ever heard of such a thing, so when the robots report it, you send an investigator. All he has to find out is how they do it. All he has to do is to parcel up what is to be kept and what eliminated when the time comes for an expeditionary force.

There's always one clean way out, thought Bril, putting his hands behind his head and looking up at the tough ceiling. Item, one Earth-normal planet, rich in natural resources, sparsely populated by innocents. You can always simply exterminate them.

But not before you find out how they communicate, how they cooperate, and how they specialize in skills they never tried before. How they manufacture superior materials out of thin air in no time.

He had a sudden heady vision of Kit Carson equipped as these people were, a billion and a half universal specialists with some heretofore unsuspected method of intercommunication, capable of building cities, fighting wars, with the measureless skill and split-second understanding and obedience with which this little house had been built.

No, these people must not be exterminated. They must be used. Kit Carson had to learn their tricks. If the tricks were—he hoped not!—inherent in Xanadu and beyond the Carson abilities, then what would be the next best thing?

Why, a cadre of the Xanadu, scattered through the cities and armies of Kit Carson, instantly obedient, instantly trainable. Instruct one and you teach them all; each could teach a group of Kit Carson's finest. Production, logistics, strategy, tactics—he saw it all in a flash.

Xanadu might be left almost exactly as is, except for its new export—aides de camp.

Dreams, these are only dreams, he told himself sternly. *Wait until you know more. Watch them make impregnable hardboard and anti-grav tea-trays.*

The thought of the tea-tray made his stomach growl.

He got up and went to it. The hot food steamed, the cold was still frosty and firm. He picked, he tasted. Then he bit. Then he gobbled.

Nina, that Nina . . .

No, they can't be exterminated, he thought drowsily, not when they can produce such a woman. In all of Kit Carson, there wasn't a cook like that.

He lay down again and dreamed, and dreamed until he fell asleep.

They were completely frank. They showed him everything, and it apparently never occurred to them to ask him why he wanted to know. Asking was strange, because they seemed to lack that special pride of accomplishment one finds in the skilled potter, metalworker, electronician, an attitude of "Isn't it remarkable that I can do it!" They gave information accurately but impersonally, as if anyone could do it.

And on Xanadu, anyone could.

At first, it seemed to Bril totally disorganized. These attractive people in their indecent garments came and went, mingling play and work and loafing, without apparent plan. But their play would take them through a flower-garden just where the weeds were, and they would take the weeds along. There seemed to be a group of girls playing jacks right outside the place they would suddenly be needed to sort some seeds.

Tanyne tried to explain it: "Say we have a shortage of something—oh, strontium, for example. The shortage itself creates a sort of vacuum. People without anything special to do feel it; they think about strontium. They come, they gather it."

"But I have seen no mines," Bril said puzzledly. "And what about shipping? Suppose the shortage is here and the mines in another district?"

"That never happens any more. Where there are deposits, of course, there are no shortages. Where there are none, we find other ways, either to use something else, or to produce it without mines."

"Transmute it?"

"Too much trouble. No, we breed a fresh-water shellfish with a strontium carbonate shell instead of calcium carbonate. The children gather them for us when we need it."

He saw their clothing industry—part shed, part cave, part forest glen. There was a pool there where the young people swam, and a field where they sunned themselves. Between times, they went into the shadows and worked by a huge vessel where chemicals occasionally boiled, turned bright green, and then precipitated. The black precipitate was raised from the bottom of the vessel on screens, dumped into forms and pressed.

Just how the presses—little more than lids for the forms —operated, the Old Tongue couldn't tell him, but in four or five seconds the precipitate had turned into the black stones used in their belts, formed and polished, with a chemical formula in Old Tongue script cut into the back of the left buckle.

"One of our few superstitions," said Tanyne. "It's the formula for the belts—even a primitive chemistry could make them. We would like to see them copied, duplicated all over the Universe. They are what we are. Wear one, Bril. You would be one of us, then."

Bril snorted in embarrassed contempt and went to watch two children deftly making up the belts, as easily, and with the same idle pleasure, as they might be making flower necklaces in a minute or two. As each was assembled, the child would strike it against his own belt. All the colors there are would appear each time this happened, in a brief, brilliant, cool flare. Then the belt, now with a short trim of vague tongued light, was tossed in a bin.

Probably the only time Bril permitted himself open astonishment on Xanadu was the first time he saw one of the natives put on this garment. It was a young man, come dripping from the pool. He snatched up a belt from the bank and clasped it around his waist, and immediately color and substance flowed up and down, a flickering, changing collar for him, a moving coruscant kilt.

"It's alive, you see," said Tanyne. "Rather, it is not nonliving matter."

He put his fingers under the hem of his own kilt and forced his fingers up and outward. They penetrated the fabric, which fluttered away—untorn.

"It is not," he said gravely, "altogether material, if you will forgive an Old Tongue pun. The nearest Old Tongue term for it is 'aura.' Anyway, it lives, in its way. It maintains itself for—oh, a year or more. Then dip it in lactic acid and it is refreshed again. And just one of them could activate a million belts or a billion—how many sticks can a fire burn?"

"But why wear such a thing?"

Tanyne laughed. "Modesty." He laughed again. "A scholar of the very old times, on Earth before the Nova, passed on to me the words of one Rudofsky: 'Modesty is not so simple a virtue as honesty.' We wear these becaue they are warm when we need warmth, and because they conceal some defects some of the time— surely all one can ask of any human affectation."

"They are certainly not modest," said Bril stiffly.

"They express modesty just to the extent that they make us more pleasant to look at with than without them. What more public expression of humility could you want than that?"

Bril turned his back on Tanyne and the discussion. He understood Tanyne's words and ways imperfectly to begin with, and this kind of talk left him bewildered, or un- reached, or both.

He found out about the hardboard. Hanging from the limb of a tree was a large vat of milky fluid—the paper, Tan explained, of a wasp they had developed, dissolved in one of the nucleic acids which they synthesized from a native weed. Under the vat was a flat metal plate and a set of movable fences. These were arranged in the desired shape and thickness of the finished panel, and then a cock was opened and the fluid ran in and filled the enclosure. Thereupon two small children pushed a roller by hand across the top of the fences. The white lake of fluid turned pale brown and solidified, and that was the hardboard.

Tanyne tried his best to explain to Bril about that roller, but the Old Tongue joined forces with Bril's technical ignorance and made the explanation incomprehensible. The coating of the roller was as simple in design, and as complex in theory, as a transistor, and Bril had to let it go at that, as he did with the selective analysis of the boulderlike "plumbing" and the anti-grav food trays (which, he discovered, had to be guided outbound, but which "homed" on the kitchen area when empty).

He had less luck, as the days went by, in discovering the nature of the skills of Xanadu. He had been quite ready to discard his own dream as a fantasy, an impossibility—the strange idea that what any could do, all could do. Tanyne tried to explain; at least, he answered every one of Bril's questions.

These wandering, indolent, joyful people could pick up anyone's work at any stage and carry it to any degree. One would pick up a flute and play a few notes, and others would stroll over, some with instruments and some without, and soon another instrument and another would join in, until there were fifty or sixty and the music was like a passion or a storm, or after-love or sleep when you think back on it.

And sometimes the bystanders would step forward and take an instrument from the hands of someone who was tiring, and play on with all the rest, pure and harmonious; and, no, Tan would aver, he didn't think they'd ever played that particular piece of music before, those fifty or sixty people.

It always got down to *feeling*, in Tan's explanations.

"It's a *feeling* you get. The violin, now; I've heard one, we'll say, but never held one. I watch someone play and I understand how the notes are made. Then I take it and do the same, and as I concentrate on making the note, and the note that follows, it comes to me not only how it should sound, but how it should *feel*—to the fingers, the bowing arm, the chin and collarbone. Out of those feelings comes the feeling of how it feels to be making such music.

"Of course, there are limitations," he admitted, "and some might do better than others. If my fingertips are soft, I can't play as long as another might. If a child's hands are too small for the intrument, he'll have to drop an octave or skip a note. But the feeling's there, when we think in that certain way."

"It's the same with anything else we do," he summed up. "If I need something in my house, a machine, a device, I won't use iron where copper is better; it wouldn't *feel* right for me. I don't mean feeling the metal with my hands; I mean thinking about the device and its parts and what it's for. When I think of all the things I could make it of, there's only one set of things that feels right to me."

"So," said Bril then. "And that, plus this—this competition between the districts, to find all elements and raw materials in the neighborhood instead of sending for them—that's why you have no commerce. Yet you say you're standardized—at any rate, you all have the same kind of devices, ways of doing things."

"We all have whatever we want and we make it ourselves, yes," Tan agreed.

In the evenings, Bril would sit in Tanyne's house and listen to the drift and swirl of conversation, or the floods of music, and wonder; and then he would guide his tray back to his cubicle and lock the door and eat, and brood. He felt at times that he was under an attack with weapons he did not understand, on a field which was strange to him.

He remembered something Tanyne had said once, casually, about men and their devices: "Ever since there were human beings, there has been conflict between Man and his machines. They will run him or he them; it's hard to say which is the less disastrous way. But a culture which is composed primarily of men has to destroy one made mostly of machines, or be destroyed. It was always that way. We lost a culture once on Xanadu. Didn't you ever wonder, Bril, why there are so few of us here? And why almost all of us have red hair?"

Bril had, and had secretly blamed the small population on the shameless lack of privacy, without which no human race seems to be able to whip up enough interest in itself to breed readily.

"We were billions, once," said Tan surprisingly. "We were wiped out. Know how many were left? *Three!*"

That was a black night for Bril, when he realized how pitiable were his efforts to learn their secret. For if a race were narrowed to a few, and a mutation took place, and it then increased again, the new strain could be present in all the new generations. He might as well, he thought, try to wrest from them the secret of having red hair. That was the night he concluded that these people would have to go; and it hurt him to think that, and he was angry at himself for thinking so. That, too, was the night of the ridiculous disaster.

He lay on his bed, grinding his teeth in helpless fury. It was past noon and he had been there since he awoke, trapped by his own stupidity, and ridiculous, ridiculous. His greatest single possession—his dignity—was stripped from him by his own carelessness, by a fiendish and unsportsmanlike gadget that—

His approach alarm hissed and he sprang to his feet in an agony of embarrassment, in spite of the strong opaque walls and the door which only he could open.

It was Tanyne; his friendly greeting bugled out and mingled with birdsong and the wind. "Bril! You there?"

Bril let him come a little closer and then barked through the vent, "I'm not coming out." Tanyne stopped dead, and even Bril himself was surprised by the harsh, squeezed sound of his voice.

"But Nina asked for you. She's going to weave today; she thought you'd like—"

"No," snapped Bril. "Today I leave. Tonight, that is. I've summoned my bubble. It will be here in two hours. After that, when it's dark, I'm going."

"Bril, you can't. Tomorrow I've set up a sintering for you; show you how we plate—"

"No!"

"Have we offended you, Bril? Have I?"

"No." Bril's voice was surly, but at least not a shout.

"What's happened?"

Bril didn't answer.

Tanyne came closer. Bril's eyes disappeared from the slit. He was cowering against the wall, sweating.

Tanyne said, "Something's happened, something's wrong. I . . . feel it. You know how I feel things, my friend, my good friend Bril."

The very thought made Bril stiffen in terror. Did Tanyne know? Could he?

He might, at that. Bril damned these people and all their devices, their planet and its sun and the fates which had brought him here.

"There is nothing in my world or in my experience you can't tell me about. You know I'll understand," Tanyne pleaded. He came closer. "Are you ill? I have all the skills of the surgeons who have lived since the Three. Let me in."

"No!" It was hardly a word; it was an explosion.

Tanyne fell back a step. "I beg your pardon, Bril. I won't ask again. But—tell me. Please tell me. I must be able to help you!"

All right, thought Bril, half hysterically, *I'll tell you and you can laugh your fool red head off. It won't matter once we seed your planet with Big Plague.* "I can't come out. I've ruined my clothes."

"Bril! What can that matter? Here, throw them out; we can fix them, no matter what it is."

"No!" He could just see what would happen with these universal talents getting hold of the most compact and deadly armory this side of the Sumner System.

"Then wear mine." Tan put his hands to the belt of black stones.

"I wouldn't be seen dead in a flimsy thing like that. Do you think I'm an exhibitionist?"

With more heat (it wasn't much) than Bril had ever seen in him, Tanyne said, "You've been a lot more conspicuous in those winding sheets you've been wearing than you ever would in this."

Bril had never thought of that. He looked longingly at

the bright nothing which flowed up and down from the belt, and then at his own black harness, humped up against the wall under its hook. He hadn't been able to bear the thought of putting them back on since the accident happened, and he had not been this long without clothes since he'd been too young to walk.

"What happened to your clothes, anyway?" Tan asked sympathetically.

Laugh, thought Bril, *and I'll kill you right now and you'll never have a chance to see your race die.* "I sat down on the—I've been using it as a chair; there's only room for one seat in here. I must have kicked the switch. I didn't even feel it until I got up. The whole back of my—" Angrily he blurted, "Why doesn't that ever happen to you people?"

"Didn't I tell you?" Tan said, passing the news item by as if it meant nothing. Well to him it probably was nothing. "The unit only accepts non-living matter."

"Leave that thing you call clothes in front of the door," Bril grunted after a strained silence. "Perhaps I'll try it."

Tanyne tossed the belt up against the door and strode away, singing softly. His voice was so big that even his soft singing seemed to go on forever.

But eventually Bril had the field to himself, the birdsong and the wind. He went to the door and away, lifted his seatless breeches sadly and folded them out of sight under the other things on the hook. He looked at the door again and actually whimpered once, very quietly. At last he put the gauntlet against the doorplate, and the door, never designed to open a little way, obediently slid wide. He squeaked, reached out, caught up the belt, scampered back and slapped at the plate.

"No one saw," he told himself urgently.

He pulled the belt around him. The buckle parts knew each other like a pair of hands.

The first thing he was aware of was the warmth. Nothing but the belt touched him anywhere and yet there was a warmth on him, soft, safe, like a bird's breast on eggs. A split second later, he gasped.

How could a mind fill so and not feel pressure? How could so much understanding flood into a brain and not break it?

He understood about the roller which treated the hardboard; it *was* a certain way and no other, and he could feel the rightness of that sole conjecture.

He understood the ions of the mold-press that made the belts, and the life-analog he wore as a garment. He understood how his finger might write on a screen, and the vacuum of demand he might send out to have this house built so, and so, and exactly so; and how the natives would hurry to fill it.

He remembered without effort Tanyne's description of the *feel* of playing an instrument, making, building, molding, holding, sharing, and how it must be to play in a milling crowd beside a task, moving randomly and only for pleasure, yet taking someone's place at vat or bench, furrow or fishnet, the very second another laid down a tool.

He stood in his own quiet flame, in his little coffin-cubicle, looking at his hands and knowing without question that they would build him a model of a city on Kit Carson if he liked, or a statue of the soul of the Sole Authority.

He knew without question that he had the skills of this people, and that he could call on any of those skills just by concentrating on a task until it came to him how the right way (for him) would *feel*. He knew without surprise that these resources transcended even death; for a man could have a skill and then it was everyman's, and if the man should die, his skill still lived in everyman.

Just by concentrating—that was the key, the keyway, the keystone to the nature of this device. A device, that was all—no mutations, nothing 'extra-sensory' (whatever that meant); only a machine like other machines. You have a skill, and a feeling about it; I have a task. Concentration on my task sets up a demand for your skill; through the living flame you wear, you transmit; through mine, I receive. Then I perform; and what bias I put upon that performance depends on my capabilities. Should I add something to that skill, then mine is the higher, the more complete; the *feeling* of it is better, and it is I who will transmit next time there is a demand.

And he understood the authority that lay in this new aura, and it came to him then how his home planet could be welded into a unit such as the Universe had never seen. Xanadu had not done it, because Xanadu had grown randomly with its gift, without the preliminary pounding and shaping and milling of authority and discipline.

But Kit Carson! Carson with all skills and all talents shared among all its people, and overall and commanding, creating that vacuum of need and instant fulfillment, the Sole Authority and the State. It must be so (even though, far down, something in him wondered why the State kept so much understanding away from its people), for with this new depth came a solemn new dedication to his home and all it stood for.

Trembling, he unbuckled the belt and turned back its left buckle. Yes, there it was, the formula for the precipitate. And now he understood the pressing process and he had the flame to strike into new belts and make them live—by the millions, Tanyne had said, the billions.

Tanyne had said . . . why had he never said that the garments of Xanadu were the source of all their wonders and perplexities?

But had Bril ever asked?

Hadn't Tanyne begged him to take a garment so he could be one with Xanadu? The poor earnest idiot, to think he could be swayed away from Carson this way! Well, then, Tanyne and his people would have an offer, too, and it would all be even; soon they could, if they would, join the shining armies of a new Kit Carson.

From his hanging black suit, a chime sounded. Bril laughed and gathered up his old harness and all the fire and shock and paralysis asleep in its mighty, compact weapons. He slapped open the door and sprang to the bubble which waited outside, and flung his old uniform in to lie crumpled on the floor, a broken chrysalis. Shining and exultant, he leaped in after it and the bubble sprang away skyward.

Within a week after Bril's return to Kit Carson in the Sumner System, the garment had been duplicated, and duplicated again, and tested.

Within a month, nearly two hundred thousand had been distributed, and eighty factories were producing round the clock.

Within a year, the whole planet, all the millions, were shining and unified as never before, moving together under their Leader's will like the cells of a hand.

And then, in shocking unison, they all flickered and dimmed, every one, so it was time for the lactic acid dip which Bril had learned of. It was done in panic, without test or hesitation; a small taste of this luminous subjection had created a mighty appetite. All was well for a week—

And then, as the designers in Xanadu had planned, all the other segments of the black belts joined the first meager two in full operation.

A billion and a half human souls, who had been given the techniques of music and the graphic arts, and the theory of technology, now had the others: philosophy and logic and love; sympathy, empathy, forbearance, unity in the idea of their species rather than in their obedience; membership in harmony with all life everywhere.

A people with such feelings and their derived skills cannot be slaves. As the light burst upon them, there was only one concentration possible to each of them—to be free, and the accomplished feeling of being free. As each found it, he was an expert in freedom, and expert succeeded expert, transcended expert, until (in a moment) a billion and a half human souls had no greater skill than the talent of freedom.

So Kit Carson, as a culture, ceased to exist, and something new started there and spread through the stars nearby.

And because Bril knew what a Senator was and wanted to be one, he became one.

In each other's arms, Tanyne and Nina were singing softly, when the goblet in the mossy niche chimed.

"Here comes another one," said Wonyne, crouched at their feet. "I wonder what will make *him* beg, borrow or steal a belt."

"Doesn't matter," said Tanyne, stretching luxuriously, "as long as he gets it. Which one is he, Wo—that noisy mechanism on the other side of the small moon?"

"No," said Wonyne, "That one's still sitting there squalling and thinking we don't know it's there. No, this is the force-field that's been hovering over Fleetwing District for the last two years."

Tanyne laughed. "That'll make conquest number eighteen for us."

"Nineteen," corrected Nina dreamily. "I remember because eighteen was the one that just left and seventeen was that funny little Bril from the Sumner System. Tan, for a time that little man loved me." But that was a small thing and did not matter.

A SPECIAL KIND
OF MORNING

Gardner R. Dozois

When this fierce and beautiful story of future war first appeared, back in 1971, Gardner Dozois was an obscure young writer, a member of that inchoate mass of hairy newcomers associated with the Clarion science-fiction writers' workshop. At last report Dozois was still young (safely under thirty) and still hairy, but he is obscure no longer: he has been nominated for Hugo and Nebula awards, has published a dozen or more major stories and is working on his first novel, has even edited an anthology or two, and is generally recognized as one of the outstanding scince-fiction writers of the decade. He appears in **Alpha** now for the first time, but surely not the last.

The Doomsday Machine is the human race.
        —grafitto in New York subway, 79th St. station

Did y'ever hear the one about the old man and the sea? Halt a minute, lordling; stop and listen. It's a fine story, full of balance and point and social pith; short and direct. It's not mine. Mine are long and rambling and parenthetical and they corrode the moral fiber right out of a man.

223

Come to think, I won't tell you that one after all. A man of my age has a right to prefer his own material, and let the critics be damned. I've a prejudice now for webs of my own weaving.

Sit down, sit down: butt against pavement, yes; it's been done before. Everything has, near about. Now that's not an expression of your black pessimism, or your futility, or what have you. Pessimism's just the common-sense knowledge that there's more ways for something to go wrong than for it to go right, from our point of view anyway—which is not necessarily that of the management, or of the mechanism, if you prefer your cosmos depersonalized. As for futility, everybody dies the true death eventually; even though executives may dodge it for a few hundred years, the hole gets them all in the end, and I imagine that's futility enough for a start. The philosophical man accepts both as constants and then doesn't let them bother him any. Sit down, damn it; don't pretend you've important business to be about. Young devil, you are in the enviable position of having absolutely nothing to do because it's going to take you a while to recover from what you've just done.

There. That's better. Comfortable? You don't look it; you look like you've just sat in a puddle of piss and're wondering what the socially appropriate reaction is. Hypocrisy's an art, boy; you'll improve with age. Now you're bemused, lordling, that you let an old soak chivy you around, and now he's making fun of you. Well, the expression on your face is worth a chuckle; if you could see it you'd laugh yourself. You will see it years from now too, on some other young man's face—that's the only kind of mirror that ever shows it clear. And *you'll* be an old soak by that time, and you'll laugh and insult the young buck's dignity, but you'll be laughing more at the reflection of the man you used to be than at that particular stud himself. And you'll probably have to tell the buck just what I've told you to cool him down, and there's a laugh in that too; listen for the echo of a million and one laughs behind you. I hear a million now.

How do I get away with such insolence? What've I got to lose, for one thing. That gives you a certain perspective. And I'm socially instructive in spite of myself—I'm valuable as an object lesson. For that matter, why is an arrogant young aristo like you sitting there and putting up with my guff? Don't even bother to answer; I knew the minute you came whistling down the street, full of steam and strut. Nobody gets up this early in the morning any more, unless they're old as I am and begrudge sleep's dry-run of death—or unless they've never been to bed in the first place. The world's your friend this morning, a toy for you to play with and examine and stuff in your mouth to taste, and you're letting your benevolence slop over onto the old degenerate you've met on the street. You're even happy enough to listen, though you're being quizzical about it, and you're sitting over there feeling benignly superior. And I'm sitting over *here* feeling benignly superior. A nice arrangement, and everyone content. Well, then, mornings make you feel that way. Especially if you're fresh from a night at the Towers, the musk of Lady Ni still warm on your flesh.

A blush—my buck, you *are* new-hatched. How did I know? Boy, you'd be surprised what I know; I'm occasionally startled myself, and I've been working longer to get it catalogued. Besides, hindsight is a comfortable substitute for omnipotence. And I'm not blind yet. You have the unmistakable look of a cub who's just found out he can do something else with it besides piss. An incredible revelation, as I recall. The blazing significance of it will wear a little with the years, though not all that much, I suppose; until you get down to the brink of the Ultimate Cold, when you stop worrying about the identity of warmth, or demanding that it pay toll in pleasure. Any hand of clay, long's the blood still runs the tiny degree that's just enough for difference. Warmth's the only definition between you and graveyard dirt. But morning's not for graveyards, though it works the other way. Did y'know they also used to use that to make babies? 'S'fact, though few know it now. It's a versatile beast. Oh *come*—buck, cub, young cocksman—

stop being so damn surprised. People ate, slept, and forni-
cated before you were born, some of them anyway, and a
few will probably even find the courage to keep on at it
after you die. You don't have to keep it secret; the thing's
been circulated in this region once or twice before. You
weren't the first to learn how to make the beast do its
trick, though I *know* you don't believe that. *I* don't believe
it concerning myself, and I've had a long time to learn.

You make me think, sitting there innocent as an egg and
twice as vulnerable; yes, you are definitely about to make
me think, and I believe I'll have to think of some things I
always regret having thought about, just to keep me from
growing maudlin. Damn it, boy, you *do* make me think.
Life's strange—wet-eared as you are, you've probably had
that thought a dozen times already, probably had it this
morning as you tumbled out of your fragrant bed to meet
the rim of the sun; well, I've four times your age, and a
ream more experience, and I still can't think of anything
better to sum up the world: life's strange. 'S been said, yes.
But *think,* boy, how strange: the two of us talking, you
coming, me going; me knowing where you've got to go,
you suspecting where I've been, and the same destination
for both. O strange, very strange. Damn it, you're a deader
already if you can't see the strangeness of that, if you can't
sniff the poetry; it reeks of it, as of blood. And I've smelt
blood, buck. It has a very distinct odor; you know it when
you smell it. You're bound for blood; for blood and passion
and high deeds and all the rest of the business, and maybe
for a little understanding if you're lucky and have eyes to
see. Me, I'm bound for nothing, literally. I've come to rest
here in Kos, and while the Red Lady spins her web of colors across the sky I sit and weave my own webs of words
and dreams and other spider stuff—

What? Yes, I do talk too much; old men like to babble,
and philosophy's a cushion for old bones. But it's my profession now, isn't it, and I've promised you a story. What
happened to my leg? That's a bloody story, but I said you're
bound for blood; I know the mark. I'll tell it to you then;
perhaps it'll help you to understand when you reach the

narrow place, perhaps it'll even help you to think, although that's a horrible weight to wish on any man. It's customary to notarize my card before I start, keep you from running off at the end without paying. Thank you, young sir. Beware of some of these beggars, buck; they have a credit tally at Central greater than either of us will ever run up. They turn a tidy profit out of poverty. I'm an honest pauper, more's the pity, exist mostly on the subsidy, if you call that existing— Yes, I know. The leg.

We'll have to go back to the Realignment for that, more than half a century ago, and half a sector away, at World. This was before World was a member of the Commonwealth. In fact, that's what the Realignment was about, the old Combine overthrown by the Quaestors, who then opted for amalgamation and forced World into the Commonwealth. That's where and when the story starts.

Start it with waiting.

A lot of things start like that, waiting. And when the thing you're waiting for is probable death, and you're lying there loving life and suddenly noticing how pretty everything is and listening to the flint hooves of darkness click closer, feeling the iron-shod boots strike relentless sparks from the surface of your mind, knowing that death is about to fall out of the sky and that there's no way to twist out from under—then, waiting can take time. Minutes become hours, hours become unthinkable horrors. Add enough horrors together, total the scaly snouts, and you've got a day and a half I once spent laying up in a mountain valley in the Blackfriars on World, almost the last day I ever spent anywhere.

This was just a few hours after D'kotta. Everything was a mess, nobody really knew what was happening, everybody's communication lines cut. I was just a buck myself then, working with the Quaestors in the field, a hunted criminal. Nobody knew what the Combine would do next, we didn't know what *we'd* do next, groups surging wildly from one place to another at random, panic and riots all over the planet, even in the Controlled Environments.

And D'kotta-on-the-Blackfriars was indescribable, a seventy-mile swath of smoking insanity, capped by boiling umbrellas of smoke that eddied ashes from the ground to the stratosphere and back. At night it pulsed with molten scum, ugly as a lanced blister, lighting up the cloud cover across the entire horizon, visible for hundreds of miles. It was this ugly glow that finally panicked even the zombies in the Environments, probably the first strong emotion in their lives.

It'd been hard to sum up the effects of the battle. We thought that we had the edge, that the Combine was close to breaking, but nobody knew for sure. If they weren't as close to folding as we thought, then we were probably finished. The Quaestors had exhausted most of their hoarded resources at D'kotta, and we certainly couldn't hit the Combine any harder. If they could shrug off the blow then they could wear us down.

Personally, I didn't see how anything could shrug *that* off. I'd watched it all and it'd shaken me considerably. There's an old-time expression, "put the fear of God into him." That's what D'kotta had done for me. There wasn't any God any more, but I'd seen fire vomit from the heavens and the earth ripped wide for rape, and it'd been an impressive enough surrogate. Few people ever realized how close the Combine and the Quaestors had come to destroying World between them, there at D'kotta.

We'd crouched that night—the team and I—on the high stone ramparts of the tallest of the Blackfriars, hopefully far away from anything that could fall on us. There were twenty miles of low, gnarly foothills between us and the rolling savannahland where the city of D'kotta had been minutes before, but the ground under our bellies heaved and quivered like a sick animal, and the rock was hot to the touch: feverish.

We could've gotten farther away, should have gotten farther away, but we had to watch. That'd been decided without anyone saying a word, without any question about it. It was impossible *not* to watch. It never even occurred to any of us to take another safer course of action. When reality is being turned inside out like a dirty sock, you

watch, or you are less than human. So we watched it all
from beginning to end: two hours that became a single
second lasting for eons. Like a still photograph of time
twisted into a scream—the scream reverberating on forever and yet taking no duration at all to experience.

We didn't talk. We *couldn't* talk—the molecules of the
air itself shrieked too loudly, and the deep roar of explo-
sions was a continual drumroll—but we wouldn't have
talked even if we'd been able. You don't speak in the
presence of an angry God. Sometimes we'd look briefly at
each other. Our faces were all nearly identical: ashen,
waxy, eyes of glass, blank, and lost as pale driftwood
stranded on a beach by the tide. We'd been driven through
the gamut of expressions into *extremus-rictus:* faces so
contorted and strained they ached—and beyond to the
quietus of shock: muscles too slack and flaccid to respond
any more. We'd only look at each other for a second,
hardly focusing, almost not aware of what we were seeing,
and then our eyes would be dragged back as if by magne-
tism to the Fire.

At the beginning we'd clutched each other, but as the
battle progressed we slowly drew apart, huddling into individual agony; the thing so big that human warmth meant
nothing, so frightening that the instinct to gather together
for protection was reversed, and the presence of others
only intensified the realization of how ultimately naked
you were. Earlier we'd set up a scattershield to filter the
worst of the hard radiation—the gamma and intense infrared and ultraviolet—blunt some of the heat and shock
and noise. We thought we had a fair chance of surviving,
then, but we couldn't have run anyway. We were fixed by
the beauty of horror/horror of beauty, surely as if by a
spike driven through our backbones into the rock.

And away over the foothills, God danced in anger, and
his feet struck the ground to ash.

What was it like?

Kos still has oceans and storms. Did y'ever watch the sea
lashed by high winds? The storm boils the water into froth,
whips it white, until it becomes an ocean of ragged lace to

the horizon, whirlpools of milk, not a fleck of blue left alive. The land looked like this at D'kotta. The hills *moved*. The Quaestors had a discontinuity projector there, and under its lash the ground stirred like sluggish batter under a baker's spoon; stirred, shuddered, groaned, cracked, broke: acres heaved themselves into new mountains, other acres collapsed into canyons.

Imagine a giant asleep just under the surface of the earth, overgrown by fields, dreaming dreams of rock and crystal. Imagine him moving restlessly, the long rhythm of his dreams touched by nightmare, tossing, moaning, tremors signaling unease in waves up and down his miles-long frame. Imagine him catapulted into waking terror, lurching suddenly to his knees with the bawling roar of ten million burning calves: a steaming claw of rock and black earth raking for the sky. Now, in a wink, imagine the adjacent land hurtling downward, sinking like a rock in a pond, opening a womb a thousand feet wide, swallowing everything and grinding it to powder. Then, almost too quick to see, imagine the mountain and the crater switching, the mountain collapsing all at once and washing the feet of the older Blackfriars with a tidal wave of earth, then tumbling down to make a pit; at the same time the sinking earth at the bottom of the other crater reversing itself and erupting upward into a quaking fist of rubble. Then they switch again, and keep switching. Like watching the same filmclip continuously run forward and backward. Now multiply that by a million and spread it out so that all you can see to the horizon is a stew of humping rock. D'y'visualize it? Not a tenth of it.

Dervishes of fire stalked the chaos, melting into each other, whirlpooling. Occasionally a tactical-nuclear explosion would punch a hole in the night, a brief intense flare that would be swallowed like a candle in a murky snowstorm. Once a tacnuke detonation coincided with the upthrusting of a rubble mountain, with an effect like that of a firecracker exploding inside a swinging sack of grain.

The city itself was gone; we could no longer see a trace of anything man-made, only the stone maelstrom. The river Delva had also vanished, flash-boiled to steam; for a while we could see the gorge of its dry bed stitching across the plain, but then the ground heaved up and obliterated it.

It was unbelievable that anything could be left alive down there. Very little was. Only the remainder of the heavy weapons sections on both sides continued to survive, invisible to us in the confusion. Still protected by powerful phasewalls and scattershields, they pounded blindly at each other—the Combine somewhat ineffectively with biodeths and tacnukes, the Quaestors responding by stepping up the discontinuity projector. There was only one, in the command module—the Quaestor technicians were praying it wouldn't be wiped out by a random strike—and it was a terraforming device and not actually a "weapon" at all, but the Combine had been completely unprepared for it, and were suffering horribly as a result.

Everything began to flicker, random swatches of savannahland shimmering and blurring, phasing in and out of focus in a jerky, mismatched manner: that filmstrip run through a spastic projector. At first we thought it must be heat eddies caused by the fires, but then the flickering increased drastically in frequency and tempo, speeding up until it was impossible to keep anything in focus even for a second, turning the wide veldt into a mad kaleidoscope of writhing, interchanging shapes and color-patterns from one horizon to the other. It was impossible to watch it for long. It hurt the eyes and filled us with an oily, inexplicable panic that we were never able to verbalize. We looked away, filled with the musty surgings of vague fear.

We didn't know then that we were watching the first practical application of a process that'd long been suppressed by both the Combine and the Commonwealth, a process based on the starship dimensional "drive" (which isn't a "drive" at all, but the word's passed into the common press) that enabled a high-cycling discontinuity projector to throw time out of phase within a limited area, so that a spot *here* would be a couple of minutes ahead or behind a spot a few inches away, in continuity sequence. That explanation would give a psychophysicist fits, since "time" is really nothing at all like the way we "experience" it, so the process "really" doesn't do what I've said it does—doing something abstruse instead—but that's close enough to what it does on a practical level, 'cause even if the time distortion is an "illusionary effect"—like the sun seeming to rise and set—they still used it to kill people. So it threw time out of phase, and kept doing it, switching the dislocation at random: so that in any given square foot of land there might be four or five discrepancies in time sequence that kept interchanging. Like, *here* might be one minute "ahead" of the base "now," and then a second later (language breaks down hopelessly under this stuff; you need the math) *here* would be two minutes behind the now, then five minutes behind, then three ahead, and so on. And all the adjacent zones in that square foot are going through the same switching process at the same time (Goddamn this language!). The Combine's machinery tore itself to pieces. So did the people: some died of suffocation because of a five-minute discrepancy between an inhaled breath and oxygen received by the lungs, some drowned in their own blood.

It took about ten minutes, at least as far as we were concerned as unaffected observers. I had a psychophysicist tell me once that "it" had both continued to "happen" forever and had never "happened" at all, and that neither statement canceled out the validity of the other, that *each* statement in fact was both "applicable" and "non-applicable" to the same situation consecutively—and I did not understand. It took ten minutes.

At the end of that time, the world got very still.

We looked up. The land had stopped churning. A tiny star appeared amongst the rubble in the middle distance, small as a pinhead but incredibly bright and clear. It seemed to suck the night into it like a vortex, as if it were a pinprick through the worldstuff into a more intense reality, as if it were gathering a great breath for a shout.

We buried our heads in our arms as one, instinctively.

There was a very bright light, a light that we could feel through the tops of our heads, a light that left dazzling afterimages even through closed and shrouded lids. The mountain leaped under us, bounced us into the air again and again, battered us into near unconsciousness. We never even heard the roar.

After a while, things got quiet again, except for a continuous low rumbling. When we looked up, there were thick, sluggish tongues of molten magma oozing up in vast flows across the veldt, punctuated here and there by spectacular shower-fountains of vomited sparks.

Our scattershield had taken the brunt of the blast, borne it just long enough to save our lives, and then overloaded and burnt itself to scrap; one of the first times *that's* ever happened.

Nobody said anything. We didn't look at each other. We just lay there.

The chrono said an hour went by, but nobody was aware of it.

Finally, a couple of us got up, in silence, and started to stumble aimlessly back and forth. One by one, the rest crawled to their feet. Still in silence, still trying not to look at each other, we automatically cleaned ourselves up. You hear someone say "it made me shit my pants," and you think it's an expression; not under the right stimuli. Automatically, we treated our bruises and lacerations, automatically we tidied the camp up, buried the ruined scatterfield generator. Automatically, we sat down again and stared numbly at the lightshow on the savannah.

Each of us knew the war was over—we knew it with the gut rather than the head. It was an emotional reaction, but very calm, very resigned, very passive. It was a thing too big for questioning; it became a self-evident fact. After D'kotta there could be nothing else. Period. The war was over.

We were almost right. But not quite.

In another hour or so a man from field HQ came up over the mountain shoulder in a stolen vacform and landed in camp. The man switched off the vac, jumped down, took two steps toward the parapet overlooking hell, stopped. We saw his stomach muscles jump, tighten. He took a stumbling half-step back, then stopped again. His hand went up to shield his throat, dropped, hesitated, went back up. We said nothing. The HQ directing the D'kotta campaign had been sensibly located behind the Blackfriars: they had been shielded by the mountainchain and had seen nothing but glare against the cloud cover. This was his first look at the city; at where the city had been. I watched the muscles play in his back, saw his shoulders hunch as if under an upraised fist. A good many of the Quaestor men involved in planning the D'kotta operation committed suicide immediately after the Realignment; a good many didn't. I don't know what category this one belonged in.

The liaison man finally turned his head, dragged himself away. His movements were jerky, and his face was an odd color, but he was under control. He pulled Heynith, our team leader, aside. They talked for a half hour. The liaison man showed Heynith a map, scribbled on a pad for Heynith to see, gave Heynith some papers. Heynith nodded occasionally. The liaison man said good-by, half-ran to his vacform. The vac lifted with an erratic surge, steadied, then disappeared in a long arc over the gnarled backs of the Blackfriars. Heynith stood in the dirtswirl kicked up by the backwash and watched impassively.

It got quiet again, but it was a little more apprehensive.

Heynith came over, studied us for a while, then told us to get ready to move out. We stared at him. He repeated it in a quiet, firm voice; unendurably patient. Hush for a second, then somebody groaned, somebody else cursed, and the spell of D'kotta was partially broken, for the moment. We awoke enough to ready our gear; there was even a little talking, though not much.

Heynith appeared at our head and led us out in a loose travel formation, diagonally across the face of the slope, then up toward the shoulder. We reached the notch we'd found earlier and started down the other side.

Everyone wanted to look back at D'kotta. No one did.

Somehow, it was still night.

We never talked much on the march, of course, but tonight the silence was spooky: you could hear boots crunch on stone, the slight rasp of breath, the muted jangle of knives occasionally bumping against thighs. You could hear our fear; you could smell it, you could see it.

We could touch it, we could taste it.

I was a member of something so old that they even had to dig up the name for it when they were rooting through the rubble of ancient history, looking for concepts to use against the Combine: a "commando team." Don't ask me what it means, but that's what it's called. Come to think, I know what it means in terms of flesh: it means ugly. Long ugly days and nights that come back in your sleep even uglier, so that you don't want to think about it at all because it squeezes your eyeballs like a vise. Cold and dark and wet, with sudden death looming up out of nothing at any time and jarring you with mortality like a rubber glove full of ice water slapped across your face. Living jittery high all the time, so that everything gets so real that it looks fake. You live in an anticipation that's pain, like straddling a fence with a knifeblade for a top rung, waiting for something to come along in the dark and push you off. You get so you like it. The pain's so consistent that you forget it's there, you forget there ever was a time when you didn't have it, and you live on the adrenalin.

We liked it. We were dedicated. We *hated*. It gave us something to do with our hate, something tangible we could see. And nobody'd done it but us for hundreds of years; there was an exultation to that. The Scholars and Antiquarians who'd started the Quaestor movement—left fullsentient and relatively unwatched so they could better piece together the muddle of prehistory from generations of inherited archives—they'd been smart. They knew their only hope of baffling the Combine was to hit them with radical concepts and tactics, things they didn't have instructions for handling, things out of the Combine's experience. So they scooped concepts out of prehistory, as far back as the archives go, even finding *written* records somewhere and having to figure out how to use them.

Out of one of these things, they got the idea of "guerrilla" war. No, I don't know what that means either, but what it *means* is playing the game by your own rules instead of the enemy's. Oh, you let the enemy keep playing by *his* rules, see, but you play by your own. Gives you a wider range of moves. You *do* things. I mean, *ridiculous* things, but so ancient they don't have any defense against it because they never thought they'd have to defend against *that*. Most of the time they never even knew *that* existed.

Like, we used to run around with these projectile weapons they'd copied from old plans and mass-produced in the autfacs on the sly by stealing computer time. The things worked by a chemical reaction inside the mechanism that would spit these tiny missiles out at a high velocity. The missile would hit you so hard it would actually lodge itself in your body, puncture internal organs, kill you. I know it sounds like an absurd concept, but there were advantages.

Don't forget how tightly controlled a society the Combine's was; even worse than the Commonwealth in its own way. We couldn't just steal energy weapons or biodeths and use them, because all those things operated on broadcast power from the Combine, and as soon as one was reported missing the Combine would just cut the relay for that particular code. We couldn't make them ourselves because unless you used the Combine's broadcast power you'd need a ton of generator equipment with each weapon to provide enough energy to operate it, and we didn't have the technology to miniaturize that much machinery. (Later some genius figured out a way to make, say, a functioning biodeth with everything but the energy source and then cut into and tap Combine broadcast power without showing up on the coding board, but that was toward the end anyway, and most of them were stockpiled for the shock troops at D'kotta.) At least the "guns" worked. And there were even unexpected advantages. We found that tanglefields, scattershields, phasewalls, personal warders, all the usual defenses, were unable to stop the "bullets" (the little missiles fired by the "guns")—they were just too sophisticated to stop anything as crude as a lump of metal moving at relatively sluggish ballistic speeds. Same with "bombs" and "grenades"—devices designed to have a chemical reaction violent enough to kill in an enclosed place. And the list went on and on. The Combine thought we couldn't move around because all vehicles were coded and worked on broadcast power. Did you ever hear of "bicycles"? They're devices for translating mechanical energy into motion, they ride on wheels that you actually make revolve with physical labor. And the bicycles didn't have enough metal/mass to trigger sentryfields or show up on sweep probes, so we could go undetected to places they thought nobody could reach. Communicate? We used mirrors to flash messages, used puffs of smoke as code, had people actually carry messages from one place to another.

More important, we personalized war. That was the most radical thing, that was the thing that turned us from kids running around and having fun breaking things into men with bitter faces, that was the thing that took the heart out of the Combine more than anything else. That's why people still talk about the Realignment with horror today, even after all these years, especially in the Commonwealth.

We killed people. We did it, ourselves. We walked up and stabbed them. I mentioned a knife before, boy, and I knew you didn't know what it was; you bluff well for a kid —that's the way to a reputation for wisdom: look sage and always keep your mouth shut about your ignorance. Well, a knife is a tapering piece of metal with a handle, sharpened on the sides and very sharp at the tapered end, sharp enough so that when you strike someone with it the metal goes right into their flesh, cuts them, rips them open, *kills* them, and there is blood on your hands which feels wet and sticky and is hard to wash off because it dries and sticks to the little hairs on the backs of your wrists. We learned how to hit people hard enough to kill them, snap the bones inside the skin like dry sticks inside oiled cloth. We did. We strangled them with lengths of wire. You're shocked. So was the Combine. They had grown used to killing at a great distance, the push of a button, the flick of a switch, using vast, clean, impersonal forces to do their annihilation. *We* killed people. We killed *people*—not statistics and abstractions. We heard their screams, we saw their faces, we smelled their blood, and their vomit and shit and urine when their systems let go after death. You have to be crazy to do things like that. We were crazy. We were a good team.

There were twelve of us in the group, although we mostly worked in sections of four. I was in the team leader's section, and it had been my family for more than two years:

Heynith, stocky, balding, leatherfaced; a hard, fair man; brilliant organizer.

Ren, impassive, withdrawn, taciturn, frighteningly competent, of a strange humor.

Goth, young, tireless, bullheaded, given to sudden enthusiasms and depressions; he'd only been with us for about four months, a replacement for Mason, who had been killed while trying to escape from a raid on Cape Itica.

And me.

We were all warped men, emotional cripples one way or the other.

We were all crazy.

The Combine could never understand that kind of craziness, in spite of the millions of people they'd killed or shriveled impersonally over the years. They were afraid of that craziness, they were baffled by it, never could plan to counter it or take it into account. They couldn't really believe it.

That's how we'd taken the Blackfriars Transmitter, hours before D'kotta. It had been impregnable—wrapped in layer after layer of defense fields against missile attack, attack by chemical or biological agents, transmitted energy, almost anything. We'd walked in. They'd never imagined anyone would do that, that it was even possible to attack that way, so there was no defense against it. The guardsystems were designed to meet more esoteric threats. And even after ten years of slowly escalating guerrilla action, they still didn't *really* believe anyone would use his body to wage war. So we walked in. And killed everybody there. The staff was a sentient techclone of ten and an executive foreman. No nulls or zombies. The ten identical technicians milled in panic, the foreman stared at us in disbelief, and what I think was distaste that we'd gone so far outside the bounds of procedure. We killed them like you kill insects, not really thinking about it much, except for that part of you that always thinks about it, that records it and replays it while you sleep. Then we blew up the transmitter with chemical explosives. Then, as the flames leaped up and ate holes in the night, we'd gotten on our bicycles and rode like hell toward the Blackfriars, the mountains hunching and looming ahead, as jagged as black snaggle-teeth against the industrial glare of the sky. A tanglefield had snatched at us for a second, but then we were gone.

That's all that I personally had to do with the "historic" Battle of D'kotta. It was enough. We'd paved the way for the whole encounter. Without the Transmitter's energy, weapons, and transportation systems—including liftshafts, slidewalks, irisdoors, and windows, heating, lighting, waste disposal—were inoperable; D'kotta was immobilized. Without the station's broadcast matter, thousands of buildings, industrial complexes, roadways, and homes had collapsed into chaos, literally collapsed. More important, without broadcast nourishment, D'kotta's four major Cerebrums—handling an incredible complexity of military/industrial/administrative tasks—were knocked out of operation, along with a number of smaller Cerebrums—the synapses need constant nourishment to function, and so do the sophont ganglion units, along with the constant flow of the psychocybernetic current to keep them from going mad from sensory deprivation, and even the nulls would soon grow intractable as hunger stung them almost to self-awareness, finally to die after a few days. Any number of the lowest-ranking sentient clones—all those without stomachs or digestive systems; mostly in the military and industrial castes—would find themselves in the same position as the nulls; without broadcast nourishment they would die within days. And without catarcs in operation to duplicate the function of atrophied intestines, the build-up of body wastes would poison them anyway, even if they could somehow get nourishment. The independent food dispensers for the smaller percentage of fullsentients and higher clones simply could not increase their output enough to feed that many people, even if converted to intravenous systems. To say nothing of the zombies in the Environments scattered throughout the city.

There were backup failsafe systems, of course, but they hadn't been used in centuries, the majority of them had fallen into disrepair and didn't work, and other Quaestor teams made sure the rest of them wouldn't work either.

Before a shot had been fired, D'kotta was already a major disaster.

The Combine had reacted as we'd hoped, as they'd been additionally prompted to react by intelligence reports of Quaestor massings in strength around D'kotta that it'd taken weeks to leak to the Combine from unimpeachable sources. The Combine was pouring forces into D'kotta within hours, nearly the full strength of the traditional military caste and a large percentage of the militia they'd cobbled together out of industrial clones when the Quaestors had begun to get seriously troublesome, plus a major portion of their heavy armament. They had hoped to surprise the Quaestors, catch them between the city and the inaccessible portion of the Blackfriars, quarter the area with so much strength it'd be impossible to dodge them, run the Quaestors down, annihilate them, break the back of the movement.

It had worked the other way around.

For years the Quaestors had stung and run, always retreating when the Combine advanced, never meeting them in conventional battle, never hitting them with anything really heavy. Then, when the Combine had risked practically all of its millitary resources on one gigantic effort calculated to be effective against the usual Quaestor behavior, we had suddenly switched tactics. The Quaestors had waited to meet the Combine's advance and had hit the Combine forces with everything they'd been able to save, steal, hoard, and buy clandestinely from sympathizers in the Commonwealth in over fifteen years of conspiracy and campaign aimed at this moment.

Within an hour of the first tacnuke exchange, the city had ceased to exist, everything leveled except two of the Cerebrums and the Escridel Creche. Then the Quaestors activated their terraforming devices, which I believe they bought from a firm here on Kos, as a matter of fact. This was completely insane—terraforming systems used indiscriminately can destroy entire planets—but it was the insanity of desperation, and they did it anyway. Within a half hour, the remaining Combine Heavy Armaments battalions and the two Cerebrums ceased to exist. A few minutes later, the supposedly invulnerable Escridel Creche ceased to exist, the first time in history a creche had ever been destroyed. Then, as the cycling energies got out of hand and filterfeedback built to a climax, everything on the veldt ceased to exist.

The carnage had been inconceivable.

Take the vast population of D'kotta as a base, the second largest city on World, one of the biggest even in this sector of the Commonwealth. The subfleets had been in, bringing the betja harvest and other goods up the Delva; river traffic was always heaviest at that time of year. The mines and factories had been in full swing, and the giant sprawl of the Westernese Shipyards and Engine Works. Add the swarming inhabitants of the six major Controlled Environments that circled the city. Add the city-within-a-city of Admin South, in charge of that hemisphere. Add the twenty generations of D'kotta Combine fullsentients whose discorporate ego-patterns had been preserved in the mountain of "indestructible" micromolecular circuitry called the Escridel Creche. (Those executives had died the irreversible true death, without hope of resurrection this time, even as disembodied intellects housed within artificial mind-environments: the records of their brain's unique pattern of electrical/chemical/psychocybernetic rhythms and balances had been destroyed, and you can't rebuild consciousness from a fused puddle of slag. This hit the Combine where they lived, literally, and had more impact than anything else.) Add the entire strength of both opposing forces; all of our men—who suspected what would happen —had been suicide volunteers. Add all of the elements together.

The total goes up into the multiples of billions.

The number was too big to grasp. Our minds fumbled at it while we marched, and gave up. It was too big.

I stared at Ren's back as we walked, a nearly invisible mannequin silhouette, and tried to multiply that out to the necessary figure. I staggered blindly along, lost and inundated beneath thousands of individual arms, legs, faces; a row of faces blurring off into infinity, all screaming—and the imagining nowhere near the actuality.

Billions.

How many restless ghosts out of that many deaders? Who do they haunt?

Billions.

Dawn caught us about two hours out. It came with no warning, as usual. We were groping through World's ink-dark, moonless night, watched only by the million icy eyes of evening, shreds of witchfire crystal, incredibly cold and distant. I'd watched them night after night for years, scrawling their indecipherable hieroglyphics across the sky, indifferent to man's incomprehension; now, as always, the night sky reminded me of a computer punch card, printed white on black. I stopped for a second on a rise, pushing back the infrared lenses, staring at the sky. What program was printed there, suns for ciphers, worlds for decimal points? An absurd question—I was nearly as foolish as you once, buck—but it was the first fully verbalized thought I'd had since I'd realized the nakedness of flesh, back there on the parapet as my life tore itself apart. I asked it again, half-expecting an answer, watching my breath turn to plumes and tatters, steaming in the silver chill of the stars.

The sun came up like a meteor. It scuttled up from the horizon with that unsettling, deceptive speed that even natives of World never quite get used to. New light washed around us, blue and raw at first, deepening the shadows and honing their edges. The sun continued to hitch itself up the sky, swallowing stars, a watery pink flush wiping the horizon clear of night. The light deepened, mellowed into gold. We floated through silver mist that swirled up around the mountain's knobby knees. I found myself crying silently as I walked the high ridge between mist and sky, absorbing the morning with a new hunger, grappling with a thought that was still too big for my mind and kept slipping elusively away, just out of reach. There was a low hum as our warmsuits adjusted to the growing warmth, polarizing from black to white, bleeding heat back into the air. Down the flanks of the Blackfriars and away across the valley below —visible now as the mists pirouetted past us to the summits —the night plants were dying, shriveling visibly in mile-long swaths of decay. In seconds the Blackfriars were gaunt and barren, turned to hills of ash and bone. The sun was now a bloated yellow disk surrounded by haloes of red and deepening scarlet, shading into the frosty blue of rarefied air. Stripped of softening vegetation, the mountains looked rough and abrasive as pumice, gouged by lunar shadows. The first of the day plants began to appear at our feet, the green spiderwebbing, poking up through cracks in the dry earth.

We came across a new stream, tumbling from melting ice, sluicing a dusty gorge.

An hour later we found the valley.

Heynith led us down onto the marshy plain that rolled away from mountains to horizon. We circled wide, cautiously approaching the valley from the lowlands. Heynith held up his hand, pointed to me, Ren, Goth. The others fanned out across the mouth of the valley, hid, settled down to wait. We went in alone. The speargrass had grown rapidly; it was chest-high. We crawled in, timing our movements to coincide with the long soughing of the morning breeze, so that any rippling of the grass would be taken for natural movement. It took us about a half hour of dusty, sweaty work. When I judged that I'd wormed my way in close enough, I stopped, slowly parted the speargrass enough to peer out without raising my head.

It was a large vacvan, five-hundred-footer, equipped with waldoes for self-loading.

It was parked near the hill flank on the side of the wide valley.

There were three men with it.

I ducked back into the grass, paused to make sure my "gun" was ready for operation, then crawled laboriously nearer to the van.

It was very near when I looked up again, about twenty-five feet away in the center of a cleared space. I could make out the hologram pictograph that pulsed identification on the side: the symbol for Urheim, World's largest city and Combine Seat of Board, half a world away in the Northern Hemisphere. They'd come a long way; still thought of as long, though ships whispered between the stars—it was still long for feet and eyes. And another longer way: from fetuses in glass wombs tò men stamping and jiggling with cold inside the fold of a mountain's thigh, watching the spreading morning. That made me feel funny to think about. I wondered if they suspected that it'd be the last morning they'd ever see. That made me feel funnier. The thought tickled my mind again, danced away. I checked my gun a second time, needlessly.

I waited, feeling troubled, pushing it down. Two of them were standing together several feet in front of the van, sharing a mild narcotic atomizer, sucking deeply, shuffling with restlessness and cold, staring out across the speargrass to where the plain opened up. They had the stiff, rumpled, puff-eyed look of people who had just spent an uncomfortable night in a cramped place. They were dressed as full-sentients uncloned, junior officers of the military caste, probably hereditary positions inherited from their families, as is the case with most of the uncloned cadet executives. Except for the cadre at Urheim and other major cities, they must have been some of the few surviving clansmen; hundreds of thousands of military cadets and officers had died at D'kotta (along with uncounted clones and semisentients of all ranks), and the caste had never been extremely large in the first place. The by-laws had demanded that the Combine maintain a Security Force, but it had become mostly traditional with minimum function, at least among the un-cloned higher ranks, almost the last stronghold of old-fashioned nepotism. That was one of the things that had favored the Quaestor uprising, and had forced the Combine to take the unpopular step of impressing large levies of industrial clones into a militia. The most junior of these two cadets was very young, even younger than me. The third man remained inside the van's cab. I could see his face blurrily through the windfield, kept on against the cold though the van was no longer in motion.

I waited. I knew the others were maneuvering into position around me. I also knew what Heynith was waiting for.

The third man jumped down from the high cab. He was older, wore an officer's hologram: a full executive. He said something to the cadets, moved a few feet toward the back of the van, started to take a piss. The column of golden liquid steamed in the cold air.

Heynith whistled.

I rolled to my knees, parted the speargrass at the edge of the cleared space, swung my gun up. The two cadets started, face muscles tensing into uncertain fear. The older cadet took an involuntary step forward, still clutching the atomizer. Ren and Goth chopped him down, firing a stream of "bullets" into him. The guns made a very loud metallic rattling sound that jarred the teeth, and fire flashed from the ejector ends. Birds screamed upward all along the mountain flank. The impact of the bullets knocked the cadet off his feet, rolled him so that he came to rest belly-down. The atomizer flew through the air, hit, bounced. The younger cadet leaped toward the cab, right into my line of fire. I pulled the trigger; bullets exploded out of the gun. The cadet was kicked backwards, arms swinging wide, slammed against the side of the cab, jerked upright as I continued to fire, spun along the van wall and rammed heavily into the ground. He tottered on one shoulder for a second, then flopped over onto his back. At the sound of the first shot, the executive had whirled—penis still dangling from pantaloons, piss spraying wildly—and dodged for the back of the van, so that Heynith's volley missed and screamed from the van wall, leaving a long scar. The executive dodged again, crouched, came up with a biodeth in one hand and swung right into a single bullet from Ren just as he began to fire. The impact twirled him in a staggering circle, his finger still pressing the trigger; the carrier beam splashed harmlessly from the van wall, traversed as the executive spun, cut a long swath through the speargrass, the plants shriveling and blackening as the beam swept over them. Heynith opened up again before the beam could reach his clump of grass, sending the executive—somehow still on his feet—lurching past the end of the van. The biodeth dropped, went out. Heynith kept firing, the executive dancing bonelessly backwards on his heels, held up by the stream of bullets. Heynith released the trigger. The executive collapsed: a heap of arms and legs at impossible angles.

When we came up to the van, the young cadet was still dying. His body shivered and arched, his heels drummed against the earth, his fingers plucked at nothing, and then he was still. There was a lot of blood.

The others moved up from the valley mouth. Heynith sent them circling around the rim, where the valley walls dipped down on three sides.

We dragged the bodies away and concealed them in some large rocks.

I was feeling numb again, like I had after D'kotta.

I continued to feel numb as we spent the rest of that morning in frantic preparation. My mind was somehow detached as my body sweated and dug and hauled. There was a lot for it to do. We had four heavy industrial lasers, rock-cutters; they were clumsy, bulky, inefficient things to use as weapons, but they'd have to do. This mission had not been planned so much as thrown together, only two hours before the liaison man had contacted us on the parapet. Anything that could possibly work at all would have to be made to work somehow; no time to do it right, just do it. We'd been the closest team in contact with the field HQ who'd received the report, so we'd been snatched; the lasers were the only things on hand that could even approach potential as a heavy weapon, so we'd use the lasers.

Now that we'd taken the van without someone alerting the Combine by radio from the cab, Heynith flashed a signal mirror back toward the shoulder of the mountain we'd quitted a few hours before. The liaison man swooped down ten minutes later, carrying one of the lasers strapped awkwardly to his platvac. He made three more trips, depositing the massive cylinders as carefully as eggs, then gunned his platvac and screamed back toward the Blackfriars in a maniac arc just this side of suicidal. His face was still gray, tight-pressed lips a bloodless white against ash, and he hadn't said a word during the whole unloading procedure. I think he was probably one of the Quaestors who followed the Way of Atonement. I never saw him again. I've sometimes wished I'd had the courage to follow his example, but I rationalize by telling myself that I have atoned with my life rather than my death, and who knows, it might even be somewhat true. It's nice to think so anyway.

It took us a couple of hours to get the lasers into position. We spotted them in four places around the valley walls, dug slanting pits into the slopes to conceal them and tilt the barrels up at the right angle. The hardest thing was figuring out elevation and trajectory, but we finally got them all zeroed on a spot about a hundred feet above the center of the valley floor, the muzzle arrangement giving each a few degrees of leeway on either side. That's where she'd have to come down anyway if she was a standard orbot, the valley being just wide enough to contain the boat and the vacvan, with a safety margin between them. Of course, if they brought her down on the plain outside the valley mouth, things were going to get very hairy; in that case we might be able to lever one or two of the lasers around to bear, or, failing that, we could try to take the orbot on foot once it'd landed, with about one chance in eight of making it. But we thought that they'd land her in the valley; that's where the vacvan had been parked, and they'd want the shelter of the high mountain walls to conceal the orbot from any

Quaestor eyes that might be around. If so, that gave us a much better chance. About one out of three.

When the lasers had been positioned, we scattered, four men to an emplacement, hiding in the camouflaged trenches alongside the big barrels. Heynith led Goth and me toward the laser we'd placed about fifty feet up the mountain flank, directly behind and above the vacvan. Ren stayed behind. He stood next to the van—shoulders characteristically slouched, thumbs hooked in his belt, face carefully void of expression—and watched us out of sight. Then he looked out over the valley mouth, hitched up his gun, spat in the direction of Urheim and climbed up into the van cab.

The valley was empty again. From our position the vacvan looked like a shiny toy, sundogs winking across its surface as it baked in the afternoon heat. An abandoned toy, lost in high weeds, waiting in loneliness to be reclaimed by owners who would never come.

Time passed.

The birds we'd frightened away began to settle back onto the hillsides.

I shifted position uneasily, trying half-heartedly to get comfortable. Heynith glared me into immobility. We were crouched in a trench about eight feet long and five feet deep, covered by a camouflage tarpaulin propped open on the valley side by pegs, a couple of inches of vegetation, and topsoil on top of the tarpaulin. Heynith was in the middle, straddling the operator's saddle of the laser. Goth was on his left, I was on his right. Heynith was going to man the laser when the time came; it only took one person. There was nothing for Goth and me to do, would be nothing to do even during the ambush, except take over the firing in the unlikely event that Heynith was killed without the shot wiping out all of us, or stand by to lever the laser around in case that became necessary. Neither was very likely to happen. No, it was Heynith's show, and we were superfluous and unoccupied.

That was bad.

We had a lot of time to think.

That was worse.

I was feeling increasingly numb, like a wall of clear glass had been slipped between me and the world and was slowly thickening, layer by layer. With the thickening came an incredible isolation (isolation though I was cramped and suffocating, though I was jammed up against Heynith's bunched thigh—I couldn't touch him, he was miles away) and with the isolation came a sick, smothering panic. It was the inverse of claustrophobia. My flesh had turned to clear plastic, my bones to glass, and I was naked, ultimately naked, and there was nothing I could wrap me in. Surrounded by an army, I would still be alone; shrouded in iron thirty feet underground, I would still be naked. One portion of my mind wondered dispassionately if I were slipping into shock; the rest of it fought to keep down the scream that gathered along tightening muscles. The isolation increased. I was unaware of my surroundings, except for the heat and the pressure of enclosure.

I was seeing the molten spider of D'kotta, lying on its back and showing its obscene blotched belly, kicking legs of flame against the sky, each leg raising a poison blister where it touched the clouds.

I was seeing the boy, face runneled by blood, beating heels against the ground.

I was beginning to doubt big, simple ideas.

Nothing moved in the valley except wind through grass, spirits circling in the form of birds.

Spider legs.

Crab dance.

The blocky shadow of the vacvan crept across the valley.

Suddenly, with the intensity of vision, I was picturing Ren sitting in the van cab, shoulders resting against the door, legs stretched out along the seat, feet propped up on the instrument board, one ankle crossed over the other, gun resting across his lap, eyes watching the valley mouth through the windfield. He would be smoking a cigarette, and he would take it from his lips occasionally, flick the ashes onto the shiny dials with a fingernail, smile his strange smile, and carefully burn holes in the plush fabric of the upholstery. The fabric (real fabric; not plastic) would smolder, send out a wisp of bad-smelling smoke, and there would be another charred black hole in the seat. Ren would smile again, put the cigarette back in his mouth, lean back, and puff slowly. Ren was waiting to answer the radio signal from the orbot, to assure them that all was well, to talk them down to death. If they suspected anything was wrong, he would be the first to die. Even if everything went perfectly, he stood a high chance of dying anyway; he was the most exposed. It was almost certainly a suicide job. Ren said that he didn't give a shit; maybe he actually didn't. Or at least had convinced himself that he didn't. He was an odd man. Older than any of us, even Heynith, he had worked most of his life as a cadet executive in Admin at Urheim, devoted his existence to his job, subjugated all of his energies to it. He had been passed over three times for promotion to executive status, years of redoubled effort and mounting anxiety between each rejection. With the third failure he had been quietly retired to live on the credit subsidy he had earned with forty years of service. The next morning, precisely at the start of his accustomed work period, he stole a biodeth from a security guard in the Admin Complex, walked into his flowsector, killed everyone there, and disappeared from Urheim. After a year on the run, he had managed to contact the Quaestors. After another year of training, he was serving with a commando team in spite of his age. That had been five years ago; I had known him for two. During all that time, he had said little. He did his job very well with a minimum of waste motion, never made mistakes, never complained, never showed emotion. But occasionally he would smile and burn a hole in something. Or someone.

The sun dived at the horizon, seeming to crash into the plain in an explosion of flame. Night swallowed us in one gulp. Black as a beast's belly.

It jerked me momentarily back into reality. I had a bad moment when I thought I'd gone blind, but then reason returned and I slipped the infrared lenses down over my eyes, activated them. The world came back in shades of gray.

Heynith was working cramped legs against the body of the laser. He spoke briefly, and we gulped some stimulus pills to keep us awake; they were bitter, and hard to swallow dry as usual, but they kicked up a familiar acid churning in my stomach, and blood began to flow faster. I glanced at Heynith. He'd been quiet, even for Heynith. I wondered what he'd been thinking. He looked at me, perhaps reading the thought, and ordered us out of the trench.

Goth and I crawled slowly out, feeling stiff and brittle, slapped our thighs and arms, stamped to restore circulation. Stars were sprinkling across the sky, salt spilled on black porcelain. I still couldn't read them, I found. The day plants had vanished, the day animals had retreated into catalepsy. The night plants were erupting from the ground, fed by the debris of the day plants. They grew rapidly, doubling, then tripling in height as we watched. They were predominately thick, ropy shrubs with wide, spearhead leaves of dull purple and black, about four feet high. Goth and I dug a number of them up, root-systems intact, and placed them on top of the tarpaulin to replace the day plants that had shriveled with the first touch of bitter evening frost. We had to handle them with padded gloves; the leaf surfaces greedily absorbed the slightest amount of heat and burned like dry ice.

Then we were back in the trench, and it was worse than ever. Motion had helped for a while, but I could feel the numbing panic creeping back, and the momentary relief made it even harder to bear. I tried to start a conversation, but it died in monosyllabic grunts, and silence sopped up the echoes. Heynith was methodically checking the laser controls for the nth time. He was tense; I could see it bunch his shoulder muscles, bulge his calves into rock as they pushed against the footplates of the saddle. Goth looked worse than I did; he was somewhat younger, and usually energetic and cheerful. Not tonight.

We should have talked, spread the pain around; I think all of us realized it. But we couldn't; we were made awkward by our own special intimacy. At one time or another every one of us had reached a point where he *had* to talk or

die, even Heynith, even Ren. So we all had talked and all
had listened, each of us switching roles sooner or later. We
had poured our fears and dreams and secret memories
upon each other, until now we knew each other too well.
It made us afraid. Each of us was afraid that he had exposed too much, let down too many barriers. We were
afraid of vulnerability, of the knife that jabs for the softest
fold of the belly. We were all scarred men already, and
twice-shy. And the resentment grew that others had seen
us that helpless, that vulnerable. So the walls went back up,
intensified. And so when we needed to talk again, we could
not. We were already too close to risk further intimacy.

Visions returned, ebbing and flowing, overlaying the
darkness.

The magma churning, belching a hot breath that stinks
of rotten eggs.

The cadet, his face inhuman in the death rictus, blood
running down in a wash from his smashed forehead, plas-
tering one eye closed, bubbling at his nostril, frothing
around his lips, the lips tautening as his head jerks forward
and then backwards, slamming the ground, the lips then
growing slack, the body slumping, the mouth sagging open,
the rush of blood and phlegm past the tombstone teeth,
down the chin and neck, soaking into the fabric of the
tunic. The feet drumming at the ground a final time, digging up clots of earth.

I groped for understanding. I had killed people before,
and it had not bothered me except in sleep. I had done it
mechanically, routine backed by hate, hate cushioned by
routine. I wondered if the night would ever end. I remembered the morning I'd watched from the mountain. I didn't
think the night would end. A big idea tickled my mind
again.

The city swallowed by stone.

The cadet falling, swinging his arms wide.

Why always the cadet and the city in conjunction? Had
one sensitized me to the other, and if so, which? I hesitated.

Could both of them be equally important?

One of the other section leaders whistled.

We all started, somehow grew even more tense. The whistle came again, warbling, sound floating on silence like oil on water. Someone was coming. After a while we heard a rustling and snapping of underbrush approaching downslope from the mountain. Whoever it was, he was making no effort to move quietly. In fact he seemed to be blundering along, bulling through the tangles, making a tremendous thrashing noise. Goth and I turned in the direction of the sound, brought our guns up to bear, primed them. That was instinct. I wondered who could be coming *down* the mountain toward us. That was reason. Heynith twisted to cover the opposite direction, away from the noise, resting his gun on the saddle rim. That was caution. The thrasher passed our position about six feet away, screened by the shrubs. There was an open space ten feet farther down, at the head of a talus bluff that slanted to the valley. We watched it. The shrubs at the edge of the clearing shook, were torn aside. A figure stumbled out into starlight.

It was a null.

Goth sucked in a long breath, let it hiss out between his teeth. Heynith remained impassive, but I could imagine his eyes narrowing behind the thick lenses. My mind was totally blank for about three heartbeats, then, surprised: a null! and I brought the gun barrel up, then, uncomprehending: a null? and I lowered the muzzle. Blank for a second, then: how? and trickling in again: how? Thoughts snarled into confusion, the gun muzzle wavered hesitantly.

The null staggered across the clearing, weaving in slow figure-eights. It almost fell down the talus bluff, one foot suspended uncertainly over the drop, then lurched away, goaded by tropism. The null shambled backward a few paces, stopped, swayed, then slowly sank to its knees.

It kneeled: head bowed, arms limp along the ground, palms up.

Heynith put his gun back in his lap, shook his head. He told us he'd be damned if he could figure out where it came from, but we'd have to get rid of it. It could spoil the ambush if it was spotted. Automatically, I raised my gun, trained it. Heynith stopped me. No noise, he said, not now. He told Goth to go out and kill it silently.

Goth refused. Heynith stared at him speechlessly, then began to flush. Goth and Heynith had had trouble before. Goth was a good man, brave as a bull, but he was stubborn, tended to follow his own lead too much, had too many streaks of sentimentality and touchiness, *thought* too much to be a really efficient cog.

They had disagreed from the beginning, something that wouldn't have been tolerated this long if the Quaestors hadn't been desperate for men. Goth was a devil in a fight when aroused, one of the best, and that had excused him a lot of obstinacy. But he had a curious squeamishness, he hadn't developed the layers of numbing scar-tissue necessary for guerrilla work, and that was almost inevitably fatal. I'd wondered before, dispassionately, how long he would last.

Goth was a hereditary fullsentient, one of the few connected with the Quaestors. He'd been a cadet executive in Admin, gained access to old archives that had slowly soured him on the Combine, been hit at the psychologically right moment by increasing Quaestor agitprop, and had defected; after a two-year proving period, he'd been allowed to participate actively. Goth was one of the only field people who was working out of idealism rather than hate, and that made us distrust him. Heynith also nurtured a traditional dislike for hereditary fullsentients. Heynith had been part of an industrial sixclone for over twenty years before joining the Quaestors. His Six had been wiped out in a production accident, caused by standard Combine negligence. Heynith had been the only survivor. The Combine had expressed mild sympathy, and told him that they planned to cut another clone from him to replace the destroyed Six; he of course would be placed in charge of the new Six, by reason of his seniority. They smiled at him, not seeing any reason why he wouldn't want to work another twenty years with biological replicas of his dead brothers and sisters, the men, additionally, reminders of what he'd been as a youth, unravaged by

years of pain. Heynith had thanked them politely, walked
out and kept walking, crossing the Voninx Waste on foot
to join the Quaestors.

I could see all this working in Heynith's face as he
raged at Goth. Goth could feel the hate too, but he stood
firm. The null was incapable of doing anybody any harm;
he wasn't going to kill it. There'd been enough slaughter.
Goth's face was bloodless, and I could see D'kotta reflected
in his eyes, but I felt no sympathy for him, in spite of my
own recent agonies. He was disobeying orders. I thought
about Mason, the man Goth had replaced, the man who
had died in my arms at Itica, and I hated Goth for being
alive instead of Mason. I had loved Mason. He'd been an
Antiquarian in the Urheim archives, and he'd worked for
the Quaestors almost from the beginning, years of vital
service before his activities were discovered by the Combine. He'd escaped the raid, but his family hadn't. He'd
been offered an admin job in Quaestor HQ, but had
turned it down and insisted on field work in spite of
warnings that it was suicidal for a man of his age. Mason
had been a tall, gentle, scholarly man who pretended to
be gruff and hard-nosed, and cried alone at night when he
thought nobody could see. I'd often thought that he could
have escaped from Itica if he'd tried harder, but he'd been
worn down, sick and guilt-ridden and tired, and his heart
hadn't really been in it; that thought had returned to
puzzle me often afterward. Mason had been the only
person I'd ever cared about, the one who'd been more
responsible than anybody for bringing me out of the
shadows and into humanity, and I could have shot Goth at
that moment because I thought he was betraying Mason's
memory.

Heynith finally ran out of steam, spat at Goth, started
to call him something, then stopped and merely glared at
him, lips white. I'd caught Heynith's quick glance at me,
a nearly invisible head-turn, just before he'd fallen silent.
He'd almost forgotten and called Goth a zombie, a wide-
spread expletive on World that had carefully not been
used by the team since I'd joined. So Heynith had never

really forgotten, though he'd treated me with scrupulous fairness. My fury turned to a cold anger, widened out from Goth to become a sick distaste for the entire world.

Heynith told Goth he would take care of him later, take care of him good, and ordered me to go kill the null, take him upslope and out of sight first, then conceal the body.

Mechanically, I pulled myself out of the trench, started downslope toward the clearing. Anger fueled me for the first few feet, and I slashed the shrubs aside with padded gloves, but it ebbed quickly, leaving me hollow and numb. I'd known how the rest of the team must actually think of me, but somehow I'd never allowed myself to admit it. Now I'd had my face jammed in it, and coming on top of all the other anguish I'd gone through the last two days, it was too much.

I pushed into the clearing.

My footsteps triggered some response in the null. It surged drunkenly to its feet, arms swinging limply, and turned to face me.

The null was slightly taller than me, built very slender, and couldn't have weighed too much more than a hundred pounds. It was bald, completely hairless. The fingers were shriveled, limp flesh dangling from the club of the hand; they had never been used. The toes had been developed to enable technicians to walk nulls from one section of the Cerebrum to another, but the feet had never had a chance to toughen or grow callus: they were a mass of blood and lacerations. The nose was a rough blob of pink meat around the nostrils, the ears similarly atrophied. The eyes were enormous, huge milky corneas and small pupils, like those of a nocturnal bird; adapted to the gloom of the Cerebrum, and allowed to function to forestall sensory deprivation; they aren't cut into the psychocybernetic current like the synapses or the ganglions. There were small messy wounds on the temples, wrists, and spine-base where electrodes had been torn loose. It had been shrouded in a pajamalike suit of non-conductive material, but that had been torn almost completely away, only a few hanging tatters remaining. There were no sex organs. The flesh under the rib-cage was curiously collapsed; no stomach or digestive tract. The body was covered with bruises, cuts, gashes, extensive swatches sun-baked to second-degree burns, other sections seriously frostbitten or marred by bad coldburns from the night shrubs.

My awe grew, deepened into archetypical dread.

It was from D'kotta, there could be no doubt about it. Somehow it had survived the destruction of its Cerebrum, somehow it had walked through the boiling hell to the foothills, somehow it had staggered up to and over the mountain shoulder. I doubted if there'd been any predilection in its actions: probably it had just walked blindly away from the ruined Cerebrum in a straight line and kept walking. Its actions with the talus bluff demonstrated that; maybe earlier some dim instinct had helped it fumble its way around obstacles in its path, but now it was exhausted, baffled, stymied. It was miraculous that it had made it this far. And the agony it must have suffered on its way was inconceivable. I shivered, spooked. The short hairs bristled on the back of my neck.

The null lurched toward me.

I whimpered and sprang backwards, nearly falling, swinging up the gun.

The null stopped, its head lolling, describing a slow semicircle. Its eyes were tracking curiously, and I doubted if it could focus on me at all. To it, I must have been a blur of darker gray.

I tried to steady my ragged breathing. It couldn't hurt me; it was harmless, nearly dead anyway. Slowly, I lowered the gun, pried my fingers from the stock, slung the gun over my shoulder.

I edged cautiously toward it. The null swayed, but remained motionless. Below, I could see the vacvan at the bottom of the bluff, a patch of dull gunmetal sheen. I stretched my hand out slowly. The null didn't move. This close, I could see its gaunt ribs rising and falling with the effort of its ragged breathing. It was trembling, an occasional convulsive spasm shuddering along its frame. I was surprised that it didn't stink; nulls were rumored to have a strong personal odor, at least according to the talk in field camps—bullshit, like so much of my knowledge at that time. I watched it for a minute, fascinated, but my training told me I couldn't stand out here for long; we were too exposed. I took another step, reached out for it, hesitated. I didn't want to touch it. Swallowing my distaste, I selected a spot on its upper arm free of burns or wounds, grabbed it firmly with one hand.

The null jerked at the touch, but made no attempt to strike out or get away. I waited warily for a second, ready to turn my grip into a wrestling hold if it should try to attack. It remained still, but its flesh crawled under my fingers, and I shivered myself in reflex. Satisfied that the null would give me no trouble, I turned and began to force it upslope, pushing it ahead of me.

It followed my shove without resistance, until we hit the first of the night shrubs, then it staggered and made a mewing, inarticulate sound. The plants were burning it, sucking warmth out of its flesh, raising fresh welts, ugly where bits of skin had adhered to the shrubs. I shrugged, pushed it forward. It mewed and lurched again. I stopped. The null's eyes tracked in my direction, and it whimpered to itself in pain. I swore at myself for wasting time, but moved ahead to break a path for the null, dragging it along behind me. The branches slapped harmlessly at my warmsuit as I bent them aside; occasionally one would slip past and lash the null, making it flinch and whimper, but it was spared the brunt of it. I wondered vaguely at my motives for doing it. Why bother to spare someone (some*thing,* I corrected nervously) pain when you're going to have to kill him (*it*) in a minute? What difference could it make? I shelved that and concentrated on the movements of my body; the null wasn't heavy, but it wasn't easy to drag it uphill either, especially as it'd stumble and go down every few yards and I'd have to pull it back to its feet again. I was soon sweating, but I didn't care, as the action helped to occupy my mind, and I didn't want to have to face the numbness I could feel taking over again.

We moved upslope until we were about thirty feet above the trench occupied by Heynith and Goth. This looked like a good place. The shrubs were almost chest-high here, tall enough to hide the null's body from an aerial search. I stopped. The null bumped blindly into me, leaned against me, its breath coming in rasps next to my ear. I shivered in horror at the contact. Gooseflesh blossomed on my arms and legs, swept across my body. Some connection sent a memory whispering at my mind, but I ignored it under the threat of rising panic. I twisted my shoulder under the null's weight, threw it off. The null slid back downslope a few feet, almost fell, recovered.

I watched it, panting. The memory returned, gnawing incessantly. This time it got through:

Mason scrambling through the sea-washed rocks of Cape Itica toward the waiting ramsub, while the fire sky-whipping behind picked us out against the shadows; Mason, too slow in vaulting over a stone ridge, balancing too long on the razor-edge in perfect silhouette against the night; Mason jerking upright as a fusor fired from the high cliff puddled his spine, melted his flesh like wax; Mason tumbling down into my arms, almost driving me to my knees; Mason, already dead, heavy in my arms, *heavy in my arms;* Mason torn away from me as a wave broke over us and deluged me in spume; Mason sinking from sight as Heynith screamed for me to come on and I fought my way through the chest-high surf to the ramsub—

That's what supporting the null had reminded me of: Mason, heavy in my arms.

Confusion and fear and nausea.

How could the null make me think of Mason?

Sick self-anger that my mind could compare Mason, gentle as the dream-father I'd never had, to something as disgusting as the null.

Anger novaed, trying to scrub out shame and guilt.

I couldn't take it. I let it spill out onto the null.

Growling, I sprang forward, shook it furiously until

its head rattled and wobbled on its limp neck, grabbed it by the shoulders and hammered it to its knees.

I yanked my knife out. The blade flamed suddenly in starlight.

I wrapped my hand around its throat to tilt its head back.

Its flesh was warm. A pulse throbbed under my palm.

All at once, my anger was gone, leaving only nausea.

I suddenly realized how cold the night was. Wind bit to the bone.

It was looking at me.

I suppose I'd been lucky. Orphans aren't as common as they once were—not in a society where reproduction has been relegated to the laboratory, but they still occur with fair regularity. I had been the son of an uncloned junior executive who'd run up an enormous credit debit, gone bankrupt, and been forced into insolvency. The Combine had cut a clone from him so that their man/hours would make up the bank discrepancy, burned out the higher levels of his brain and put him in one of the nonsentient penal Controlled Environments. His wife was also cloned, but avoided brainscrub and went back to work in a lower capacity in Admin. I, as a baby, then became a ward of the State, and was sent to one of the institutional Environments. Imagine an endless series of low noises, repeating over and over again forever, no high or low spots, everything level: MMMMMMMMMMM MMMMMMMMMMMMMMMMMMMMMMMMMMMMMM MMMMMMM. Like that. That's the only way to describe the years in the Environments. We were fed, we were kept warm, we worked on conveyor belts piecing together miniaturized equipment, we were put to sleep electronically, we woke with our fingers already busy in the monotonous, rhythmical motions that we couldn't remember learning, motions we had repeated a million times a day since infancy. Once a day we were fed a bar of food-concentrates and vitamins. Occasionally, at carefully calculated intervals, we would be exercised to keep up muscle tone. After reaching puberty, we were occasionally masturbated by electric stimulation, the seed saved for sperm banks. The administrators of the Environment were not cruel; we almost never saw them. Punishment was by machine shocks; never severe, very rarely needed. The executives had no need to be cruel. All they needed was MMMMM MMMMMMMMMMM MMMMMMMMMMMM. We had been taught at some early stage, probably by shock and stimulation, to put the proper part in the proper slot as the blocks of equipment passed in front of us. We had never been taught to talk, although an extremely limited language of several mood-sounds had independently developed among us; the executives never spoke on the rare intervals when they came to check the machinery that regulated us. We had never been told who we were, where we were; we had never been told anything. We didn't care about any of these things, the concepts had never formed in our minds, we were only semi-conscious at best anyway. There was nothing but MMMMMMMM MMMMMMMMMMMMMM. The executives weren't concerned with our spiritual development, there was no graduation from the Environment; there was no place else for us to go in a rigidly stratified society. The Combine had discharged its obligation by keeping us alive, in a place where we could even be minimally useful. Though our jobs were sinecures that could have been more efficiently performed by computer, they gave the expense of our survival a socially justifiable excuse, they put us comfortably in a pigeonhole. We were there for life. We would grow up from infancy, grow old, and die, bathed in MMMMMM MMMMMMMMMMMMMMM. The first real, separate and distinct memory of my life is when the Quaestors raided the Environment, when the wall of the assembly chamber suddenly glowed red, buckled, collapsed inward, when Mason pushed out of the smoke and debris-cloud, gun at the ready, and walked slowly toward me. That's hindsight. At the time, it was only a sudden invasion of incomprehensible sounds and lights and shapes and colors, too much to possibly comprehend, incredibly alien. It was the first discordant note ever struck in our lives:

MMMMMMMMMMM!!!! shattering our world in an instant, plunging us into another dimension of existence. The Quaestors kidnaped all of us, loaded us onto vacvans, took us into the hills, tried to undo some of the harm. That'd been six years ago. Even with the facilities available at the Quaestor underground complex—hypnotrainers and analysis computers to plunge me back to childhood and patiently lead me out again step by step for ten thousand years of subjective time, while my body slumbered in stasis—even with all of that, I'd been lucky to emerge somewhat sane. The majority had died, or been driven into catalepsy. I'd been lucky even to be a Ward of the State, the way things had turned out. Lucky to be a zombie. I could have been a low-ranked clone, without a digestive system, tied forever to the Combine by unbreakable strings. Or I could have been one of the thousands of tank-grown creatures whose brains are used as organic-computer storage banks in the Cerebrum gestalts, completely unsentient: I could have been a null.

Enormous eyes staring at me, unblinking.

Warmth under my fingers.

I wondered if I was going to throw up.

Wind moaned steadily through the valley with a sound like MMMMMMMMMMMMMMMM.

Heynith hissed for me to hurry up, sound riding the wind, barely audible. I shifted my grip on the knife. I was telling myself: it's never been really sentient anyway. Its brain has only been used as a computer unit for a biological gestalt, there's no individual intelligence in there. It wouldn't make any difference. I was telling myself: it's dying anyway from a dozen causes. It's in pain. It would be kinder to kill it.

I brought up the knife, placing it against the null's throat. I pressed the point in slowly, until it was pricking flesh.

The null's eyes tracked, focused on the knifeblade.

My stomach turned over. I looked away, out across the valley. I felt my carefully created world trembling and blurring around me, I felt again on the point of being catapulted into another level of comprehension, previously unexpected. I was afraid.

The vacvan's headlights flashed on and off, twice.

I found myself on the ground, hidden by the ropy shrubs. I had dragged the null down with me, without thinking about it, pinned him flat to the ground, arm over back. That had been the signal that Ren had received a call from the orbot, had given it the proper radio code reply to bring it down. I could imagine him grinning in the darkened cab as he worked the instruments.

I raised myself on an elbow, jerked the knife up, suspending it while I looked for the junction of spine and neck that would be the best place to strike. If I was going to kill him (*it*), I would have to kill him (*it!*) now. In quick succession, like a series of slides, like a computer equation running, I got: D'kotta—the cadet—Mason—the null. *It* and *him* tumbled in selection. Came up *him*. Lowered the knife. I couldn't do it. He was human. Everybody was.

For better or worse, I was changed. I was no longer the same person.

I looked up. Somewhere up there, hanging at the edge of the atmosphere, was the tinsel collection of forces in opposition called a starship, delicately invulnerable as an iron butterfly. It would be phasing in and out of "reality" to hold its position above World, maintaining only the most tenuous of contacts with this continuum. It had launched an orbot, headed for a rendezvous with the vacvan in this valley. The orbot was filled with the gene cultures that could be used to create hundreds of thousands of nonsentient clones who could be imprinted with behavior patterns and turned into computer-directed soldiers; crude but effective. The orbot was filled with millions of tiny metal blocks, kept under enormous compression: when released from tension, molecular memory would reshape them into a wide range of weapons needing only a powersource to be functional. The orbot was carrying, in effect, a vast army and its combat equipment, in a form that could be transported in a five hundred-foot vacvan and slipped into Urheim, where there were machines that could put it into use. It was the Combine's last chance, the second wind they needed in order to survive. It had been financed and arranged by various industrial firms in the Commonwealth who had vested interests in the Combine's survival on World. The orbot's cargo had been assembled and sent off before D'kotta, when it had been calculated that the reinforcements would be significant in insuring a Combine victory; now it was indispensable. D'kotta had made the Combine afraid that an attack on Urheim might be next, that the orbot might be intercepted by the Quaestors if the city was under siege when it tried to land. So the Combine had decided to land the orbot elsewhere and sneak the cargo in. The Blackfriars had been selected as a rendezvous, since it was unlikely the Quaestors would be on the alert for Combine activity in that area so soon after D'kotta, and even if stopped, the van might be taken for fleeing survivors and ignored. The starship had been contacted by esper in route, and the change in plan made.

Four men had died to learn of the original plan. Two more had died in order to learn of the new landing site and get the information to the Quaestors in time.

The orbot came down.

I watched it as in a dream, coming to my knees, head above the shrubs. The null stirred under my hand, pushed against the ground, sat up.

The orbot was a speck, a dot, a ball, a toy. It was gliding silently in on gravs, directly overhead.

I could imagine Heynith readying the laser, Goth looking up and chewing his lip the way he always did in stress. I knew that my place should be with them, but I couldn't move. Fear and tension were still there, but they were under glass. I was already emotionally drained. I could sum up nothing else, even to face death.

The orbot had swelled into a huge, spherical mountain. It continued to settle, toward the spot where we'd calculated it must land. Now it hung just over the valley center, nearly brushing the mountain walls on either side.

The orbot filled the sky, and I leaned away from it instinctively. It dropped lower—

Heynith was the first to fire.

An intense beam of light erupted from the ground down-slope, stabbed into the side of the orbot. Another followed from the opposite side of the valley, then the remaining two at once.

The orbot hung, transfixed by four steady, unbearably bright columns.

For a while, it seemed as if nothing was happening.

I could imagine the consternation aboard the orbot as the pilot tried to reverse gravs in time.

The boat's hull had become cherry-red in four widening spots. Slowly, the spots turned white.

I could hear the null getting up beside me, near enough to touch. I had risen automatically, shading eyes against glare.

The orbot exploded.

The reactor didn't go, of course; they're built so that can't happen. It was just the conventional auxiliary engines, used for steering and for powering internal systems. But that was enough.

Imagine a building humping itself into a giant stone fist, and bringing that fist down on you: *squash*. Pain so intense that it snuffs your consciousness before you can feel it.

Warned by instinct, I had time to do two things.

I thought, distinctly: so night will never end.

And I stepped in front of the null to shield him.

Then I was kicked into oblivion.

I awoke briefly to agony, the world a solid, blank red. Very, very far away, I could hear someone screaming. It was me.

I awoke again. The pain had lessened. I could see. It was day, and the night plants had died. The sun was dazzling on bare rock. The null was standing over me, seeming to stretch up for miles into the sky. I screamed in preternatural terror. The world vanished.

The next time I opened my eyes, the sky was heavily overcast and it was raining, one of those torrential southern downpours. A Quaestor medic was doing something to my legs, and there was a platvac nearby. The null was lying on his back a few feet away, a bullet in his chest. His head was tilted up toward the scuttling gray clouds. His eyes mirrored the rain.

That's what happened to my leg. So much nerve tissue destroyed that they couldn't grow me a new one, and I had to put up with this stiff prosthetic. But I got used to it. I considered it my tuition fee.

I'd learned two things; that everybody is human, and that the universe doesn't care one way or the other; only people do. The universe just doesn't give a damn. Isn't that wonderful? Isn't that a relief? It isn't out to get you, and it isn't going to help you either. You're on your own. We all are, and we all have to answer to ourselves. We make our own heavens and hells; we can't pass the buck any further. How much easier when we could blame our guilt or goodness on God.

Oh, I could read supernatural significance into it all— that I was spared because I'd spared the null, that some benevolent force was rewarding me—but what about Goth? Killed, and if he hadn't balked in the first place, the null wouldn't have stayed alive long enough for me to be entangled. What about the other team members, all dead —wasn't there a man among them as good as me and as much worth saving? No, there's a more direct reason why I survived. Prompted by the knowledge of his humanity, I had shielded him from the explosion. Three other men survived that explosion, but they died from exposure in the hours before the med team got there, baked to death by the sun. I didn't die because the null stood over me during the hours when the sun was rising and frying the rocks, *and his shadow shielded me from the sun*. I'm not saying that he consciously figured that out, deliberately shielded me (though who knows), but I had given him the only warmth he'd known in a long nightmare of pain, and so he remained by me when there was nothing stopping him from running away—and it came to the same result. You don't need intelligence or words to respond to empathy, it can be communicated through the touch of fingers—you know that if you've ever had a pet, ever been in love. So that's why I was spared, warmth for warmth, the same reason anything good ever happens in this life. When the med team arrived, they shot the null down because they thought it was trying to harm me. So much for supernatural rewards for the Just.

So, empathy's the thing that binds life together; it's the flame we share against fear. Warmth's the only answer to the old cold questions.

So I went through life, boy; made mistakes, did a lot of things, got kicked around a lot more, loved a little, and ended up on Kos, waiting for evening.

But night's a relative thing. It always ends. It does; because even if you're not around to watch it, the sun always comes up, and someone'll be there to see.

It's a fine, beautiful morning.

It's always a beautiful morning somewhere, even on the day you die.

You're young—that doesn't comfort you yet.

But you'll learn.

SELECTIONS FROM THE PUBLISHER OF THE BEST SCIENCE FICTION IN THE WORLD

far away places . . . visitors from other worlds . . .
the wonders of ancient civilizations . . .
the ancestors of Man . . .

from **Ballantine**

ANCIENT ENGINEERS, by L. Sprague de Camp.
From the pyramids of Egypt and the Great Wall of China to the "no parking" signs at Nineveh and the water alarm clock of Plato.
From the author of **Citadels of Mystery** $1.75
As fascinating as Chariot of the Gods

TEMPLE OF THE STARS, by Brinsley le Poer Trench.
An examination of Mankind's ancient link with visitors from distant stars as seen in astrological theories.
By the former editor of **Flying Saucer Review** $1.50

PILTDOWN MEN, by Ronald Millar.
Here is the story, as fascinating as a whodunit, of how the Piltdown skull came to be discovered; how the hoax was exposed; and who the hoaxer may have been.   **$1.75**

IN SEARCH OF THE MAYA, by Robert L. Brunhouse.
The wonder, the disbelief, the unfolding of the idea of a unique culture as sophisticated as that of the Old World was a genuine discovery and as fascinating an adventure as any that can be found in exploration or archeology.   **$1.65**

"A shining example of what can be done by the technologically oriented writer of science fiction."

—Algis Budrys

LARRY NIVEN

PROTECTOR

Larry Niven's new science fiction novel in which Phssthpok the Pak attempts to save, develop and protect the group of Pak Breeders sent into space some 2½ million years before.

WORLD OF PTAVVS

In which a telepathic alien almost takes over the planet.

A GIFT FROM EARTH

Which saves the inhabitants of Mount LookitThat from the organbanks, (human organs that is).

NEUTRON STAR

A superb collection which includes the Nebula Award winning title story.

RINGWORLD

An excellent . . . s.f. story. Contains one genuinely mind-boggling concept—a ring-shaped artificial world, large enough to circle its sun . . ."

—A.J.

To order by mail, send $1.25 per book plus 25¢ per order for handling to Ballantine Cash Sales, P.O. Box 505, Westminster, Maryland 21157. Please allow three weeks for delivery.

SCIENCE FICTION
from

BALLANTINE BOOKS

WALK TO THE END OF THE WORLD,
    S. M. Charnas $1.25
ICERIGGER, Alan Dean Foster $1.25
UNDER PRESSURE, Frank Herbert $1.25
THE LEGEND OF MIAREE, Zach Hughes $1.25

THE BEST OF STANLEY G. WEINBAUM
    With an INTRODUCTION by Isaac Asimov and an
    Afterword by Robert Bloch $1.65

launching a new series of Sci Fi Greats

SCIENCE FICTION EMPHASIS 1
    David Gerrold, Ed. $1.25
THE GINGER STAR
    Leigh Brackett $1.25
A HOLE IN SPACE
    Larry Niven $1.25
STAR TREK LOG ONE
    Alan Dean Foster $ .95
PATRON OF THE ARTS
    William Rotsler $1.25
THE BEST SCIENCE FICTION OF THE YEAR #3
    Terry Carr, Ed. $1.50

---

available at your local bookstore

To order by mail, send price of book(s)
plus 25¢ per order for handling to Ballantine Cash Sales, P.O. Box 505, Westmin-
ster, Maryland 21157. Please allow three
weeks for delivery.